BLOOD
OF
DAWN

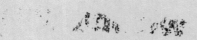

Also by Tami Dane:

Blood of Eden

Blood of Innocence

"Werewolves in Chic Clothing"
in
The Real Werewives of Vampire County

BLOOD
OF
DAWN

TAMI DANE

KENSINGTON PUBLISHING CORP.
http://www.kensingtonbooks.com

KENSINGTON BOOKS are published by

Kensington Publishing Corp.
119 West 40th Street
New York, NY 10018

All Kensington titles, imprints, and distributed lines are available at special quantity discounts for bulk purchases for sales promotions, premiums, fund-raising, and educational or institutional use.

Special book excerpts or customized printings can also be created to fit specific needs. For details, write or phone the office of the Kensington Special Sales Manager: Kensington Publishing Corp., 119 West 40th Street, New York, NY 10018, attn: Special Sales Department. Phone: 1-800-221-2647.

Kensington and the K logo Reg. U.S. Pat & TM Off.

ISBN-13: 978-0-7582-6711-5
ISBN-10: 0-7582-6711-8

First Printing: December 2012

10 9 8 7 6 5 4 3 2 1

Printed in the United States of America

BLOOD
OF
DAWN

All that is necessary for the triumph of evil is that good men do nothing.

—Edmund Burke

PROLOGUE

Joe Malone's party was rocking. The sound of music and laughter echoed through the thick night air. A couple of girls, drunk off their asses, staggered by, laughing.

Stephanie Barnett tugged down her top, exposing as much boobage as possible, and adjusted her skirt so it barely covered her ass. "How do I look?" she asked, doing a three-sixty for her friend Megan.

"Like a total whore."

"Good. So do you."

"I hope Nate's here tonight," Megan said as she smoothed some gloss on her lips.

"He will be. Let's go."

Together, they sauntered up the front walk. As they were clunking up the steps, a bolt of lightning sliced through the still night, followed by an earsplitting *craaaaack* and a resonating *kaboom.* Startled, Megan and Stephanie jumped, grabbed the door, and scurried inside, just as the sky opened up and a torrent of rain saturated the house, the street, and the weedy yard.

"Whew. We got here just in time," Stephanie said, glancing outside. The wind picked up, catching the branches of the mature oak tree standing between the sidewalk and street. The two drunk girls who'd stumbled by them screeched, then started laughing hysterically as their hair whipped around their heads and their clothes became sodden.

"Whoa," said someone behind them. A male.

Stephanie turned around.

It was Derik Sutton. "Hey," he said, giving her a look that made her skin crawl.

"Yeah. Whatever. Megan!" She shrugged past him, following Megan. "Wait for me." They wove through the thick crowd, working their way toward the kitchen, where the keg would be. "See anyone yet?"

"Not yet," Megan said over her shoulder. "Whew, it's hotter than hell in here."

At the end of the hall, they shoved through a wall of people, only to face another wall. And another.

"Damn, this place is packed," Stephanie yelled, wincing as someone elbowed her rib cage. "I'm getting claustrophobic, and we just got here."

"Matt Shelton tweeted about the party this afternoon," Megan yelled over her shoulder. "He has something like five thousand followers."

Something or someone tapped her ass and Stephanie jumped. If that was that psycho Sutton, she was going to kick him in the nuts. She jerked around.

It was Kyle.

"You're here." She flung her arms around his neck, pressed her body against his, letting him know, under no uncertain terms, how glad she was to see him.

He kissed her back.

When they came up for air, Kyle slid his arm around her waist, pulling her tighter against him. "That was nice. How about we go somewhere else and do some more of that?"

"I'm game. Let me tell . . ." She looked left, right. No Megan. Figuring her bestie was on the hunt for Nate, Stephanie dug her phone out of her purse and hit speed dial. The call went straight to voice mail. After screaming a message to the friend who had deserted her, she clicked off, shoved her phone back in her purse, and smiled. "Let's go."

With Kyle following closely, she wove through the packed kitchen and ducked out the back door, sucking in some much needed air. Then, turning a one-eighty, she smashed her body against him and tipped her head up for another kiss. The air was thick and warm and smelled like wet grass. The rain had stopped. So had the thunder. But she was burning up inside. Tight and hot and buzzing with energy. "How's this?"

"Hmm. Better." He cupped her chin, brushing his mouth over hers. But just as he was about to kiss her again, some asshole slammed into him. He jerked a look over his shoulder, wrapping a protective arm around her. "Let's go somewhere quiet."

"We can go to my house. Mom's out of it by this time of night. She takes sleeping pills. A 747 could land on our roof and she wouldn't hear it."

"Okay."

The walk was short. It was only a handful of blocks. Her dad's house was closer, but he'd be awake. They stopped a couple of times, crushed their bodies together and kissed until they were dizzy and aching and breathless. Once, next to a big lilac bush, which made the air smell sweet, he nipped and nibbled on her neck and her earlobe. She'd nearly crumpled to the ground right there. By the time they'd made it to her mom's house, she was nervous and excited. Her legs were a little wobbly; her heart was thumping hard against her rib cage. She knew what was about to happen. There could be no doubt. It would be her first time.

Moving carefully, to be quiet, she unlocked the door and led Kyle up the steps to her room. Nothing from Mom. Not a peep. Exactly as she had expected.

She scurried down the hall to her room, with Kyle on her heels, and closed the door. As she twisted the lock, her hands were shaking a little. "Wait here. I'll be right back." Trying to keep on the sexy, she swung her hips as she sauntered toward the bathroom. Once she had herself safely shut in, she freshened up, dug out the condoms she'd stashed in the bottom of her makeup drawer, and brushed her teeth. Outside, thunder boomed and lightning flashed in the window. Rain pounded on the roof, the storm making her even more anxious and jittery. She'd never liked storms—especially at night.

A brilliant bolt zigzagged through the sky, and in a blink an eardrum-splitting bang followed. Startled, she flung herself through the door, into her bedroom. "That was too close!" she muttered to herself.

"There you are." Kyle was standing next to her dresser, shoulder against the wall.

"Sorry it took so long. I wanted to freshen up." Running her palms down her legs, she went to the window. She needed some fresh air, but the storm was scaring her. She inched it open a crack.

Kyle stalked closer, stopping right behind her. "Are you nervous?" he whispered in her ear as he flattened his body against her back.

A wave of heat crashed through her body. He was so close and he smelled so good. And—oh, my God—she was about to have sex for the first time. She nodded. "Yes."

Reaching around her, he cupped her chin, tilting her head to one side. "You should be." His voice was strange. Cold.

A blade of icy dread shot up her spine. What did he mean by that? Was he joking? Trying to scare her? The hairs on her nape stood on end. Goose bumps prickled the skin of her arms and shoulders. Twisting, she glanced over her shoulder. "What are you trying to do? Talk me out of it?"

His lips curled into a toothy smile, and the faint light seeping into her room through her window flashed on his pearly whites. "Why would I do a thing like that?" He licked his lips, and her gaze locked on his mouth, on the fangs that hadn't been there a fraction of a second ago. "You taste so good."

The air around her crackled.

Time is a great teacher, but unfortunately it kills all its pupils.

—Louis Hector Berlioz

I

My father once wrote: *If you want to find the bizarre, the impossible, the fantastic, you just have to open your fucking eyes. As scientists, it's our responsibility to tell the truth. Monsters are everywhere.* It was shortly after publishing that little nugget of brilliance that he'd lost his job and became the laughingstock of academia.

On the other hand, my mother once told me, "Marijuana is the world's most perfect substance. It expands one's consciousness. It restores health and balance. And it just makes me feel real fucking good."

I'm the product of those combined genes . . . and minds.

I'm Sloan Skye, now starting the second month of my internship with the FBI's Paranormal Behavioral Analysis Unit, or the PBAU. We profile criminals, just like the oh-so-popular BAU, but our bad guys have fangs and fur . . . and they aren't your average, monstrous Homo sapiens.

My father was right. There are monsters everywhere. In fact, the world was teeming with all kinds of paranormal creatures. We call them Mythics. *Adzes* and *aswangs* living in the burbs, masquerading as soccer moms. And honest-to-God, literal bloodsucking lawyers.

But on my off-hours—which are few and far between this

summer—I'm just your average daughter to a tree-hugging, pot-smoking, pregnant forty-something hippie schizophrenic and a man who faked his death twenty years ago, all in the name of protecting his precious family (me and my mom).

Dad just recently resurrected. And the newly reborn Dad wasted no time getting Mom knocked up. The jury's still out on whether the whole pretending-to-be-dead thing was necessary. But I hope this time he sticks around to see his kid grow up. As far as missing my childhood—first words, first steps, first Junior Nobel Prize award—I'm not the grudge-holding type, so I've decided to let it go.

You never know, he could have been telling the truth about our being in danger. There's a lot going on in the shadows of our world. And right in front of our faces too. He should know. He was the head of security for the queen of the elves.

Don't you wish you were me?

Don't answer that question too soon. My cell phone just rang.

Mom.

"Pie craving," she screamed in my ear. "It's bad."

I blinked bleary eyes at the red glowing numbers on my clock. I saw a 1, two vertically aligned dots, a 2, and a 3. I pushed myself upright and rubbed the sleep from my eyes. "Mom, should you be eating pie at this hour?"

"I. Need. Pie," she enunciated. Her voice vibrated, like she was sitting on a clothes dryer.

I didn't ask.

"Where's Dad?" I flipped the covers back and swung my legs over the edge of the bed. "Isn't he there with you?"

"No, he's not. He's doing the queen a favor—don't ask. He won't be back until sometime tomorrow. I can't wait until then. I'd drive myself to the store, but I can't find the car keys. I've looked everywhere."

I had a feeling there was a reason why the car keys were

a *rei absentis*—aka, missing. "Okay. I'll be there in a little bit. What kind of pie do you want?"

"Something smooth and creamy and chocolaty. Mmm," she purred, like a kitten. "Oh, and something tart. Cherry. With whipped cream."

"Okay. So one chocolate cream pie and one cherry."

"You'd better get lemon meringue too."

"Fine. Bye." I ended the call, stumbled over to the dresser, grabbed the first pair of sweatpants and T-shirt I found, and stuffed my half-asleep body into them. After making myself halfway presentable, so nobody at the twenty-four-hour grocery store would mistake me for a vagrant, I shuffled out to my car, hopping over puddles in the driveway. I dove into the driver's seat, cranked on the motor, and had a myocardial infarction when someone pounded on my window.

After my heart stopped hopping around in my chest like electrons in a microwave, I rolled down the window and glared at the individual responsible for my near-fatal arrhythmia.

"What are you doing here?" I asked my ex-fiancé, whose appearance would give most girls a heart attack, and I'm not saying that to be mean.

Elmer Schmickle is a prince. How many girls grow up thinking all princes are tall, dark, and handsome, right? Not this royal.

Elmer is the prince of the *Sluagh*. For those who aren't in the know, the *Sluagh* are the spirits of the restless dead. And he is the exact opposite of a Disney prince. At least in looks. Fairy-tale princes are all handsome, tall, with perfect hair. This prince is short, with spindly arms and legs, and a face that not even a mother could love.

"I need your help," Elmer said, wringing his hands. His buggy eyes flicked back and forth from my car to my apartment building and back again. "Please."

My phone rang. Mom.

I lifted an index finger. "I'm sort of busy right now. Can it wait?" I asked him.

"No."

"Not even an hour?"

His expression soured.

I motioned to the passenger seat. "Fine. I need to run a quick errand. You can tell me what's up on the way."

In a blink, Elmer was strapping himself in; and less than a minute later, we were zooming through silent streets of Virginia, toward the nearest all-night grocery store.

Elmer glanced out the window. "Where are we headed?"

"Pie run. For Mom."

"Oh, pie." Elmer narrowed his eyes. "I love pie." His eyes became squinty. "I love pie *a lot.*"

"I hear you."

"It's your fault that I'm still waiting to eat pie. If you had married me, I could be eating pie right now." He sighed. "I could have had pie last night too. And tomorrow. And the day after that."

"It's not my fault that you can't eat or drink, Elmer. I have no problems helping out my friends, but marrying you—just so you could eat pie—is asking a lot."

"Says the girl who can eat pie anytime she wants." He sulked the rest of the drive to the store. Because my room-mate and I are poor—and we can't afford to live close to DC, where my folks' new *house* is located (it's more a freaking mansion than a house)—that was a long time, almost an hour.

"Are you coming inside?" I asked as I zoomed into the closest parking spot in front of the Giant grocery store.

"Are you kidding? I never go near food stores. They're hell on earth for a guy like me. Nothing like walking by mountains of food I can smell and see, but can't eat."

"I see your point." I shut off the engine and pocketed the keys. "Okay. I'll be out in a few."

"Make sure you double bag."

"Got it." My phone rang at least ten times as I raced

through the store, loading pies into my cart. Mom. Elmer. My roommate, Katie. Ignoring them all, I paid, double bagged everything, and wheeled the contraband out to my car.

After dumping the load into the trunk, I flopped into the driver's seat.

"I can smell them," Elmer said on a sigh.

"I double bagged everything." Looking over my shoulder, I maneuvered out of the parking spot. Once the car was rolling forward again, I asked, "So what was so urgent that it couldn't wait until morning?"

"Uh." He gave me that you-know-what look. "You know what happens to me at sunrise."

"How could I forget? Right. You vanish." I turned the car out of the lot, heading toward my parents' swanky neighborhood in Alexandria. "Anyway . . . ?"

"Tomorrow night's the first night of taping. I'm not ready."

"Ah. Have a bad case of stage fright, do you?"

He slid me some squinty eyes. "It's not a 'bad case' of anything. And I do not get any kind of 'fright,' stage or otherwise."

Clearly, I'd struck a raw nerve. "Of course. What do you want me to do?"

"I could use some acting lessons."

"I'm not an actress," I pointed out. "I've never even been in a school play."

Elmer grunted.

"Shouldn't your producer be helping you with this?"

"I asked her, and she told me she didn't want me taking acting lessons because then I might not come off as real. Since the show's a *reality* program, she didn't want that."

"Well, then, maybe you should trust her judgment."

Elmer scowled. "I don't want to make an ass out of myself."

I pulled up to a red light and glanced at him. He was looking paler than normal. And his thin lips were thinner too.

"This was *your* idea," he pointed out.

That was true. It was my idea. Sort of. I'd mentioned it as a joke. Kind of. But then I'd found out my father knew some people who could make the show happen for real; and before I knew it, Elmer was signing a contract to film eight episodes of *Who Wants to Marry an Undead Prince?*

I was hoping the show would be an answer to my prayers. Elmer was desperate to find a bride. He'd kidnapped me not too long ago, and had nearly dragged me, kicking and screaming, down the aisle. But I'd talked myself out of that close scrape by promising to help him find a replacement bride. Easier said than done. We've tried speed dating, online dating. No deal. Elmer had some physical limitations to work around—his inability to materialize before sunset, specifically—but they didn't get in his way as much as his appearance. It seemed most girls couldn't look past his Halloween-ghoulish mug to see the man inside. It also didn't help that Elmer had one very significant stipulation: his future bride had to be 100 percent elf.

I turned into the folks' driveway, parked in front of the house, and killed the engine.

Elmer's eyes glittered as he took in the glory that was Mom and Dad's new place. "Wow."

"I guess Dad felt like he had some making up to do, leaving Mom living in that rattrap apartment for twenty years." I grabbed the bag out of the trunk and hustled to the front door. On the porch, I poked the doorbell and listened to the *ding dong, ding dong,* of the chime.

No answer.

I rang the bell again.

"Maybe she fell asleep," Elmer suggested.

"I didn't just drive over here for nothing." I poked the button a third time; when that didn't work, I handed the bag to Elmer and went back to the car for my phone. I hit 1 on my speed dial and listened to the phone ring. It rang ten times before my mother picked up.

"Hello?" Mom said, sounding sleepy.

"Mom, I'm outside. With pie."

"I called. Didn't you get my message?"

"No."

She yawned. "I'll be right there."

I clicked off and rejoined Elmer on the porch. Grimacing, he shoved the bag into my hands.

The door finally opened, and a very rumpled Mom poked her head out. "Sloan, I'm sorry. I told you not to bother. Your father called right after I talked to you. He came home early. And he brought me some pie."

I shoved the bag at her. "But I bought all of this, and I don't want to eat it."

She snorted, jerking backward, like I'd just shoved a bag of radioactive plutonium at her. "Get it away. I can't look at another pie. I ate too much already."

"But it's the middle of the night, and I drove an hour to get here. And I have to be at work by nine—"

"Not my fault, Sloan. You didn't answer your phone. I think you should hurry home and get into bed. You can still catch a few more hours if you don't waste any time." Her eyes started watering, and her face turned the shade of a turnip. "Oh, no. I told you to get that pie away from me. Gotta go. Bye." She clapped her hand over her mouth and slammed the door in my face.

My arm dropped to my side, and I slid a sidelong glance at Elmer. I give him credit. He was looking outraged on my behalf.

"I can't believe she slammed the door in your face," he said.

"That's my mother for you. She's a strange bird." I headed back to the car, dumped the bag of pies in the trunk, and climbed behind the steering wheel. Elmer was already in the passenger seat.

I glanced at the red glowing numbers on the clock. Now, I was seeing a 2, two dots, a 4, and a 9. I had almost an hour drive ahead of me before I could climb back into my bed. My eyes were gritty and blurry, my head foggy.

I started the car, shifted into reverse, then shifted back into park before the car had rolled a single inch. "To heck with this. I'm not driving home. She called me out here, so she can let me sleep over. It isn't like she doesn't have room for me. There are five bedrooms in this place." I poked my cell phone, calling Mom.

"Sloan," Elmer said, "there's something else we need to talk about. It's about a certain debt you owe me."

"Oh, yeah, right." I was hoping he'd forgotten about that.

"You remember, I said we'd meet at midnight . . . several nights ago."

"Um, no. I forgot. Sorry."

Elmer's daytime invisibility had come in handy in my last case. We were chasing a bloodthirsty *aswang* and I had been desperate. The problem was, his help had come with strings attached. At this point, I still had no idea how thick those strings were.

"So, were you thinking cash?" I asked.

"Money?" Elmer shook his head. "I don't need more money. I already have enough of that. No, I was thinking about something else. Maybe something to add to my collection."

"What collection?" A quiver of dread wound through my insides. To be fair, my father had warned me about the dangers of striking a deal with a *Sluagh*. But I'd chosen to ignore his warning, in the interest of serving the greater good, of course.

My phone rang. I checked it. Katie.

Was it unusual that Katie was calling at almost three in the morning? Not necessarily. The girl kept crazy hours. But calling multiple times in the last hour? That was a reason for concern. Not to mention, I was glad for the distraction.

I answered, "What's up?"

"You need to come home. Right now. Right. Now!"

The line went dead.

"Elmer, we'll have to talk about this later. Something's wrong with Katie."

Elmer humphed. "There's always something wrong. I'm not going anywhere."

2

I made it as far as my street before my phone rang yet again. This time it wasn't Mom. It wasn't Katie either. It was Jordan Thomas, one of my coworkers and also the subject of more than a few steamy dreams since I'd started working for the PBAU.

I answered, "JT, what's wrong?"

"Where are you?"

I suppose there was good reason for him to ask that. He probably would have assumed any normal person would be in bed at this hour, sound asleep. I'm not any normal person, though. Which is partly why I was interning for the FBI in the first place.

"I'm heading home. Why?"

"The chief needs you to get to the following address ASAP." He paused.

"Go ahead," I told him. There was no need for me to write down the address. Not that I'm bragging, but my memory is insanely good. Since taking this job a few weeks ago, I've memorized roughly half of my father's research on paranormal creatures. That's somewhere around ten years' worth of work.

He rattled off an address in Baltimore, then added, "I'll meet you there."

"Okay. I need to run home and change first. I don't think anyone's going to take me seriously in what I'm wearing right now."

"Why not?"

I glanced down at my shirt. "Just trust me."

"Okay. But you're going to have to show me what you're wearing another time. I'm intrigued." At the hint of naughtiness in his voice, parts of my anatomy started tingling.

That was not a good thing.

Ever since my first day on the job, I've had a thing for JT. Who wouldn't? He's sexy. He's smart. He's brave. And I've been doing everything in my power to keep from throwing myself at him like a shameless hussy and begging him to take me. Because I have big hopes for a long-term future with the FBI, I have resisted the urge. But there have been times when my self-control has been pushed to the limit. Like when he'd caught me coming out of the shower, and I was wrapped only in a towel. And when he'd been taping the microphone wire to me, and the only piece of clothing between my nipples and his hands was my lace bra.

For the most part, JT has been good about respecting my wishes to maintain a respectable, professional distance. But every now and then, his voice goes low and husky, or his eyes grow come-hithery. It doesn't help that our boss, Chief Peyton, keeps pairing us together to work on cases.

Or she gives us undercover assignments where we have to sleep together.

"Gotta go, bye." I clicked off.

Elmer gave me a raised-brow look.

"Sorry, work calls."

"But we need to talk. About my acting lessons. And that debt. You owe me, Sloan Skye. You have to pay."

"I will. Say, would the acting lessons count as payment?"

"No."

Stubborn, stubborn undead guy.

"But where am I going to find an acting coach at three-thirty in the morning?" I asked. "This is no small favor you're asking."

He shrugged. "This whole TV thing was your idea. You figure it out."

Once again, I was going to have to call my father. I hated doing that. I'd lived without the man for twenty years. It irritated me how often I found myself groveling for his help since his return. Granted, technically speaking, it was *his* fault that I'd had to find Elmer an alternative wife in the first place. He'd promised me to Elmer a long, long time ago. Like, while I was still in diapers.

"I'll call my father after I change my clothes. That's the best I can do." I steered into my apartment complex, rounded the bend, then stomped on the brakes.

"Oh, no," I said.

Our building was on fire. There were fire trucks and police cars everywhere.

"So much for changing your clothes, eh?" Elmer said, his voice sounding a little too cheerful.

"What did she do?" I muttered as I cut a sharp U-turn. I parked in the first lot that had an open parking spot and dialed Katie.

"Sloan!" she shouted.

"What happened?"

"It wasn't my fault. I swear. The fire didn't even start in our apartment."

"Are you sure?"

"Positive. I was asleep when the smoke alarms started shrieking. Where are you?"

"First lot, behind the rental office."

"I'll drive over."

Five minutes later, we were both standing between our cars, staring at our building, watching the glowing flames poke out of broken-out windows in our apartment. "It doesn't look like we'll be able to salvage anything," Katie said sadly. "My research."

A chill swept up my spine. "My father's research."

Katie slumped against the car. She was a mess. "I need to get some sleep. I guess I'll check in to a hotel for the night."

"I'll call my folks later. Their house is huge. There's plenty of room for both of us."

"No, Sloan."

"Really, it won't be a problem."

"Before you do that, let me check with the apartment complex, see if they have a vacant unit," Katie suggested.

"Fair enough. Let me know when you hear something."

Katie nodded. "Will do."

My phone rang. It was JT. No doubt he was expecting me to roll up to Brookline Street within the next fifteen minutes or so. Wasn't going to happen. "I have to go," I told Katie. "Do you have money for the hotel room?"

"I grabbed my purse on the way out." Katie opened her car door and flopped into the driver's seat. "There's no point in hanging around here any longer, I guess. It's just making me more depressed, thinking about all my hard work, gone."

"Oh, hon." I gave my depressed roommate a hug. "Didn't you back up?"

"Sure. But I backed up most of it on my portable hard drive. And you can guess where that is." She tipped her head toward the building, which was now spewing thick clouds of toxic smoke and ash into the air.

"I'll get in touch with Mom."

"And I'll call you once I hear from the complex manager." Katie closed her door, started the car, and opened the window. I was strolling toward my car when she yelled, "Sloan!"

I turned around.

"Thanks. You're a good friend."

"You're my best friend. I'm here for you, no matter what. Even if the fire had been your fault." Then I remembered the pies. "Hang on! I have something that'll make you feel better."

Stephanie Barnett lived in a quaint, little tan stucco-and-brick Cape Cod in Hunting Ridge, a neighborhood sitting on the western fringes of Baltimore. Like its neighbors, the house was neat, well maintained. And both inside and outside, it was full of charming character.

Sadly, it was teeming with police personnel combing every inch in an effort to solve the murder of a teenage girl.

I found JT upstairs, in what I had to assume was the teenager's bedroom. The walls were painted with black-chalkboard paint. And bizarre chalk illustrations covered nearly every inch of the walls: Gruesome faces with fangs. Skeletal, emaciated beings with buggy eyes. This was a girl who had been either fascinated by things that were dark and scary or was severely disturbed.

JT was talking to a woman who had the look in her eyes of a bereft parent who'd just walked into her worst nightmare.

"Mrs. Barnett, this is Sloan Skye," JT said as I stepped up to them. "Why don't you tell Miss Skye what you just told me?"

"Sure. You need to take a look at my ex-husband. That bastard's behind this," Mrs. Barnett said as she dabbed at her watery eyes. "I know it. He did this to get back at me."

"What makes you say that?" JT asked as he scribbled some notes in the little notebook he carried with him.

"Because he's a sick freak who doesn't want me to be happy," she snapped. "Mike's done some low-down stuff before, but nothing . . ." She sniffled, blinked, then sobbed. "Things were starting to look up for us. Finally. And he had to ruin it, like he always did. He was jealous, because I'd found someone and he hadn't."

JT and I exchanged looks. Jealousy was a powerful motivator for some people. I'd read about some heinous crimes committed in the name of jealousy. But to kill his own child . . . ?

"Has your ex-husband made any threats to you or your daughter before?" I asked.

"Sure. He's made plenty. It's no secret the man wanted me dead."

"But your daughter?"

"Well"—the woman faltered—"most of the threats were directed toward me. But he's such a psycho. I wouldn't put it past him to take out his anger on Stephanie. He'd never been close to her." She pointed at the walls. "See all of this?" She sneered. "It's because of him. And there's something else."

"What's that?" I asked, taking a closer look at the artwork on the nearest wall. It was drawn well, the work of someone who'd spent many hours honing her craft. The subject matter was odd, but kids sometimes expressed themselves in strange ways.

"He filled my daughter's head with a bunch of crazy talk about vampires. He believes in that kind of thing. In fact, he told her he's a vampire. I was so mad when I found out about that. I went over to talk to him yesterday. Things turned ugly. It can't be a coincidence that we had a fight just yesterday and I find my only daughter dead in her room this morning. That's *Mike—Michael—Barnett*," she said, enunciating his name.

"Thank you for the information, Mrs. Barnett," JT said, writing in his notebook. "Do you have an address for your ex-husband?"

"Sure. He lives less than a mile away." She rattled off the address; then she grabbed JT's arm and turned beseeching eyes to him. "Please, please don't let him get away with this. My daughter. My little girl." She sank down, boneless, landing on the mattress. She covered her face with her hands. The sound of her sobs was heart-wrenching. It was something I knew I wouldn't forget for a long time.

JT tucked his notebook in his pocket and squatted in front of the crying woman. "We will do our very best to catch your daughter's killer. I promise."

"Thank you." The trembling mother motioned toward the door. "If you don't need me anymore . . ."

"Yes, of course. We'll find you if we have any more questions. Standing, JT turned to me. I saw the glimmer of unshed tears in his eyes for a fraction of a second. Then he blinked and they were gone. Speaking softly, he pointed at the taped silhouette on the floor. "The victim was found here. Cause of death is undetermined, but there were puncture wounds on the neck." Next to where she'd been lying was an alarm clock. I nudged it with my toe. Broken.

"Again? Do we have another *adze* or *aswang* on the loose?"

"I don't know. But if it is an *aswang* . . ." He didn't finish his sentence. I could understand why. The *aswang* preyed on pregnant women. We were investigating the death of a sixteen-year-old girl. Sixteen was awfully young to become a mother, but it was entirely possible.

"Should we ask?" I tipped my head toward the door.

"No. Chances are, if the girl was pregnant, she might have kept it from her parents, anyway. The ME will catch it when he does the autopsy."

"Okay." I pointed at the outline. To me, it seemed the position of the victim was odd. She was found lying on her side, curled in a fetal position, arms and legs tucked in. Unlike the victims of the *aswang* we had recently caught, Stephanie Barnett had left her bed before being killed. On the other hand, the victims of the *adze*—the first unsub we had profiled—had died from a variety of infectious diseases, contracted when they were bitten. "What do you think about the victim's position? Do you generally find murder victims curled up like that?"

"Based on her position, I'd say she was lying there for a while. She might have been trying to protect herself. Or maybe she was in pain."

A shiver crept up my spine. I jerked my gaze away, scanning the rest of the room. "Nothing else appears to be disturbed. Have they found the point of entry for the unsub yet?"

"No. There was no sign of forced entry. Doors and windows on the ground level were locked. Basement windows too."

I turned my attention to the window at the far end of the room. After our last case, I knew that paranormal creatures could access victims on upper-level floors, without the aid of a ladder. The window was closed and locked. "Was this window closed all night?"

"I don't know. I'll ask the mother before we leave," JT said as he circled around the room, checking the floor, walls, bedding, for any missed clues.

At the opposite end of the room, I ducked down, checking under the bed. Lots of dust bunnies. One cardboard box. No weapons. No blood. Nothing.

"The place is clean. No blood. Not a single drop. Did the ME find any other puncture wounds on the victim?"

"No. Just the two. On the neck." He tipped his head toward the door. "Ready to go? I'd like to have a chat with the victim's father before the detective takes him in for questioning. We have puncture wounds on the neck and a guy who says he's a vampire. Makes sense, right? Then we can review the case notes, see if there's anything we missed here."

"Sounds like a plan."

We both headed toward the door; but before we stepped out into the hallway, JT caught my arm, stopping me. His lips curled into the hint of a wicked smile, and my heart did a little hop in my chest. His gaze flicked to roughly boob level. "I wanted to say something sooner, but it wasn't the right time. Nice shirt."

Feeling my face turn red, I smacked my arms over my

chest. "If there'd been any way I could have changed, I would have."

"I thought that was why it took you so long to get here." His smile drooped a bit. "You mean, you didn't wear that for my benefit?"

"Absolutely not." I shoved him back. He was getting much too close, and looking way too scrumptious. What those sexy glitters in his eyes did to me! "While I was out playing delivery girl for my mother—it was a pie emergency—my apartment building burned to the ground."

"Oh." *Poof,* the sparkles were gone. "Sorry, Sloan."

"Yeah, sorry. My father's work was in my apartment. I've only memorized half of it. Unless he kept a copy somewhere, the rest of it is lost."

His eyes widened. "Oh."

"I'll call him later. Hopefully, he stowed a backup copy somewhere. If not, the rest of the summer could be really rough. His research helped us catch two killers already."

You cannot teach a man anything; you can only help him discover it in himself.
                                    —Galileo Galilei

3

Mike Barnett might live less than a mile away from his former wife and daughter, but in terms of neighborhood, his was light-years away. Whereas Brookline Street was lined with pretty Cape Cods and stately Colonials, with nicely landscaped lots, wide driveways, and a very large wooded park, Woodbine Street looked tired and bleak. None of the neglected homes had driveways. The lawns were weedy, and the only color brightening the area was the mustard-yellow hue of dandelions. The cars lining the narrow roads were just as neglected and as tired as the houses.

An unmarked police car angled up to the curb in front of Mike Barnett's house as we were trotting up the walk from opposite directions.

"We're too late," I said when I met JT on the sloping front porch of the vinyl-clad, two-story house.

"Maybe not." JT knocked. And knocked. And knocked.

"Maybe he's not home." I suggested the obvious, since it seemed JT wasn't aware of it.

He pointed at the small window on the upper level, facing the street. "Someone just peeked out at us."

The detective came stomping up the front steps. "No answer?"

Knocking yet again, JT shook his head. "Not so far, but

he's in there. Sloan Skye." JT pointed at me. "Detective Forrester."

Forrester acknowledged me with a nod, then hooked a thumb over his shoulder. "That's Barnett's truck parked across the street. The one with the trailer." He stepped up to the door and banged hard with his fist.

Finally we heard the sound of movement inside. The door swung open, and a man who looked like he'd been to hell and back, or on a three-week bender, blinked bloodshot eyes at us. "Yeah?" he said. The odor of alcohol on his breath was so strong, it made my eyes water.

"Good morning, sir. Are you Michael Barnett?" Forrester said.

"Yeah." Mike Barnett's eyes narrowed. "Why?"

"Detective Forrester, Baltimore Police Department. Can I come in for a minute?"

Barnett's eyes became even more squinted. "What for?"

"We'd like to ask you a few questions."

"About what?"

Forrester wasn't earning this guy's trust. I decided to poke in, see if I could help. "Your daughter, sir," I said, donning my most convincing I'm-no-threat look.

Barnett's gaze jerked from me to JT to Forrester, then back to me again. Finally, the self-proclaimed vampire stepped aside. I took a few mental notes. First, if he was an honest-to-God vampire, he had no problem with direct sunlight. And second, he was able to consume at least one variety of beverage, and it would appear, from his swaying, that the beverage had the desired effect on him. "Fine. But I don't have a lot of time. Need to get to work."

"This won't take long," Forrester said, leading the charge through the front door.

Inside, we congregated inches from the entry.

Mike Barnett crossed his arms over his chest. Not the friendliest body language. "What about my daughter? What's she done now?"

The girl was an honor student and not the kind to get into

trouble, from what we'd been told by her mother. Why he'd say such a thing escaped me, but I was anxious to find out. Perhaps her mother either didn't realize her daughter was in trouble or was in denial.

Before I could ask a question, though, Forrester said, "I'm sorry to inform you, sir, but your daughter passed away last night."

The man's expression shifted from confusion to disbelief to confusion again. "What?"

"Sir, your daughter is deceased," JT said gently.

The stunned father said nothing for several long moments, merely stared at me, brows scrunched, mouth agape. It was a convincing display of surprise. Then he started shaking, and his eyes watered. The sobs followed as he stumbled to a nearby chair and sat. After several painful minutes, he stuttered, "I . . . W-when? How?"

"She was found collapsed in her home. The medical examiner hasn't determined a cause of death yet. When was the last time you saw your daughter?" Forrester asked.

Mike Barnett shook his head. "Wait, if she collapsed, why are you asking . . . ? Was she . . . murdered?"

"There is a possibility," Forrester said.

The grieving father jerked ever so slightly. His gaze dropped to the floor, then moved to the left. "I . . . haven't seen her in days."

That, right there, was a sign he was lying, if you believed Richard Bandler's and John Grinder's research on Neuro-Linguistic Programming.

I glanced at JT. If he'd caught Barnett's eye movement, he was keeping it to himself. His gaze found mine for a brief moment; then it wandered off, taking in our surroundings. I turned my attention back to the father, who was doing a lot of stammering, also a sign of deception.

"My ex-wife and I haven't been on the best of—of terms lately," he said. "But—but still . . . you're not thinking . . . ?" He shook his head.

Something buzzed.

Forrester pulled a cell phone out of his pocket and glanced at it. He lifted an index finger. "I need to take this." Out he went, to take his call, leaving JT and me alone with a man who was lying.

That man focused on me. "My daughter was murdered?"

"There is reason to suspect it," I answered. "There will be an investigation."

"I'm guessing her mother told you it was me." His jaw clenched. "We've had our problems, her and me. But I have never, and would never, hurt the girl."

"The girl?" I silently repeated his odd description of his daughter.

"Where were you last night, between the hours of ten and two?" JT asked as he scrutinized a nearby side table, piled with soiled paper plates and crumpled napkins.

"Right here." Mike Barnett pointed at the worn recliner. "I watched a movie until midnight, then went to bed."

"Were you alone?" I asked.

"Yeah, I was alone."

"Can anyone verify you were home last night?" JT asked.

"I doubt it. My neighbors don't give a damn about my comings and goings." He sat, shoving his fingers through hair the color and texture of steel wool. "I can't believe this."

"Sir, when we first mentioned your daughter," I said, "you asked what she'd done *this time*. Why did you say that?"

"Well, lately Stephanie's been having some problems with her mother. Nothing too bad. Sneaking out. Normal teenage stuff. Her mother has been going off the deep end, though. Overreacting, if you ask me. I thought maybe she'd been caught at a party or something."

"I see."

"Maybe her mother wasn't overreacting, after all," Mike Barnett said to the floor.

JT lifted his phone, signaling he'd received a call too.

"Thank you for answering our questions. If you happen

to think of anything, why someone would want to harm your daughter, please feel free to call me." JT handed him a card, poked the button on his cell phone, and headed toward the door. "Thomas," he said. "What do you have?"

I thanked the extremely remorseful-looking father and followed JT outside. I noticed Forrester's car was gone. After JT hung up, I motioned to the empty spot where the detective's car had been parked. "Does this mean Mike Barnett has been cleared?"

"No. Forrester was called on another case. He'll be back later."

"Ah. And what's our next step?" I asked. "You didn't mention anything about the mother saying he was a vampire."

"No, I don't want him knowing about the bite marks. Yet. We're heading back to the office. I need to get on a computer."

"Okay. See you there." I tossed him a wave and we each climbed into our respective vehicles and motored down I-95, toward Quantico. I put in a call to Dad while I was driving. He didn't answer, so I left a message on his voice mail, asking if he had backup copies of his research somewhere. I wasn't expecting good news on that front. When I'd asked him for some help with our last case, he'd pretty much told me he didn't remember anything and hadn't kept copies.

Just as I was pulling into our building's lot, my phone rang. I was hoping it was my father, telling me he'd found something. It wasn't. It was Katie.

"I have good news and bad news," Katie said, sounding unhappy. "Which do you want first?"

I'd already had more than my share of bad news today, and it wasn't even noon yet. "The good."

"The complex has units for everyone in our building."

"That's great! So what's the bad news?"

"It's going to be at least two weeks before our new apartment will be ready," she said.

Not the news I was hoping for, but I wasn't surprised.

Our complex had very few vacancies. When we'd first applied for a unit, we'd had to wait a couple of months for one to open up.

This left us with a couple of options. One: find a new complex, which made no sense, since we'd probably face at least a two-week wait no matter where we went. Two: stay in a hotel, which would be insanely expensive. Neither of us could afford that. Or three: stay with my parents.

"I was really hoping . . . ," Katie said.

"I know. Living with Mom can be difficult, but their new house is huge. It'll be nothing like when she came to stay with us in our little apartment."

"Call me back after you talk to her?" Katie's voice was laced with doubt.

"You bet. Bye." I ended that call. After I parked, I hit the speed dial for my parents' place. Sergio, Mom and Dad's full-time pool boy/butler/eye candy/whatever, answered on the third ring.

"Irvine residence," he said. His accent was so thick that I could barely understand him.

"Hi, it's Sloan. Is my mother available?"

"She's . . . occupied at the moment. May I take a message?"

"That's okay. I'll call her back later."

"Okay. Good-bye."

I dropped my phone into my bag and headed inside.

The PBAU is located in the same building that houses the Behavioral Analysis Unit. Like the other units in the National Center for the Analysis of Violent Crime, or NCAVC, the PBAU's primary mission is to provide behavioral-based operational support to law enforcement agencies involved in the investigation of unusual or repetitive violent crimes. Both units have a chief in charge of operations. Both units have agents who travel across the country to work cases. But that was where the similarities ended. I was a summer intern. If I'd kept my original assignment, working for the BAU, I'd be schlepping coffee and lunch orders to agents and performing other mindless tasks that nobody else wanted to do—just like other interns. Instead, I've spent a fair amount of my internship working undercover, while trying to develop a profile that would help police determine what species our unsub (that's FBI speak for "unknown subject") was.

After I dumped my laptop bag on my desk, I wandered back to JT's cubicle to see what he was up to.

As it turned out, he wasn't there. But on my way back to my cubby, I was intercepted by another intern, one I had known, very well, for many, many years. Gabe Wagner gave me a little wave and flashed a smile that would stop traffic. "What's new, Skye?" he purred.

I waved back. "If you haven't read today's ScienceDaily, it's been reported that injected progenitor cells can slow the aging of mice with progeria. But that comes as no surprise to me. And we're working a new case. A teenage girl. Puncture wounds on the neck."

"Interesting."

"Which? The research or the case?"

"The fact that you haven't mentioned your shirt." He pointed.

I swear, my internal temperature must have rose to nearly fatal levels. I slammed my arms across my chest and tried not to act like I was about to experience spontaneous combustion. "Oh. That. I . . . Our building caught fire, and I was wearing this . . . to sleep in. . . ." I clamped my lips shut when his brows rose at the word "sleep." While he said nothing, I knew his dirty mind was painting pictures of me in bed. "I need to make a quick run." I snatched my purse and scurried toward the door leading out to the hallway.

Until recently, Gabe and I had been more enemies than friends. After an ugly breakup a long time ago, we'd gone from swapping DNA to ugly insults. But things have changed lately. Right before he'd been shipped out of state to work on another case, Gabe admitted he still had feelings for me. Romantic feelings.

I've had some time to think about how I felt about his

confession. I've decided I had no interest in traveling down that bumpy road again. Sure, his body makes my heart rate, breathing, and blood pressure increase, and certain parts of my anatomy get warm and tingly, but we share too much ancient history. Starting over just wasn't going to work.

But that didn't mean I was completely immune to his charms. Or that the raised-brow, twinkly-eyed look wasn't making bits of my anatomy stand up and take notice. Oh, no, quite the contrary. Already I was hoping he would be called off to somewhere far, far away, where I wouldn't have to be subjected to his irritatingly amusing dry wit, his perfectly symmetrical features, or his rip-off-his-clothes body.

For now, I would just have to stay strong. Stay focused.

"Skye?" JT called to my back just as I was about to head out. I had no idea where he'd come from.

I jerked a look over my shoulder. "I'll be back in a half hour. That's all I need. Thirty minutes."

"For what?" JT asked, his gaze settling on my arms, which were still covering my chest.

"I need to go shopping."

"Why?" both guys said in unison.

"Because clearly you both have dirty minds." I unfolded my arms and jerked up my chin. There was nothing wrong with my shirt, and I was mad at myself for letting those two . . . *boys* . . . make me think there was. The picture in the center was of a peapod . . . that did look a little like a penis—but only if you squinted. It didn't help that the stupid pod had a smiley face. The text said: Obey Mendelian principles. It's the laws of inheritance. I'd picked it up during my last visit to the Smithsonian. "You're immature children. Both of you."

They didn't look a bit remorseful.

"A half hour," I said. My phone rang. Mom. "Consider it my lunch break."

"Fine, Skye." JT waved me off. "See you in a half hour."

I punched the button, taking Mom's call as I stepped out into the hall. I poked the down elevator button. "Mom. Katie and I need a place to stay for a couple of weeks. Can we camp out at your house?"

"Why? Did you have another firefly infestation?" Mom asked. You might wonder why she'd ask such a crazy question. There was a good reason for it. "No."

"Lose power from a major electrical short?"

"Not that either." We only had those when Mom was staying with us. Among her many bizarre habits was the building of contraptions she called inventions. So far, one, in hundreds, maybe thousands—I'd lost count—had been somewhat useful. She'd actually built a trap for our last unsub. It had failed at trapping the killer, but it had saved a life.

"There was a fire," I admitted. The elevator door opened and I stepped into an empty car. "Not our fault—this time."

"You know I love Katie, but . . . ," Mom said, sighing. "Sloan, I'm pregnant. I can't have any benzene in my kitchen."

"I promise, your kitchen will remain benzene free." I pushed the lobby button.

"Yes, you said that last time—"

"You weren't pregnant then, and Katie was working on an important project. Besides, she's using toluene these days. The solvent properties are almost identical, but toluene is less toxic."

"No toluene either," Mom warned.

"You have my word." The elevator landed, bouncing a little.

"Fine."

"Thank you." I stepped out into the main-floor lobby and set my sights on the exit. "I'll call Katie and let her know. See you later, Mom."

"Okay. And, Sloan?"

"Yes?"

"Would you mind picking up some pie on your way home?"

The main door swooshed open. "You bet. Let me guess. Something tangy and something sweet?"

"That's perfect. I think I'm going to like having you living at home. Yes, I think it'll be just fine."

Exactly what I was afraid of.

Why—oh, why—did it have to be our building that burned down?

A sudden bold and unexpected question doth many times surprise a man and lay him open.

—Francis Bacon

4

Five hours later, all I'd accomplished was procuring a basic wardrobe, a new toothbrush, and two pies—French silk and cherry. We'd made no headway on the case. There'd been little to go on, and we were still waiting for the ME to give us a final determination on the cause of death. I was now whizzing along I-95, a few miles from my exit, pondering the COD, when my phone rang.

It was Damen Sylver.

Gorgeous, sexy, make-me-quiver Damen.

A little flash of excitement zoomed through me as I hit the button, answering the call. "Hello," I said, my voice all smiley. I couldn't help it. Damen Sylver made me feel girly. He was gorgeous. He was polite. He was intelligent. And he wasn't a coworker, an ex-boyfriend, or otherwise completely off-limits like Gabe and JT were.

Albeit, he was also an FBI agent. He'd convinced me that wouldn't be a problem.

"I have a surprise for you," he said. "But . . . I noticed your building looks a little vacant."

"Yeah. There was a fire last night. I have to stay with my parents for the next couple of weeks. Where are you?"

"In your parking lot."

"I'm sorry. I didn't think to tell you." Why would I? We weren't an item. We hadn't done enough stuff to be considered an item yet.

"That's okay. Would you mind if I stopped by your parents' place?"

"Absolutely not." I glanced in the mirror and scowled. I'd been walking around looking like the undead all day. I had no makeup. My hair was a mess. The only thing going for me was the fact that he was sitting in my parking lot, and I was minutes from Mom and Dad's, which gave me time to make myself presentable. I rattled off the address, asked if he needed directions, and when he said no—GPS—ended the call. Then I lead-footed it to my temporary home, hauled in my bags, and dashed up to my new bedroom. Moving quickly, I gathered up some supplies from Mom's stash, showered, shaved, loofahed, primped, spritzed, flat-ironed, and plucked until I was looking date ready. I was putting the finishing touches on my hair when Sergio knocked, announcing I had a visitor downstairs. He was waiting in the den.

I found him sitting across from Mom. He looked amazing, from the top of his shaggy-haired head to his well-shod toes. What he was doing here, waiting for plain old me . . . I couldn't imagine.

"There she is." He bent over the side of the chair and grabbed something; then, keeping his hands behind his back, he strolled to me. Intriguing. Curious to find out what he was hiding, I did my part to decrease the distance separating our bodies. Within seconds, we were standing mere inches apart. He produced a medium-sized, gift-wrapped box from behind his back.

"What's this?" I asked, staring down at the box. "It's not my birthday."

"It's just a little something. I saw it and thought of you." Smiling so big that little crinkles fanned the outsides of his eyes, he handed it over. "Open it."

"Okay." I untied the ribbon, then ripped the paper away.

It was a book. I flipped it over to read the title: *Comparative Analysis of Vampiric Species,* by James Skye.

As far as I knew, that book had been out of print for decades. "Where did you find this?" Considering the fire, and the fact that I'd lost all of my father's research, this was the find of the century.

But the statistical likelihood that this was merely a lucky coincidence was almost nil.

"It was collecting dust in a little used-book store I like to visit from time to time. . . . Okay, I confess. Jim—er, your father—called and told me what had happened. I had this copy at home. To be honest, I thought I'd sold it. But I checked, anyway. Obviously, I hadn't sold it. I thought you could use it more than me."

"Thank you." I hugged the book to my chest and stared up into his eyes. "This is sure going to come in handy."

"Glad to hear that."

Mom cleared her throat. "Oh, my." She yawned loudly. It was a complete fake. "I'm exhausted. I think I'll head up to bed."

"Did you have some of your pie?" I asked her. "I bought French silk."

"French silk." Mom's eyes sparkled, but then they flicked to Damen. All the sparkle vanished. *Poof.* Gone. "My doctor told me that I need to cut back." She shuffled past my gentleman caller, stopped next to me, and whispered, "Good night, Sloan. I gave Sergio the rest of the night off, and your father's working late." She waggled her eyebrows. Then, continuing on, she turned to Damen. "It was good seeing you again, Mr. Sylver."

"It was good seeing you too," he said, the corners of his lips twitching.

Once she was out of earshot, I shook my head. "I knew living with her was going to be tough, but I had no idea—"

Before I could finish, Damen hauled me into his arms. I looked up, my mouth agape. And he tipped his head down, lower, lower. He was going to kiss me; and oh, my God, was I happy about it! When his lips came into contact with mine, my whole body felt like it was electrified. Every single cell. I heard the book hit the floor long before I realized I had dropped it. I threw my arms around Damen's neck and held on while he kissed me. The world seemed to close in on itself, until all that existed was his big, hard body and little, trembling me.

When he finally broke the kiss, I blinked a couple of times and muttered something unintelligible.

"Are you okay?" he asked.

"S-sure."

With his arm still curved around my waist, he bent over and picked up the book. "You dropped this."

"Th-thanks."

I couldn't seem to produce more than one syllable at a time. My insides were zooming and swooping and flip-flopping. My head was spinning. I wasn't sure which way was up. I was brain-dead. And as much as I wanted to shake myself out of it, I couldn't.

"Sloan, come here." He guided me to the couch and helped me sit. Then he went to the kitchen. He grabbed a bottled water out of the refrigerator and handed it to me. After I guzzled half of it, he asked, "Better?"

"What was that?" I asked. Three words. Three syllables. That was an improvement.

"I'd like to think it was the result of my overwhelming charm." He winked.

"I've never been struck dumb before. It was weird."

"Weird, bad?"

"Weird, weird. But not necessarily bad." I set down the bottle. "In the name of science, maybe we should try that again. To see if we get the same results."

His smile broadened. "Of course, in the name of science." Our mouths met. An explosion of colors blasted behind my closed eyelids. I swear, there couldn't be a nerve in my body that wasn't on fire.

It was magic.

"Excuse me," someone said.

No. Not now.

The offending interrupter cleared his throat. "Thith is life or death."

So was this. I didn't just want to keep kissing Damen. I *needed* to keep kissing him. I couldn't stop. Not a chance.

Damen stopped. He leaned back. I pried open my eyelids and cut a mean look at Elmer.

"I don't care," Elmer hissed. "You didn't help me thith morning, and now it'th too late."

My gaze wandered up and down his form. He was wearing a suit. Black. Black shirt. Black tie. His hair was covermodel perfect—and much, much thicker than it had been this morning. And his skin was the shade of a *Baywatch* lifeguard's. His teeth were no longer barracuda-pointy. And his hair was a lot darker, too.

"Why . . . What's wrong with your mouth? Is it your teeth?" I mumbled.

"Capths." He pursed his lips. "I'm thill getting uthed to them. Do I talk funny?"

"Not at all," I lied. "They definitely make you look less . . . er, scary. Are you wearing a toupee?"

He grunted; then he slapped his hand on the top of his head and yanked the hairpiece off. "I told her it wouldn't fool anybody." He wound up for the pitch; his target was the trash can in the kitchen.

"No, no, no." I caught his spindly arm. "I didn't mean to make you think it looks bad. It doesn't."

"They hired a thylist to guthy me up. But I don't feel like it'th me."

"It is an improvement." I released his arm.

He didn't look convinced. "If you thay." His gaze slid to

Damen, who was sitting very quietly by my side, one arm draped across the back of the couch. "I need Thloan to come with me. They're filming the first epithode in a few. She got me into thith. . . ."

That was, at best, a slight tweak of the truth, but I didn't bother to correct him.

"That's fine. I need to get going, anyway." Damen stood, leaned over me, and gave me a quick kiss on the lips. The kiss was much too brief. "When can I see you again?"

I gazed up into his deep eyes. "I'm pretty much free every night this week, assuming I don't get called in to work."

"Good. I'll be back tomorrow. Don't eat dinner."

"Great. See you then." I basked in the brilliance of his smile before standing. "If you want to wait a minute, I can walk you to the door. I need to grab my purse."

"Sure."

Elmer shot him some mean eyes.

"Actually, I should get going," Damen said, looking a bit nervous.

Was he really going to let that little creep chase him away?

I bit back a comment that he might not have liked and threw him a little dismissive wave. "That's fine. I'll see you tomorrow." He made a beeline for the front door; I glared at Elmer. "Why'd you do that?"

"What?"

"You scared my friend."

Elmer blinked his creepy, little, beady eyes at me. "I didn't mean to."

"Yeah. Right."

"Whatever. Can we get going? Dale Nethinger hath been calling me every five minutes thince I left. I think she'th getting nervouth."

"You could have called her and explained the problem."

Inside my car, I shoved the key into the ignition and gave it a twist.

"I'm not a freaking geniuth like thome people, but even I know that wouldn't have worked."

"Okay, so why don't you just *poof* to wherever they're filming and I'll meet you there?"

"Becauthe I'm not filming even one minute without you being there. Consider yourthelf my agent."

What had I gotten myself into?

A jagged bolt of lightning lit up the sky.

Emma Walker could hardly believe this was happening. She was alone. With Kyle Quinn. *The* Kyle Quinn. "I thought you'd hooked up with Stephanie Barnett?" she asked, finding herself leaning into him. He smelled so good. Looked even better. And she hoped to find out how he tasted soon too.

His brows scrunched. "Who told you that? I didn't hook up with her or anyone else."

"I thought I saw you together at Joe Malone's party."

"No. I didn't go to Malone's party."

"Oh." The house had been crammed full of people. She supposed she could have mistaken someone else for him. Now that she thought about it, she hadn't gotten a clear view of him . . . or whoever that had been. "Anyway, I really appreciate the help with algebra." She pulled open the door. "It would take me hours to do this stupid homework if you didn't help."

"No problem." Kyle stepped inside after her, then waited for her to shut the door. "Where's your mom?"

"Working. She's on afternoons all week. Then she switches to midnights. The joys of being a nurse."

"That sucks for her." Moving swiftly, he hooked her waist in his arm and jerked her to him. The air left her lungs, and her heart started pounding in her chest.

"Yeah, sucks for her," she whispered, smiling up into Kyle Quinn's dark eyes. Little currents of electricity seemed to be buzzing up and down through her body.

He tipped his head. "I've been wanting to do this for a long time," he said as his mouth moved toward hers.

She swore that she'd just died and gone to heaven.

It was almost three A.M. before I'd been able to hit the road. My eyes felt like they'd been plucked out of my head, rolled in sand, and stuffed back into their sockets. I was probably incapable of passing a field sobriety test. Not because I was drunk, but just because I was so freaking exhausted. And all I could think about was landing in my big, soft bed.

The filming had gone okay. Not great. But not disastrous either. As it turned out, Elmer could act charming when the cameras were rolling. Even I found myself looking past his ghoulish features to admire his sense of humor. When he was *on,* he wasn't a goofy cutup. Nor was he socially awkward. He was witty and intelligent.

At any rate, by some miracle, I made it back to the parents' mansion without being pulled over, hitting something, or going the wrong way on the freeway. I dragged my stiff, achy body up the front walk and tried the door. Locked. I knocked. I rang the bell. I called Mom and left her a message. And once everything else failed, I went back to my car, slumped into the driver's seat, reclined it as far back as it would go, and shut my eyes.

A knock on my window woke me up sometime later. Much later. It was light outside.

Mom was standing there, munching on a piece of toast, staring at me like I was Shamu at SeaWorld.

I turned on the car so I could power down the window. The clock's digital display glowed green. Seven-thirty. And the windshield was covered with water droplets. It had stormed again while I'd been sleeping.

My phone rang.

"Sloan? Why are you sleeping in your car?" Mom asked.

"Because it's more comfortable—and drier—than the front porch. You locked me out."

Mom gave me stink eye. "I didn't lock you out. You locked yourself out. I was in bed when you left."

"You're right. Technically, I did lock myself out."

Mom handed me her nibbled toast. "Are you hungry? Here. Come inside and I'll make you some pancakes while you shower."

I haven't had Mom's pancakes in years. That's a good thing. She's the only person I know who can mess up a perfectly good Aunt Jemima batter. It's the additives she tries to sneak in, to make them healthy: crunchy twigs, little leaves. And don't get me started on the brown liquid—labeled sugar-free syrup—that she douses them in. "That's a very kind offer, but I've got to go." As if on cue, my phone rang again. I snatched it. Expecting it to be either Chief Peyton or JT, I checked the display. It was the latter. "See? Work's calling me. I'm late." I grabbed my phone and purse and hurried out of the car. "I need to change clothes."

Mom shrugged, then fell into step beside me. "I guess that leaves more for Katie. She's a little skinny, anyway. And her diet is absolutely horrible. Did you know she eats a ham sandwich every single day?"

"Terrible, isn't it? I've tried telling her how bad those processed meats are, but she won't stop. Maybe she'll listen to you." Inside, I hustled up the steps. There was no time for a shower. I would have to freshen up, pull my hair back, put on a little makeup, and head out. I still had a long drive to Quantico ahead of me.

"You can bet I'll try my best. I love that girl like she's my own daughter."

"I know you do, Mom. And she's so, so lucky."

After I changed, slapped on some makeup, and plastered my hair back, I hurried back downstairs. I checked my messages before heading out to my car.

JT: "Sloan, call me. ASAP. We've got a second victim." My insides twisted. Bad news already. "Damn."

Every man casts a shadow; not his body only, but his imperfectly mingled spirit. This is his grief. Let him turn which way he will, it falls opposite to the sun; short at noon, long at eve. Did you never see it?

—Henry David Thoreau

5

Within an hour, I'd parked down the street from the middle-class residence of Emma Walker, the second victim. Wasting no time, I bustled out of the vehicle and jogged down the sidewalk toward the cordoned-off area in front of the house. The similarities between the girls, at least from the outside, were apparent right away. Like Stephanie Barnett, Emma Walker lived in a nice, well-kept home on a quiet suburban street. Their houses were mere blocks from each other, which suggested the killer was probably local, targeting girls he knew personally. My first thought, as I hurried up the front steps, was to check what schools the girls attended. If we were dealing with a teen killer, chances were good they were students of the same school.

Inside, I found JT standing in the living room, talking to a woman who had to be the girl's mother—judging by the bloodshot eyes and tear-streaked face. My heart did a little jerk in my chest at the sight of the bereft woman, and I wondered if I'd ever get used to seeing such wretched human suffering. My insides twisted, and my stomach churned. I took a couple of deep breaths and approached JT and the girl's mom.

JT introduced me. "Mrs. Walker, this is Sloan Skye. She's going to help us profile the person who did this."

Dabbing her splotchy face, Mrs. Walker merely acknowledged me with a nod before turning back to JT. "I don't understand why anyone would do this. My daughter was an innocent girl. A good girl. She was liked by everyone. Had lots of friends. Never got into trouble. Why?" She started sobbing again, and JT glanced at me.

He said, "I know this is hard for you, but the more information we can get about your daughter, the more accurate our profile will be." I could see that he was having a hard time with this one too. The man did have a good heart.

I tried to encourage him with a tiny nod.

The woman's sobs finally settled down a little, and she blew her nose. "I'm trying." She sniffled.

"Take your time," he said gently; his eyes were very soft and kind.

"What was it you wanted?" she asked. "I don't remember."

"We'd like a list of all of her friends at school," he answered.

The woman looked left and then right. "I don't know. . . . Wait, her phone. Let me see what I can come up with."

"We'll stay right here."

"Okay." She lifted an index finger. Her lip quivering, she asked, "Does it make me a bad mother that I don't know most of her friends' names?"

JT shook his head. "No, ma'am. It doesn't."

She nodded and shuffled away, shoulders sagging.

"I feel for her," I told him, once I was sure she was out of earshot.

"Me too. She lost her only daughter."

Staring at the photographs lining one wall of the living room, I grumbled, "I hate that so many of our cases involve children. The kidnapping in the first one, the stolen babies in the second, and now this."

"Yeah." JT shoved his fingers through his hair. "Makes it hard to sleep at night."

"I thought I was the only one."

JT's gaze locked onto mine. "You're not."

I forced myself to look away before things became uncomfortable. Not so long ago, we'd gone out. On a date. And it was nice. Very nice. But I had decided, even though there was enough chemistry between us to cause a nuclear reactor meltdown, that we had to keep things professional. I had high hopes for a career in the FBI. Any rumors about my sleeping with a superior would pretty much put an end to that dream.

At any rate, every now and then, things got a little strained between JT and me. Even though I was now kind of, sort of, seeing Damen. I'd read that a person's brain could rule the body, that thoughts could cure disease, lengthen life, and improve health. So why was it so hard for a person's mind to seize control over an overactive libido?

Thankfully, Mrs. Walker came back. "The detective wants to take Emma's phone for evidence, so I copied down the names and numbers for you." She handed JT a piece of paper.

"Thanks." JT turned around and gave me the paper. "Now, one more time, what can you tell us about what happened last night?"

"I don't know. I came home from work at a little after midnight—I'm a nurse, working afternoons this week. I found my daughter upstairs in her room. She was . . ." She stopped and blinked once, twice. "She was on the floor. No pulse. Nothing. And she had these strange marks on her neck."

"When was the last time you talked to her?"

"I called her after school, right before cheerleading practice."

"Did she say anything unusual?" JT scribbled some details in his little notebook.

"Nothing. After practice, she was going to the library to study and then she was coming home."

JT asked, "Is it possible your daughter brought someone into your home without your knowledge?"

The mother's lips thinned. "Yes, I suppose so. But I've warned her never to bring anyone in our home when I'm not there. I trusted her." She placed her shaking hands over her mouth. "If only I'd known . . . If only . . ." She started shaking all over, hard sobs cutting through the silence.

Not sure what to do, I stood mute at JT's side. Would I ever know what to say in these situations? Or would they always be uncomfortable and awkward?

JT gave the woman a moment to collect herself. When it seemed she was able to speak again, he asked in a soft voice, "Outside of your daughter, did you notice anything else unusual? Anything out of place?"

Mrs. Walker's eyes darted around the room, as if she was searching. "No. But I wasn't looking. I just went upstairs to check on Emma when she didn't respond. Once I found her, I called 911 right away. After that, I don't really know what I was doing. I'm a nurse with over twenty years of experience, and I've seen just about anything you could imagine. But this . . . Well, even I couldn't handle this."

"I'm so sorry," I said.

Forrester came down the stairs and turned the corner, joining our little circle. "We're just about done upstairs. We'll be out of your way soon, ma'am. I'd like a phone number to reach you in case we have any more questions," the BPD detective inquired.

She nodded, then enclosed her body in her arms. "I . . . I don't know if I can stay here tonight." Her eyes cut to the stairs. "No, I don't think I can. My sister lives a few miles from here. I'll probably go stay with her for a few days. You can call my cell phone. I'll give you her number as well." She rattled off the numbers for the officer.

Meanwhile, JT and I were getting antsy. We were standing around, accomplishing absolutely nothing. We had two dead teenagers. Two. Killed within twenty-four hours of each other. This guy was going to kill again. Soon. We needed to be doing something.

"What's next?" I asked JT.

He was skimming his notes. "We've got nothing." His brows scrunched. "Not a goddamn thing."

"Have you asked if Emma Walker knew Stephanie Barnett? Or what about Barnett's father?"

"I . . . No."

I did a three-sixty, looking for Mrs. Walker. She'd been right there, behind us, a few minutes ago. Not any more. Forrester was gone too. I dashed outside and found Forrester. "Where is Mrs. Walker?"

"She went to stay with a family member."

"Address?"

He flipped his notebook open, ripped a sheet out, and wrote something on it. I thanked him and turned back toward the house, figuring I'd find JT inside. He wasn't. He was outside, walking toward his car.

"Where are you going?" I asked.

"I don't know." Leaning past me, he grabbed the door handle.

I set my hand on his arm. "Is everything okay? You're acting a little strange."

"I had a rough night."

"What happened?"

"I don't want to talk about it right now." His jaw clenched a little as he pulled open the door. "I'm heading back to Quantico."

"But what about Mrs. Walker? I have the address where she's staying. Shouldn't we talk to her about Barnett?"

"You talk to her. I need . . . to go." He sat and slammed the door. With me standing outside, wondering what was going on, he started the car and zoomed off.

I haven't known JT long, but I knew him well enough to realize something was very wrong.

Shoving aside my concern, I dashed to my car and motored over to the address Forrester had given me. There were three cars crowded on the double-wide driveway. I hoped one of them was Mrs. Walker's.

I wasted no time running up to the house and knocking.

A woman, who looked a lot like Mrs. Walker, answered. "May I help you?"

"Hi, I'm Sloan Skye. FBI. I was wondering if Mrs. Walker was here?"

"She is, but she's resting."

"We had only a couple more questions for her, if there's any chance she might be able to speak with me. It won't take long."

The woman stepped aside, inviting me in. "Let me go check with her. FBI, right?"

"Yes."

I stood in the tiled foyer of a pretty Federal-style Colonial and watched the woman shuffle up the wood staircase. At the top, she knocked on a closed door. Seconds later, she stepped into a room. Mrs. Walker emerged, looking worse than she had a little while ago. Very pale. Her face. Her lips. She staggered slightly at the top of the stairs. And then, she just collapsed. I saw her falling. It was like time had slowed and every second lasted minutes. I tried to stop her, tried to catch her, but I couldn't get there fast enough. Before I knew it, the thumping had stopped and I was staring into her eyes, wide open but unseeing. I couldn't move. Not a muscle. I couldn't believe what I'd just seen. Was it real?

Someone screamed, snapping me out of my stupor. Finally able to move, I ran to her, felt her neck for a pulse, and shouted, "Call 911!" I didn't know if anyone had heard me.

Not that it mattered.

There was no pulse.

There were no respirations.

She was dead. The poor woman was dead.

Hours later, I was finally given the green light to leave. No sooner was I on the road than the chief called, asking when I would be in. She needed to discuss something with me. As soon as possible.

I haven't been working with the PBAU for long, and thus I don't have a lot of experience in these things. However, I've already learned that when one was called into the chief's office for a private chat, the news generally wasn't good. My heart started thumping irregularly the minute JT informed me that Chief Peyton was waiting for me in her office.

I fussed with my clothes, self-consciously, as I hurried toward her office. These days, Mom had the money to shop at the finest stores. And she took full advantage of that fact. But her taste hadn't elevated. Not one iota. Instead of owning ugly clothes sewn from cheap materials, she now owned hordes of ugly clothes sewn from expensive materials. Lucky me, I got to wear them.

I did my best to bolster my confidence as I knocked on the chief's door. She responded with an invitation to come in. I opened the door and saw she was on the phone. There was a grim look on her face. I sat in the chair that faced her desk; my hands clasped together in my lap.

She cut off the call, placed the phone back on the cradle, and then smiled at me. The smile wasn't genuine.

I was in for something horrid. I could tell.

"I heard about your unfortunate accident, Sloan. The fire. If there's anything we can do to help, please don't be afraid to ask."

"That's very kind of you to offer," I said, knowing the fire couldn't be the reason for my being called in for a private tête-à-tête with Alice Peyton. "Thank you."

"You're welcome." The chief hesitated. This was just a lead-in to the real purpose of our meeting. "Sloan, you have done an exceptional job for us since your very first day on the job."

"Thank you. It's been an excellent experience. I'm grateful for the opportunity."

"So glad you feel that way. I'm sure you realize your activities go far beyond those of the average summer intern."

"I do."

"We're walking a very fine line with you, and I want to make sure you're not feeling pressured to take on more than you can handle. At times, your work has put you directly in the line of fire. That's something no intern has experienced before."

I wasn't sure where this conversation was leading. Was it possible that someone, maybe one of her superiors, was blaming me for what had happened to Mrs. Walker? I had a witness who could testify to my innocence. Immediately after she had collapsed, her sister came out of the room with an empty pill bottle. Mrs. Walker had overdosed.

Preparing myself mentally to defend my innocence, I said, "I've always felt you took calculated risks and reasonable measures to protect me."

"We have done our best."

"I know." And I did. What I wanted to know now was where this conversation was headed. "Does this have anything to do with Mrs. Walker's death?"

"No."

No? If not, then what is it?

Was this the result of some kind of disciplinary action? Had someone reported what I was doing and decided the bureau needed to put a stop to it, pronto?

"Chief, I realize I don't have the training to be a full

member of this team yet, and maybe you're bending the rules a bit—"

"Sloan, I haven't bent the rules. I've looped them up and tied them in knots. My superior reviewed our work on the last case, and there is talk of my facing a disciplinary review."

Oh, no. "I'm sorry."

"You have nothing to be sorry for. You followed my direction, and we got the job done, thanks to you. I knew from the start I was taking a risk. The bottom line is my superior has determined you should be facing no more dangerous tasks than driving in."

I sighed. *Bureaucracy.* "What can I do?"

"Nothing. I've informed my superiors that you will be delegated tasks that are more suited to your current position with the bureau."

In other words, the fun was over. I would be, from this point forward, filing and fetching coffee. "I understand."

"In the meantime, I've secured your spot in the next FBI Academy class. You've just finished up your master's. I don't know what your plans are for the fall. But the slot is yours, if you want it."

My insides did a somersault. "You bet I do. Thank you." When I'd applied for the internship, I'd hoped I might receive some kind of recommendation for the academy. I hadn't expected the path to be paved for me.

"Excellent. I know you'll be a very valuable member of the bureau for years to come. And I hope you'll choose to join our team when you graduate."

"I would be honored."

"Good." She steepled her fingers under her chin. "Another thing: Hough is out on medical. She miscarried last night. The unit is putting together a care package, if you'd like to contribute."

Miscarried.

That explained JT's sour mood earlier.

"I'm sorry to hear that. Of course, I'll contribute."

"Very well. Thomas is handling all the specifics. You can get with him later. Now, about our current case. We're having a status meeting tomorrow morning. I want you there. I have an assignment for you. I don't know how anyone could argue with this one. It's no more dangerous for you than it would be for any teenager."

I was intrigued. On the one hand, she'd just been warned to pull me out of danger. While on the other hand, it appeared as though she was sending me undercover again. "I'm all ears, so to speak."

Her lips curled into a slightly devious smile. "I knew I could count on you."

If you only do what you know you can do—you never do very much.

—Tom Krause

6

The day I said *"sayonara"* to Osbourn High School was the happiest day of my life. Over were the days of being teased and tormented by students who were years older than me, but dozens of IQ points beneath me. I had endured being stuffed into trash cans and lockers, called any number of derogatory names, humiliated and harassed from the day I stepped into the concrete-and-tile building until the day I stepped out of it.

And now, I was about to dive right back into the shark-infested waters of high school. Oh, the joy. I hoped Fitzgerald High wasn't as bad as Osbourn.

This time, in the interest of fitting in somewhat, I was pretending to be a below-average student. If not for the mean girls and obnoxious boys, it might have been an interesting experiment. But for whatever reason, I seemed to be a bully magnet, attracting them no matter what I did.

I hoped I wouldn't be playing the part of a below-average high-school junior for long.

Standing in the FBI Academy parking lot, I made a few adjustments to my clothes before I tumbled out of the car. I'd done some shopping yesterday, after my meeting with the chief. She let me know Mom's clothes just weren't going to cut it for this assignment. Thus, instead of the wool trousers and ugly silk blouse I'd been wearing yesterday when I'd come in, I was now sporting the unofficial uniform of the high-school student: miniskirt, top, and sandals.

The skirt was too short. The top was too tight. The heels were too high. The ensemble screamed "slut."

I yanked on the skirt's hem again. I felt ridiculous, more ridiculous than the time I had to pretend to be nine months pregnant and had to wear one of Brittany Hough's castaway maternity dresses. The ugly thing had a freaking bib, and still I felt worse in this getup. Especially when I caught the look on JT's face as I pushed my car door shut. He parked his car and shoved open his door. "Not one word," I warned him as I tried to pretend his obvious staring wasn't making me feel a little warm.

"I didn't say anything."

"You said it with your eyes."

His lips curled into an adorable half smile as he sauntered over to me. I couldn't help noticing the smile didn't reach his eyes. "I just can't hide anything from you, Sloan, can I?"

"I don't think you even tried."

"You're right. I didn't." His gaze dropped to boob level.

I pushed on his chin, forcing him to lift his head. "Do."

He chuckled and the two of us headed inside. Despite my suspicion that his semi-inappropriate leer was just an act, to cover up his pain, I was glad to see he was acting a little more like himself. I'd never been pregnant. I couldn't even imagine how it felt to lose a child.

One of the reasons why I'd decided to draw the proverbial line in the sand with JT was finding out he had *donated* his sperm to Hough, and she was carrying his child. Granted, their situation was somewhat unique. She was a lesbian, despite having conceived the child the old-fashioned "Tab A, Slot B" way. She'd initially intended to raise the baby with her wife. But since she'd suffered an ugly breakup— which, rumor had it, was leading to what promised to be an even uglier divorce—JT had been taking a more active role in preparing to parent. And a more active interest in Hough's pregnancy. Thus, I suspected he might have felt the loss more keenly than he'd expected.

Inside the building, as we waited for the elevator to rumble its way down to us, I asked, "How's Hough doing? The chief told me yesterday."

"She's doing as well as could be expected, I guess. She took it hard."

"I'm sorry." The bell chimed, and the door rolled open. A couple of guys in suits stepped out; their gazes flicked to me as they walked past. I smashed my arms over my chest. "This is ridiculous. I want to change."

"You look fine," JT said, poking the button for our floor.

"People are staring."

"That's only because you appear younger than you are. You look out of place."

"I don't know." I glanced down. My boobs looked mighty big in this shirt.

"I'm telling the truth."

The car bounced to a stop at our floor, and I scurried into the sanctuary of the unit, dropped my stuff on my desk, and grabbed a legal pad and pen. Then I headed up to the conference room, situated at the back of the open space, elevated slightly. A raised walk led to the entrance. I clomped up the steps in my high-school "ho heels" and plopped down in a chair at the huge table. Within minutes, the others joined me. JT, Chad Fischer, our media liaison, some man I didn't know, Gabe Wagner, who seemed to appreciate my outfit more than JT, and the chief.

Chief Peyton cleared her throat. "Good morning." She motioned to the stranger. "This is Steve McBride. He'll be handling Hough's duties while she's on medical leave."

We all uttered a polite hello, to which he gave each of us a little nod.

"Now let's go over the case." Peyton motioned to the board she'd set up. There were two pictures on it—one of each of our victims. There was a line drawn from each photo to the words "Fitzgerald High School." Another line was drawn from Stephanie Barnett to Michael Barnett. "This is what we have so far. The only connection between our victims is their school. They share nothing else in common, outside of gender. Different races—one Caucasian, the other black. Different body types. We've found no link between our one person of interest, Michael Barnett, and Emma Walker."

"But they both live in single-parent households. Middle-class," I pointed out.

"True." She uncapped a whiteboard Magic Marker and wrote some notes below the high school.

"They are geographically linked too," JT pointed out. "Their homes are located within blocks of each other. Michael Barnett's house is close to both."

"Has cause of death been confirmed for either victim yet?" I asked.

"Yes. The official COD for both Barnett and Walker is fibrillation and heart failure caused by electrocution."

"Electrocution?" I echoed, completely surprised.

"Yes." Peyton turned on a projector, displaying a set of two photographs, both of the young women's torsos. One was a smooth ivory color, the other a deep mocha. A series of branching red marks, like those found on lightning-strike victims, fanned out from the center of their chests.

"Lightning strikes generally cause no entry or exit wounds. No muscle damage," I recited. Back when I was little, after our neighbor had been struck by lightning, I'd done some reading on it. It seemed that it might come in handy in this case.

"That is consistent with our victims," the chief said, pointing at the photos. "The current interrupted the normal electrical activity of the heart, causing the cells to beat independently from each other, rather than as one coordinated system."

"What about the bite marks?" I asked as I jotted down some info. "Is our unsub vampiric?"

"It appears he may be. Both victims were bit, but the level of blood loss was not lethal."

"Electrocution," I repeated. I'd read a lot of my father's research before I'd lost it. But I didn't recall any Mythic that used electricity to kill its victims. I was going to have to skim through the book Damen had given me. ASAP.

"Is it possible we're dealing with a mortal unsub, pretending to be Mythic?" Chad Fischer asked. "Someone who is using some kind of electrical device to deliver the current and is merely biting, to throw us off?"

"We may be. But the markings don't support that theory. Either way, we need to find out why he is using this mode of killing. I haven't done any research yet, but it seems to be his signature, unique to our unsub." Peyton pointed to Gabe Wagner. "I'd like you to see what you can find out on electrocution. See if there have been any serial killers who've used it as their method of killing."

"Will do, Chief," he said, standing.

To me, Peyton said, "You know what your assignment is, Skye. It's July. Summer classes are just getting started. You've registered, correct? If you register yourself, I'm not technically sending you undercover . . ." At my nod, she added, "Excellent. Keep your ear to the ground. See what you can learn about our two victims."

"I'll do my best," I said, yanking once again on my skirt.

"And the clothes are perfect. Good job."

Perfect? It was no wonder I was a social outcast back in the day. I wouldn't have been caught dead in a getup like this.

This assignment was nothing like the last. I wasn't putting myself directly in the line of fire, so to speak. I wasn't setting myself up as bait. But, by the same token, I was about to revisit a time in my life I would have gladly forgotten. And I was doing it dressed like a ho.

"I know you will do a great job." She turned to JT next. "Thomas, you, Fischer, and I are going to have to sit down and hammer out a plan. Thomas, Fischer will be focusing on the victimology, looking for any common connections between the girls. I want you to work with McBride. See what you can dig up on Michael Barnett."

I gathered my things and scurried back to my desk. Class would be starting in a little over a half hour. I needed to get myself mentally prepared for this. And I might have to bend a few traffic laws to make it to class on time.

I grabbed my purse, a notebook, and a pen; then I hauled ass out of the building, eliciting more than a handful of curious stares along the way. Outside, I cranked on my car and zoomed out of the parking lot.

I was about to reenter the third level of hell. Yay, me!

I read Dante's *Divine Comedy* when I was in third grade. I never forgot it. This is why I can say with absolute certainty that he missed the mark, particularly when it came to his description of the deepest bowels of hell. I know this because I was in it.

The teacher was droning on and on about nothing in particular. This was supposed to be an economics class, but he was talking about dodging the draft during the Vietnam War. I was getting the stink eye from the gaggle of girls in the back row. There was no air-conditioning, and it had to be at least 120 degrees in the classroom. And my phone, set on vibrate, was ringing nonstop.

How the heck would I convince anyone that I belonged here? That I was one of them?

Moving carefully, I slid my hand into my new backpack to check my phone. The last call was from Katie. I gave a mental sigh.

"Excuse me, Miss Skye," the teacher said. "Care to answer my question?"

I zipped my backpack, snapping, "What question is that?"

The class broke out into riotous laughter.

At first, my face flamed. But then, as I noticed that more

than one student was giving me a friendly smile, a virtual high five, my mortification lifted.

Could it have been so easy? Could I have avoided years of torment if only I'd dressed like a prostitute and acted like I was stupid?

Now the teacher's face was turning colors. That shade didn't look so great on him. It deepened when a few residual snickers echoed through the room. He pointed toward the door.

I was being excused from class. I'd never been thrown out of a class. I'll admit, I was a little embarrassed. But I did my damned best to hide it as I gathered my things. Just before leaving, I glanced at the gaggle. One of them acknowledged me with a little tip of the head.

I headed out into the hall, wandered down to the principal's office, and sat outside it. Principal Glover knew why I was here, at the school. He knew I was working undercover. But, as far as I knew, he was the only one. He gave me a look as he rushed in from somewhere, waved me into his office, and closed us in.

"What's this?" he asked.

"I'm trying to fit in."

"Got it. Just try not to piss them off too badly."

"Will do." The bell rang. I checked my printed-out schedule. "I guess it's off to introductory algebra next."

"Good luck." He opened the door, stepping aside to let me pass.

"Thanks." I donned a grim expression and shuffled out into the packed hallway. It was loud and chaotic, exactly as I remembered it. I joined the stream of bodies heading toward the math classrooms.

"That was hilarious," someone said behind me.

I glanced over my shoulder. "Thanks." I stepped to the side so I wouldn't be trampled. A girl, the one I surmised had spoken, followed me. "He wasn't even talking about economics. I was dying from boredom," I added.

"So was everyone else." Jostling her books, the girl

leaned closer. "If you want to skip class, we all go down to the bathroom on the D Wing. Nobody ever checks it."

"Thanks. D Wing. Where are you headed next?"

"Algebra."

"Me too. I'm Sloan, by the way." I extended a hand.

"Cool name. I'm Megan Carter." She took it and gave it a shake. We began to walk down the corridor together.

"Thanks. I hated my name when I was a kid. I thought it was weird. It's grown on me. Good to meet you, Megan."

"You too."

I made a point to look around, as if nervous. "I heard about this school on the news. Two girls were killed. Just this week. That's crazy."

Megan's expression sobered. "One of them was my friend."

"Oh. Sorry I mentioned it."

"It's okay. You didn't know. How could you?"

We were now standing outside our algebra classroom.

A young man sauntered up, gave us a look, and sneered. "Hey, Megan. Looking good today," he said to her boobs.

We looked at each other.

"Did you say D Wing?" I asked.

"Yeah." She motioned with her hand. "It's this way."

"Who was that?" I asked, following her.

"Derik Sutton. He's a creep. Everyone hates him." She peered over her shoulder, as though afraid he might be following us.

Finally we ducked into the bathroom, which was empty. It was no wonder nobody checked it. This wing seemed to be unused right now. The hall lights were illuminated, but I noticed not a single classroom was lit up.

Inside, we flipped on the light. Megan went to the counter, dropped her backpack on the floor, and stared into the mirror. "It was my fault," she said, eyes reddening. "I haven't told anyone."

"What was your fault?"

"Stephanie's death."

A little shiver buzzed up my spine. "Why do you think it's your fault?"

"Because I left her. At Joe's party." She wrapped her arms around herself and closed her eyes. "I don't know why I'm telling you this. I don't even know you. I guess I just needed to tell someone."

"That's a hard secret to keep."

"Yeah, it is."

I watched her struggle to contain her grief and guilt. My heart ached for her. It wasn't fair that she was blaming herself, but I doubted I'd be able to convince her of that.

"Did you know someone wanted to hurt her?"

"No way." She rubbed her thumb along her lower lashes, wiping away the raccoon eyes that were forming.

"Then there's no reason to blame yourself."

"If I'd walked home with her, instead of dumping her so I could hook up with that asshole Nate, maybe she'd still be alive."

"And maybe not."

Megan's hands shook as she bent over to dig into her backpack. She pulled out a water bottle, flipped open the top, and took a swig. She handed it to me. "Drink? It's vodka. The teachers can't smell it on your breath."

I shook my head. I knew for a fact that wasn't true. Any form of alcohol could be detected on someone's breath. "No thanks."

"Suit yourself." She took another swallow, capped the bottle, and stuffed it back into her bag. "I don't want to be here."

"Me neither."

She turned around, ass resting on the sink. "I don't want to talk anymore. What's your story?"

"Me? I don't have a story. I'm just here because I have to be. I wasn't happy when I heard about it."

"Nobody is. School sucks balls. It's summertime. I should be working on my tan, not doing fucking algebra."

"Yeah." I wasn't about to tell her that baking in the hot sun was about as enjoyable to me as having a tooth extraction.

"My friends are all going to the shore today. And here I am." Something in her backpack buzzed. She shoved her hand in and pulled out a phone.

I smoothed on some lip gloss, trying not to cringe at my reflection in the mirror as I listened in on her end of the conversation. Unfortunately, she said very little. When the call ended, she looked at me, said, "Fuck this," and left.

I guessed she was heading to the beach.

I debated whether I should hang out in the bathroom, alone, until the bell rang or head to algebra. The thought of sitting in a classroom, learning how to solve uber easy linear equations I could do with my eyes closed, made my brain ache. But sitting in the girls' bathroom all day wasn't going to get me a permanent gig with the FBI.

Steeling myself for an hour of simplifying expressions, I took a deep breath and headed out.

I have known a vast quantity of nonsense talked about bad men not looking you in the face. Don't trust that conventional idea. Dishonesty will stare honesty out of countenance any day in the week, if there is anything to be got by it.

—Charles Dickens

7

The rest of the day crept by at a snail's pace. It was torture, but not in the way I'd expected. The subject matter was dull. Most of the teachers were trying their best to get the students involved and interested, but they were failing. In a nutshell, I was very glad to be leaving, and I was dreading going back tomorrow. The one highlight had been that little chat I'd had with Megan. She hadn't given me any useful details, but I now knew that Stephanie Barnett had sneaked out to a party. Others had to have seen her. Maybe even with the killer.

I tossed my backpack onto the backseat and flopped into the driver's seat. My phone was in my fist, and I was about to call JT to bring him up to speed when his ringtone sounded.

I hit the button. "Great timing. I was about to call you."

"I just got off the phone with Forrester. A third girl is dead."

"Already? This guy's moving fast." I stuffed the key into

the ignition and cranked it. "I'm at the school. What's the address?"

"He's thinking this one isn't a murder. If it is, the MO is completely different. He's on his way to the scene now."

"Do you have the address?"

"I do. But you can't go. Chief's orders."

"But I can be there in five."

"And what if some of the students see you? Your cover will be blown."

I glanced out the window, watching the parking lot empty. A few stragglers were just leaving the building. "You're right. It's bad enough I couldn't use a fake name to go undercover. I'm trying to keep my last name quiet. I guess that means I won't be able to go to any of the crime scenes from this point forward. At least, not until I'm done with this assignment."

"Are you complaining?"

I thought about the nausea, the jangling nerves, and the awkward conversations with grieving parents. "Of course not. I'd never complain. Anyway, I had an interesting conversation with a friend of Stephanie Barnett's today. Barnett sneaked out to a party the night she died."

"Interesting. What else did the friend know?"

"That's it. Nothing else. They split up. She dumped her at the party and left with a boy. But maybe someone else saw Barnett."

"It's something."

"It isn't much. I don't even know who was at the party, where it was, nothing."

"The fact that you somehow managed to find a friend of Barnett's already tells me you won't have any problems getting more information."

"That was dumb luck."

"We'll see about that. Nothing about you is dumb, Sloan."

"And we'll see about that." The parking lot was clear now. I drove to the exit and steered out into traffic. I was headed toward the freeway, but I didn't know which way to go once I got there. "What should I do now? Go back to the unit?"

"No, there isn't anything you can do there now. Might as well call it a day. I'll call you as soon as I know more about the dead girl."

"Okay. I'll talk to you later, then."

"Good-bye, Sloan."

"Bye. Um, JT?"

"Yeah?"

"Are you okay?"

"Yeah. I'm fine." There was a heaviness to his voice. I couldn't miss it.

"If you need to talk, I'm here."

"Thanks."

"You're welcome." When he didn't say anything else, I added, "I'll talk to you later."

"Yep. Bye."

I clicked off and called Katie. No answer. I dropped my phone onto the passenger seat and pointed my car toward my "home away from home."

When I rolled into my folks' driveway, I noticed a certain car was parked front and center. It would seem I had company. Again.

He was early. It wasn't even close to dinnertime.

"Hello, gorgeous." Damen took a slow, winding visual perusal of my person before lifting his gaze to my face. "That is some outfit you're wearing."

"Yeah." Feeling very uncomfortable, I hugged myself as I clomped up to the door. "It's for work."

His brows rose. He shouldered the door frame as I knocked. I'd forgotten to ask Mom for a house key again.

"I guess I shouldn't ask?"

"Probably not. But, based on your expression, I feel it's pretty safe to say it isn't what you're thinking."

Sergio opened the door for us, gave me a little nod, then disappeared to take care of some other pressing matter.

Damen cornered me in the foyer. "It's going to take some getting used to, knowing you're out there, risking your life—"

"I'm an intern," I pointed out. "Interns generally don't risk their life . . . unless you consider going out for coffee or lunch a death-defying act." I decided it wasn't a good idea telling him the truth. Not yet.

His chuckle was warm and his eyes sparkled, and I liked those sparkles very much. "Fair enough. I'll worry no more." He grabbed me at the waist and pulled me closer. "May I?" he asked, tipping his head.

"You may."

I swear, my feet left the floor when he kissed me. My head was spinning when the kiss ended, and I opened my eyes to find I'd smashed my body against his and was holding on for dear life.

"W-wow," I stammered.

"I agree. Maybe we should do that again." He kissed me once more, and it was all I could do to resist begging him to take me right there, on the foyer's cold marble floor.

Sadly, a soft cough cut that one short. Then again, that was probably for the better.

Still plastered to his front, I turned to give the interrupting party a half smile. In my mind's eye, I imagined I was looking completely stumble-to-your-ass drunk.

Mom's brows lifted so high, her forehead looked like the skin of a shar-pei. "Sorry to interrupt, but, Sloan, your father needs to speak with you."

Odd. "Sure." I gave Damen an apologetic grin and stumbled away, heading toward my father's home office. The door was open, and he was sitting in front of his computer.

"Sloan, have a seat."

I pulled up the big armchair angled in the small room's corner so I was looking across the desk at my father. "Is something wrong?"

"No. Not at all. But after your reaction to the last time, I thought I'd better run this one by you."

I had no clue what he was talking about. "What 'one'?"

"Damen Sylver has formally proposed that you and he should court."

"'Court'?"

"To court is to date with the intention of marriage."

"Marriage? Um . . ." I wrung my hands. Court? Courtship? Marriage? I'd just broken an arranged engagement, and here I was staring at the possibility of diving into another? A lot of what-ifs flooded my mind. What if I decided Damen wasn't the right one for me? How hard would it be to end this courtship? What if I started to like him, to love him, and he backed out? What if? . . . What if? . . . What if?

"Tell me what you're thinking," my father said, clearly keying into my mixed emotions. A part of me was flattered that a man who seemed so great wanted to take our relationship to the next level. But it was so fast, and we barely knew each other.

Maybe there was a reason why he was pushing toward a commitment so soon.

If something seems too good to be true, it probably is.

"Why is he moving so fast? Why even think about marriage already?"

"It may seem fast to you, but it isn't. Not in the world of the elves. Arranged marriages are still very common. Many times a man meets his wife for the first time on the day of their wedding. If it makes you feel any better, I don't see a wedding in your immediate future. When Her Majesty approached me with her concerns—"

"She has concerns?"

"It's nothing personal. She has a great deal of respect and admiration for you, of course."

"Of course." Yes, there was a touch of sarcasm there. It just sort of slipped out.

My father paused for a few seconds, as if to give me a moment to gather myself. It wasn't necessary. I had full control of my emotions. If I didn't, he'd know it. "Sloan, maybe you don't realize, but that man out there is the future king of the elves. Things don't work the same with royalty as they do with an average FBI profiler."

"I'm not dating any FBI profiler, average or otherwise. But that's beside the point. I realize Damen is the potential inheritor of a throne, but isn't he down the line of succession? Like, way down the line?"

"No. He's at the top."

"What? Didn't someone mention something about the fertility of the elves? Doesn't he have like . . . I don't know . . . dozens of siblings?"

"He does. But they all relinquished their claim."

"Why?"

My father leaned back in his chair. "Because there are certain requirements, expectations, responsibilities."

"In other words, none of them wanted it, so he's stuck with it?"

My father shrugged. "I guess you could say that. What matters is that you understand what you're walking into here. And what will be expected of you."

If it wasn't for the fact that Damen seemed to be a great man, honorable, responsible, charming, adorable, sexy—the list of adjectives could go on and on—I would've told my father to forget it and walked away. But I couldn't. Because Damen was all those things, and so many more. I liked the way he made me feel. Not just physically, but also emotionally. I didn't just feel smart. I felt pretty. And desirable.

"What's involved in this courtship thing?" I asked.

"It's pretty much just a fancy way of saying you'll be appearing in public together, as a couple."

I thought about it for a moment or two. Was that so bad? Really, it wasn't. In fact, maybe I was making too much out of this whole courtship thing. "Okay, I guess I can handle that. No commitment, right?"

"None. But there is something else. You'll have to be chaperoned. And there cannot be any physical intimacy beyond a kiss."

Considering how warm I became when Damen kissed me, that restraint could prove to be a challenge.

"Chaperone?" I repeated. Then again, that was probably exactly what I needed.

Immediately my mind went back to that night with Gabe, the first time we made love. That night had been one I'd never forgotten. Bittersweet. And many times, I'd wished it hadn't happened because later, when we did break up, it was the regret of that night that haunted me.

Yes, smart kids, even kids with IQs over 190, make stupid mistakes. Don't I know it.

"I know it's a lot to think about," my father said.

"It is. But it isn't. Damen seems to be a good man. Tell me, is he a good man?"

My father's shoulders lifted. "I'd like to say I had picked a good man for you, but it seems we have a different opinion there. So I'll say I've known Damen Sylver since he was a boy, and he's never done anything illegal, immoral, or otherwise objectionable."

"Well, then, I guess that means he checks out. You'd know, being the head of security, if there was something to worry about."

"Yes, I would." His gaze focused on the desk.

For just an instant, I questioned my father's honesty. But then I shook off my doubt. He wouldn't lie to me. He was my father. He would feel an obligation to protect me. "Okay." I stood. "I'll head out and give him the good news."

"All right." My father stopped me at the door. "Sloan, if you have any problems, my door is always open."

"You're acting like you expect this thing to fail already."

"That's not what concerns me. Sloan, until you've dealt with Her Highness, you have no idea what you're in for."

The tone in his voice made a little quiver quake up my spine.

With mixed emotions, I left my father's office. Damen was waiting in the living room with Mom. She was beaming. So was he. Me . . . I doubt it.

Mom stood. She looked like a kid who was waiting to talk to Santa. "Well?"

I turned to Damen.

He stood and strolled toward me with strong, sure strides. He took my hands in his and looked into my eyes. "Sloan, it would make me a very happy man if you'd agree to a courtship."

How could I not melt, the way he was looking at me? It was as if his next breath hinged upon my answer. I didn't have the heart to make him wait a single second more.

"Yes. I'll court you."

He grabbed me in a bone-crushing embrace and whispered, "I swear, I'll make you the happiest woman on earth."

I tipped my head back. "Now, don't you go starting things off by making promises you can't keep."

Memory believes before knowing remembers. Believes longer than recollects, longer than knowing even wonders.

—William Faulkner

8

There haven't been many things in life I couldn't grasp. I could understand the Yang-Mills theory, the Many Worlds theory, and the theory of Quantum Entanglement. But trying to comprehend how anyone under the age of thirty could see a future so bleak, he or she felt there was no reason to go on living was beyond the scope of my understanding. And believe me, there've been times when I've been downright miserable.

I've suffered loss. I've suffered disappointment. I've suffered guilt and regret. Still, not once did I feel life wasn't worth living. And so, when JT called me to tell me our potential third victim had been a suicide, I'd been slightly taken aback.

That was nothing, as I soon learned.

"The girl's name was Megan Carter," JT said.

"Oh." I clapped my hand over my mouth. It was shaking. *Megan Carter.* I'd spoken to Megan Carter. In the bathroom in the D Wing. Had I said something to set her off? Was her death somehow my fault?

"She left a letter for her mother, Sloan. In her letter, she said Stephanie Barnett's death was her fault. Do you know what she meant by that?"

"She told me she left Stephanie at a party. That's all. She felt that if she'd walked home with Stephanie, rather than ditching her, Stephanie might still be alive. I tried to tell her there was no reason to believe it was her fault."

JT's end of the phone line was silent.

"JT, did I do something wrong?"

"No, Sloan. You didn't. I read the letter."

"I need to read it."

"I have a copy. I can show it to you."

"Please. Thanks."

"I'll be out in your area tomorrow morning. I'll run by."

"Okay. Thanks. Bye." My hands were still shaking as I set my phone down.

Damen keyed to my reaction right away. "What's wrong?" he asked.

My eyes were burning. My nose too. I sniffled, glancing around for a tissue.

He took my hands in his. "Sloan?"

I rubbed my drippy cheek on my shoulder. "She was so young. Both of them were. I hate this case."

"You don't have to do this," he said, thumbing away the tear that had dribbled down my other cheek. "If it's too much, quit."

"But the unit needs me. I've helped them profile two killers already."

"That's extraordinary, Sloan, but you're still young, and that kind of work takes its toll on people. Being exposed to too much of humanity's ugliness can make you callous."

I could see that happening to some people. I wasn't sure if it would for me. And maybe that was why I briefly considered doing exactly what he suggested. Because I had a feeling either I'd have to learn to separate myself from my cases, or I'd end up having a breakdown. Considering the genes I inherited, risking that kind of trauma was probably dodgy.

But then I reminded myself that I'd been working my whole life toward this goal. If I walked away from my dream, what would I do? What would my future be?

I shook my head. "I'm not ready to call it quits yet."

"Okay." He ran his hands up and down my arms. It was a soothing gesture, and it made my heart stop thumping so hard. "I know you can't say a lot about your work, but I'm here for you."

"Thanks." Appreciative of his broad shoulders, I leaned in and let him support me. "I haven't been at this for long. I think with time it'll get easier."

"I hope it does. For your sake."

We sat there, like that, on my parents' couch. His warmth and strength embraced me like a cocoon, until my eyelids became heavy and I couldn't keep them open any longer. He stretched, gently moving out from under me. "I need to get going." Offering me a hand up, he turned a worry-filled gaze down to me.

"I'm okay. Better." I climbed to my feet.

"Okay."

Together we walked through the house, toward the front foyer. At the door, he caught my chin, lifting it. "Promise me, if it gets to be too much, you'll say something."

"I promise."

He tipped his head down, brushing his lips over mine. The kiss was soft, a teasing temptation that made my toes curl and the gears in my head come to a clunking halt. "Good night, Sloan."

"Good night," I whispered back.

Damen left.

Physically and mentally beat, I dragged myself upstairs. In my room, I changed into a pair of Mom's old velour lounge pants and a T-shirt. After taking care of the bedtime essentials, I crawled into bed and shut my eyes. Megan's tormented face instantly flashed in my mind.

Could I have done or said anything different? Could I have talked her out of killing herself if I'd known?

* * *

"If I give you a kiss, will you proclaim your undying love or punch me in the nose?"

I knew that voice.

Not so long ago, I'd thought it was coming from a nightmare. Then I learned the truth.

I didn't open my eyes, but I did roll onto my side to protect my mouth. I did not want a kiss. Not from this guy. "Elmer, I don't think you'll like my answer."

"Darn."

I cracked open one eye.

The lights were off, and the room was pretty dark, but I could still sense that Elmer was close. It was the smell. The way the air felt cold and void of life.

"Back off, *Sluagh*," I grumbled.

"Backing."

I opened the other eye, squinting at the glowing numbers on my clock. Of course, it was the middle of the freaking night. "Why are you here in my bedroom? Aren't you supposed to be filming your TV show right now?"

"Yeah, well, I walked off the set."

A wave of dread swept through me. My first thought was for myself. If the show failed, then I was probably going to have to step in and become the next queen of the *Sluagh*. Then my next thought was for Damen. He would be hurt, disappointed. I hadn't filled him in on all the ugly details of my arrangement with Elmer. If I had, I suppose he might not have dove into the whole courtship thing.

"Elmer, you shouldn't have done that."

"Why not?"

"You signed a contract."

He crossed his skinny, little arms over his chest and jerked up his pointy chin. I noticed his teeth were back to barracuda pointy. The wig was gone. And his skin was back to the pale white of a fish belly. "Yeah? So? You signed a contract too. With me. And so far, you've reneged."

"I have not. We just haven't come to an agreement on the terms of repayment."

He plopped on the bed. The temperature of the air around me dropped by at least twenty degrees. "Let's talk about that."

"Not now." My breath turned to mist. I inched back, outside of the cold/dead zone. "We need to discuss the terms of your agreement with the production company. I didn't read the contract. Do you remember what it said?"

"No." He mumbled something I couldn't make out; then, "I didn't really read it myself."

I was beginning to get a very bad feeling about this. "Do you have a copy? They did give you one, right?"

"Sure. Somewhere."

"Okay." I scrubbed my face with my hands and glanced at the clock. If only my creepy, little friend could pay me visits during normal hours, rather than in the middle of the night, things would be so much simpler. "You have two choices. You can either go back and finish what you started, or you can find your contract and see if quitting is even an option."

Clearly, Elmer didn't like either suggestion. The air around me grew chillier. The heavy sigh I expelled turned into a white cloud.

He cleared his throat. "About your debt—"

"Take care of this problem first."

Elmer's eyes narrowed. "No, Sloan. No more excuses. No more putting it off. I will have what's coming to me. Now."

There could be no doubt: I'd run out of time. I'd run out of excuses too. It wasn't that I don't like to pay my debts. I hate having something like this hanging over my head. But in this case, I was very nervous. When we'd struck our deal, my end of the bargain had been left wide open. There was no saying what it was going to cost me. None whatsoever. With my father's warning ringing in my ear, I nodded. "What do you want?"

"Take this." Elmer handed me a stone. It was smooth and cool to the touch. Slightly translucent. Oblong. Smaller than a Ping-Pong ball.

I stared at the stone, wondering what it had to do with my debt. Was it some kind of precious gem? Topaz, perhaps? There were no sharp edges. The surface was smooth, as if it had been polished for years by flowing water. "What is it?"

"A very precious gem," he said. "Now close your eyes."

Intrigued, and a little confused, I did as he asked.

"I want you to bring to mind a precious memory. Something you've held on to for many years. Don't think too hard, just let it come to your mind."

The image of me with Gabe in college flashed in my head. We were behind the science building. I had found this cozy little spot, situated in the center of a copse of trees. I liked to go there and think sometimes. It was quiet. Private. So different from my dorm room. I'd been sitting on the ground. My back was leaning against the trunk of an old oak. Up above, a squirrel chattered. Birds twittered. A soft breeze carried the scent of earth and fallen leaves to my nose. . . .

"Gabe, what are you doing here?"

My heart pittered and pattered. He was so good-looking. How many times I'd wanted him to notice me. I'd caught him watching Lisa Flemming with the glitter of hard male appreciation in his eyes. But not once had I ever caught that glimmer in his eyes when he'd looked at me.

Until now.

"Looking for you." His lips curved slightly, pulling into a sexy half smile.

"Why? Did you need some help with the organic-chem homework?"

"No." He squatted, putting us more at eye-to-eye level. "What are you doing here, Sloan Skye?" He reached for me, caught the collar of my jacket in his fingertips. "Are you hiding?"

"From whom?" I asked. I was breathless. I was nervous.

I was wondering what he'd do or say next. Was he going to tease me? Mock me? Or . . . or . . . ?

"Are you hiding from me?" he asked. He extended his other arm, flattening his hand on the tree trunk. That position put him even closer. Mere inches away.

I could smell his cologne. I could smell his soap too. And the hint of man—that sweet musk that was only his. My insides buzzed and twitched. I'd never been this close to a man who was so incredibly sexy.

"Are you afraid of me, Sloan Skye?" He eased closer still.

I froze. Not that I wanted to run from him; but if I had, there was no way I could have. Not a chance.

"N-no. Should I be?"

"Yes," he whispered. "You should. And here's why." He kissed me, and every inch of my body responded. My toes curled. My heart banged against my breastbone. My skin, from the top of my head to the balls of my feet, burned and tingled.

Unable to stop myself, I threw my arms around his neck and kissed him back. A moan bubbled up in my throat, slipped out of my mouth to echo in my ears.

His tongue swept into my mouth, filling it with his decadent flavor. And I knew, then and there, that if he asked me to make love, I would be his.

"Sloan Skye," he whispered between stabs and strokes. "I want you. I've wanted you for a very long time. And I won't ever stop wanting you." He backed away slightly, regarding me with heavy-lidded eyes. "Do you believe me?"

"Y-yes."

"Then trust me." He slid his hands beneath my shirt.

My mind went blank. As if I'd been watching a movie and a heavy black curtain had fallen over the screen, shutting it off from my view. My hand burned and my eyelids snapped open. The stone was glowing red.

"That's good. Very good." Elmer snatched it from me and pocketed it.

"What happened?" My gaze bounced back and forth from my hand to Elmer.

"We're even now," he said.

"We are? How? All I did was hold a rock."

"You've paid my price. You've given me a treasured memory. It's mine now, and your debt is paid. In full."

"Memory? Of what?" I searched my brain, trying to recall whatever images I'd just seen. Nothing was there. Not one little glimmer. "What memory did I give you?"

Elmer shrugged. "I wouldn't know. Yet. I haven't taken a look at it. But I will. Soon." *Poof,* he vanished.

I stared at the empty spot where he'd just been sitting, and I tried to figure out what I should be feeling.

There was a touch on my shoulder. A soft tap.

I turned.

"I'm sorry, Sloan," my father said, looking extremely apologetic. He was standing in my room, fully dressed as if he'd just come home from work. "I tried to warn you about the *Sluagh*. He's a good man. But when it comes to collecting a debt, he's merciless."

"What just happened?"

"Remember, when you asked him for his help, I warned you that the *Sluagh* are collectors. The price he asked—in return for his help—was 'I'm gathering a very special memory you've been carrying around with you for years.'"

"I got that. But how do I figure out what memory it was? Is there any way to get it back? To remind myself?"

My father shook his head. "Once it's gone, it's gone forever. Unless you can find a way to strike another deal with the *Sluagh*. If you can do him as great a favor as he did for you, he will be honor-bound to return it to you."

Me do him a favor? Haven't I already done several?

"Really? Another favor? I've done a lot of favors for that man already. I've been helping him find a wife, gone to a horrid speed-dating night, found a way for him to get his stupid *Who Wants to Marry an Undead Prince?* show filmed, so he could meet women. What more can I do?"

"Those favors served your interests as well as his," my father said, patting my knee. "Whatever favor it is, it has to be only for him. Maybe something will come up. Either that, or you'll live without that memory. If you're fortunate, it wasn't something that led to a lot more memories. To a life you didn't realize you'd lived. A wife you hadn't remembered marrying. A child you didn't recall holding."

"Are you saying . . . ?"

My father sat in the exact same spot where Elmer had been only moments ago. He stared down at the floor for several seconds. "I didn't know how to tell you the truth, so I lied. There was no threat to your lives, at least none that I was aware of."

Aha! "I didn't believe that excuse. I knew there was something else going on."

"There was."

"So let me get this straight. Because of a deal you made with a *Sluagh,* I grew up without a father, and Mom without a husband. You didn't remember us at all? Nothing?"

Dark shadows filled his eyes. "Absolutely nothing about either of you. I remembered everything else, so I didn't realize what I had lost."

Something about his story still wasn't making sense. "What about the money you were sending to Mom?"

"I didn't send her any money. If she was receiving something, I'm guessing it was the *Sluagh* who was sending it. I guess he had something of a conscience."

I stood. I sat. I stood again.

This story was true. I knew it in my gut. The pieces fit.

"But what about your research?" I asked as my mind went to work, shifting ideas, sorting through conversations. "You said you'd caught meningitis and had forgotten your research."

"That much is true. I did have meningitis, and I cannot recall much of my research."

"Okay, so you didn't realize you had a wife and child. You forgot your research. How did you end up coming back and finding us?"

"That's a long, complicated story."

"It's okay. It looks like I have plenty of time tonight." I sat back down. After settling in, I grabbed my father's hand. "Dad, I'm sorry I didn't trust you. I was confused. Your story, about trying to protect us by staying away, made no sense. I thought you were lying."

"I would've thought the same thing." My Dad took my other hand in his, cupping them both in his palms. "It's okay. We have a lot to do, to make up for all that lost time. At least we have the chance to do that now."

"Yes, we do. And I'm going to make sure we take advantage of every minute we get."

Dad's smile was a little shadowed, happy but with a ghost of sadness lurking at the corners. "I've missed so much. You're such a wonderful young woman now. Intelligent. Capable. Responsible. Independent. Kind. My last memory of you was when you were a tiny infant. You smiled up at me. And I saw something special in your eyes. Even then. Before you could speak. Before you could read. Before you could do anything."

"I'd like to think I got some of those special qualities from you."

He blinked a few times. "Maybe you did."

"At least, it seems, Elmer didn't take my memory of you away."

"Like I said, he has a conscience."

"It was *him*? Elmer?"

My father nodded. "None other."

If you don't make mistakes, you're not working on hard enough problems. And that's a big mistake.

—F. Wikzek

9

The next morning, JT was standing on my parents' front porch when I came sprinting outside, bedecked in an outfit that made me grateful my high-school days were far, far behind me. He handed me an envelope and followed me. I pulled the piece of paper from the envelope as I walked, but I didn't unfold it until I was sitting behind the wheel of my car.

JT made himself comfortable in the passenger seat. He remained completely silent while I read the copy of Megan's final words. It was hard to get through. When I was done, I couldn't help exhaling a little harder than normal.

"This is so sad," I said as I returned the copy to the envelope. I handed it back to JT. "We have to stop this guy. I don't care what it takes. He's destroying so many lives—not just the victims'. There's Megan. And Mrs. Walker."

"We're doing our best." JT fiddled with the envelope's flap.

"Has Forrester come up with anything? Has anyone come up with anything?"

"No. So far, all we've found is that the two girls attend the same school. They don't look alike. Don't share the same circle of friends. We're really hoping you can get something at the school."

I stuffed the key into the ignition. "It isn't going to be easy. Teens don't just openly embrace a new student. I'm the new kid, with no friends. I'm not going to hear much."

"All you can do is try."

"I'm trying."

"You've done more than that. In one day, you found this girl." He shook the envelope. "She might have been a witness."

"But I couldn't save her life." A horrible thought crossed my mind. "What if the killer saw us talking and killed Megan, making her death look like a suicide?"

"I guess that's possible. We'll take another look at it, see if there's any way she might have been murdered."

My insides twisted into a tight coil. "If she was killed because someone heard us talking, then I don't think I can go through with this assignment."

"One step at a time, Skye. One step at a time." Once again, he looked at me. This time, I got the vibe he was trying to tell me something else, more personal. "Sloan . . ."

"What is it?"

He cupped my cheek and I lifted my hand to his, curling my fingers around it. I wanted to pull it away. I really did. But when his gaze snagged mine, and I was swept up in all the emotions I saw in his eyes, I froze.

He pulled gently, coaxing me to lean into him. I knew where this was going. There was not a single shred of doubt. And I also knew I couldn't let it happen. My mind was screaming. Warning sirens were shrieking. Still, I didn't fight it. His lips brushed across mine in the softest kiss of my life. I sucked in a gasp and gulped it down.

But the minute his mouth settled more firmly over mine, I pulled back.

"JT, there's a lot going on right now. You've just lost a child. You're grieving. This shouldn't be happening. I shouldn't let it happen. It's wrong."

"You're not doing anything wrong." His fingers grazed my jaw. He tried to cup my head again, but this time I moved out of his reach. "You want to comfort me. There's nothing wrong with that. You're attracted to me. There's nothing wrong with that either. I'm attracted to you. And again, there's nothing wrong with that. You've tried to hide it. And maybe you've convinced everyone else that you don't want me—maybe even convinced yourself. But you haven't fooled me."

"I am attracted to you. I won't deny that. But that doesn't mean we should go there."

Moving quickly, he jerked me into his arms and kissed me again. This time, it wasn't soft. It wasn't shy. It was hard and demanding and convincing. And I almost lost control and let it continue. But I didn't. I flattened my hands against his chest and pushed. And to make sure it didn't happen again, I leaned backward and opened the door. If I had to, I'd leave the car.

"JT, I said *no*."

JT's jaw clenched. "Damn it," he muttered as he stared out the windshield. He visibly exhaled. "I apologize, Sloan. I'm fucked up in the head right now."

"I understand. You're upset. At least you're letting your emotions out now. I'm sorry. So sorry. I don't want to be rude or hurt your feelings. I want to help. Please tell me what I can do." I closed my door and crossed my arms over my chest, trying not to look conflicted and confused, which was exactly how I was feeling. Here I had a great guy who liked me. We had a lot in common. And the chemistry was definitely sizzling. But I also felt that way about someone else— a man who wasn't a coworker.

"You're just trying to be a good friend. Shit, Sloan. I pushed too hard."

"Don't worry about it. We're still friends."

"The fact is, I don't want to be friends with you." He shook his head. "I don't."

"I don't know what to say, JT. You know what I think about that." I gave the key a twist, starting the car. "I don't think now is a good time to deal with this, anyway. Obviously, you're hurting."

I glanced at the clock. It was ten to eight. I was going to be late for my first class. Very late. "I need to go."

His eyes drilled into me, seeming to peer deep into my soul. "Yeah, you're right. Now is not the time to talk about this." JT reached for the door handle. "Good luck."

"Thanks, I'm going to need it."

After JT climbed out, I drove to the school, parked in the very last parking spot in the whole lot, and hiked what felt like a mile inside. When I entered, the hallways were empty. I went straight to my first class and slinked into the room, sliding into a seat at the very back.

The teacher cleared his throat and said, "Well, look who decided to join us."

Everyone turned around. A few dozen sets of eyes focused on me.

I was mortified.

When I'd signed on to be an intern at the FBI, I'd imagined myself in all kinds of situations, but not once did I visualize anything like this.

I smiled and waved.

The teacher humphed.

A few of the students smirked.

The smartest kids—who couldn't be all that smart, since they were attending summer school—gave me a look of disdain. I immediately confessed my sins for doing something similar when I was in high school.

Thankfully, the teacher let it drop after that and went back to rambling on about the economy of post–USSR Russia. A fascinating subject. *Not.* I pretended to take notes while trying to overhear whispered conversations among students. I heard one girl mention Megan's name. But that was it. Evidently, there'd been a very brief announcement made at the beginning of class about Megan's death, with no details shared. When the bell rang, signaling the end of the period, I had nothing more to go on than I did when I'd stepped into the building. Already I was beginning to think this undercover assignment might be a waste of time. Whether it was better or worse than sitting around the PBAU, waiting for the phones to ring, was still undecided.

During my second and third classes of the day, I had the same experiences. I caught a few muttered mentions of Megan, some speculation about her having committed suicide, but nothing more. By the time the final bell rang, I was ready to head to the unit and ask the chief if I could be reassigned to another task. This was getting us nowhere.

But then, as I was walking out to my car, I heard two girls talking about a party. It was tonight. At someone's house. Supposedly, the student's parents were out of town.

Alcohol. Teens. It was going to be an ugly scene. But I would be far more likely to hear something useful at a party than I would here.

It was decided; I would attend my first high-school keg party tonight.

Feeling a little better about my lack of progress, I stopped on the way back to the unit and grabbed a submarine sandwich and a bag of chips. I rolled into the parking lot a little while later. I hauled my lunch-in-a-bag inside and made a beeline for my cubicle. The unit was quiet.

I powered up my laptop and skimmed my e-mail while I munched on the six-inch turkey-and-Swiss sub, cheddar-flavored chips, and slurped down diet cola. Just as I was finishing up, I heard the unit's door open. I glanced up.

Gabe Wagner? What was he doing here?

"Hey, Skye," he said as he strolled toward my cubicle.

I blinked. "Hi," I said, unable to hide my confusion and disbelief. I hadn't seen Gabe Wagner in years, since college. What was he doing here?

His brows scrunched together. "What's wrong?" he asked.

"N-nothing." I didn't ask him why he was standing in the middle of the PBAU, acting like he belonged there. For some reason, I felt like I'd look like an idiot if I did that. Why? I had no idea. "I'm just eating my lunch."

"What do you have there?" He rested his butt on my desk. I couldn't believe it. He'd never acted so friendly to me before. What was going on? He shoved his hand in my almost empty chip bag, pulled out a couple of chips, and stuffed them into his mouth. He crunched, and I sat there, gaping, I'm sure. "Mmm. Good." His brows scrunched. "Skye, why are you looking at me like I grew a second head?"

"Um." I glanced right. I glanced left. "Um." I felt so stupid and confused. I clamped my jaw. "Nothing. I was just thinking . . . about the case. Yes, that's what I was doing."

"What were you thinking about the case?" he asked.

Why had he asked that? He wasn't a part of our unit. He didn't belong here. Come to think of it, how the hell did he even get in here? Our offices were located on a U.S. Marine base. There were guards at the gate.

His father must've pulled some strings, somehow. His father was a fairly influential man. He was a state senator, with dreams of running for the U.S. Senate someday.

Had his father talked the PBAU into hiring him?

Just in case Gabe wasn't there legally, I decided not to tell him anything about the case. I'd clear it up with the chief when she came in. "I was thinking I need to get to work." I shoved the remainders of my lunch into the bag and stuffed it in the trash can. Then I poked my computer's power button, waking it up from sleep mode.

"Okay. Give me a holler if you need some help." He removed his butt from my desktop. I tried not to look at it as he strolled away. I failed.

Imagine that. Gabe Wagner. Here.

And he'd looked at me with some sparkly eyes.

And he'd smiled at me too.

Sheesh, I sounded like a sixth grader. I was somewhat socially challenged, but I wasn't *that* bad. Usually. In this case, it was Gabe Wagner. He had been my secret crush in college.

Shoving my thoughts of Gabe Wagner aside, I went on a fact-hunting mission on Google. As of right now, we had very little information about this unsub. We knew he or she was killing at night and using some sort of tool that produced a current of electricity. There were no clues at the scenes, which would lead me to the conclusion that we were dealing with an organized killer.

Speaking in the most general terms, the FBI classified serial killers in one of three broad categories—organized, disorganized, or mixed. Organized killers were the Ted Bundys and John Wayne Gacys of the world. They were intelligent, selected their victims with care, generally killed strangers, and planned their crimes methodically. And they took measures to cover up their crimes and avoid capture.

Disorganized killers, like Ed Gein, were very different. They tended to have average or below-average IQs, were impulsive killers, using whatever weapon was available at the crime scene, and tended not to hide the body. Their crime scenes often showed excessive violence and sometimes necrophilia or sexual violence.

It was fairly clear, by the lack of evidence, as well as the lack of violence, that we were dealing with an organized killer.

As far as gender went, I was leaning toward a male killer, but I didn't have any facts to support my theory. Female killers tended to kill for material gain. They often had a relationship with their victims. They killed their spouses, their children, or elderly friends or family members. And they frequently employed covert methods to kill, like poison. At this point, I wasn't seeing the fingerprint of a female killer. But I wasn't going to completely dismiss the idea either.

And then there was motive. This was the big question mark in our case. Why? Why were Stephanie Barnett and Emma Walker dead?

The motives of serial killers were generally classified into four categories: visionary, mission-oriented, hedonistic, and power or control. Killers motivated by lust, thrill, and profit fell under the hedonistic category. Because we weren't seeing any sexual torture or mutilation, I was willing to eliminate lust from the list of potential motives. I also didn't see any signs that the victims were being killed for profit. Their belongings were left at the crime scene. But the remaining motives couldn't be crossed off the list yet, including thrill.

Thus, we had a very sketchy picture of our killer.

The one thing we had was the signature.

Unfortunately, as I scoured the Web for information about killers who used electrocution to murder, I found more about killers who had been electrocuted. As in, put to death using the electric chair.

I tweaked my search terms and hit pay dirt.

One man in Russia had electrocuted six people using his home-built electric chair. The power station worker also claimed to have made an electrified carpet that would kill people when they stepped on it, as well as a camera that would blast victims with an electromagnetic ray. That was the only case I'd found. And the reason for his choice of MO seemed obvious.

I wondered why our unsub had chosen electrocution as his method. Maybe he had some kind of unusual fascination with electricity. Interesting. If he was a student, that kind of thing might be noticed by a perceptive science teacher, like my chemistry teacher, Mr. Hollerbach. I made a mental note to share my idea with JT. Being undercover, I couldn't question the teachers without raising suspicion. He could.

Deciding I needed to know more about electrocution, I searched that term next. I skimmed several articles on electrocution. One thing that leapt out at me was our victims' lack of burns. From what I was reading, burns were common in electrical shock, and they fell into three broad categories: electrical burns, arc burns, and thermal-contact burns. Our victims weren't showing any of the three, outside of the strange branching red marks. And yet, the ME was convinced they had received a large enough shock to stop their hearts. According to what I read, it would take as little as one-tenth of an amp to do that. There were no exit wounds, where the electricity left the body. Nor were there any marks where it had entered. I wondered if a Taser or some other stun gun could be the source of the jolt.

As I was about to look up stun gun injuries, JT wandered into the unit, glanced at me, then went to his cubby. He sat down, dumped his stuff on his desk, and just stared.

I waited at least a minute for him to say or do something. When he didn't move, didn't speak, I walked over to his cubicle and said in a quiet voice, "Knock, knock?" He didn't respond, so I said it again. Finally, when I said it a third time, he seemed to shake himself out of his stupor. He looked at me. "Skye."

"JT, what's wrong? Did something happen? Was there another killing?"

"No." His gaze dropped to his desk.

"Are you ill?"

"No." He was still staring down at his desk. Something was wrong. I hadn't seen him act this strangely since he was clobbered on the head at the bagel shop during my first week. His shaggy hair wouldn't let me see if he'd suffered some kind of head injury. His forehead was clear. No bumps. But that didn't mean anything. If his head had been jarred, like in a car accident, he could still have an injury. I crouched down to get a look at his eyes. "JT, did you have some kind of accident?"

"No." He blinked, then met my gaze. "I'm just wiped out."

"What are you doing here, then?"

"I didn't want to go home. Didn't want to be alone."

Gabe Wagner came over too. He leaned against the cubby wall. "I was about to head out for some dinner. Do you two want to join me?"

JT gazed up. He didn't look surprised to see a strange man inviting him to dinner. Then again, he didn't seem to be all that responsive about anything. "No thanks. I'm not hungry."

"I just ate," I said. "I'm heading out in a few. Thanks, anyway."

"Okay. I'll be back in a bit." Gabe left.

JT stared at his desk.

I stared at him. "JT, I had a thought at school. I wonder if any of the science teachers might have noticed a student who has an unusual interest in electricity." I tapped his shoulder. "JT?"

Nothing.

Finally I gave his shoulders a little shake. "JT, you're scaring me. What's wrong? Is it something I did? Was it about that situation this morning? Things have been awkward between us, but I care about you. If I've done something to upset you—"

"It's nothing like that. You're fine."

"Then what is it? I can see you're upset. Is it about Hough?"

He didn't respond right away. He just sat there, staring down at his hands, deep in thought. I was beginning to think he couldn't talk to me.

Even with his eyes averted, I could see they were becoming red and watery. His face was flushing. Was he . . . crying?

"JT?"

"When we first talked about it, everything was set," he murmured. "I knew what I was doing and why, and I was okay with it. I was helping out a friend. Giving her something she wanted very badly. But when her marriage fell apart, things changed."

Okay, so this was about Brittany and the child she was carrying. But what exactly was going on?

He continued to share. "I took Brittany to her ultrasound. And when I saw that first image . . ." He visibly swallowed. And finally his gaze lifted to my face. The hurt in his eyes nearly took my breath away.

"JT, did something else happen to Brittany?"

His head fell forward again. He shoved his fingers into

his hair and pulled. "She attempted suicide last night." A sob echoed through the empty room. "I just found out. A little while ago."

My knees suddenly felt soft and gooey. I sat on his desk to avoid falling over and lifted my hand. I needed to touch him, to give him some small sign of comfort. But I pulled it back before it had made contact with his shoulder. As much as I wanted to do it, I couldn't.

I clapped one hand over my mouth. Through my fingers, I said, "Oh, JT. I don't know what to say. Is she . . . ?"

"Critical condition. At Bon Secours. I've already lost our child. I can't lose her too." He started to cry harder, and every sob tore at my heart. It was awkward and painful, and I wanted to do something to help him, but I had no idea what that something should be. It continued for a while, and I sat there, helpless and useless, wishing I could take away his pain, but knowing I couldn't. When his crying let up a bit, I breathed a little easier. I heard something. A noise. My head spun as I lifted it to check the door. Nobody was there.

With his hands flattened on top of his downturned head, he said, between sniffles, "I realize now not only how much I wanted that child, but also everything that went along with her. I want a wife. A family. All of it. I want Brittany."

"Wow. JT." I took a long, slow inhalation and let it out. He was right. He was messed up. This morning, he was trying to shove his tongue down my throat; and now, hours later, he was telling me he wanted to *marry* Brittany Hough? My gaze switched to the clock. As much as I wanted to be there for JT and help him sort through his feelings, I was under some pressure to get going. I had a couple of hours before the house party, but I calculated that Mom and Dad's place was a decent drive from the Baltimore suburb where the party was going to happen. And it was an even longer drive from Quantico to my folks' place. I needed to change my clothes. I didn't have any party-appropriate outfit in my go bag. "Can I get you something to eat? Something to drink?"

"No. Thanks." He pulled his laptop out of his bag and hit the power button. "I need to keep busy. That's the only way I'm going to get through this."

"I can't stick around much longer. But do you want to see what I was working on?"

"Sure."

I hurried back to my cubby, grabbed my laptop, and hauled it to JT's desk. "I was looking into stun gun injuries."

"Stun gun?"

"That's the only way I can think of for our unsub to deliver a potentially fatal charge, but I wonder about burns or other marks."

"Interesting. Let me see what I can find."

My eyes flicked to the clock again. I really needed to get home if I was going to make it to the party. I stood.

"Where are you going?" he asked.

"I need to head out."

"Why? Do you have a date?" His face flushed. His lips thinned. "Sorry, that's none of my business."

"Actually, it's work related. I'm going to a kegger."

One of his brows lifted.

"Stephanie Barnett died shortly after going to a party."

He stood. He didn't look very steady on his feet. "I'll go with you."

"Are you sure you're in the frame of mind to deal with a bunch of rowdy, obnoxious, drunk high-school kids?"

"No, I'm probably not." He stuffed his hand into his pocket and rooted around in there. Probably looking for the keys that were sitting on his desk. "I don't want you to go to a party like that by yourself."

"I'll be fine." I handed him his keys.

"Thanks." He shut his laptop. "I'm going."

"But what about the research?"

"It can wait."

I gave him an up-and-down look. His crisp button-down shirt, rolled up to the elbows, and dress pants weren't going to cut it. "You need to change your clothes."

"I can do that. We'll stop at my place first."

My timeline just got a whole lot tighter. "Are you sure about this, JT? It really isn't necessary."

"I'm sure. You're not going by yourself."

"Fine." I scurried to my desk, threw my laptop in its case, flung it over my shoulder, and, with JT at my heels, headed for the exit. We met Gabe out in the hall. He stepped out of the elevator and gave us a questioning look.

"See you tomorrow, Wagner," JT said.

"Yeah." Gabe's gaze captured mine as I stepped into the elevator. And it didn't let go until the door shut, cutting him off from me.

At the end of your life, you will never regret not having passed one more test, not winning one more verdict, or not closing one more deal. You will regret time not spent with a husband, a friend, a child, or a parent.

—Barbara Bush

10

A half hour later, I was sitting in JT's living room, waiting for him to change his clothes. We'd taken separate cars, so I could have gone straight home. But I hadn't wanted to leave him alone. Despite his repeated assurances that he was okay, he didn't look okay. He looked depressed and on the verge of breaking down.

I wandered over to the hallway leading to the bedrooms and shouted, "Why don't you plan on spending the night at my folks' house tonight? We can pick up your car tomorrow morning, on the way to work."

"I'll think about it."

I headed back to the living room, checking the clock on the wall as I sat. Time was slipping away; and if we didn't get going soon, I wasn't going to have much time to make myself look party ready. Anxious, I stood and paced a few times. What was taking the man so long? I knew from our past undercover work that even if he showered, he would be ready to head out in no more than twenty minutes. It had been almost an hour since he'd closed himself in his room.

I knocked. No answer. I pressed an ear to the door. Was that . . . crying?

The poor man. He was brokenhearted.

I knocked again. "JT?"

I listened to his heavy footsteps as he came to the door. It swung open, revealing a red-faced, watery-eyed JT. "Sorry, Sloan. It's taking me a little longer than normal to get ready. But I'm going to get my shit together. I promise."

"JT." I stood there, watching a grown man struggle to contain his emotions. And I felt like an ass for even thinking about putting pressure on him. I wasn't sure what to do. I needed to get to that party. And yet I didn't like the idea of JT sitting home alone. He needed to have someone there with him. "Is there news about Brittany?"

"Nothing new. She's still in critical condition."

"You have no business going to a party tonight," I said, stepping into the room.

He headed toward the en suite bathroom, located off the far side of his bedroom. "I said I'll be fine." The sound of him blowing his nose echoed in the small, tiled room.

"But—"

"Stop it." He charged out of the bathroom like a bull that had been prodded in the ass. "I'm ready. Let's go."

He was halfway to the front door before I realized it. The man could move fast when he wanted.

When we headed outside, he made a beeline for his car, and I went for mine. "Leave your car here," he shouted. "We'll pick it up tomorrow."

I hated being stranded without a car. But I guessed JT hated it more. It wouldn't kill me to ride shotgun—as long as JT was in an okay condition to drive. I grabbed my laptop case and locked up; then I hurried over to his car. Off we zoomed, heading toward the freeway.

His jaw was clenching, I noticed, as he drove. We were bending the speed limit laws slightly, weaving between cars and trucks that weren't. I needed JT to slow down—but more than that, I needed him to concentrate on keeping us alive.

When we hit an open patch of road, I said, "JT, we have plenty of time. No need to risk a ticket."

His gaze shot to the speedometer. "Shit. I didn't realize I was going so fast. Sorry."

"It's okay. You're not yourself today. I understand. If you need me to drive, I can." When I'd first started with the PBAU, I'd had to drive JT's old car. He'd been clobbered over the head and had a concussion, so I had to drive him to the hospital. That was a different car. It had had a manual transmission. I think I'd pretty much destroyed the clutch by the time I'd pulled up to the emergency entry. That car burned to a crisp after a hard rain, and now JT was driving a Ford Fusion. And it was an automatic. I could handle this car just fine.

"I can drive," he growled for the third time. Typical male. He wasn't about to admit anything that might be viewed as a weakness. He continued, "I got top marks in my driving class. We're not talking about puttering along at fifty-five here. We're talking about high-speed maneuvering."

And la-dee-dah to you. "Fine." I tightened my hold on the handle above my window and stared straight ahead.

Forty hair-raising minutes later, I was standing on solid ground, outside of Mom and Dad's place. I'd never been happier to be out of a vehicle. JT was being a stubborn ass. As I stomped up to the back door, I vowed that I wouldn't get near that vehicle again if he was driving. The man had almost killed us at least a dozen times.

Inside, I shouted a greeting to Mom, Dad, and Katie, and received nothing in return. The house was quiet. Not even Sergio was anywhere to be seen.

As I had been doing since I was at the PBAU, I checked the clock. It was after nine now. The party was probably getting going, and I wouldn't have time to shower or blow-dry and straighten my hair. I opted for a quick change into something sluttier than my daytime outfit; then I went to the bathroom to do what I could with my hair and makeup. It was about nine-thirty when I click-clacked down the stairs.

JT was in the den, staring at Dad's ginormous TV. When he heard me, he glanced my way. His eyeballs protruded. His gaze dropped to my toes, then wandered north again. It seemed to hesitate at the hem of my skirt—and at my Victoria's Secret–enhanced boobs—before climbing up to my face.

"Wow," he said.

"Is that a bad 'wow' or a good 'wow'?"

"Um . . . good. But I think my job as your bodyguard just got a hell of a lot harder."

"Stop it. All the girls dress like this."

"No girls dressed like that when I went to school."

"Where'd you go to school?"

"Catholic."

"Ah, I see." I teetered toward the door. "Ready?"

"Sure." He stuffed his hand in his pocket and pulled out the keys. I snatched them away before he realized what I was doing. And then, because I was pretty sure he would put up a fight, I ran as fast as I could in three-inch heels toward the car. He beat me. He wasn't even out of breath.

Standing sentry in front of the driver's-side door, he gave me stink eyes and crossed his arms over his chest. "What do you think you're doing?"

"I'm driving."

"No, you're not."

"Either I drive, or—"

He took a step closer. "Or what?"

"I'm thinking."

His eyes traveled to the keys.

Out of sheer instinct, I stuffed my hand down my shirt, shoving the keys into my bra.

I'd never done anything like that before. Now I knew why.

Bras weren't meant to house anything sharp or cold. I gritted my teeth and jerked my chin up. "You won't get your keys."

"You want to bet?" His eyeballs honed in on my boobs.

Maybe this wasn't such a good idea.

Before things got carried away, I back-stepped, holding my hands palms out. "Look, I'm not trying to cause any trouble. I just want to stay alive long enough to catch this unsub. And whether you want to admit it or not, you were driving like an ass earlier. I was scared for my life. So . . . if you want to go to the party with me, you'll get your butt in the passenger seat and buckle yourself in."

That was telling him.

He lifted a brow. Then his eyes became shadowed and his expression darkened. "You're right. I'm sorry." He circled the car, leaving me to fish his keys out of my Miracle Bra in peace. However, as I was working my hand down to where the keys had settled—*gravity*—there was a little *poof,* and the air grew cold and still.

"Need some help?" Elmer asked, sneering.

This night was getting better by the minute.

"No thanks," I said through gritted teeth. I turned my back to the leering undead guy. "I can take care of this myself."

"Nice outfit," he said. "You never dressed like that for me. Going on a date?"

"No. I'm working undercover." *Success!* Keys in hand, I headed toward the car.

"Cool. Can I help?" he asked.

"No. Absolutely not."

"Please?"

I already knew better than to accept the help of a *Sluagh,* though I still had no clue what he'd taken from me. The fact was, by inviting him along, I would be accepting another favor from him. It wasn't worth the price he'd make me pay. "Aren't you supposed to be filming your television show?"

"I quit. Remember?"

"You signed a contract. You can't quit."

"I can quit, and I have. I'm wasting my time. Those women are a bunch of flaky nutcases. I can't marry any of them."

"Ask the producer to find some better brides." I opened the door and angled behind the steering wheel. I reached for the door, to close it, but Elmer stepped in the way.

"I did talk to Dale. She told me this was the best she could do. I'm telling you, Sloan, they're all bat shit crazy. Every single one of them. There isn't a normal woman in the whole batch. You've got to do something."

"I'll call her." I pulled on the door. It struck him in the ass. He didn't budge. "It won't help."

"It's worth a try." I jerked my head. "Now I need to go. Please move."

His squinty eyes narrowed. "Fine." He stepped out of the way, but only so he could open the back door. Before I had the car started, he was in the backseat. "Where are we going? A nightclub? Maybe I'll meet a nice elf at a nightclub."

"We're going to a party."

"Better yet. Will there be elves at the party?" Elmer's eyes found mine in the rearview mirror.

"No, no elves."

"Well . . . what kind of party is that? Everyone knows elves are the life of any party."

"This party is for kids."

Elmer's eyes slitted. "Why are you going to a kids' party? And dressed like that? What kind of role model are you trying to be?"

"I'm not trying to be a role model. I'm trying to fit in with them."

There was a snort. Then a guffaw. "Like that'll ever happen. Sloan, you didn't fit in when *you were* a kid."

"Don't remind me."

I shifted the car into reverse, ready to hit the road. We still had a pretty decent drive back to Baltimore, but I expected the party would go on well past midnight . . . if it wasn't raided by the police.

But just as I was about to back out of the parking spot, Katie's car came zooming up the double-wide drive, curved into the spot next to JT's car, and screeched to a halt.

I'd never seen her drive like that. Worried, I shifted into park and powered down the window.

"Katie, are you okay?" I yelled.

Katie shoved open her door and stomped over to me. "My life sucks."

"What's wrong?"

"What isn't wrong?" She glanced at JT, then at Elmer in the backseat. Then her gaze lurched back to me. "Where are you going? Somewhere, perhaps, where they sell alcohol?"

"Um, not legally."

"What's that mean?" Katie opened the back door and joined Elmer. It was my assumption she didn't care where we were going. So I went ahead and started backing out.

"We're going to a kegger," I told her.

"Now you're talking," Katie said, her voice smiley.

"It isn't like that," I explained as I turned the car around and pointed it toward the street. "It's a high-school keg party. I'm working undercover again."

"That's okay," she said. "Beer is beer. I haven't been to a keg party in ages."

Why did it seem I was just now really getting to know all of the important people in my life? "You were at a keg party? *You?*"

"Yes. Believe it or not, I did have some crazy moments as a party girl."

I felt like this was a whole side of Katie I'd missed. "No way. Tell me."

Katie leaned forward, looking through the gap between the two front seats. "When I was in high school, I had a friend whose father lived on a farm in Pennsylvania. Every fall, he would have this big pig roast/keg party and invite all his friends and family. They would eat and drink all night, watching the stupid pig turn on the big roaster thingy. His kids were allowed to invite as many friends as they wanted, but they had to promise not to leave the property."

"Did you get totally drunk?" I asked as I waited for a gap in traffic so I could turn onto Woodmont Street.

"Not exactly. I had one small paper cup of beer, nursed it until it was as warm as pee, and then I dumped it out. Not a fan of beer."

"We're heading to a keg party," I pointed out. "You said, 'Beer is beer.'"

"Yeah, I know. But I'm desperate enough, I think, to choke down more than one Dixie cup this time."

One hour later, we were curving down Glenn Street, nearing the party. When we drove within a block of the house, both sides of the road were lined with cars, and the thrum of loud music echoed in the night. It was a wonder the neighbors hadn't called the police by now. I passed the party house, went down another block, pulled into a driveway, turned around, and found a parking spot roughly a quarter mile away. When I cut off the motor, I turned toward my entourage.

The drive over had given us plenty of time to formulate a plan. JT and Elmer were going to stick together, pretending to be friends, and Katie and I would do the same. We would spread out, covering as much ground as possible, and then try to eavesdrop for any mention of the dead girls.

"Okay," I said, pocketing my keys, "since we have two people who aren't in the bureau, I'll remind everyone—*no drinking*."

"Won't we stick out if we're the only ones who aren't drinking? It's a beer party," Katie reasoned.

"Right. We don't need to draw attention to ourselves. So, it's okay to get a beer. But nurse it."

"Right," Katie said. "No real drinking. Only sipping. That's okay. Like I said, I'm not a big fan of beer."

"You're taking all the fun out of this," Elmer grumbled. "Do you think there will be any elves here? At least it'll be worth it if I can find an elf—"

"They're underage," I reminded him. "Jailbait."

Elmer grumbled something I couldn't make out.

"Hey, it was your choice to come." I opened my door. "You could always—*poof*—materialize right back on the set and film the next episode of *Who Wants to Marry*—"

"I'm good."

My phone rang. It was Dale, the producer of *Who Wants to Marry an Undead Prince?* "Speaking of the devil." I held up my phone.

"Don't answer it," Elmer said.

I answered, "Hello."

"Hello, Ms. Skye, this is Dale Nessinger. I'm trying to locate Elmer Schmickle. I realize you're no longer his agent." *I'm not? This is definitely news to me.* "But I wonder if you might know how I can reach him. He walked off the set two nights ago, saying he was ill, and we haven't heard from him since. He's now in breach of his contract, and he's costing me a lot of money. I need to get in touch with him immediately."

I squinted at Elmer. "Since I'm no longer his agent, I haven't been informed of his whereabouts. But I can see if I can track him down for you. I'm sure there's just been a misunderstanding."

"I hope so. This is very serious. I appreciate your help. We can't delay the filming any longer. I need him here tonight."

"I'll see what I can do."

"Thank you."

I clicked off, pushed out of the car and pocketed my phone. To Elmer, I said, "You're going back. *Tonight*. As soon as we're done here."

Elmer shook his head. "No."

"Elmer, if you don't, she's going to sue you for breach of contract. That could cost you millions of dollars."

Elmer shrugged. "I don't care."

I couldn't imagine not caring about the loss of millions of dollars. It made me wonder exactly how rich Elmer Schmickle was. "Since my father helped you make this connection, it's going to reflect poorly on him too," I pointed out.

Elmer considered that statement. "I'll make it up to him."

"Elmer." I glared. I stomped ahead of him a few paces, then stopped and turned. "If you don't keep your end of the bargain, then I'll have no choice but to break mine too. I won't be your backup bride. Nor will I help you find a wife. You'll be on your own, and who knows how long it'll take for you to find a decent elf who will be willing to marry you? Especially if you're destitute."

Elmer laughed. "A few million isn't going to leave me destitute." Then his expression sobered. "But I don't appreciate your blackmailing me."

"Take it or leave it."

"I'll give you back your memory. The one I took for payment for that little favor I did. . . ."

"I have no idea what memory you took."

"Have you noticed anyone sort of popping into your life in the last twenty-four hours? Someone you haven't seen in years?"

I searched my brain.

"Someone who you had a little crush on in college?"

"Gabe Wagner?"

Elmer pointed at his nose. "Wouldn't you like to recall what's happened with your Gabe Wagner between your freshman year in college and this morning?"

In the time we'd had our little discussion, we'd made our way up to the party house. Katie was walking at my side, listening in. JT was trailing behind. He'd been uncharacteristically quiet since we'd left my parents' house. I glanced over my shoulder to make sure he was still back there. He was.

"What is the little freak talking about, Sloan?" Katie demanded. She shot Elmer some mean eyes.

"We need to get inside. I'll tell you later." To Elmer, I said, "You'll do the right thing *or else*."

Elmer humphed.

Katie crossed her arms over her chest and gave her head a short nod. "Yes, do the right thing."

JT nudged me. "Let's get this over with."

A life spent making mistakes is not only more honorable, but more useful than a life spent doing nothing.

—George Bernard Shaw

I I

I was squashed on all sides, pinned between sweaty teen bodies, unable to breathe or move—or see more than twelve inches in front of me. This was no party. It was a sweltering pack of inebriated humanity.

Trying to make the best of things, I did what I could to listen in on conversations nearby. The problem was, it was nearly impossible to hear much of anything. The music was cranking so loud that my eardrums were ready to burst, and the bass was vibrating my fillings loose. When the scent of rotten eggs hit the back of my throat, I inched around, facing Katie, and pointed at the exit. I mouthed, "Let's go!" She nodded.

I'd never in my life wondered what a salmon swimming downstream might feel as he fought to go the wrong way. But now I knew. We tried to wriggle ourselves into tiny gaps amid people, but it just wasn't working. Katie gave me a forlorn shrug and we went back to moving with the flow, rather than against it. At least, we hoped, we'd eventually make our way into a room that had some space to breathe.

A half hour later, and we'd traveled maybe eight feet.

"I can't believe this. It's insane," I shouted into Katie's ear. "The minute you see an exit—be it a window, a door, a hole in the wall, anything—tell me. I've got to get out of here. It smells like old gym shoes soaked in beer."

Katie nodded. She was a few inches taller than I am, so she rose on tiptoes—a dangerous move, when you consider people were pushing against us from all sides. "I think I see something." She grabbed my wrist and pulled, shoving her way past a few smaller kids toward the rear of the kitchen. A few agonizing moments later, we were standing outside, sucking in huge gulps of fresh air.

I pulled on my earlobes. "My ears are ringing."

Katie yelled back, "Mine too!" She glanced around. "Where to now?"

"Back to the car." I checked my phone. We'd agreed to meet at the vehicle in an hour. We weren't off by much. When we shuffled up to the car, we saw the guys hadn't made it back yet. I took the driver's seat; Katie took the front passenger seat. We watched a couple of kids stagger down the road. They fell over, knocking someone's garden gnome on his face. They laughed, then hauled each other back on their feet. "That was a *total* waste of time. It was too loud and too crowded to see or hear anything!" I yelled.

"What were you expecting?" Katie asked.

"Nothing like that."

"No need to ask if you've ever been to a keg party." Katie gave me a little nudge with her elbow. "Check that out." She pointed out her window at a couple that was grinding and pawing at each other next to a tree. The girl had silvery hair. It flashed in the moonlight, making her look almost unearthly.

"I never did that when I was in high school either," I said, unable to tear my gaze away. It was a shocking display of underage lust. The kids involved were practically having sex right out there on the street. Why couldn't I look away?

I honked my horn, and the lovebirds broke it up. Both of

them glanced our way before turning around and heading down the street.

Katie sighed. "That was the most action I'm probably going to see in a while."

"Why's that? What happened with Viktor?"

"I wish I knew. I haven't heard from him since the day after your mom and dad's wedding. Everything was great the last time I talked to him. He said he had to go out of town on business, and he would call, but then . . . nothing." Katie fiddled with her necklace, a gift from the man we were talking about. "I guess I scared him away."

"Do you want me to talk to Damen? See if he knows anything?"

"No."

"But brothers talk."

"That's exactly what I'm worried about. He'll tell Viktor that I was asking about him, and then I'll look like a crazy stalker. No. If he wants to talk to me or see me again, he'll call."

"Okay. If you change your mind—"

"I won't. But thanks, anyway. To hell with him. I'm not going to sit around like a pathetic, lonely, old . . . chemist . . . and wait for him." She visibly perked up a bit. "Oh, I didn't tell you, I heard from our complex. They have a vacancy for us. It'll be ready a week from today."

"Wow, that was fast."

"I know. I guess we caught a lucky break. No offense, but I'm ready to get out of your parents' house. I can't do my work, and your mother is driving me nuts, begging me to run errands for her all the time."

"Is that why I haven't seen you around much?"

"I've been camping out in the chemistry department's office. At least it's quiet, and I can get my work done."

"Sorry."

"It's not your fault. You didn't start that fire. And it's still a roof over my head. Better than living under a bridge."

"I'd never let you do that."

The back door swung open, and JT fell into the car. Literally fell. He mumbled something, and instantly the stench of beer filled the tiny space.

Katie fanned her face, eyes blinking. "Whoa, smells like someone made it to the keg."

The other door opened, and Elmer shoved JT into an upright position, then took his seat. "Your friend nearly got us beat up," he snapped.

I swiveled around. "What happened?"

"He did something involving a lot of beer, a long plastic hose, and a funnel—more than once. And then he got in some guy's face—and he was huge—and started yelling at him about how he was treating his girlfriend. Sloan, I know it's none of my business, but you need to be more careful about who you pick for your friends."

"He just received some very painful news today," I said, feeling I needed to defend him. "He's not himself."

Elmer humphed and buckled himself in.

JT groaned. His skin turned a little green.

This wasn't going to be a pleasant drive home.

But there was one somewhat-bright spot. At least it wasn't my car.

JT was lying facedown on my parents' lawn.

Katie was inside, drowning her sorrows in chocolate.

And I was sitting on Mom and Dad's front porch, on the phone, answering yet another hysterical call from Dale Nessinger. Meanwhile, Elmer flapped his hands, trying to convince me that I didn't need to tell her he was standing right there.

He failed.

"As it turns out, he's right here," I said.

Elmer's face turned the shade of flour paste.

I mouthed, "Do it or else"; then I made a slashing gesture across my neck.

Elmer took the phone from me, cupped his hand over it, and said, "Fine. You win. I'll go, but only if you go with me."

"I can't." I pointed at JT, whose nose was buried in the grass. "Someone needs to make sure he doesn't suffocate."

"Bring him with you."

JT groaned and snorted.

I snorted too. "Are you kidding?"

"He'll fit right in. Take my word for it. Besides, there's always a medic on the set. We need one with all the insane girls getting drunk and cracking their heads open, falling down stairs and stuff. You can have her keep an eye on him. She could at least make sure he doesn't dehydrate."

That part actually sounded good. In fact, it sounded darn good. "Okay."

"I'll be there within the hour," Elmer said into the phone. After clicking off, he handed it back to me. "You have no idea what you're in for. But at least now you'll see what I mean."

"It can't be that bad."

And this time, Elmer snorted.

"Are you kidding me?" I was standing in the center of a melee. At least, that's how it appeared to me. All around me were nearly naked, sexy women, staggering around, calling each other names, pulling hair, stripping off clothes—and worse.

"See what I mean?" Elmer said, grinning. "I wasn't exaggerating. These women are all freaking nuts. I can't marry any of them."

"Let me see what I can do." Leaving Elmer, I went to find a quiet spot, where I could make a phone call. I had to go a long, long way. I dialed Dale Nessinger's number. It rang no less than fifty times, or so it seemed, before it clicked to voice mail.

"This is Sloan Skye. I need to speak with you as soon as possible regarding *Who Wants to Marry an Undead Prince?*

Thank you." I hung up and returned to the set, making myself invisible behind the director. Standing there, I watched in horror as Elmer was subjected to the insanity of over twenty vicious, sleazy, wannabe actresses. This wasn't what either of us had had in mind when we'd signed on.

"Bitch!" screamed one, a redhead.

"He's mine," shrieked another as she threw herself at Elmer and plastered her fake boobs against his chest.

Elmer's face turned the shade of bleached rice.

"Cut!" shouted the director. "Prince, I need you to look like you're not completely repulsed by Jessica."

Elmer's lips thinned. "I'll try."

"She's not repulsive," the one who'd called Jessica a bitch said. "What's your problem?"

"Thanks, hon." Jessica blew the screamer a kiss.

So much for reality.

Elmer's sad eyes found me. He mouthed, "Get me out of here."

I wished I could. I mouthed back, "I'm sorry."

"Let's take it from the top. And . . . action!" the director yelled.

"You bitch," the screamer screeched.

Jessica threw herself at Elmer, smooshing her fake boobs against his chest, and snarled, "Get lost, whore! He's mine."

The water is crystal clear. The gorgeous, cloudless summer sky reflects on its mirror-like surface. The sun is warming my back. I sigh. Content. Relaxed.

Hands work the tight knots out of my shoulders.

Now, this is the way to spend a summer day.

Turning my head to the side, I take in the sight. There are at least four men surrounding me. All drop-dead gorgeous. All naked from the waist up. Mom must have hired some new help.

I love my mom.

"A little lower," I murmur to the one rubbing my back.

The hands move down, finding the tight spot, right between the shoulder blades.

"*Yesss. That's it. Right there.*"

A bumblebee buzzes in my ear. I swat it away, but it comes back. Getting louder. Louder.

Sheesh, what kind of bee is that?

"Sloan," someone said.

"Ignore it," I whispered. "It's nothing."

"No, it's time to wake up," he said.

"What are you talking about?"

"Sloan. Get up."

I jerked upright.

I wasn't lying by a pool. There were no beautiful men surrounding me, lavishing me with their undivided attention.

Reality was such a downer sometimes.

JT was standing next to my bed, looking a lot better than I would've expected. I had to attribute his miraculous recovery to the IV fluids he'd been given on the show set.

"You look like hell," he said.

"Gee, thanks. Excuse me while I go make myself presentable." I threw the covers off and sidestepped around JT to get to the bathroom.

"There's been another murder," JT called after me. "The chief called about an hour ago."

"Damn. But I'm working undercover. I shouldn't go."

"It's a little after five A.M. on a Saturday. Most of the kids are nursing hangovers—at least, the ones we need to worry about probably are. Nobody's going to see you."

"All right. If you think it's okay, I'll go with you. I'll hurry." I closed the bathroom door and went about the business of preparing to visit yet another grisly crime scene. Roughly a half hour later, I smelled much better and my hair wasn't sticking out like I'd stepped on a live wire. A layer of cover-up was somewhat hiding the dark circles under my eyes. But nothing was taking care of the red eye, not even Visine.

After throwing on some of Mom's nicer, non-slutty clothes—a somewhat cute skirt, a lightweight knit top, and a pair of comfy kitten-heeled shoes—I headed down to the kitchen in search of large amounts of caffeine.

JT was sitting at the breakfast counter, a protein bar in one hand and a bottle of vitamin water in the other. "Ready to go?" JT pushed out of his seat.

"In a few. I need caffeine."

JT returned his butt to his chair. "You've got five." He guzzled about half of his water. "Um, what happened last night?"

"You don't remember?"

"No." He glanced at the bandage on his forearm. "Did someone poke me with something?"

"Do you remember the party?"

JT scrunched up his face and lifted his eyes. "Um . . . no. Not really."

"So you don't remember sucking a gallon of beer down a plastic tube?" I filled the coffeemaker with grounds and powered it up.

JT's eyes bugged. "I . . . ? Oh. I do kind of remember doing something like that." His face turned the shade of his car—officially called "Ruby Red." He muttered, "Shit."

"Hey, you were upset. People do things when they're upset."

"I don't drink."

Anticipating the first glorious drips would be exiting the coffeemaker any minute now, I grabbed a clean travel mug from the cupboard and put it where the carafe normally sat. "You did last night." I motioned to his head. "At least you're not hungover. You can thank Elmer for that."

"What's he have to do with anything?"

"He arranged for the IV." The mug full, I put the glass pot back where it belonged and then dug in the cupboard for something portable to eat.

JT's gaze dropped to his arm again. "Ah, I see."

"So, no harm, no foul. You went on a little binge, but nothing bad came out of it. Oh, except . . ." I crinkled my nose. "We're going to have to borrow my mom's car today. Yours is going to need to be cleaned out. The drive home was a little rough."

JT dropped his head into his hands. "Are you saying I . . . ?"

"You vomited all over your floor. We managed to keep it off the leather seats . . . for the most part."

"I guess I owe you my gratitude, then."

"Accepted." I pocketed two boxed brownies—I'd save them for later, an hour or so after we'd left the crime scene—and motioned toward the door. "Now I'm ready. I hope this time we find something useful."

"You and me both. Forrester's had a guy on Barnett since Stephanie's murder. I don't think he's our guy."

Out we went, into a sauna. It was very early, and the birds were just waking up. Already the air was so thick and hot, I could practically see it. The interior of Mom's car was like an oven. I cranked open the windows and set the air-conditioning on high.

JT slumped into the passenger seat. "You have the air on. Shouldn't you close the windows?"

"I have my ways of cooling a car." I motored down the driveway and stopped at the street, waiting for a break in traffic. "What do you know about this latest victim? Anything?"

"I know she's a female. And she attends Fitzgerald. That's all I have right now. The chief is tied up in meetings until noon. Fischer's handling the press, and, of course, you know about Hough. McBride has been called in, but he hasn't answered. That leaves the two of us to handle this. And Wagner. He's on his way up too. We're closer, so we'll probably beat him there."

Something clicked in my head, just then, as JT talked about Gabe. What had Elmer said last night? Then it came to me: *"Have you noticed anyone sort of popping into your life in the last twenty-four hours? Someone you haven't seen in years?"*

"Damn it!" I grumbled. "How could I forget?"

"Forget what?" JT asked.

"It's nothing. Absolutely nothing." I felt my jaw clenching. My teeth were aching. "What exactly did he take?"

"Who?"

"Nobody."

"Skye, are you okay?"

"Yeah, I'm fine." I maneuvered onto I-95 and hit the gas. As soon as the sun set tonight, I was going to track down that memory-stealing creep and make him give back what he'd taken. I couldn't work with Gabe like this. Not when I didn't remember what had been happening with him for so long. What if we'd been . . . intimate? What if he expected to be intimate again? From his rather friendly behavior, this was a very real possibility.

Sunset couldn't come soon enough for me.

"It's the girl from last night," I whispered, staring at the photograph hanging on the wall. Yet again, we were standing in a nice, middle-class, suburban home in Hunting Ridge. "At least I think it is. . . ."

"You saw this girl?" JT asked.

But this time, we were standing next to a grieving woman and a man. They'd learned only a short time ago that their daughter, Hailey Roberts, was dead. My heart ached for them. Damn it, this guy needed to be stopped. Today. Now. Right now.

"What time did your daughter return home last night?" I asked them.

"She never left home," the mother stated.

"Are you sure it's her?" JT whispered.

I scrutinized the photo. "Almost certain. It was somewhat

dark, but that hair is difficult to forget." I pointed at the picture. The girl had silver-platinum hair. It wasn't every day I saw a kid with hair that color.

"Our daughter was home last night," Mr. Roberts stated, pretty much telling me with his voice that I was full of baloney.

"Okay." JT was listening and writing in his little notebook. "Did you have any visitors to your home last night?"

The father shook his head. "No."

"Did you see or hear anything unusual?" JT continued.

The parents glanced at each other.

Mr. Roberts said, "No."

"Do you know anyone who would have a reason to harm your daughter?"

"No," the father said.

"Actually . . ." Mrs. Roberts took a step away from her husband. I found that to be a telling gesture. "Recently there'd been a little blowup on the Internet between Hailey and another girl."

"What kind of blowup?" the father snapped. "How could there be a blowup recently? We took Hailey's computer away."

"Well"—the mother took a second step away from her husband—"I let her use it a few times."

"What? After—"

"She told me she needed it for homework."

Mr. Roberts's eyes narrowed to slits. And his neck started glowing red. "If she was doing homework with it, how could there be a blowup?"

Mrs. Roberts pressed her fingers to her mouth. They were trembling. So were her lips. "She . . . Okay, I felt bad about cutting her completely off. So I told her she could use it for just a half hour a night."

The veins running down Mr. Roberts's neck started protruding. I was beginning to worry about Mrs. Roberts's safety. "You did what?"

Mrs. Roberts clenched her jaw. Her eyes widened. "You were being unreasonable. Completely blew that first situation out of proportion. Isolating our daughter wasn't going to help her learn to handle these things. It was going to make things worse."

"You think? Take a look, Teresa!" He motioned at the crime scene technicians carrying cameras and evidence bags. "Do you still think giving her computer back helped our daughter learn to solve her problems?"

The mother's mouth gaped open. The color drained from her face. "Oh, my God. What have I done?" She crumpled to the floor like a deflated weather balloon.

A family is a place where minds come in contact with one another. If these minds love one another, the home will be as beautiful as a flower garden. But if these minds get out of harmony with one another, it is like a storm that plays havoc with the garden.

—Buddha

12

After Mrs. Roberts's collapse, JT and I called for some medical help for her; then we went to check out their daughter's bedroom, the crime scene. A quick look around suggested we were facing the same lack of physical evidence we'd had at the other scenes, but that didn't stop us from trying to find something. It was a statistical improbability of enormous proportions that our unsub had come into this space, committed a crime, and left without leaving something behind—even if he took the effort to cover his tracks. One of the first things I learned in Forensic Science 101 was Locard's theory. *Every contact leaves a trace.* We were missing whatever it was he hadn't cleaned/covered/removed.

The BPD crime techs were doing their best, combing the carpet, searching the bed, using lights, tweezers, any tool in their arsenal, to find that *one thing.* It was frustrating work. Tedious too. I gave them a lot of credit.

A half hour later, I asked one of the techs if he'd found anything.

"Nothing."

Another one called him over. "Hey, take a look at this."

He raised an index finger. "Hang on." He followed his coworker, and I followed him.

"Check out this stereo. It's fried."

"Yeah. And?"

"Do you remember the Barnett house? The clock was blown. It's like they both were hit by a huge electrical surge."

"Do you have any idea of how much electricity it would take to do this kind of damage?" I asked the one who'd noticed it.

"Not a clue. You'd have to ask an electronics engineer," he replied. "Crime Tech Two" shot some pictures of the stereo.

"I'll do that. Thanks," I said, motioning to the stereo. "Will you be taking that in as evidence?"

"Crime Tech One" shrugged. "Not sure. It's an interesting coincidence, especially when we're dealing with an electrocution, but I doubt it'll lead us to the unsub."

"Can I take it, then?"

"Sure. Just in case, don't dispose of it."

"Okay."

While JT wandered off to talk to the other techs, I disconnected the bookshelf stereo from the speakers and wall socket. As I was reaching behind the dresser to unplug it, I noticed something. It was a small piece of paper, folded into a tiny, dense rectangle. On the paper, I found two words:

Your dead.

Was that a threat? If so, it was grammatically incorrect. Should have been "You're."

Glad I was wearing gloves, I found the closest tech and handed it to him. "I found this behind the dresser. I doubt it's a coincidence. Can I snap a picture of it with my phone before you take it?"

"Sure." He slid it into a clear bag, then handed it back to me so I could snap a photo too.

After returning the bagged note, I went in search of JT, stereo in hand. I found him downstairs, talking to Gabe Wagner.

"I found a note," I told them.

"What did it say?" JT asked, eyeballing the stereo.

"'You're dead,' but spelled y-o-u-r. That's it. No name. But the handwriting was unique. I'd recognize it if I saw it again. I took a picture of it with my phone."

"Good. Now what's with the radio?"

"It's a bookshelf stereo."

Wagner glanced from me to JT. "Well, I guess I'll get back to the unit, since you two have this scene covered."

"See you in a bit." JT stuffed his little notebook back in his pocket.

"Are we leaving too?" I asked him.

"I'm done here. What about you?"

"I'd like to ask the parents if Hailey had a yearbook. It was dark last night, but maybe I'd recognize the boy she was with if I saw a picture of him."

"It's worth a try." JT motioned to the mother, who was now sitting on the couch. She wasn't looking very good, but at least she was conscious. "Do you want me to ask?"

"No, I can do it." Handing the stereo off to him, I headed over to her. "Mrs. Roberts, did your daughter have a recent yearbook?"

"Sure. We buy her one every year."

"Is it possible for me to borrow the most recent one?"

"I . . . suppose."

"Thank you. I appreciate it, and I understand it's probably not something you want to part with right now. I promise I'll return it as soon as possible."

Mrs. Roberts stood. I moved closer, in case she collapsed again. "Why do you need it?"

"Because I believe I saw your daughter last night," I explained in a low voice. "She left a party with a boy."

"What party? Where?"

"It was only a couple of blocks away."

"At whose house? I'd like to know. Whoever held that party is responsible for my daughter's death."

"No, Mrs. Roberts. Please don't lay that blame at their feet. It's not their fault. It's not your fault either. It's the killer's fault. Only his. And we're working hard to catch him so he can't do this again."

She stared down at her hands, wringing a wadded-up tissue. "But I didn't protect her. I failed."

"You did the best you could. No parent is perfect."

"True, but not every parent's failing leads to her child's death."

"Don't blame yourself—"

"Don't do that!" the anguished mother screeched. "Don't tell me what I can or can't feel."

"I'm sorry. I didn't mean—"

She clapped her hands over her face and started sobbing. I stood there, mute, feeling like crap for making her cry again. I wanted to leave the poor woman in peace, but I needed to get my hands on that yearbook.

JT nudged me. "Maybe we can get a copy from the school. Let's go."

I nodded. "I think I've done enough damage here."

We headed out to Mom's car. JT dumped the stereo onto the backseat while I cranked the engine, powered down the windows, and tried not to sweat. Of course, I failed. And within minutes, as we wove through the narrow streets of the subdivision, my face was shiny and little rivulets of sweat were dribbling down my cleavage.

JT was quiet, staring out the passenger window. He said nothing until we were almost back in Quantico. "Thanks for stepping up back there, Sloan. I'm the agent. You're the intern. But you're doing most of the work on this one."

"It's okay."

He rubbed his temples. "I want to get my head together. I'm trying. It's just so fucking hard."

"It takes time. Everyone handles grief differently, but there are four stages and it generally takes—"

"Sloan, please. I don't need to hear a psychological analysis right now."

"Sorry."

"Do me a favor. Take me back to my place."

We drove the rest of the way to JT's apartment in silence. Strained silence. Luckily, traffic was light. Saturday morning. No rush hour.

We rolled up and I let him out. I popped the trunk so he could get his go bag.

He stepped up to my window. "Are you heading into the office for a while?"

"Yes, I think I'm going to make some calls, see if I can get anyone to take a look at that thing." I hooked my thumb over my shoulder at the backseat.

"I think I'm going to call it a day. Ring me if anything comes up."

"Will do."

He disappeared into his building as I backed out of the parking spot.

When I strolled into the PBAU a little while later, a bag of food in one fist, the portable stereo cradled in my arms, I was greeted by Gabe, who appeared to be packed up and ready to head home for the day.

"What'cha have there?" he asked, flicking his gaze to my hands.

"A stereo." I lifted it up.

"Yeah, I see that. Is there a reason why you took it from the last victim's house? Wanting to crank the jams while you're doing your Sloan-super-profiling thing?"

He was so silly. "No. It's fried. The crime scene techs didn't want it so I thought I'd get someone to look at it."

Wagner's brows furrowed as he shouldered my cubby wall. "Why?"

"I don't know. Maybe, if the unsub caused the damage, we can find out something about him from it. I wanted to get someone to look at it."

"I have a friend who plays around with stuff like that. Want me to ask him to take a look at it?"

"Sure. That would be great. Thanks." I handed off the

stereo to Gabe. Our fingers brushed as he slid his arms around it, and my face started warming. I backed up.

Gabe's eyes locked on mine.

I swear, the earth stopped spinning for a split second. Then it started again, and I felt this lurch. Or maybe that was just my imagination. I silently muttered a curse, vowing to find a way to get my memories of Gabe back before things got weird.

"What are you doing here on a Saturday, Sloan?"

That was a silly question. Not to mention, I could easily turn it right back on him. Stating the obvious, I said, "Working. What about you?"

"No plans?" He set the stereo on his desk; then he came back to my cubby to harass me some more.

"No." I didn't want to talk about my personal life with Gabe Wagner, though I sensed he knew plenty about it. I was really hating Elmer right now.

"How about we head out for some lunch?" He stepped closer, leaning his butt against the edge of my desk. His arms were crossed, and he was wearing a short-sleeved shirt. His biceps looked huge, a lot bigger than I remembered. His skin looked a little darker too. His teeth were whiter.

I plunged my hand into the paper bag I'd hauled in and pulled out a wrapped six-inch sub. "I'm all set. Thanks."

"Hmm." He dug into the bag, produced a bag of Sun-Chips, and tore them open. "Mind if I have a couple?"

This was getting to be a regular thing with us.

"Not at all." I took a big bite of my turkey and Swiss and chewed as I fished my laptop out of its bag.

Gabe stood there, watching me, crunching. "Need some help?"

"No thanks."

"What are you working on?"

"Just poking around the Internet. Doing some research."

"On . . . ?"

"Electricity, electrocution, that kind of thing." I took another bite of sandwich while Windows loaded. "I wish my father's research hadn't burned up in the fire. I'd love to see if there are Mythics tied to electricity. The one book I do have only contained a small portion of his body of work."

"I haven't read any of your dad's research, but I know there's at least one."

"You know this?"

"Sure. I've read ghosts can create electrical disturbances. And then there's the Mongolian Death Worm, which may or may not be a Mythic—there's no evidence to support it's real, which means it's technically a cryptid. It is said to be able to produce bursts of electrical energy."

"'Mongolian Death Worm'?" I repeated.

"Yeah. I've been doing some online research. It lives in the Gobi Desert, and only surfaces after a rain."

"Interesting." It took me no time at all to see a connection I'd missed before. All three victims had died after a storm. "Do you have more information on this worm? Could one have made its way here from Mongolia somehow?"

"Who knows? We import somewhere around twelve million dollars of goods a year from there. Mostly food products, sugar, salt. Maybe it found its way into a shipping container, burrowed underground once it landed here. In Mongolia, it lives in sand dunes and only surfaces during the hottest months of the year."

"We've had some muggy, hot weather lately."

"We have."

"And it has rained before every attack."

"It has."

"Could we be onto something? Why didn't you mention this possibility to the chief?" I asked while I typed *Mongolian Death Worm* into a Web search.

"Because I see one major issue with the Mongolian Death Worm theory. Its skin is supposedly toxic to the touch, and victims die instantly. Since we've found every one of our victims on the second floor of their homes, that would suggest the worm is entering their houses and traveling up the stairs by its own means. The victims couldn't carry the worm without dying."

That just blew a small hole in the Mongolian Death Worm theory. "I see what you mean. But would it be impossible? How do they move? Can they fly?"

"Nope. They use a rolling form of locomotion. I can't see a two- to five-foot snake rolling up a staircase."

"Hmm. Still deserves some further investigation." I hit the enter button. The screen filled with links: 115,000. I was going to have plenty of reading ahead of me. "Thanks for the information. And for getting your friend to look at that stereo."

"No problem." He didn't leave.

I elevated my eyes up at him, giving him the okay-you-can-leave look.

"Listen, Sloan, about all the stuff that's been going on between us lately."

I wish I could recall what that "stuff" was. "Gabe, we need to work together. So I'd rather keep things professional."

"So you've said. But . . ." He leaned closer, invading my personal-space bubble; for some crazy reason, I didn't want to back away.

His gaze flicked to my mouth, and warning sirens squealed in my head. A flash of heat blazed through my body. And I suddenly found myself facing the possibility that a longtime fantasy was about to come true.

Gabe was going to kiss me.

One thought raced through my head: *What about Damen? I'm supposed to be courting him. That has to mean something.*

Gabe's face descended toward mine. Seconds dragged by; time seemed to slow to a crawl. I had plenty of opportunity to react. But I just couldn't seem to comprehend what was about to happen.

His mouth hovered over mine. "Sloan?" he whispered.

My eyelids fluttered shut.

The image of Damen's face flashed in my head.

I smacked my hands on Gabe's chest and gave him a shove. "I can't do this."

Gabe moved back, not fighting me. His gaze searched my face. "I'm not going to apologize. Sloan, I've cared about you for years. Waited for my chance to tell you how I feel. And I did, and I can tell you have feelings for me too."

"There's someone else," I enunciated.

"No, there's not. If there really was someone else, I wouldn't have even made it that close." Without saying another word, he went back to his desk, grabbed the stereo, and left the unit.

His words echoed in my head as I watched the glass door swing shut behind him.

What he'd said—it was true.

All that is necessary to break the spell of inertia and frustration is to . . . act as if it were impossible to fail.

—Dorothea Brande

13

After that little episode with Gabe, I couldn't concentrate. I had no choice but to pack up my computer and head home. During the entire drive, I chastised myself for what I'd almost done. He was right, damn it. If I cared about Damen as much as I said, Gabe shouldn't have been able to get that close.

I called myself several unflattering names as I zoomed up the Capital Beltway toward Mom and Dad's. I wasn't feeling any better about my actions when I pulled into the driveway.

Or when I let myself inside.

"Sloan, is that you?" Mom shouted when I tromped through the house, heading toward the stairs.

"Yes, it's me, Mom."

She yelled, "There's a package in the front hall for you."

"A package?"

I hadn't placed any orders. I wasn't expecting a package.

"Yes. Also, we'll be leaving in a few hours. We decided to take a honeymoon now, before the baby's born. We're flying to Tahiti."

"Tahiti, that's great." Much more curious about the package than Mom and Dad's travel plans, I went out to the front hall, finding a large box sitting on the table next to the front door. The return address was Amazon. I took it, along with my loaner computer, upstairs.

Katie intercepted me in the hallway. "Sloan, I need a girls' night out." Her mascara had run down her cheeks. She looked like a very bad impressionist's representation of a *Procyon lotor*—aka, a raccoon.

"Oh, hon, what's wrong?"

"I finally heard from Viktor."

A flare of guilt buzzed through me. Why had I let her talk me out of calling Damen to see if I could find out what was going on with him? I might have been able to ease the blow if I'd known what was coming. "You did?"

"He called to tell me he'd left something in my car. That was it. Didn't mention seeing me again." She started sniffling. Her eyes started watering once more.

I set the box on the floor, then grabbed and hugged her. "Men are such jerks."

"Jerks," she said, snuffling and sobbing.

Stepping out of the embrace, I rubbed her arms. "You deserve so much better than that. You realize that, right?"

She sniffed. She dripped. She nodded. "I know."

"You're intelligent and beautiful. Sooner or later, you'll meet the one. I promise."

"I hope you're right." She eased out of my hold, smiling and crying at the same time. "I hate that I get so worked up about this stuff."

"We all do. It's part of being a woman."

She snorted. Her gaze gravitated to the box I'd all but forgotten about. "What's that?"

"I don't know."

Her brows lifted. "Open it."

"Sure. Okay." I hauled it into my room and set it on my bed. I broke several fingernails, trying to pull off the tape, before Katie sighed, went to her room, and returned with something slender and silver. She pushed a button and, *click*, a knife blade sprung out. "What the heck is that?"

"It's a knife." She ran the tip of the blade along the seam between the box flaps, slicing through the tape like it was tissue.

"I can see that. But where did you get it? I mean, is that even legal?"

"It depends." She hit the button and, *snap,* the blade went back in.

"Upon . . . ?"

"What state we're in. It's legal to possess in Maryland."

"We're not in Maryland," I pointed out.

"This, I'm aware of." She handed the opened box to me and returned the deadly weapon to its home. "My father bought it for me ages ago. It usually sits in my dresser. I've thought about getting rid of it a few times, but it's one of the few things I have that he gave me. Plus, you never know when it might come in handy."

"I guess I see your point." I folded the box flaps out, revealing a lot of white foam peanuts. I slid my hand in, found a smaller box, and pulled it out.

"What's that?" she asked.

"Another box."

"I can see that. Any idea who sent it?"

"No."

I opened the smaller box, and inside that one was yet another box. "Sheesh, reminds me of those Russian nesting dolls." Borrowing Katie's knife again, I opened the third box. The outside of this box had a familiar logo on it. And inside the box, I found an Alienware laptop with practically enough memory to run the National Archives and Records Administration database. At the bottom of the receipt was typed:

I thought you could use this. Had to leave town for a few days. Will be thinking about you. Damen.

My phone rang.

JT.

"Sloan, I just received a call from Mrs. Roberts. She has her daughter's yearbook. Would you like to call her?"

"Yes. Thank you."

He recited the number; then, after another quick thank-you on my part, he hung up. I was on my way to the Roberts house ten minutes later, after calling to make sure she'd be there. Katie rode shotgun. I didn't have the heart to leave her at home. Not in her condition. Could I have waited until to-morrow? Probably. But I couldn't get my hands on that book fast enough. Not with three girls dead now. Luckily, traffic was relatively light. I was on the Roberts family's front porch in record time.

"If this will help you catch whoever did this, before they kill someone else's daughter, then it's the least I can do. Right?" the grieving mother said as she reluctantly handed over the book.

"I promise I'll take care of it. You'll get it back very soon."

Eyes tearing, she nodded and thanked me.

I forced myself to wait before flipping through the pages. While I drove back to Mom and Dad's, Katie complained about men, highlighting every fault she'd found in all the male Homo sapiens she'd ever met. Of course, being her best friend, I agreed with her. Men sucked. Men were rotten. Men were downright evil. And we women were better off without them.

The minute we got back to Mom and Dad's, I started poring over the pages of the yearbook, looking for the kid I saw in the dark.

I found him on page twenty-two. I called JT first. Then Chief Peyton.

And then I called Elmer. We had some business to discuss.

I talked to JT. He returned my call within ten minutes.

I talked to the chief. She returned my call within twenty minutes.

I didn't hear back from Elmer.

He was not going to be able to avoid me forever.

* * *

On Sunday morning, JT and I met at the BPD's Southwest District police station. I was driving JT's freshly cleaned car. He had caught a ride from someone. He would take me home later, once the interview of the student I recognized, Benjamin Gardener, was over.

Inside, we exchanged pleasantries. JT was most definitely still not himself.

"Any news on Brittany?" I asked as we checked in at the front desk.

"She's stabilized."

"That's good news."

"Yeah. But she's a long way from being okay."

"She's lucky to have such a dedicated friend."

"Yeah, 'friend,'" he echoed.

Forrester intercepted us on the way back to Interview Room C.

"We haven't talked to him yet." To me, he said, "Are you absolutely sure this is the one?"

"I have an eidetic memory. I can tell you what he was wearing, what she was wearing, what they were doing, and where they were doing it."

Forrester's gaze slid to JT. "Good enough. I'm going to let you two have a go at him first. Good luck."

JT leaned toward me. "We're interviewing a minor. Please let me handle this."

"Understood." I made a zipper motion across my mouth, and in we went. The door shut behind us.

A man, the boy's father, no doubt, was sitting in a chair next to his son. He watched us enter with caution-filled eyes.

"Mr. Gardener?" JT offered the man his hand. "I'm Agent Thomas. FBI. Thank you for bringing your son in this morning. I'm sure this is the last thing you wanted to do on a Sunday."

"Tom Gardener." He looked my way as he shook JT's hand. "Is my son in some kind of trouble?"

"Not at all." JT motioned for him to sit. "I am a criminal profiler, a psychologist, investigating some crimes in the area and am interviewing kids who attend a local high school, to see if I can find a connection among the victims."

The father slid his son a sideways glance. "Okay, but if I get uncomfortable with this at any point, I'm going to put the brakes on."

"Fair enough." JT leaned back in his chair. I guess he was trying to look relaxed and trustworthy. Nonthreatening. He turned his focus on Benjamin. "Hello, Benjamin. Thanks for coming down to answer our questions."

The kid shrugged. "Sure. But it's Ben. Just Ben."

"Ben, do you know Hailey Roberts?"

The boy glanced at his father before answering. "Yes. Sort of."

"What does that mean, 'sort of'?" JT asked.

"It means I know she goes to Fitzgerald. She was in a couple of my classes last year."

"That's it? That's all you know about her?"

"Yeah."

The father leaned forward, but he said nothing.

"What about Stephanie Barnett and Emma Walker?" JT asked.

"Yeah. I know them too. No better than Hailey."

JT nodded. "So you'd call them . . . 'acquaintances'?"

"Yeah. *Acquaintances,*" the kid echoed. He had a very interesting definition of the word. I wouldn't call someone I'd swapped DNA with an "acquaintance." But then, maybe that was just me.

JT continued, in a friendly, just-help-me-out kind of voice. "We're having a hard time figuring out who killed the girls and why. I'm hoping someone at your school can help. Maybe you. Can you tell me if there are any obvious connections among the three girls? Did they share the same friends? Or enemies?"

"I didn't know them that well."

"None of them?"

"Nope."

JT paused. I had a feeling the hey-we're-buddies chat was

over. "We've been told you were seen leaving a party with Hailey Roberts the night she died."

"That's it." The father smacked his flattened hands on the table. "Interview's over. Ben, we're leaving." He stood, grabbed his son's arm, and hauled him to his feet.

JT remained seated; his expression was calm and cool. "We're not implying your son had anything to do with anyone's death. We're trying to find out what happened after they parted ways."

"It's okay, Dad. I don't have anything to hide. I did leave the party with Hailey. We hooked up, messed around a little. But that was it."

"Shut your mouth, Ben," his father snapped.

"I didn't kill *nobody*. If I don't talk, then they're going to think I'm trying to hide something."

I agreed.

His father probably didn't.

JT asked, "Where did you 'mess around'?"

"In my friend's front yard. I kissed her a little. That's all. Then I walked her home and went back to the party. People saw me there, when I came back."

"Which people?" JT asked.

"Lots. There were a lot of people there."

"Can you give us some names?"

"Sure. Jake, Matt, and Dalton."

JT wrote the names in his notebook. "When you dropped her off, did she go directly into her house?"

"Yes, I think so. I mean, I didn't watch her go in."

"Was anyone else with her, besides you?"

"No."

"Did you see anyone else in the vicinity? Or anything suspicious?"

His gaze lifted up and to the right. "Hmm. Come to think of it, I might have seen something. Maybe."

"What did you see?"

"There was a car parked across the street. The engine was running, but the headlights were out."

"Did you see who was in the car?"

"No. It was dark." His gaze jerked to his dad, and his lips pursed for a brief instant. So far, I'd seen nothing to indicate he might be lying . . . until now.

"Could you estimate what time that would have been?" JT asked.

"I guess around eleven-thirty." That was shortly after we'd seen him kissing Hailey. He was right on the money there.

JT asked, "What can you tell me about the car?"

"It was a small-sized sedan. Dark. Maybe black."

The father sat mute, eyes sharp, jaw a little tight. He hadn't interrupted again. Not yet.

"That's it?" JT asked. "A dark sedan?"

"Yeah, sorry. I didn't really think much about it until now."

"Can you think of any reason why anyone would want to harm Stephanie, Emma, and Hailey?"

"No, sorry. Like I said, I didn't know them very well. Not even Hailey. We just hooked up that night, made out a little. We didn't talk much."

"I understand."

"Wish I could be more help. If I hear any rumors, I'll let you know."

"Thanks. I'd appreciate that."

"No problem." Ben stood. "Can I go now?"

"Sure." JT motioned to the door. "You're free to leave at any time. Do you have any questions for me?"

The kid sat. "Maybe I do. Say I wanted to be an FBI profiler like you, what would I need to do?"

JT smiled. "You'd need a Ph.D. in psychology for starters. Then you'd need to apply to the FBI Academy."

The kid's eyes widened. "Wow, all that? Just to make up stuff about serial killers?"

Make stuff up! Isn't he cute?

"We don't 'make up stuff,'" JT corrected. "We develop a profile of a killer, to help police target suspects in a murder investigation."

"Sure." Ben headed for the door. "Come on, Dad. I'm hungry. How about we grab a burger somewhere?"

"Sure, son."

I said absolutely nothing until I was sure Ben and Tom Gardener couldn't overhear us. "Obviously, he doesn't have a lot of respect for criminal profilers." I chuckled.

"Yeah. Obviously." JT was staring up at the LCD monitor hanging on the back wall, a remote control in his hand. He hit the button and the screen lit up. "I want to play that last part back. Did you see what I saw?"

"If you're talking about the microexpression?" I watched the video playback.

"Yeah. That." JT hit the button, pausing the video at the exact moment when Ben's lips pursed after he'd mentioned the car.

"Maybe he isn't the killer, but I think he was lying about the car."

"So what does that mean?" JT asked.

"If he's making up a mysterious car—and maybe he isn't, microexpression theory isn't one hundred percent reliable in identifying deceit—then I'm guessing he saw something else, something that might incriminate someone he knows."

"We need to keep a close eye on him, find out what he's covering up. I'm going to see if Forrester can get someone to tail him." JT hit the power button, shutting off the monitor.

"Sounds like a plan." We headed toward the exit together. "What's next?"

"After I take you home, I'm heading to the hospital to see Brittany. I'd like to interview more kids tomorrow. Someone at that school knows something. It's just a matter of finding out who that someone is."

"I have Hailey Roberts's yearbook. It's been autographed. We could start by compiling a list of names from that."

"Sounds good, Sloan. Thanks again for your help. You're doing a damn good job. Just remember, don't let this job take over your life. You're an intern. It's summertime. Go. Live a little. Go to the shore. Do something that doesn't involve chasing monsters with a hunger for blood."

"Okay, if you insist." Of course, I had no intention of doing any such thing. Three girls were murdered and a fourth dead. That was four too many in my book. There would be plenty of time for fun in the sun . . . after this effing killer was caught.

Monday morning, I donned my slutty-teen garb, and packed up my list of names for JT, my go bag, and my new superpowerful computer. Then I motored to Fitzgerald High School. I heard a lot of muttering in the halls during breaks between classes. A lot more than normal. I tried to catch bits and pieces of conversations as I made my way from economics to "Intro to Algebra" to chemistry, but it was hard to get more than a few words here and there before I was forced to move on or risk being found out.

This was frustrating.

Since joining the PBAU, I'd pretended to be a suburbanite with an exercise fetish and a very pregnant wife to JT. Those had been tough assignments. Physically and mentally. But this was really bad. Not just because I was living the worst days of my life over again—I was no more popular now than I was then, even dressed in my smut-tastic finery—but I was getting absolutely nowhere. *No friends* meant nobody would talk to me. Nobody would talk to me, except the girl who'd killed herself.

Somehow I had to find someone willing to befriend the new girl.

When I was in school, I'd made a couple of friends. Science nerds. I was tempted to hunt down this school's science-nerd clique, but I knew for a fact that they wouldn't be attending summer school. Summer school wasn't for smart kids.

And then an idea struck me. A brilliant idea.

I approached Mr. Hollerbach and asked if he could recommend a tutor. He said he'd get a list together by the end of the day, tomorrow at the latest. Then he asked me for my phone number, promising to pass it on if he found someone who was interested. I figured I'd have a prospective contact within the next twenty-four hours.

Which was a good thing, because by the end of the day, I had absolutely nothing for the team other than a list of kids who'd autographed Hailey Roberts's yearbook.

But later, as I was pulling into the McDonald's drive-through lane, my cell phone rang. The number was a Baltimore area code. I answered and sweet-talked a senior named Jia Wu into agreeing to a tutoring session that afternoon. I did a little celebratory fist pump as my car rolled up to the drive-through window.

Maybe these tedious days of torture were about to come to an end.

Maybe.

You may be deceived if you trust too much, but you will live in torment if you do not trust enough.

—Frank Crane

14

"Allotropes are different forms of the same element in the same state of matter."

This I've known since I was six. Examples included O_2, oxygen gas, and O_3, ozone. But, playing the part of a clueless high-school flunk out, I gave my new tutor, Jia, a look of complete bewilderment. "What? Same what of what?"

"Look here." Jia drew two circles on a piece of paper. "These are oxygen atoms. They're both oxygen. Same element. And when there are two of them like this, we have oxygen in a gaseous form." Then she drew three circles interlinked. "And now we have three oxygen atoms stuck together. They're still a gas, but this is ozone."

I donned a "eureka" expression. "Ah, I get it now."

"Good. We can move on." My tutor looked slightly surprised. Maybe I'd made it too easy for her. "A molecule is a neutral group of bonded atoms."

I plastered on my confused face again. "Uh?"

To her credit, Jia didn't pull out her hair, like I had been tempted to do back when I was a tutor.

"Can I ask you something?"

"Sure," Jia said as she flipped the paper over and started drawing more circles, illustrating the difference between an atom, unbonded atoms, and molecules.

"Are you worried about the murderer who is targeting girls at our school?"

"What murderer?"

Jia didn't even look up from what she was doing. No reaction whatsoever. Was she intentionally avoiding the subject? If so, why?

"What are you talking about?" she asked again.

"You haven't heard? It was on the news last night. Three girls have been killed, and they all go to Fitzgerald High."

"No way. Who?"

How could she not have heard? "Stephanie Barnett, Emma Walker, and Hailey Roberts. Do you know them?"

"I knew Emma. I tutored her last year. Geometry."

"Not the other two?"

"I knew *of* them, but I never talked to them. Our school isn't huge. My freshman year, I had a couple of classes with Stephanie. But that's it."

"So, do you think there's any reason to be worried? I mean, I don't know why those three girls were killed. So I don't know if I might be the next one."

"Hmm." She was labeling her pictures. And from the look of it, caring more about that than our conversation about the dead girls. Either she was one very focused tutor, or she was trying to avoid the topic.

"I heard the FBI's investigating the murders," I added, fishing for some kind of reaction or information. "They're calling in students and interviewing them. I wonder if they think it's one of us. A student?"

"I can think of one or two students who might be capable of doing something like this."

Now that was more like it! At last, I was getting somewhere. I should've thought of this angle a long time ago. "Who?"

Jia looked left. She looked right. She leaned close. Was she afraid someone was listening? "Don't say a word about this to anyone."

"Sure. I promise. Hell, I'm the new girl. Nobody talks to me, anyway."

"I heard Ben Gardener spent three years in juvie up in Indiana. Nobody's ever said what he did. But if it's true, three years is a long time. He must've done something pretty bad. Maybe something violent."

"Could be."

She leaned closer still. "And then there's Zoey Urish. I've known her since kindergarten. She's crazy. Absolutely insane. She was in my third-grade class and lives one block from me. In fact, I even remember once, when we were in fifth grade, a friend of mine, who lives across the street from my house, was giving her a hard time about her hair during recess. She was being kind of mean, and that wasn't right. But that night, my friend let her dog out to do his business, and someone broke his neck. The next day, Zoey asked her how her dog was. My friend's mother called the police right away. We knew she did it, but the police couldn't get enough evidence, so they couldn't press charges. After that, both my friend and I have stayed away from her. She'll do *anything* to anyone who crosses her."

"Wow." I was making mental notes. Zoey Urish and Ben Gardener. Forrester hadn't mentioned anything about Gardener's juvenile record. I wondered why.

"You won't say anything to anyone, right?"

"No, I won't tell anyone." *Any students.* "I promise. Thanks. Now I know who to stay away from."

"That's the only reason why I said anything. Now let's get back to bonded atoms."

"Okay. But can I ask you one more question first?"

"I . . . guess."

"Do you know Derik Sutton? I've heard he's kind of creepy."

"I . . . um, don't know." Jia glanced at the clock. "We're running out of time. We'd better get back to chemistry."

She pointed at the drawing. "Here we have two hydrogen atoms. . . ."

I called JT as soon as I was back in my car. He didn't answer, so I left him a message, including what Jia had told me. Then I clicked off and drove home. During the entire drive, I wondered why Jia had been willing to talk about Ben and Zoey, but she seemed to shut down once I mentioned Derik Sutton's name. Was it a coincidence? Or was there a reason why she'd cut off our conversation at that point? I really, really wanted to know. Fortunately, I had another tutoring session tomorrow. The tutoring was going to cost the FBI some cash; but if she continued to talk, it would be well worth the investment.

I headed to the unit. Empty. There wasn't a soul in the place. Not even McBride, our techie geek. After spending some time on Facebook, checking out all of the kids who'd signed Hailey Roberts's yearbook, including Ben and Zoey, as well as sketching out a preliminary profile, I packed it up and headed home.

Just like at the office, I found myself alone. Mom and Dad were winging their way to Tahiti, and Katie was nowhere to be found. Sergio was gone for the night, too. The big house felt cold and a little creepy. I made myself a sandwich and took it upstairs to my room. I ate while reading over my preliminary profile. Then I powered up the new supercomputer, transferred all my files over, and hunted down everything I could find on the Mongolian Death Worm. Gabe had made some good points about its mode of locomotion. Logrolling up a set of steps would be difficult, if not impossible. However, I wasn't willing to dismiss the possibility of our unsub being a Death Worm—*if* it was able to shape-shift.

Hours later, I had read pretty much everything published on the Internet about the Death Worm. And I'd watched a documentary. Not one source mentioned the ability to shape-shift. I wasn't sure whether that was because it couldn't, or if people simply didn't realize it yet. Regardless, I was tired, and I had another long day ahead of me. I shut down the laptop, put in another call to Elmer, and went to bed, knowing I'd be having dreams about ugly worms that spit acid and shot lightning out of their rectums and creepy undead men who stole from me.

The next morning, I cussed out Elmer for not paying me a visit and then did my usual thing. Showered, dressed, infused my bloodstream with ample quantities of caffeine, and flounced out to school in my high-school ho outfit. I sat through an hour and a half of economics (yawn), another hour and a half of algebra (another yawn), a lunch hour spent eating by myself while getting odd looks from my fellow students (evidently, dressing like a ho wasn't making me fit in better), and finally one last hour and a half sitting through chemistry (which wouldn't have been so bad if we weren't covering material I'd learned when I was six).

By two o'clock, I was *so* glad to say *"sayonara"* to Fitzgerald High. I rounded the north corner of the building, heading to my car. Derik Sutton was approaching from the opposite direction. His gaze flicked to me, but he didn't acknowledge me. Not with a nod or a wave or even a smile. Just like everyone else in this school.

But as our paths crossed, he suddenly slammed into me, flattening me against the wall. His body held me pinned to the brick building.

"I heard you were asking questions about me," he said, his voice barely above a whisper.

"I—I'm new. I just . . . saw you at the party, and I wanted to know more about you."

"Why?"

"B-because." I was shaking all over now. I couldn't help it. "I thought you were cute."

He cupped my chin and stared into my eyes, and I felt like

he was somehow rummaging around in my brain, trying to dig up all my hidden secrets.

"Sorry," he said, his lips curling into a sneer, "but you're not my type." And he strolled away as if he hadn't just assaulted me.

Sheesh, I'd known this assignment wasn't going to be pleasant, but I'd thought it would at least be safer than coaxing an *adze* out of hiding.

My knees felt like gelatin as I pushed away from the building. For a brief moment, I questioned whether I had the stomach for this line of work. Maybe something less risky, like researching the cures for virulent diseases, would be more my thing.

I practically made it to my car when I remembered I'd forgotten my chemistry book in my locker. After checking the time on my cell phone, I hurried back inside to get it. It was a quick trip to my locker and back outside.

But when I rounded the north corner, there he was again, Derik Sutton. He seemed to be waiting for me. My insides crept and crawled. I tried to pretend I didn't see him there. He made a little noise. Our gazes met. He came closer as I continued forward. My heart started thumping. My chest grew tight. I glanced around, searching the area for other students. None? Why didn't anyone else walk this way?

"Hello there, Sloan Skye," he said in a smooth voice, which was probably intended to be seductive. It wasn't.

"Hi." Donning a don't-get-too-near expression, I crossed my arms over my chest and kept going.

"Really? You're going to blow me off?"

I didn't say a thing. He was behind me now, and I was doing my damned best to make sure it stayed that way. Unfortunately, he didn't like it. He grabbed my arm and jerked me around.

"Why do you have to be so fucking rude?"

"I'm not trying to be rude. I'm in a hurry."

"Yes. Need to get to your tutoring session with Jia, right?"

So Jia had told him what I'd said? After she'd asked me to keep her secret? I felt betrayed. "Yes. You know her?"

"Yeah, I know her. She's my stepsister."

"Oh." Why hadn't Jia mentioned that? It did explain her unwillingness to talk about him.

"Anyway," he said, invading my personal-space bubble, "I wanted to talk to you about something else." His hand, the one that had been clamped around my wrist like a metal vise, skimmed up my arm. "I think I've been a little hasty in judging you."

Lucky me. *Not.*

He licked his lips. "You are rather sexy." His gaze flicked south of my face. "And you have great tits."

Gag.

I couldn't do this. There was no freaking way. The FBI couldn't pay me enough money to put up with nasty, little punks pawing me, leering at me. "You know what? I was wrong too. You're not cute. Not at all." I stomped past him, throwing some mean eyes over my shoulder. "And if you touch me again, I'll file harassment charges."

"You'll be sorry, bitch."

His words echoed in my head for the next hour.

God, I hoped I hadn't just made myself the target of a serial killer.

On the drive over to the library, I thought long and hard about whether to say something to Jia about her step-brother's threat. I decided to keep it to myself and called JT, instead. He answered.

"Hey, what's up?" he said, sounding like the happy-go-lucky, kick-ass agent I've known since my first day. I hoped *this* JT would stick around. I really needed him.

"JT, has anyone gotten anything on Ben Gardener yet?"

I was driving toward the library. "Rumor has it he was in juvenile detention in Indiana."

"No. The rumor's wrong. I ran a background on him and his father. Both came up clean. BPD's got a guy watching him."

"Okay, we need to do a check on another student, named Derik Sutton. There's something not quite right about him. And he's been harassing me at school."

"Okay, I'll check him out. Is it possible he likes you? Kids that age have strange ways of showing girls how they feel."

"It's possible, but I sort of blew him off. He got mad and said I'd be sorry." I turned into the library's parking lot.

"Hmm. So it's not so much a harassment but more a threat."

"It was most definitely a threat. I'm telling you, it was creepy. The way he was looking at me, touching me." I shuddered as I pulled into an empty spot.

"I'll run a full background on him. Can you avoid him?"

"A part of me wants to. Another doesn't. I need to figure out whether he's our unsub. Then again, if he is, he could hunt me down and . . . you know." My gaze flicked to the clock on my dash. "His stepsister is my tutor, so I'm going to see what I can learn about him from her. Without calling too much attention to myself. This undercover stuff is tricky. I want to get close enough, but not too close to put myself in danger."

"I need to call the chief. She should know about this. Do you want to stay at my place tonight?"

"No thanks. I'm probably just being paranoid."

"I wouldn't be so quick to dismiss your intuition. If you ask me, I think we should pull you from the school. The chief's already taken some heat for putting you in danger."

"You know what? I wouldn't complain if you did pull me out. The kids aren't talking to me, anyway."

"Your parents' place has a security system, right?"

"Yes, it does. My father's the head of security for a queen. Security's kind of his thing."

"Good. As long as the system is armed, you should be safe."

"Unless creepy boy is some kind of Mythic that can vaporize and seep through the crack under the front door."

"Now you're talking crazy, Sloan." His chuckle made me feel better. I'd made him laugh. I hadn't heard that sound in a while. I hadn't realized how much I had missed it. "I'll call the chief and see what she thinks. I'm guessing you've spent your last day at summer school."

The all-too-famous Alice Cooper song "School's Out" played in my head. I felt my lips curl into a smile. "I'd be glad to do lunch runs and make coffee for the rest of the summer, if it means I don't have to go back."

"You'd better be careful there, Sloan. You may get exactly what you wished for. Later." He clicked off.

I glanced at the clock in my car for the second time, shoved my phone into my pocket, and headed inside. Even if I was dropping out of summer school, I still wanted to get in this final tutoring session—see if I could get anything else out of Jia. One thing I would be sure to do, though—avoid mentioning Derik's name.

I found her sitting exactly where she'd been last time, at a table in the back, near the romance section. She waved me over when she saw me approaching. I donned a smile and plunked down on the chair.

"So how'd your quiz go?" she asked.

"I got a seventy."

Her brows scrunched. "A seventy? You knew that material."

"I have problems taking tests."

The brows didn't unscrunch. "Huh. I guess we'd better work harder." She reached for my book, which I'd dropped on the table, and started leafing through the pages. "What chapter are you doing now?"

"Three."

"Okay." She found the start of the chapter and skimmed the pages. "All right. This stuff is easy. We can get that grade up." She hesitated. "But before we dig in, I need to tell you something," she whispered.

"What?" I whispered back.

"You mentioned Derik last time, when we were talking about . . . what's been going on. Anyway, I was talking to my mom about it, and I think he might've overheard me."

"He did."

Her face paled. "I'm sorry. What happened?"

"He pinned me to the wall and asked why I was talking about him."

"And . . . ?"

"I told him I thought he was cute."

"You did? I mean, do you?"

"Um . . . I'd rather not talk about this with you."

"No, it's okay. I swear I won't tell anyone."

Right. "You're his stepsister."

"Not legally. Our parents aren't married. They're just dating. They say they're engaged."

"I see."

She inched closer. "The truth is, I've been telling my mom for a long time that there's something creepy about Derik. There's a strange vibe coming off him, but she doesn't believe me." She paused. "But you agree with me, don't you?"

"Yes, I do. Especially now. He's very pushy with girls. And more than a little scary."

"You don't think . . ." She tipped her head down and cupped her hand over her mouth. "Could he be the killer?"

"I don't know. Do you know where he was the nights of the murders?"

"I don't know when the murders happened."

"The last one was this past Friday."

She looked up and tapped her fingers on the tabletop. "Hmm. He stayed at our house that night. He left at around nine. Don't know where he went. He didn't tell me, and I didn't ask. But he came home around eleven."

Eleven was too early. The ME set the time of death at after two A.M.

"Are you sure about that time?" I asked.

"Yes. I was awake, watching a movie."

"Could he have left again, after you saw him?"

"I know he didn't leave between eleven and about three A.M. That's when I went to bed."

Damn. He had an alibi. An airtight one—unless Jia was lying. I'd seen no signs of deception, though. Not one. And why would she bring up this whole thing and then lie? That made no sense. The other alternative was that she was mistaken about the time.

"Did anyone else see him at home that night?"

"Why are you asking me that? Do you think I'm lying?"

"Of course not. But maybe you're mistaken. Or maybe he slipped out for a while and then came back in, making you think he'd been there that whole time. Criminals do that when they want to establish an alibi."

"No, there's no mistake. He wasn't faking anything. We saw him—I mean, I saw him."

"There was someone else there? Your parents?"

Jia went silent again. Several seconds later, she mumbled, "Let's get to work. I shouldn't have said anything. Just forget it, okay? Why are you so interested in this, anyway?"

"Jia, he threatened me. So you see now why I'm worried! If he's the killer, I need to tell someone."

"I don't think he's the killer."

"But you just said there's something not right about him."

"Yeah. . . ."

What was this girl hiding? Was she covering for him because he threatened her too? Or was it something else?

"Jia, has he threatened you too?"

"No."

"Then why do I get the feeling you're hiding something?"

"Damn it, you don't give up, do you? You should become

a cop. You'd be good at it, I think." She stared down at the table for several moments. I said absolutely nothing, hoping she'd feel compelled to speak, to fill the silence. "It has nothing to do with my stepbrother. If you must know, I wasn't alone Friday night." Her cheeks turned deep red, but her lips curled a little into a shy but slightly wicked smile. "I'd rather not say who I was with."

I was curious. Much too curious not to ask, "Who?"

She stared at me for a heartbeat, two, three. "Promise me you won't tell anyone."

"Again, who am I going to tell? Nobody at school will even say hello."

"Mr. Hollerbach."

I tried to hide my shock. I felt my mouth gape open, but I snapped it shut. "The chemistry teacher?"

"You can't tell. He'll be fired."

Oh, this was bad. The notion of this young woman having some kind of illicit affair with a teacher hadn't crossed my mind. She was bright. She seemed to have her act together. Why would she do something so foolish?

Smart kids do stupid things sometimes.

"I won't tell anyone, but you really need to think hard about what you're doing." I hadn't noticed if Mr. Hollerbach wore a wedding ring. Even though, technically, I wasn't a student, I didn't go around checking teachers' ring fingers out, to see if they might be single.

"We haven't done a lot . . . yet." The color in her cheeks deepened. "Why am I talking about this? We're supposed to be studying."

"Forget about chemistry. This is more important." I grabbed her hand and locked my eyes with hers. "I don't care if Mr. Hollerbach is single and all you've done is sit around and talk about organic compounds. You're making a mistake. A big mistake. And he . . . That bastard shouldn't have even entertained the thought of coming to your house at night."

Jia's lip started quivering. "But he's one of the few people I can talk to. He says I'm beautiful and smart, and he loves me."

Oh, God. It was worse than I thought. "You need to find an adult you can trust, and you need to get some help with this. If you don't, you will eventually be hurt, and I would hate to see that happen."

The quiver got worse. "But he loves me. He'd never hurt me."

"We all want to believe that. The sad truth is, people stop loving."

"He said he's going to leave his wife and marry me."

He was married. Even worse. "Don't believe him. Chances are, he has no intention of leaving his wife."

All the color drained from Jia's face.

Now I felt crappy. "I'm sorry. I'm not saying this to be mean. It's the truth."

"You don't know him. How could you know what he will or won't do?"

"I can't, but I know this. Infidelity in marriage doesn't just hurt the people directly involved. It hurts everyone—the spouse, the children, the entire family. You're a smart young woman, with a brilliant future ahead of you. Don't you want a man in your life who you can trust? A man who won't cheat on you someday, when he gets tired of you, or you've lost your youth? Don't you want a man who will respect you?"

"Of course, I do. But why are you so emotional about this?"

"Because my father cheated on my mother," I confessed. "I've seen the ugly side of infidelity."

"I'm sorry. What happened?"

"They're married. They're having another child soon. And I'm praying for my mother's sake, and the unborn baby's, that my father meant it when he promised it won't ever happen again."

"I guess I never looked at it from that perspective." She

glanced down at her hand. A small gold band with tiny diamonds was circling her left ring finger. She twisted it. "He gave me this. A promise ring." She blinked a few times. "He said we'd be married as soon as I graduate."

"He's a lying jerk. And even if he's not lying about marrying you, you will eventually regret it. He'll do to you what he's doing now. He'll dump you for someone else."

"I trust him."

"You're trusting the wrong man."

"I don't want to talk about it anymore." She pushed the book in front of me. "We're running out of time, and we haven't studied anything yet. If you flunk another test, I'm going to feel like crap."

My supposed flunking was the least of her problems. But clearly, she wasn't ready to hear that yet.

"All right. If it'll make you feel better, we'll study."

Mourning is not forgetting. . . . It is an undoing. Every minute tie has to be untied and something permanent and valuable recovered and assimilated from the dust. The end is gain, of course. Blessed are they that mourn, for they shall be made strong, in fact. But the process is like all other human births, painful and long and dangerous.

—Margery Allingham

15

After that conversation with Jia, I pretty much decided we had nothing on our case but a sketchy profile. We had no viable suspects, no solid persons of interest. No motive. No clues, outside of the marks on the victims and a couple of burned-up electronics. I needed to do something about that.

I pointed my car southeast, toward Quantico.

Using speakerphone, I called JT as I was pulling onto Dumfries Road. He answered on the second ring.

"I talked to the chief," he said.

"And . . . ?"

"Consider yourself a summer school dropout. You're through."

Those words were music to my ears. "That's a relief. I just finished up my second tutoring session. My tutor states that she not only can vouch for Derik Sutton's whereabouts on the night of Hailey's death, but she also can produce—though not exactly willingly—a second witness to support her statement. Derik Sutton was at home when Hailey was killed."

"I guess that should make you feel better, right? Do you think we can trust her?"

"I believe we can trust her witness more than her. But my gut says we can also trust her. She had no problems stating she doesn't feel comfortable around Derik. But she doesn't feel threatened by him either. So why would she lie? Not to mention, she confessed something else to me. And this something else could get her witness in a lot of hot water. As common belief dictates, when a witness starts telling the interviewer the truth, she becomes increasingly less capable of lying. The likelihood of her telling a lie is low."

"Well, damn," JT responded. "Look at you, all grown-up. I'm impressed. I knew when I first met you that you'd catch on quickly. But it's only been a few short weeks. I can't wait to see what you're doing by the end of the summer."

"That's all fine and dandy, but we're back to square one on this case. Once again."

"Where are you headed now?" he asked.

"To get some dinner. Then Quantico."

"Where are you eating?"

"I haven't thought about it yet. I'm on Dumfries, heading that way."

"Meet me at Sam's, on Potomac. We'll have a working dinner. I think we need to sit down and put our heads together on this case. I haven't been with it for this one. I'm going to correct that, starting now."

This was good. I was feeling a little overwhelmed. And extremely frustrated. If JT's head was in the right place, I wondered if we might be closer to profiling this unsub. I checked my dash clock. "I can be there in maybe thirty-five minutes, depending upon traffic."

"See you then."

* * *

Exactly thirty-eight minutes later, I pulled into the parking lot of Sam's Inn. As I was maneuvering into an empty spot, I caught sight of JT's car, parked down the row. My stomach rumbled. I was starving. Hopefully, we wouldn't be waiting for a table.

In I scurried; I glanced around the waiting area. No JT. I approached the hostess, who was reaching for menus from a shelf. "I'm meeting someone. My name's Sloan."

"This way." She led me to a table in the back corner of the restaurant. JT stood as I came closer.

"Forty minutes. Not bad," he said.

"Can I get you something to drink?" the hostess asked as she set my menu on the table.

I made myself comfortable and ordered a diet cola.

She scurried off.

JT and I exchanged gazes.

"Well," I said, feeling a little awkward.

"Well," he echoed. "Derik Sutton has an alibi. Not the best news I've heard."

"Yeah. He's creepy enough to be a killer, if you ask me. I thought we had something there." I picked up my menu and skimmed the selections.

JT sipped his water, then set his glass down. "This case is frustrating me. We're getting nowhere fast. Three young women are dead. We're no closer to a profile today than we were four days ago. And I realize I'm partially to blame. I haven't been one hundred percent this week. But I'm working on it."

"Who would be, JT?"

He shrugged. "Wagner brought back your stereo. He said it was shorted out. Power surge. That's all he could get. And Zoey Urish has a solid alibi as well."

I had no comment about the stereo or Urish. What was there to say? They were both dead ends. I set the menu aside. "How's Hough?"

"She's doing better. They've moved her into a regular

room. And she's getting some help. Now that she's stable, it's actually better that I have this case to focus on. If I don't keep busy, I'll be sitting around, thinking." His mouth tightened. "That's not a good thing right now."

The waitress brought my cola. I thanked her and took a sip, waiting for JT to order his food.

After I placed my order, and the waitress hurried off to turn it in, I said, "I'm glad she's doing better, and I understand why you want to keep busy. Are you sure you're okay?"

"I have my moments. I just try to keep those moments to limited times."

"I understand. Is there anything I can do? Anything we should be doing for you or for Brittany?"

"I'm fine. As far as Britt goes, honestly, I don't know. She's grieving. That's to be expected." He sighed, and his mouth went tight again. "The timing was rough, with the breakup. Nothing I've done has helped much." He drank some more water. I noticed his eyes were getting watery again.

"I hate feeling so useless." I said.

"Believe me, so do I."

We didn't say anything for a long time. Long enough that it felt awkward. I did some thinking while I sat there, watching the ice melt in my cola.

Finally I broke the silence. "JT, our case. I'm thinking we should go to Hailey Roberts's wake tonight."

"Okay." He was staring at his water glass, blinking a lot.

"Maybe we'll see something. If nothing else, it'll give us some more people to interview."

"Okay."

JT had mentally shut down.

So much for the working dinner.

And so much for his being okay.

After our dinner, which ran longer than I had expected, I ran home to change before heading to Ambrose Funeral

Home. It was a pretty, vinyl-sided white structure—an old house, turned commercial—situated at the end of a quiet residential street. As I pulled up, I noticed the cars packing the lot. I circled the block, finding an open spot down at the far end, and hoofed it to the building.

I prayed for a clue, some insight, anything that might help us nail this profile.

Inside, I met a wall of bodies the instant I walked through the door, mostly teenagers huddled in groups, whispering. I saw very few with teary eyes. I wriggled my way through the lobby and entered Viewing Room A.

The casket was positioned at the room's end; stands displaying large photograph collages stood on either side of it. And more framed photos sat on every horizontal surface. Large clusters of people were gathered here and there; some were sitting in the rows of tightly packed chairs, some standing. I recognized Hailey's mother, standing next to an easel, talking to a woman. Her arms were wrapped around herself, and her face was very pale. A stab of pain jabbed me at the sight.

I knew I should at least greet her, but I didn't want to interrupt. The woman she was speaking to left a moment later, offering me the chance.

"Hello, Mrs. Roberts," I said, offering my hand. "I'm very sorry for your loss."

"Thank you." She gave my hand a very weak shake, then released it. "Have you found my daughter's killer yet?"

"No, not yet."

She blinked. Her lips tightened. They quivered slightly. "I can't believe this is real." Her gaze drifted to the coffin. "Since that awful night, I've been waiting, expecting to wake up and find out it was all a nightmare. I go to my daughter's bedroom every morning, praying she'll be there, in her bed, sleeping."

I had no idea what to say. There was nothing that would take away the pain I saw in her eyes. Nothing to give her hope or ease her guilt. I nodded.

Mrs. Roberts said, her voice shaky, "I want to know why. I need to know why. Until I have that, I don't think I can go on."

"We're doing our best to get that answer for you."

Someone nudged my back. I glanced over my shoulder. It was JT.

He reached around me to extend his hand to Mrs. Roberts. And as they shook hands, he offered his condolences.

A woman approached, leaned into Mrs. Roberts, and whispered something into her ear. Mrs. Roberts nodded. "I'm sorry, Agents. I have to go handle something."

"Of course. Before you go, is there any chance we can get a copy of the guest log?" I asked.

"I suppose. Why? Do you think the killer is here?"

"It's not likely, but I thought I'd ask, anyway."

Her gaze lurched around the room, and her face paled even more. "You think he could be watching us? Would he enjoy this? Seeing people suffer?" A tear dribbled down her cheek, and she sniffled.

"It's not very likely he's here," JT repeated, stepping in a little closer. "The list will help us find people to interview, friends and fellow students who might have seen her that night."

"I see." She dabbed at her nose. "I'll ask the funeral director to make copies before we leave."

"Thank you." I watched her walk away, shoulders slumped forward, head lowered. Who wouldn't feel bad for that woman? "Look at her. She's absolutely torn apart. She's blaming herself." I glanced around the room. "Where's her husband?"

"This is the side we don't see very often," JT said, tugging on my elbow, moving me toward the back of the room. "In my years with the FBI, this is only the second wake I've attended."

"Sure makes it hard to remain objective when you see so much pain and suffering."

"It does." He steered me toward a chair in the back row. "We need to stay out of the way, just watch people."

"Do you think the killer is here?" I whispered.

"It's possible. Some organized killers like to watch the fallout from their crimes. They enjoy the suffering."

"I know, that's so twisted."

"It is."

We watched for a few minutes. My gaze kept finding Mrs. Roberts. And every time I saw her, my heart jerked in my chest. This just wasn't right. That girl up there shouldn't be dead. The longer we sat there, the worse I felt. I needed to solve this case. *Needed to.* What if I couldn't? What if I failed? And even if I did do my very best, what if it wasn't enough?

For the first time, I was doubting myself.

I asked, "JT, when you first started, did you ever question whether you could handle this job?"

"Yes, I did. And I still do."

"You haven't quit yet."

"No. I tell myself that this stuff would still happen, even if I walked away. But at least by staying, I'm doing something about it. I'm helping, instead of closing my eyes and pretending it doesn't exist."

"But do you worry that seeing so much is changing you?"

"It probably has. It's probably made me more cynical and less trusting of human beings in general. I see the dark side of human nature." His eyes searched mine. "Sloan, if you're worried the darkness will somehow taint you—eat away your soul—there's still time to walk away. I'd hate to see you do that. You're so intelligent. You'd make a damn good agent. But that doesn't mean this is the right career for you. That's something you have to determine for yourself."

"I guess it's good that I'm only an intern. I haven't made any commitments yet."

"Exactly."

We sat in silence for a while, watching packs of teens

wander into the room, shuffle up to the casket. Girls cried. Boys stared, their expressions unreadable for the most part. Nobody stood out. Not one teen looked any more or less grief-stricken. I recognized a few faces from summer school. Nobody approached me, though I saw a few curious glances.

"Are we wasting our time here?" I whispered an hour later. We hadn't moved from our seats. My butt was aching a little. My back was sore. I needed to get up and walk around. More than that, I needed to do something besides sit and wait. I could be doing more research. Interviewing someone. *Something*.

"If we weren't here, where would we be? At home, Googling more?"

"Yeah. I get your point. At least we're doing something different. As Albert Einstein said, 'Insanity is doing the same thing over and over again and expecting different re-sults.'" I stretched. "I think I'm going to head downstairs and see if I can find some water."

"Okay, I'll stay here."

I headed out of the room, sidestepped my way among mobs of teens, until I found the stairs. I headed down to the open space below, where the snacks and drinks were kept. Down I went, finding that area less crowded. Along one wall ran a counter, stacked with trays of cookies, fruit, crackers, probably brought by friends and family of the deceased. And sitting off to one side was an open cooler with bottles of water. I helped myself to a cookie and a bottle of water, then stepped into a corner to watch and listen.

I finally saw Hailey's father, sitting in a chair not far away, talking to a group of adults who were roughly his age. One of them asked if he'd heard anything from the police, and he shook his head.

"They supposedly have the FBI working on the case, but they don't seem to be doing a damn thing to find the bastard who did this."

We are trying. We really are.

The guy to his left shook his head. "You'd think they'd be all over a case like this. Three dead teen girls."

We are all over this case. I'm practically living and breathing this case. What more do they expect?

"I told Forrester, the detective on the case, that I think it's Hollerbach. There's something not right about that bastard. I can tell. But did he do anything with that? No. The asshole's still teaching."

Hollerbach? That name hadn't come up before tonight, not in connection with this case. I already knew he was inappropriately involved with one student. That meant he was capable of making poor decisions. But did that mean he was a killer?

A young man approached the group and offered a hand. I recognized him right away. "Sir, I'm sorry for your loss." They shook hands.

Mr. Roberts nodded. "Thank you. You were a friend? I don't believe I've met you before."

"Yeah, I'm Ben. I knew Hailey from school."

Her father's eyes reddened. "Thank you."

"I didn't know her very well, but she seemed to be a nice girl."

Mr. Roberts nodded.

Ben stepped back. "Again, I'm sorry. I was shocked when I heard what happened."

"Weren't we all?"

I headed back upstairs and sat next to JT. I whispered, "There's a teacher we need to check out. His name's Hollerbach."

"A teacher. That makes sense. Older. Confident. It would be easy to gain the girls' trust. What's the connection?"

"At this point, I don't have a solid one," I said to JT's profile. "He was mentioned by Roberts's father, just now."

"Okay." JT nodded, and his gaze still moved around the room without coming to me.

"Here's the thing. You remember the alibi I mentioned for

Derik Sutton? The other witness who can vouch for him is none other than Carl Hollerbach. Hollerbach's having an affair with Sutton's stepsister."

JT's gaze jerked to me. "Hmm. Interesting. If that's the case, then he couldn't be the killer. He has an alibi. Jia."

"True, but I think we should still take a look at him," I continued, making sure to keep my voice very low so nobody could eavesdrop. "He'd fit the lust-motivated serial-killer profile. Between twenty-five and thirty-five years old, above-average to average intellect, married guy next door."

"The crimes don't look like your typical lust-motivated crimes. There's no sexual torture, no mutilation, no flagellation, no necrophilia."

"But there is the electrocution. That could be a form of torture. And what about the vampirism? We could be dealing with your run-of-the-mill, lust-motivated killer—of the Homo sapiens variety, not Mythic."

"Interesting theory." Looking thoughtful, he nodded; then he went back to scanning the room. "We'll see what we can dig up on the teacher. We've already found one skeleton in his closet. Let's see if we can find some more."

I waited a beat to add, "And, JT, I've decided I'm not dropping out of summer school. Not yet."

JT's jaw clenched. "Sloan—"

"I can handle it. Don't worry."

"That's exactly what Wayne Roth said before he died."

"Who's Wayne Roth?" I asked.

"Some moron who was bit by a cobra and refused to go to the hospital. He was a Darwin Award nominee."

"Ah, it's wonderful being compared to someone who improved humanity's gene pool by removing himself from it."

"No offense, of course." JT's lips curved up in a ghost of a smile.

"None taken."

There are only two mistakes one can make along the road to truth; not going all the way, and not starting.

—Buddha

16

The next morning, during the drive to school, I repeated my mantra, "I will make a friend. I will make a friend. I will make a friend." And I didn't stop until the very last bell had rung, and I was heading out to the parking lot, having yet again failed at making a connection with one single student.

It was no use. These kids weren't going to accept me.

I was strolling along the far end of the building, chastising myself, when Derik Sutton, my best buddy, came around the corner from the opposite direction.

Once again, there we were: he was glaring at me, and I was trying to pretend not to notice.

Damn it. If I'd been more aware of what I was doing, I wouldn't have come this way.

Since pretending he wasn't there hadn't worked last time, I went for a different approach. I warned him, "Touch me, and I swear you'll be sorry."

He laughed. He laughed hard. And then he sauntered over and clamped his hands around my wrists. "Oh, yeah? What are you going to—"

My knee went up. It made contact.

He fell to the ground, curled in a fetal position.

"Really? Were you so sure I wouldn't do anything that

you'd leave yourself hanging out like that?" I said over his whimpering form.

Behind me, I heard a gasp. I turned, finding two students standing about ten feet away: the female, a short brunette, skittered away without looking at me; the male, a tall, lanky boy, who had braces, didn't.

"Braces Boy" and I exchanged looks; then I jerked up my chin, squared my shoulders, and headed for the parking lot. I made it as far as the second row before hearing a distant shout of "Wait!"

I paused, unsure whether the yeller was speaking to me or someone else.

It was Braces Boy. And he was looking right at me. So I waited.

"That was awesome." He jerked his head toward the building. "Sutton's an asshole, but all the girls are afraid of him. You're the first girl who actually put him in his place."

"Why are they all afraid of him? I mean, he is sort of creepy. But it wasn't that hard to stop him."

"Didn't you know?" Braces Boy adjusted his backpack.

"Know what?"

"There's a rumor that he killed a girl. At his old school."

"No, I didn't know that." Immediately, I wondered why Jia hadn't mentioned it. Maybe she knew it wasn't true, so she didn't bother mentioning it? Or maybe she was afraid to tell me?

"I hope, for your sake, it's just a rumor."

"Me too."

"Name's Nate."

"I'm Sloan." We exchanged head nods. "Are there any other rumors I should be aware of?"

Nate's lips curled. "How much time do you have?"

"How much time do *you* have?"

He started toward the sidewalk, motioning for me to

follow. "Come with me. I live down the road. We can walk. I'll fill you in."

Twenty minutes later, I was sitting in Nate's kitchen, watching him make tuna salad sandwiches on wheat. His sister, as it turned out, was the short brunette who'd been standing next to him. She'd disappeared the instant I stepped into the house, whispering something to herself as she clomped up the stairs to the second floor.

"Your sister doesn't like me," I said, watching her hasty retreat.

"She likes you. She's just afraid to be associated with you. In case, Sutton . . . you know."

"Speaking of that, what exactly did Sutton do? Has anyone ever said?"

"I believe he strangled his ex-girlfriend."

That wasn't our killer's MO. But this conversation was still very interesting.

"Strangled?" My mind flashed back to that moment when he'd had me pinned against the wall. Had his gaze flicked to my neck? Now that I thought about it, it had. "I knew he was creepy, but I wouldn't have guessed he might be a murderer. You said there are other rumors. About him or someone else?"

"Lots of rumors, but no more about him. Supposedly, Hailey Roberts was pregnant over Christmas break and had an abortion. The father was Mr. Hollerbach."

"The teacher!"

"Yep."

"If that's the case, why's he still teaching?"

"The school did an investigation, but Hailey's parents didn't report it until after the fact. No DNA meant the police couldn't find enough evidence to indict him."

"Wow." I needed to have a chat with Jia. If she didn't know about the other girl, she needed to be told.

"And then there's the rumor about Zoey Urish. I heard she's addicted to 'bath salts' and was thrown into the hospital a couple of nights ago, after having hallucinations about some undead spirit monster trying to kidnap her."

That hallucination, ironically, sounded mighty familiar. Speaking of which, I hadn't heard from Elmer in a couple of nights, since I'd left that threatening message, demanding the return of my memory. I made a mental note to call him again. Of course, we'd already crossed Urish off the list. JT hadn't told me details, but now I knew why she couldn't be our killer.

"Bath salts?" I questioned, not sure what that addiction could be.

"They're not the smelly kind you dump in a bathtub. It's a synthetic drug marketed as Up Energizing Aromatherapy Powder." He made quotation marks in the air. "I guess it's real popular in the West."

That was a sad story. Addiction destroyed lives, but it didn't pertain to our investigation. "Anyone else I should avoid?"

Nate set a plate on the counter in front of me; then he sat on the stool at my right, his plate in front of him. "Um . . . you should probably steer clear from most of the football players. But that's not because they've killed anyone." He took a bite of his sandwich. Chewed.

"What about the girls who've died? Any rumors about what happened to them?"

He swallowed before answering. "Lots of rumors, but none that make any sense. I heard Stephanie Barnett had been in a fight with Hailey Roberts the week before she died. But I know for a fact that wasn't true. I also heard Emma Walker said Stephanie stole her iPod."

"Both those rumors are false?"

"Yes, I think so. I was . . . kind of seeing Megan, Stephanie's best friend. She told me about it."

Megan, the girl who'd killed herself.

Interesting.

He didn't seem very upset about Megan's death. I decided not to tell him about the conversation in the girls' room. "What do you think happened to Stephanie, Emma, and Hailey?"

"I have no idea. But what I can say is that the three girls were all seen with a guy—not the same one—within hours of their deaths. I'm wondering if there isn't one killer, but maybe two or more of them."

I hadn't thought of that possibility. "Do you think it's a gang? Maybe hazing of some kind?"

"Maybe."

"Great. I guess I'll just avoid being with any guy until the police sort out what's happening." I gave him a sheepish look. "Oh, no!"

"What?"

"I left school with you. We were alone. We *are* alone. . . ."

He shook his head hard. "I promise, I haven't killed anyone. I wouldn't. Couldn't. I'm not a part of the crowd those guys hang with. You're safe. I promise."

"I hope you're right."

"On the other hand, you did knee Sutton in the balls. I wouldn't walk that way tomorrow. He's not going to be so friendly the next time you run into him."

"You have my word on that." My backpack started playing JT's ringtone. "That's my mom. She's probably wondering where I am." I lifted one index finger while I rooted around in the bottom of my backpack with the other hand, searching for my phone. By the time I found it, it had stopped ringing. I hit the green button, returning the call.

"Hey," I said when JT answered.

"Where are you? You promised you'd be here by three-thirty."

"Oh." I checked the clock hanging on the kitchen wall. "Um, I'm having some lunch with a friend."

"Do you know how freaked out I was? What friend? Where are you?"

"I'm at Nate's house."

"Who's Nate?"

"A friend." I didn't like how this conversation was going. Ironic, that I'd told Nate my mother had called, and JT was sounding a lot like an over-protective mother. "There's nothing to worry about."

"Yes, there is. . . ."

As JT lectured me, I started feeling guiltier and guiltier. I could understand why JT was stressing out. I'd basically told him yesterday that I was too scared to go back to school; then I changed my mind and told him I was going back, anyway, even though the chief had told him I was done. And I had disappeared. JT continued ranting and I couldn't get a word in, so I sat and waited for him to stop to inhale.

"Sloan, you're part of a team. A team. We work together. Where are you? What's the address?"

"I don't know the exact address. I'm less than a half of a block from the school."

"Which way?"

"'Which way,'" I echoed, leaning in my seat to look out the living-room window in front of me, which faced the street. "Where are you?"

"In the school parking lot . . . staring at what remains of your car."

"What do you mean 'what remains'?" A cold shiver buzzed up my spine. I glanced at Nate. He was listening to my end of the conversation. "The house is north of the school, on the right. I'll come outside." I clicked off, shoved my phone in my backpack, and stood. "I'm sorry, but I have to leave."

"Is everything okay?"

"I guess not. That was a friend . . . of my mother's. Something happened to my car."

"No way. I bet it was Sutton. It has to be." He was on his feet too, his footsteps pounding after me as I sprinted for the front door. Before I left, I cautioned, "Maybe you shouldn't come with me. Maybe your sister was onto something by avoiding me?"

"To hell with that. I'm going."

He was over six feet tall and determined. There was no stopping him.

Out we went. JT's car came roaring up, skidding to a stop in front of the house.

JT powered down the window. "Get in. The fire department's just about got the fire out."

"Fire?" I glanced over my shoulder at Nate.

His eyes got a little buggy. "On second thought, I'd better stay here." He looked left, then right, and raced back into his house, like a roach caught in the middle of the kitchen floor.

I flung my bag onto JT's backseat; then I flopped into the passenger seat.

JT jerked his head toward Nate's house. "Looks like your new friend doesn't want to be friends anymore. Is it maybe because you've made yourself a new enemy?"

"What makes you think that?" I smirked.

JT actually laughed.

We drove back down the street, parked as close as we could to the lot where my car had been parked, and walked the rest of the way. The first thing I noticed was the blackened skeleton of my car and the stench of toxic fumes. The fire had been extinguished, but I could still hear the faint hiss of water evaporating off the hot metal.

"It was only a knee in the crotch," I grumbled, staring at my crispy car.

"Hmm. I guess you kneed the wrong guy's nuts."

"It sure looks that way. Can we prove it was him?"

"I don't know." JT glanced around at the firemen, who were packing up their equipment. "Let's see if they've found the cause of the fire." He turned a full three-sixty before finally saying, "There's the chief." With purpose-filled strides, he cut across the lot. I trailed behind him, unable to keep up.

When I reached them, they were already discussing the suspected cause of the fire.

JT turned to me. "The fire started in the front passenger seat."

That was where my laptop bag had been sitting. Inside my laptop bag had been my flashy new computer. Had the battery been the culprit, or did Derik Sutton decide I needed to pay for what I'd done?

"Is there any way to tell exactly what caused the fire?" I asked.

The fireman answered, "We have several witnesses who state they saw nobody tampering with the vehicle before the fire. We also have the investigators reviewing the school's security tape. That should give us the information we need. But at this point, we're thinking something in your car's front seat may have been the culprit."

Wasn't that just great? I hadn't even had the computer for a week, and already it had been converted into landfill fodder.

"What rotten luck," I grumbled.

"Sorry, Sloan." JT patted my back. "I guess I jumped to conclusions."

"That was easy enough to do. Aren't we lucky?" I partially joked. "Your car was torched, thanks to some faulty wiring and a heavy rainstorm, and today it's mine."

"Maybe someone's trying to tell us we need to start using public transit."

"Like that's possible. I put on almost five hundred miles last week, driving back and forth to Quantico." I sighed. "On the bright side, with my folks away on their honeymoon, at least I have access to a car while I'm waiting for the insurance claim to be paid."

"At least there's that." JT steered me back toward his vehicle. "How about we head over to the PBAU first? Before all of this, I think you had some information about the case?"

"Sure. We can work for a while. That'll take my mind off this."

* * *

An hour later, I wasn't in my cubby, talking to JT about Mr. Hollerbach and his thing for teenage girls, like I'd expected to be. Instead, I was sitting in the chief's office, informing her about the vehicle fire and the incident with Derik Sutton. The chief appeared sympathetic about the fire. The knee-in-the-nuts situation was entirely different.

When I told her, her lips clamped. She didn't speak for several excruciating seconds. I took her silence as a bad, bad sign.

"Skye, you have every right to defend yourself if you feel threatened. However, you must be extremely cautious about using physical force when you're working undercover—particularly when you're dealing with underage minors."

She kindly didn't mention the fact that she had ordered me to withdraw from my undercover assignment prior to the incident.

I nodded. "I did think about that, Chief, but this individual has physically assaulted me more than once, and has a history—"

"And you were pulled from the assignment," she interrupted, her jaw a little tighter.

And there it was.

I had no response. I had been pulled. And I decided to go back, which was in direct opposition to her command. "I take full responsibility for my poor judgment. However, because of my decision, I was able to gain some valuable information about the student in question, as well as a teacher who is rumored to have been in more than one affair with several others—"

"Skye, you disregarded my direct order. As a result, you put yourself in a position where you physically assaulted a minor. If anything comes of the assault—if charges are entered—I'll be forced to terminate you. And you'll have forfeited your chance to join our team as a full member.

Please"—she leveled a serious look at me—"do not make that mistake again."

"I'm so sorry. I promise, I won't."

"Good. I realize I've set a bad example by sending you out into the field, against my superior's direct orders as well. But that's ending right now. From this point forward, you're to be either here or in the company of Thomas or myself during working hours. I screwed up. We were skating on thin ice by having you work the field. I trusted you to make wise decisions and limit your risk."

Wow, I had really messed up. "But I registered for summer school, myself. Technically, you didn't send me."

"True. But—"

"I'd be happy to talk to anyone you want, explain how I decided to go to the school—"

"No, Sloan. That's okay. It's better if I handle this situation."

"I'm sorry, Chief. I hope this doesn't blow up into something really bad. I thought I was doing what was best for the team. And for the potential victims."

"I know. Your heart was in the right place, but not your head." She pointed at my forehead. "You need to think, Skye. Always think. I'm talking to myself here, too. There sometimes is a difference between doing what is best for the team and doing what is best for the victims. If you can't recognize that line, or decide to cross it, anyway, you'll eventually do something you'll regret."

"Got it. Think first, act second."

"Yes. Now I'll need a thorough report of the incident. And I also want a report of any information you've gained during the last twenty-four hours." Her phone rang, and she glanced down at the glowing button. "I hope the risk was worth it, Skye."

"I'll get both written up today."

I headed out of her office, feeling like I'd been thoroughly flogged.

What a mess I'd made. My first instinct was to call Jia

and see if she would talk to Derik on my behalf, convince him not to report the incident to anyone. But if that backfired, I'd be in even more trouble.

No. As the chief had clearly stated, I needed to think carefully through every movement I made before I did anything.

I slumped into my chair and stared at my loaner laptop. I flipped the top up and hit the power button, waiting for the hard drive to start spinning.

"You look like your puppy has been stolen." Sitting in his cubby, JT leaned back in his chair so he could peer into my cubicle.

"I feel like crap." I was staring at the stupid, slow-as-a-slug computer. I couldn't face him. I was ashamed, embarrassed.

"Everyone makes mistakes, Skye."

"But I don't. Not these kinds of mistakes."

JT pulled his chair from his cubby and rolled it up next to mine. He sat, then grabbed my armrests, turning me to face him. "Nobody's perfect."

"I know. But I've always been the good student, the good daughter."

"And you still are. You just let yourself get carried away. Every agent I've ever worked with has made that kind of mistake, at least once in his career. It happens. Especially when a case hits you personally, when you can relate to the victims on some level."

I dropped my head into my hands. "We weren't getting anywhere. I didn't know what else to do. I hope the chief doesn't get into trouble."

JT set one hand on my shoulder. "Don't beat yourself up over this. It'll blow over, and you'll be back in the field."

"Maybe I shouldn't be in the field. Maybe I'm not capable of working a case without getting too emotionally involved?"

"Maybe. Maybe not. It's too soon to say. Like I told you,

we've all made the same mistake, me, the chief. Does that mean none of us should be agents? That none of us are cut out to do this job?"

He made a good point.

"I suppose not," I said on a sigh.

"It's tough work."

"That it is." I finally looked up. There wasn't any hint of disappointment or condemnation in his eyes. I expected to see at least a little.

"Feel any better?" he asked.

"Not really."

"Okay, how about if I tell you about the case I screwed up?"

"That probably won't make me feel better, but you've stirred my curiosity."

He leaned back and rested an ankle on his knee. "Get comfortable. This is going to take a while."

To make no mistakes is not in the power of man; but from their errors and mistakes the wise and good learn wisdom for the future.

—Plutarch

17

Thursday morning—day number ten of this case—I was sitting in my cubicle alone. Just me. Nobody else. The chief was gone—meetings. Gabe Wagner was gone—with Fischer. JT was gone—interviewing some more students.

It was just me and the phones, which weren't ringing.

I was bored.

I was lonely.

And for the first time since I started with the PBAU, I felt like a lowly intern. It sucked.

Trying to make good use of my time, I opened a new word-processing document and poised my fingers over the keys. Just as I was about to type the first word, the phone rang.

Hallelujah.

I had never answered a phone so fast. "PBAU, this is Sloan Skye speaking. How may I help you?"

"Hello, my name's Fran Doonan. I'm calling for Agent Jordan Thomas. I got his card from a neighbor."

"I'm sorry, he's out of the office. May I help you?"

"I suppose so. I was told Agent Thomas is investigating the Fitzgerald High murderer. I have a photograph I need to show him. I live next door to Emma Walker. I was taking pictures of my cat, when I caught something on film. I was hoping he—or someone—could come to my home so I could show him the photograph."

A few days ago, this would have been a simple situation. I would have taken the woman's address and told her I'd be there within the hour.

Not so, now.

"May I please have your address and phone number, and I'll try to reach Agent Thomas and give him the message?"

She rattled off the information, and I thanked her for calling. Then I ended the call with a promise to get back to her ASAP. I grabbed my cell phone and called JT.

It rang.

And rang.

And rang.

No answer.

Finally it clicked over to voice mail. I left him a message, giving him all the pertinent details; then I tried the chief.

Her phone rang.

And rang.

And rang.

No answer.

Same with Chad Fischer's.

It seemed everyone was too busy to answer ringing cell phones.

There was nothing more I could do, though there was plenty I *wanted* to do.

Frustrated and annoyed, I went back to my blank word-processing page to write out our sketchy profile as it currently stood:

Gender: Male

Race: Caucasian

Age: Undetermined, though my gut tells me we aren't dealing with an inexperienced teenager here. This killer has been killing for some time. There are no signs of inexperience or hesitation.

Species: Undetermined, possibly Homo sapiens

MO: Debilitate the victim with an electrical charge strong enough to cause cardiac arrest. Vampirism afterward.

Motivation: Possibly lust driven, deriving pleasure from the torture of the victims. Vampirism afterward for sexual gratification. As perverse as that sounds, there have been many such serial killers throughout history. It isn't completely out of the scope of possibility.

Using the Internet, I delved deeper into the lust-driven, vampiric serial killer, reading biographies, looking for clues and commonalities that might be helpful. It appeared that a certain percentage of vampiric killers were psychotic—insane. They suffered from delusions and hallucinations.

This did not fit our profile. Psychotic killers left clues; they didn't hide evidence. They chose their victims at random and used whatever means at hand to make their kill.

And then there was the story of Rod Ferrell, a teenager who had come to believe he was a vampire after becoming addicted to role-playing games. Ferrell had killed two people for the purpose of helping a friend and fellow vampire. Now, that was an interesting case. I could see some parallels there.

Were we dealing with a group of kids playing dangerous games?

As I read the biography, I was sickened by the violence, shocked by the horrific life the boy had led. But I came away with some valuable information, some things to look for.

Sudden lack of interest in school and notable change in behavior.

A heavy interest in role-playing games.

Cutting.

Bizarre behavior and knowledge of occult practices and rituals.

Drug use.

I added those elements to my in-process profile; then I went back to reading. After a while, my back grew achy and my butt numb. I stretched, checked the clock, and decided it was time to make a lunch run. I'd just gathered my keys and wallet when my cell phone rang.

JT. *Finally.* "Hey, Skye, what's up?"

"Did you listen to your message? I received a call from the neighbor of one of our victims. She said she obtained your card from Emma Walker's parents. She caught something on film that she felt might be important to our case."

"Interesting. I'll head over. How are you doing?"

"I'm bored. But I've found some interesting stuff on the Internet about vampiric serial killers. I gathered a list of traits to add to our profile."

"Excellent. I'm about to pull into the lot. How about you come with me? You can go over that list while we're driving."

"I'm ready to go."

"Good. Meet me downstairs."

I clicked off and dashed out the door.

It didn't take me long to update JT on my Internet research. That left the rest of the trip for awkward silence, broken up by bits of uncomfortable small talk. Not since I'd started working with the PBAU had I felt so uncomfortable around JT. By the time we'd reached the Walkers' street, I was jittery, had a bad case of car claustrophobia—not to mention, a full bladder. After taking a detour to make a pit stop at a local bagel shop for doughnuts, coffee, and a trip to the ladies' room, I was ready to head over to Fran Doonan's to see what this photograph thing was all about.

JT slanted his eyes at me when I climbed back into the car with my loot. "I thought you had to use the bathroom."

"I did. But this place requires you to buy something in order to use the bathroom."

His lips twitched. "I see."

I shoved my hand in the bag, producing a custard-filled doughnut. "Want one?"

"Sure."

We munched on custard-filled, deep-fried dough for the next few minutes, which was just long enough to get back to Fran Doonan's street. I did a quick mirror check to make sure I didn't have any crumbs on my chin or custard on my lips and then followed JT up the front walk.

The door swung open after the first knock. Fran Doonan had been waiting for us.

JT extended a hand. "Agent Jordan Thomas."

The woman grabbed his hand; but instead of shaking it, she hauled him through the door. He tripped over the threshold on his way in. I followed, and the door was slammed shut and locked behind us.

Immediately sirens started shrieking in my head. This lady, who looked the epitome of a middle-class, suburban soccer mom, was either paranoid or terrified for her life.

"I was beginning to think you weren't coming," the woman said. She sounded like she'd just run a marathon. Her eyes were bugged. Her lips were the shade of milk.

"There was an accident on I-95," JT said, sending a glance my way.

I motioned to her camera, sitting on the console table. "You said you had a photograph to show us?"

"I do." The woman lifted the camera, picking up a large white envelope that was sitting under it. Her hands were visibly shaking. "Before I give this to you, I have to assure you it's one hundred percent real. I had the print blown up so you can see the details better."

Now I was really curious. "All right." I extended an arm, but Fran Doonan handed the envelope to JT, instead. Her hands were clasped as she waited for JT to take a look.

His brows rose to the top of his forehead, then scrunched together. Saying nothing, he handed the print to me.

At first, I had no idea what I was looking at. But then, I saw it. It was the form of a bird. This bird was enormous—the height of a man, black, with white on its chest, with legs the deep scarlet color of blood.

"What is it?" the woman asked. "That bird is enormous. At least six feet tall."

"We can't say . . . yet." I handed the picture back to JT.

He pointed at the window next to the bird's head. "Is this the Walkers' house?"

"It is." She grabbed the camera and shoved it into JT's hands. "There are more shots, but none as clear as that one. I had the shutter set to snap a series of shots a second apart, so you'll see that there's a brilliant blue flash, like lightning. Then the . . . bird . . . appears. It stands there for roughly ten seconds before another blue flash happens, and he's gone. I've never seen anything like it."

"Thank you. We can take the memory card out, and let you keep the camera—"

"No. Take it. I won't touch that thing again. I mean, I realize that monster isn't in there." She waved her hands. "But I just can't."

"All right. Thank you." JT cradled the camera in his hands and motioned to the door. "We should get going. We'll give this to our technicians—see what they can make of it. Thank you."

"Will you tell me what you find?"

"Sure."

I knew that was a lie. We couldn't tell her. That was against the bureau's policy. But I was guessing JT said that so the poor woman might be able to sleep at night.

"Thank you." Reaching around JT, she unlocked the door and opened it. "I haven't stepped outside since I saw that picture. A six-foot-tall bird. I still can't believe it's possible.

If anyone else had shown me that picture, I would've told them it was a fake. But the image is there, not just on the print, but on the memory card too. It isn't fake."

"We'll check it out, Mrs. Doonan. Thank you again." JT stepped outside.

I thanked her too, then followed him out.

The door slammed the minute we'd cleared the doorway.

JT rounded the front of the Doonans' house. "Before we leave, I'd like to check out the spot where the bird appeared. Let's see if we can find anything to prove it was really there."

"Sure."

We tromped up to the Walkers' house and knocked. No answer.

JT looked at me. I looked at him. We shrugged, then circled the side of the house. Fortunately, we ran into no obstacles. No fence. No landscaping.

We stopped.

"What is that?" JT asked, staring at the strange mark on the grass. Neither of us had noticed it before.

I had a feeling I knew what it was.

I stepped around him, looking down at the center of the mark, where the grass was brown. Branching out from the central patch, almost like bent spokes on a wheel, were lines that looked like veins, with smaller lines branching off those.

I stooped. "Lightning strike. It looks just like the marks on the girls."

JT glanced at the Doonans' house, then back at the Walkers' home. "What a strange coincidence that there was a lightning strike at the exact same spot Doonan had seen the giant bird."

"It's no coincidence. It can't be."

I started parting the grass, searching for something—anything—that would lead me to the answers I needed.

I had no doubt we were onto something here: the lightning

strike, the man-sized bird, the victims, all showing signs of electrocution, and the burned-out appliances.

"Finally we have a break," I said.

"What are you talking about? Did you find anything in the grass?"

"No. But, JT, that photo . . . It's a picture of our unsub. Now all we have to do is profile him."

No man chooses evil because it is evil; he only mistakes it for happiness, the good he seeks.

—Mary Wollstonecraft Shelley

18

The instant we returned to the PBAU, I powered up my uberslow loaner laptop and, after waiting eons for it to connect, started searching the Web. I hit pay dirt literally seconds later. Three little search terms, and I had a profile of our unsub.

I printed out the Web page and raced over to JT's cubby. He was on the phone, talking low. I set the printout on his desk and returned to mine.

Finally, after working this case for ten long days, we had our profile.

Thank God.

I tried to sit, but I couldn't. I tried to concentrate, but I couldn't.

I wanted to talk to JT, figure out our next step.

Why was he still sitting over there in his cubby?

I stood, peering over the top of my cubicle wall to see if he was still on the phone. He was.

Big, heavy sigh.

I opened the word-processing file in which I'd written my preliminary profile and started tinkering with it, adding the details I'd just found.

What felt like ten hours later, JT came strolling over.

He wasn't beaming. He didn't look happy at all. This wasn't the reaction I was expecting.

"What's wrong?" I asked.

"I was talking to Brittany."

Ah, now the down-in-the-dumps expression made sense. "Is she okay?"

"No."

"I'm sorry."

He pulled up a chair and, more or less, fell into it. "I want to help her, but I have no idea what to do. She's taking this loss so hard."

"I can't imagine how bad it is to lose a child."

He shook his head. "She's alone. Her marriage is over. It's all too much."

I had no idea what to say. My life hadn't been all magical ponies and National Science Fair wins, but I'd also never experienced such a huge loss. Yes, I'd lost my father. But when that had happened, I hadn't been old enough to understand or grieve.

"Her doctor's talking about releasing her already. I don't think she's ready for that." He fiddled with my printout. "Maybe this is crazy, but I'm thinking of asking her to move in with me."

Those words struck me like a kick in the gut. Not long ago, JT and I had been shoving our tongues into each other's mouth. Granted, I'd put a stop to it pretty quickly.

But still . . . it was time for some brutal honesty.

Despite this courtship thing with Damen, I'd kept the possibility, in the back of my mind, of JT and me becoming an item. If he shacked up with Brittany, that possibility would never happen.

I gave myself a mental slap to the head. What was I thinking? I was in something of a relationship. Damen and I were courting. What kind of selfish bitch was I, to think I should be able to keep JT to myself as a backup, in case things didn't work out with Damen?

I decided I would be supportive—as a friend should be. "I thought she was a lesbian?"

"Yeah." He gnawed on his lip. "She was married to a woman, but I don't think she was one hundred percent lesbian."

I didn't want to know why he thought that. It could have something to do with the fact that he had been, after all, fully capable of reaching the Big O with her, thus impregnating her. It could also be that they'd both enjoyed the act of coitus more than either had anticipated.

"Um . . ?"

"Sorry." JT flipped the pages. "I'm raining on your parade." His lips curved, but the expression wasn't a smile. "You've done it again, Skye. You've profiled our unsub."

"Yes, and no." I pointed at the pages. "Did you read those?"

"Er . . . not yet."

"I kind of thought not."

He poked a button on his cell. "I'm calling the chief. She'll want an update immediately. In the meantime, are you going to give me a hint?"

"Sure. In a nutshell, we have a lot more work to do." I shoved his chair, sending it rolling toward his cubby. "Now go, read."

After calling the chief, JT made an attempt to help me draft the final profile while we waited for the rest of the team to come in. I could see him making the effort. Sadly, though, his concentration was shot, and he kept asking me the same questions over and over and over. And when his phone rang, he'd launched out of his chair like a rocket, phone clapped to his ear, as he scurried away to take the call.

Each time, he'd come back, looking a little breathless and on edge. "Sorry."

"Not a problem. Is everything okay?" I asked.

"Yeah." He didn't elaborate, so I didn't ask.

When Gabe Wagner came in, on the heels of Chad Fischer, I was relieved and anxious, both. JT wasn't in any shape to help me with the case. I needed some fresh minds.

The chief came in a few minutes later, and we all gathered in the conference room. She took her place at the head of the table. "Skye has some important information to share with all of you." She focused on me. "Sloan, we're all ears."

I began, "After receiving a tip from one of the victim's neighbors, JT and I visited the location of an unusual sighting. This witness was able to produce a photograph that, combined with some evidence we found at the site, led to my identifying his species." While I spoke, JT handed each one a copy of Fran Doonan's photo. "That is an *impundulu* or *thekwane*. A lightning bird. This species is a creature of South African folklore. The lightning bird is able to take the form of a human-sized black-and-white bird. Plus, depending upon which myth you read, it is able not only to produce lightning at will, but it is able to take the form of lightning. It can travel at the speed of light. It is also able to take the form of an attractive man. In this form, he is able to seduce young women."

Everyone was taking notes.

After letting them get caught up, I continued my presentation. "The *impundulu* is known to act on behalf of a witch or witch doctor, acting as his or her familiar, and enacting revenge against enemies. If we make the assumption that our *impundulu* is doing the same, we are searching for not one but two unsubs. The *impundulu* himself and the witch or witch doctor he serves. The second could be either male or female. We need to generate two sets of motives—one for each unsub. And we'll need to produce two profiles as well."

The chief nodded. "Then we are searching for an attractive, confident young man who may be popular among his peers. Sloan, do any of the students you met while attending summer school fit that description?"

"No. Until we had this lead, the most promising person of interest we had was a young man who had the opposite problem. He was overly pushy, due to a lack of success and to compensate for his low confidence. We might consider the possibility that he is the master of the *impundulu*—we'll call him unsub two. And as far as the *impundulu* goes, he may or may not be a student. He is able to change identities. I had one source tell me the victims were all seen with a young man prior to their deaths, but not the same one. I'm thinking he's adopting an identity that makes it easy to gain access to the victims."

"And what would be unsub two's motivation to kill, then?" Fischer asked.

"Perhaps revenge for having been rejected." The instant I said those words, a sick feeling knotted my gut. Logic would dictate that if Derik Sutton was the one pulling the strings of the *impundulu,* I could be the next victim—or, at the least, a future victim. I'd rejected Derik Sutton in a big way. A very public way.

"Sloan," the chief said, eyeballing me with concern.

I nodded, hiding a shudder. "I might have put myself in the path of an *impundulu*."

The chief slid a glance JT's way, and I knew what was coming. Once again, we would be shacking up. The timing couldn't be worse.

One glance at JT and I knew he was none too thrilled about it. Deciding a preemptive strike was in order, I blurted out, "I'd rather stay with Wagner."

The chief's brows shot to the top of her forehead, and her skin wrinkled like a rhino's hide. "Wagner's not an agent. I can't place you with Wagner—"

"Fischer, then."

Fischer's eyes just about popped out of his head. He shot a look at the chief, and some kind of silent exchange between the two of them played out.

"Fischer has other obligations," Chief Payton said.

"Then you. I'll stay with you."

The chief stared at me. She blinked. Finally she slanted a look at JT and said, "Very well. You can stay with me until the identity of the second unsub is determined." She gave each member of the team a weighted look. "We must complete our profiles as soon as possible. If there's another killing, we're facing heat from the media and my superiors."

With those closing remarks, she ended the meeting. "Sloan, we'll be heading out in an hour."

"I'll be ready."

Wondering if I'd made the right decision in putting up a fight, I left the conference room. I made it roughly ten feet before JT caught me by the arm, pulled me to a quiet corner, not far from Hough's "Cave of Wonders."

"What was that?" he snapped.

"I thought you'd rather I stayed with someone else, considering . . . what we talked about earlier."

"Yes, well . . . sure, I do. But do you have any idea how bad that looked for both of us when you, more or less, refused to stay with me?"

"Well, come on." I tossed my hands, like any girl in my position would do. "You don't want me to stay with you because that might ruin your chances with Hough. And yet you don't want me to do something to stop it. Would you like me to go talk to the chief? Tell her I overreacted?"

"Yes."

I took a step.

He grabbed my arm. "No. Don't."

I love reading philosophy. Anyone who reads philosophy can appreciate conflicting thoughts and gray areas. This, I could handle in a theoretical sense. In application, however? No. It turned out that I preferred life to be more black-and-white nuanced.

"Which is it? Yes? Or no?" I asked.

"No."

"All right, then. I'll stay with the chief. Good luck with Hough." Once again, I started to walk away. And yet again, JT stopped me. "You have something else to say to me?"

"Skye, I'm sorry."

"For what now, JT?"

"For being such an ass. We didn't start out on the right foot, with . . ." He motioned between us. "You know."

Oh, did I ever know. I wished I didn't.

"Anyway," he continued, "thank you for being so good about everything."

"You're welcome." I leveled a look at him. "Now, am I free to go?"

He released my arm. "Yes."

The chief's home was nothing like I'd expected.

Maybe I shouldn't have assumed that she would live in a tidy Colonial in the Baltimore burbs. And that she'd have at least a couple of kids a few years younger than me blaring music from stereos or lounging on an enormous sectional sofa, staring at a flat-screen TV. But for whatever reason, that was how I'd pictured her life, outside of the PBAU.

Was I wrong!

Driving my mom's car, I followed her into a nondescript condo complex about ten minutes from Quantico. The buildings were typical Maryland construction. Adequate. Mid-1980s brick-and-vinyl exteriors. We parked, and I grabbed my go bag and followed her up to the front door.

She shoved her key into the lock, but she didn't turn it. Over her shoulder, she said, "I don't have guests, so I apologize for the mess." And with that, she pushed open the door and stepped inside. I followed.

Once, when we were bored out of our minds, Katie and I had channel surfed, trying to find something amusing to watch on TV. We stumbled upon this show about hoarding and, for whatever reason, had watched it for a few hours.

The chief could be the poster child for hoarders.

My first instinct was to clap my hand over my mouth, do a one-eighty and leave. I squashed that impulse right away. Doing that would insult my boss—the boss who was kind enough to take me in, especially when it was my fault that I was in danger in the first place.

Stepping among stacks of boxes and clothes, I tried not to notice the filth on the narrow path of poop-brown carpet under my feet. In my head, I was listing all the possible contaminants I was exposing myself to. Rodent droppings—bubonic plague, salmonella, leptospirosis. Insect excrement—dysentery, typhoid, gastroenteritis. Completely oblivious to the possibility that she might be walking in a disease-riddled minefield, Chief Peyton was a few feet ahead of me, pointing out landmarks: "The half bath is down here. The kitchen, over there."

The narrow, crowded hallway widened to a relatively open space housing what was probably a dining table on the right—the top was stacked high with papers and boxes and books. To my left was a tiny kitchen. There wasn't an inch of countertop clear. Beyond the dining space, and down a few steps, was the sunken living room. Or, at least, that's what I assumed it was. The chief seemed to be using it as a storage unit.

"There are two bedrooms upstairs," she said, leading the way around the table mountain toward a narrow, steep staircase. At the top of the steps, she opened a door, revealing what appeared to be a usable bathroom . . . as long as I didn't look too closely. And I kept the lights off. "Your bathroom." Taking a left, she opened a door. "You can sleep in here." She scurried in and started clearing off what I had to assume was a bed.

"I—I . . . I'm sorry for the inconvenience," I said, stepping up to grab an armload of clothes. They smelled clean. I was grateful for that. I added them to the pile that she'd started off to one side.

"I can't afford for anything to happen to my interns," she said as she scurried around, trying to empty the bed.

"I'm sorry I put you in this position."

She nodded, grabbing more clothes; then she stopped to stare at me. "I try to stay out of my agents' personal lives, but since you've made this my business, what's your problem with Thomas?"

"I don't have a problem with him."

"Then why wouldn't you stay with him? I got the impression the two of you got along well, which is why I've been encouraging you to work together."

"We do get along well. In a professional way. Only professional."

"So?"

Hmm. I was tiptoeing onto thin ice here. I didn't want this to reflect poorly on JT. If I told the chief he needed some personal space, she might question his commitment to the team. "I felt it was important, as an intern, to work with some of the other agents in the unit, learn how they do things."

The chief's gaze sharpened, but she didn't question me. She finished building "Mount Clothesmore," which I'd noticed was comprised of dozens of unworn garments, all still sporting their store tags. "There you are. A bed." She stepped back and glanced around the room. She shook her head, and then left.

I plopped onto the bed and a cloud of dust choked my throat. After hacking a few times, I dug out my loaner laptop, thinking I'd do some more research on lightning birds. My phone rang as I was powering up the computer.

It was Jia.

"Hi, Sloan? It's J-Jia." Jia was whispering. And stammering.

"Is everything all right?"

"Um, no. I need to talk to you."

"What's wrong?"

"Can you m-meet me?"

I glanced at my computer. It wasn't too late; but at this time of night, I wouldn't make it all the way to the Baltimore burbs before the library closed. "Sure. Where? It's going to take me a while to get there. I'm . . . at a friend's house."

"How about the coffee shop on Frederick Road, in Catonsville?"

"Okay."

"Sloan, hurry. P-please."

An earsplitting boom vibrated from the phone.

"Jia? What was that?"

"Just thunder."

She screamed.

"Jia!" I shouted.

"I'm here. I think lightning struck my house. I'm leaving right now. Hurry. Please."

The phone cut off.

Adversity is like a strong wind. It tears away from us all but the things that cannot be torn, so that we see ourselves as we really are.

—Arthur Golden

19

Something had happened to Jia. And with that thunder . . . I was absolutely terrified I wouldn't get there in time. Of course, I looked for the chief first. She was in the shower.

Jia's scream echoed in my head.

Oh, hell!

Zigging and zagging, I wove through the chief's condo and raced outside. I was holding my phone, ready to call for help, but I was running too fast to dial. And when I launched myself into my car, I was too busy strapping myself in, starting the motor, and navigating out of my parking spot.

I thought about calling 9-1-1 but I was pretty sure the dispatcher would think I was a nutcase. I tried Detective Forrester's number, but got his voicemail. I tried Jia again. The line went directly to voicemail. It wasn't until I was halfway to Catonsville before I finally put in the call to the chief.

She didn't answer. Probably still in the shower.

After leaving a message for her, I tried JT.

Again, no answer.

Well . . . what the hell was I supposed to do now?

I flipped through my contacts. Gabe Wagner. I tried him. He answered.

"Well, thank God!" I blurted.

"Hey, I'm just a man. No need to put me on a pedestal or make me divine," he said, chuckling.

"I wasn't trying—" I cut myself off. Gabe Wagner was irritating and adorable, and I had no time for either. It was time for action. "Forget about that. I need your help."

"Sure, Sloan. What's going on? You sound a little frazzled."

"'Frazzled' isn't the word for it. I'm panicked. I'm on my way to . . ." Did I think Jia had made it out of her house? I wanted to believe she had. For one thing, I didn't know where she lived. Catonsville wasn't out of the way. It was worth a try. In the meantime, I needed to get an address for her. "Catonsville. Meet me at the coffee shop on Frederick Road."

"Okay. Can I ask why?"

"I just received a call from my informant. She's in some kind of trouble. It might be the unsub."

"Which unsub?"

"She called me, sounding scared and upset. Then there was a loud boom. Thunder. And she screamed."

"Then shouldn't we be going to her house?"

"I wish we could. I don't have her address. Plus, she said she'd meet me at the coffee shop. And that was after the thunder." I glanced over my shoulder as I fought to wedge Mom's car into the space the size of a tricycle between a semi and an SUV traveling at almost eighty miles per hour.

"Damn. Do we know how to stop that lightning thing?"

"Lightning bird," I corrected. "No. Not yet. I'm just hoping I can get to her before he seduces her and—and . . . bites her."

"Sloan, shouldn't you be calling the chief on this?"

"I tried."

"You're staying with her, right? You didn't tell her you were leaving?"

"I tried. She was in the shower. And I was in a hurry."

"Sloan . . ."

"I know. I left a message. And I called JT. No answer. And I called Forrester. You were my fourth call."

"Nothing like making me feel special." Before I could respond, he added, "That was a joke. Let me see if I can get Fischer."

"Okay. You will hurry, right?"

"Yes. But don't go to that coffee shop until I get there. Park down the street."

"Will do. Thanks." I hung up, tossed my phone on the passenger seat, and pressed the gas pedal a little harder, inching up to eighty-five miles per hour. I roared up to the car in front of me in my lane, zigged into the left lane to pass him, and zagged back into the right lane. *Rinse. Repeat.* Until I was at my exit.

My phone hadn't rung. Not once. Where the heck was everyone?

I zoomed around the exit ramp, tires barely holding. I jerked to a stop at the light, took a hard right onto Frederick. And in five minutes, I was pulling up to the coffee shop parking lot.

I slowed.

I glanced at my phone.

Then I turned, parked in the first open spot I found, grabbed my phone, and tried Jia's number again.

No answer.

Well, damn it.

I tried Wagner's.

He answered, and I just about burst out in song. "Tell me you're not sitting in the coffee shop parking lot," he said.

"Okay, I won't. Where are you? Are you here?"

"Yes."

A nervous chuckle gurgled up my throat. "You jerk."

"Give me some credit. I broke at least a half-dozen traffic laws to get here before you, because I knew you wouldn't wait for me."

Still holding my phone to my ear, I grabbed my purse, shoved the strap over my shoulder, and jumped out of my car. "Where are you hiding?"

"On the side of the building. I'm walking around to the front now."

I saw him and clicked off. I dropped my phone into the front pocket of my purse and ran toward the door. "Thank you," I said as he pulled the door open for me. "Did you reach Fischer?"

"Yes, he's on his way. I told him we'd wait."

"I can see you're not any better than me at keeping your word."

"If I could get away with it, I would slap some handcuffs on you and drag you back to my car."

"You wouldn't dare."

"You bet I'd dare. And I will, if you do anything dangerous."

I believed him. Thus, I hoped I wouldn't be forced to do something dangerous.

With Wagner on my heels, I rushed inside. My gaze jerked from one table to the next. No sign of Jia. I checked the line. No sign of Jia.

Adrenaline was pumping through my system, making me jittery, as if I'd mainlined a full pot of coffee. I skittered around the perimeter of the room, mumbling, "Where is she? Where is she?"

"Problem?" Wagner asked.

"Maybe she's hiding in the bathroom. Keep your eyes open for a petite Asian woman." I raised a hand, palm down, at about my eye level. "About this tall."

"Will do."

"Thanks. Maybe you should call Fischer, have him try to get Jia's address. Be right back." I dashed across the space, almost slamming into a woman who'd stood up when I hadn't expected her to. I tossed an apology her way as I dodged a man on his way toward the door. I yanked open the bathroom door and hurried inside. "Jia? Are you in here? It's me, Sloan."

No answer.

I hurried down the full length of the room, checking for feet under stall doors. I saw just one set, in the very last stall.

"Jia?" I called out.

No one answered.

I raised my hand to knock; but before I'd made contact with the metal, the stall door opened and a shocked-looking woman of roughly thirty stared at me.

"Sorry. I'm looking for someone, and I was hoping you were my friend."

The woman nodded, giving me some suspicious eyes as she stepped around me. Yes, she thought I was insane. No big deal. Wouldn't be the first time . . . or the last.

I followed her toward the front, double-checking each stall. I even pushed open the doors to make sure Jia wasn't hiding by standing on a toilet.

No deal.

I headed back out. "Any sight of her?"

"Nope."

"Well . . . now what?" My gaze hopped around the coffee shop again.

I grabbed my phone, poked the button, trying Jia's number again. It rang. And rang. And eventually clicked over to voice mail. I left a message, letting her know I was worried and cut off the call.

"I guess we head home," Gabe said.

"Are you kidding me?"

He grinned. "Yes."

"We need to go to her house. Problem is, I don't know where she lives."

"I might be able to help you there. Do you know her last name?"

"Sure."

He lifted his phone. "This thing can do pretty much

anything. And I might have"—he coughed—"access to certain databases that might come in handy, thanks to my father."

I almost kissed him. "Why didn't you tell me sooner?"

"You didn't give me the chance. And you didn't tell me her last name."

"Do it! Her name's Jia Wu. And I know she lives around here somewhere."

Gabe's fingers poked at his phone's touch screen. He gnawed on his lip as he waited for the results to come up. I gnawed on mine too, and did a little foot shuffle as well. My gaze kept sweeping the coffee shop. I was hoping Jia would come wandering in any moment now.

Any moment.

Please.

"Got it!" Wagner grabbed my hand. Our fingers wove together, and I couldn't help but glance down. Why did it feel so natural, to be holding his hand like this?

Immediately I shook myself out of that little moment and together we sprinted out of the store, piled in his car—he insisted I wasn't in any condition to drive—and drove east on Frederick. It took us less than five minutes to locate her house. I noticed it was dark, but there was a Toyota parked in the driveway.

I didn't wait for Wagner to cut off the engine. I bailed out, ran up the front walk, and knocked on the door.

No answer.

I knocked again.

And again.

Wagner was at my side when I knocked a fourth time.

"There's nobody home," I said, wringing my hands. "Where is she?"

"I don't know, Sloan. I called Fischer and told him not to bother coming. I have a feeling we've been had. It's some kind of practical joke. A prank."

"I don't believe that."

"She's a teenager. Teens do that sort of thing. I did."

"Yeah, well, that doesn't surprise me about you, but I know this girl, and there's no way she'd pull this kind of prank. No. It was real. She screamed." I clomped down the front porch steps, hesitating at the bottom.

What now?

I started toward the side of the house, thinking it wouldn't hurt to peek in a few windows. I also wanted to check the grass for signs of a lightning strike.

"Where are you going?" Wagner asked, following me.

"I want to take a look around, see if there's anything that looks suspicious." I stopped. Looked down. Looked up.

My heart literally stopped beating.

"Look." I pointed at the ground. There, under the window, was a brown patch. And branching from it, in all directions, were bent, jig-jaggy lines, with smaller branches going off those. "There's the lightning strike."

"I see that."

"Just like Emma Walker's house. It was here. The lightning bird." I hopped up and down, trying to look in the window, but I was too freaking short to see in. I dashed toward the fence walling in the backyard. "We need to get back there."

"Sloan . . ."

I turned a one-eighty and headed back toward the front of the house, thinking there might be a gate on the other side, where the driveway cut along the opposite side of the house and angled into the attached garage. Sure enough, there was.

I hit the latch. Locked.

"Damn it."

"Sloan," Wagner repeated as he ran up behind me. He grabbed my elbow. "Stop for a minute."

"I need to make sure she isn't in there, hurt. If he . . . If she's been attacked, her heart may have stopped."

"Why don't we try calling the BPD? They can send a car out?"

"Do you really think the dispatcher is going to believe me when I tell her I think a man-sized lightning bird has attacked Jia?"

"Well . . . what if you didn't give any details?"

"Then we could be sending innocent police officers into a dangerous situation. They should know what they're dealing with. I already tried Forrester. I left a message. If we wait for him to call back, it could be too late. Do you know what happens to someone when they've been struck by lightning?"

"Um . . . no."

"In fifteen cases out of a hundred, their heart goes into arrhythmia. That's what kills them. Not the heat. The charge skims over the outside of their body, which is why so many people live. And why they aren't burned to ashes."

"That's all fine and good, but you're this close to breaking into someone's house. I'm calling 9-1-1."

"Fine. You do that. I'm going to see if I can find her. She called me." I tried the door leading into the garage. Unlocked. "Yes!" I pushed in, blinking in the semidarkness. There were no cars parked in the garage. But there were oil stains on the floor, as if someone parked there frequently. One stain was still wet. "She's home alone."

"You don't know that," Wagner shouted from outside.

"I'm just going to check this door," I said, stepping up to the door leading into the house. Unlocked. "Look at that, it's open."

"Don't do it."

I turned the knob and pushed.

"Sloan, if something has happened to Jia, you could be considered a suspect if you go inside."

"No way. I have you as my witness." I stuck my head inside. I heard no sounds. No TVs. No people talking. Nothing. "Jia? Are you in there?"

No answer.

"Jia! If you're in there, please say something. Do you need help?"

I held my breath and listened.

One second passed.

Another.

Then, a sound. Was that . . . a cry for help?

"I think she's in here." I ignored Wagner's barked no and dove through the door. I was standing in a mudroom. "Jia? I'm here to help. Where are you?" I listened; but my heart was pounding so freaking loudly, I couldn't hear. I stepped around shoes and headed toward the doorway, which opened into a narrow hall. That hall opened into an open kitchen and family room. "Jia?"

Thump. Upstairs.

I took a left, running through a dining room and past a home office, turned left again, and took the steps two at a time.

"Jia?" I called.

Thump.

I followed the sound to a closed door. I pushed it open. Looked around. Nobody.

"Jia?"

A softer sound drew me toward the far side of the bed.

She was there, lying on the floor, curled into a fetal position.

"Jia!" I dropped on one knee and rolled her onto her back. My hand went to her throat, to check for a pulse. But she blinked; her mouth opened.

"Help." Her hand shook as she pointed at the window, then at herself. She dragged in a deep breath.

I screamed for Wagner, hoping he was standing close enough to hear. "I found her! She's alive. But she needs help!"

She wasn't looking good. Pale. Very shaky. I went ahead and put my finger to her artery and tried to count the beats.

I was too shaken to count—and maybe it was me, but the beats didn't feel normal, strong. "Help's on the way. Can you speak? Tell me what happened."

"A man," she said, her voice barely audible.

"Did you know him? Who was he?"

Her head rolled from side to side. She swallowed. "Don't know."

"What did he do?"

"Kissed me." Her hand went to her neck. "So good." She blinked once, twice. "But then he said . . . He said . . ."

"What?"

Her head rolled to the side and her eyes shut.

Checking again for a pulse, and finding none, I prayed Jia hadn't just become the lightning bird's fourth victim.

All that we see or seem, is but a dream within a dream.

—Edgar Allan Poe

20

Not long afterward, we were at the hospital being told we couldn't speak to Jia. She was in serious condition, but her doctors were expecting her to make a full recovery. That was good news. What wasn't good news was what came next.

Detective Forrester came over to me and, wearing his mean-cop expression, asked if he could speak with me . . . alone.

I had nothing to hide—not really—so I went with him. Gabe didn't look particularly thrilled to watch me being escorted away for questioning. But what was he going to do about it?

Expecting to be taken to a private room somewhere, I followed the detective's lead down the hall. But at the end, he pushed through a doorway, leading outside. His car was angled up to the building, along with a marked Baltimore Police Department car.

"Um . . ." I hesitated. "Am I in trouble?"

"No, not at all," Forrester said, his bad-cop expression fading slightly. "We'd like to ask you some questions."

"All right." Not 100 percent sure I believed him, I climbed into the back of his car, trying not to think about the fact that nine times out of ten the seat was inhabited by criminals.

The ride to Baltimore's Southwest District police station

was marked by my concentrating on breathing slowly so that I wouldn't get too nervous. Funny, but I'd paid a visit to this building before and hadn't felt this way. My nerves were really jittery.

After Forrester parked, he opened my door for me—the door was locked so I couldn't open it from the inside. He motioned for me to precede him into the building, leading me down a corridor to a room I'd visited before. It was an interview—aka interrogation—room.

I sat.

"Can I get you something to drink? Coffee?" he asked.

"No thanks."

An hour later, I was glad I'd declined.

An hour and a multitude of questions after that, I was pretty sure I was being arrested. Maybe it was for breaking and entering, or maybe for something far worse.

And an hour after that, I was tired; I needed to pee bad—when I'm nervous, my bladder spasms; I'd answered the same questions a dozen times, at least, and the beginning of a migraine was throbbing in my temples.

"When am I free to go?" I finally asked, after telling him, yet again, why I'd let myself into the Wu home without permission. "Am I being charged with a crime?"

"At this time, no charges have been entered," the detective told me.

"At this time" echoed in my head.

"Then I can leave?" I asked.

"Yes. But—"

I stood, walked to the door, and tried to open it. Locked. I turned, brows raised.

"It's standard procedure." He waved at the big mirror hanging on the wall, the one that was really a one-way-window.

The lock went *click.*

I opened the door and oriented myself. Then I turned, asking over my shoulder, "Ladies' room?"

"Down the hall, make a left."

"Thank you."

"Thank you. And Miss Skye?"

"Yes?" I answered.

"We need to ask you to stay in state, please. That is, until these issues can be sorted out."

"Of course."

"In state" reverberated in my mind.

Baltimore was in Maryland.

Mom and Dad's house was in Virginia.

So was Quantico.

I went into the ladies' room, took care of the most pressing matter first. As I was washing my hands, I took a look at my reflection. Not pretty. At all.

I went back to the front desk and reclaimed my purse. After hauling ass out of the building, I checked my cell. Five messages. The first was Mom, telling me she and Dad had gone swimming with dolphins. The second was Chief Peyton. So was the third. And the fourth. The fifth was Gabe, checking to make sure I was okay.

I wasn't okay.

I was standing outside the police station, having been questioned for hours. I suspected I was this close to being arrested. For all I knew, that was still a distinct possibility.

I had no way to get home.

I couldn't go home, anyway, because home was in another freaking state.

And it was possible the real killer wanted me dead.

Gah!

How had this happened? How had things gotten so out of control?

I knew the answer to those questions. It was painful to admit the truth.

It was all my fault.

I was pretty sure the chief was going to chew me up and spit me out for what I'd done. And it was, no doubt, deserved. I wasn't generally the type to avoid the unpleasant;

but tonight I wasn't in the frame of mind to listen to what was going to be a lecture.

I called Katie. No answer.

My next call was to Gabe.

Again, no answer.

I was running out of options.

In fact, I was down to two. The chief. Or JT.

I dialed JT's number. After three rings, the phone was answered. He said, "Hello? Skye?"

"It's me. I need a favor."

"Um . . . sure."

"Can you pick me up? I'm at the BPD. Southwest Precinct."

"Okay. What are you doing there?" he asked.

"Long story."

"I'll be there in thirty."

"I'm going to walk down to the restaurant down the street, grab something to drink."

"All right. I'll see you soon."

"JT?"

"Yes, Sloan."

"I'm sorry for calling you so late." The dam burst and the tears started flowing. I tried to hold them back, but I couldn't. I ended the call, not wanting JT to hear me cry. I walked down the street slowly, hiding my face from passing cars. I didn't enter the restaurant until I'd quit sobbing. Once I was inside, I ducked into the restaurant's bathroom and tried to tidy myself up a little before facing the hostess.

She gave me a wary look; then she led me to a table.

I hid behind the menu for a while, until the waitress bounced over to take my drink order. Even after she left, and I'd placed an order for a cola and some fries, I kept that menu up in front of my face. I was in the frame of mind to find a cave, crawl into it, and curl into a ball. I had a feeling I was about to lose my job. I was on the verge of being arrested. And I hadn't heard from Damen in four nights.

About three hours later, or so it seemed, the waitress brought my drink and fries. I forced them down my throat while distracting myself with a game of Angry Birds on my phone. JT arrived after I'd lost my tenth game.

He slid into the seat across from me. "Skye, you look like . . . Er, what's going on?"

"I was questioned. I think I might be spending some time in jail in the near future."

His eyes nearly bugged out of his head. "What?"

"I know. Can you believe it?"

"No, I can't. What the hell happened?"

"I let myself into someone's home. Without permission. But I didn't break in. The door was unlocked. And I had a solid reason for not waiting for the police."

"Hmm. You realize, there are procedures we generally follow—"

"Damn it, the door was unlocked, and I had a good reason to believe an innocent girl was in danger. And, as it turned out, I was right. If I hadn't . . . er . . . let myself in, she might have died."

JT's forehead arched. He said nothing.

"I think the chief is going to fire me," I added, figuring I might as well lay all my cards on the table. "I sneaked out of her house after Jia called me."

"Why didn't you tell her where you were going?"

"I tried, but she was in the shower, and I didn't want to wait for her to finish. If it sounds any better, I called her after I left. She can check her messages. There is one there."

JT helped himself to a handful of fries. He shook one of them at me. "You didn't tell her because you knew she'd stop you."

"Maybe."

"Sloan." He shook his head. "This goes beyond what even an agent should do. An agent can't run off on his own and chase down an unsub. That's the job of the local police." He shoved the fry he'd been shaking at me in his mouth and chewed. "This is the problem here, Sloan. You're not follow-ing procedure."

"But I wasn't *chasing* the *unsub*. I was saving a friend. A young woman . . . a girl." I pushed my nearly full plate toward him.

He dunked another fry in ketchup. "Did you call it in?"

"No."

"You weren't saving a friend. You were playing the hero."

"Heroine."

"Whatever." JT's sigh was loud enough to be heard outside. "You're a brilliant woman. I've never met anyone so intelligent. And yet, when it comes to some things, you're incredibly—"

"Stupid?" I finished for him, feeling the stab of his words.

"No. Not 'stupid.'" He visibly searched for more appropriate words. "Maybe it's your age. You're young, only twenty, and maybe it isn't fair to expect you to act older."

"What are you saying? Am I a flighty twit?"

"I'd rather not put a label on you."

"I am a flighty twit?" Once again, my eyes burned. I was on the verge of another pity party/sob attack. I was so *not* going to let that happen.

Oh, hell.

The first sob slipped from between my lips, even though I'd clamped them tightly shut.

I grabbed a handful of napkins and smothered myself in them.

"Sloan, I'm not trying to be cruel."

Sure, I knew he wasn't.

"I think we've all dumped too much on you, thinking you were so intelligent you could handle it. We made a mistake."

Another sob slipped out. I tried to swallow it back down, but it came out sounding like a hiccup.

"I'll call the chief and talk to her. I don't think it's fair to fire you for our mistakes."

At this point, I didn't give a damn about the stupid job. I was feeling abandoned and pitied, and I hated both of those feelings.

After forcing down a few more sobs, I was confident I

could speak without another one sneaking out. I said, "Don't bother. I quit."

"But, Skye. Sloan—"

"No, JT. I've had second thoughts about the FBI all week. This is it. I've had enough. I can't sit in an office and pretend to be useful, drafting profiles of criminals, while leaving the real work to the police. That's not good enough. No. But thank you for helping me realize I don't belong in the FBI. At least I figured it out sooner rather than later."

"Sloan, that wasn't what I was trying to say."

I slapped a ten-dollar bill on the table and stood. "I'm done here. Again, I apologize for calling you so late and making you drag out here to pick me up. If there was anyone else I could've called, you know I would have." I headed for the door; JT followed behind.

Outside, we strolled toward his car, parked in the first spot. "Where do you want me to take you?"

"I don't know. I'm not supposed to leave the state. I left Mom's car at the coffee shop. I could get it. And then I could go . . . ?"

"Get in." He opened his door.

I opened the passenger side and slumped into the seat. "Where are you taking me?"

"My house."

"But you live in—"

"I'll call Forrester."

"And what about—"

"We'll get your car tomorrow. It's late. And I don't want you out, running around by yourself."

"Because you're afraid I'll get myself in trouble again and make the unit look bad?"

"No, because I don't want you to get hurt. Damn it, Sloan! You're pissing me off! I care about you. We all do. Even Hough."

"Speaking of her—"

"Don't even go there. Do you think I'm so damn selfish

that I'd leave you to fend for yourself because it would be inconvenient?"

"No. I guess not."

Once again, he sighed loudly. "Sloan, you're enough to drive anyone insane."

"Thanks. I love you too."

Thankfully, JT refrained from lecturing me during the rest of the drive. We parked, and I dragged into his house. And there was Hough, lounging on the couch in her pajamas, looking like she lived there.

She gave me a weak smile. "Skye."

"I'm sorry for interrupting." I turned to JT. "Where would you like me to sleep?"

"Um . . ." His gaze slid to Hough, then jumped back to me. "Why don't you get yourself something to drink while I figure that out."

"Okay." Wishing I could get the hell out of Dodge now, I shuffled off to the kitchen so the lovebirds could figure out the sleeping arrangements. I wasn't thirsty, so I put a little ice in a glass and added a splash of water. Then I tiptoed to the corner, where I could eavesdrop without being seen.

"I felt bad for her. She may be in danger, and she had nowhere else to go." That was JT.

"It seems she's always in danger, JT. You see? This is why this thing between us isn't going to work. I know how you feel about Skye."

"I told you, she and I are friends. We're only friends."

I could see why Hough wouldn't believe that. I'd heard that "we're only friends" bit from him too. Then I'd learned he'd fathered her child—and without the use of sterilized test tubes and pipettes. Of course she was questioning his motives.

Odd, how things had completely flipped around in such a short time. Once, she'd been the one trying to reassure me that there was nothing going on between her and JT. Now I was in that position. Oh, lucky me.

It was time for me to take control of this situation. I rounded the bend; my mind was made up.

"JT, in the interest of keeping the peace, I think it would be best if you drove me to the nearest hotel."

"But, Sloan, what about the *impundulu*?"

"What about it? How would it know where I'm staying?"

His mouth twisted into a grimace. "I don't know. If something happened to you—"

"I'll be fine."

He exchanged a look with Hough. She said absolutely nothing.

"All right." He stuffed his hand into his pants pocket. "I'll be back in twenty," he told Hough. Evidently, things had progressed fairly quickly. Already he was at the must-report-all-movements stage of their relationship. I was impressed. He worked fast.

Back out to his car we went. I buckled in while JT stuffed his key into the ignition. "Promise me you won't do anything dangerous?" he grumbled as he navigated the car out of the driveway.

"Dangerous? Like take a shower with a blow-dryer?" I joked.

JT wasn't amused.

"I'm sorry I effed up your evening."

"It's not your fault."

"Yes, it is. At least Hough will be glad when I'm gone."

"I hope you'll reconsider quitting, Sloan. You've done a lot of good work for the PBAU."

"I'm not a quitter. I've never quit anything in my life. But this, I can see now it's not for me."

JT pulled in front of a Red Roof Inn and opened his door. I opened mine. He walked me inside, handed over the company credit card—despite my protestations—muttering something about protective custody. Once I had my key card in my hand, he gave me a stiff-faced good-bye and left. I headed up to room 209, took a long, hot shower, and tried calling Katie again. Still, no answer. After leaving a message for her, telling her where I was, and that I'd need a ride in the morning, I lay in bed and turned on the TV. There was no way I was going to sleep.

Hours dragged. There was nothing worth watching on television . . . unless you were in the market for the latest miracle vacuum cleaner or wrinkle-reducing system. At dawn, I dragged down to the breakfast room to check out the free Continental breakfast. Coffee. Danishes. Some sad-looking fruit. I helped myself and went back up to my room. My cell phone's indicator light was blinking. Someone had called.

That someone wasn't who I was expecting.

We are each on our own journey. Each of us is on our very own adventure; encountering all kinds of challenges, and the choices we make on that adventure will shape us as we go; these choices will stretch us, test us and push us to our limit; and our adventure will make us stronger than we ever knew we could be.

—Aamnah Akram

21

"Sloan, it's Mom." Of course, I knew it was Mom. Caller ID. "Dad said the alarm company received an alert last night, at about one in the morning. They sent a cruiser out to the house to check things out, but everything appeared to be fine. Are you and Katie okay? Call me, please, so I don't drive your father batty, nagging him to take me home."

End of message.

I dialed Katie's cell first. It rang about ten times before kicking over to voice mail. And once again, I left a message for her to call. This time, I asked her to call ASAP. Then I started scrolling down to Gabe Wagner's number, but he rang me first. I answered.

"Sloan, where are you?" he asked.

"Red Roof Inn, Baltimore. Why?"

"We're at a crime scene. You need to get over here ASAP."

"I can't. My mom's car is still sitting at the coffee shop."

"Shit. Okay. I'll be out there to pick you up in about forty-five."

"But, Gabe—"

"Yeah, JT told me. You're quitting. But you have to get over here."

"Why is it so important I get over there? You and JT are already at the scene."

"The address is 6036 Grove Street."

That was Mom and Dad's place. The alarm! "Was it . . . Katie?"

"She's alive. The pool guy knew CPR."

"Oh, my God." I started pacing, wringing my hands. "Is she okay?"

"They're taking her to the hospital to keep an eye on her, but she was alert and talking when I got here."

I never thought I'd say this, but . . . "Thank God for Sergio." I was pacing faster now, stomping from one end of the room to the other. Suddenly I felt trapped and powerless and antsy.

"He saved her life, for sure. There are some inconsistencies between this scene and the others. I'm not sure what we're dealing with here."

"Damn it, I wish I had a car!" I flopped my free hand to unclench the muscles. My eyes were burning, making me blink, blink, blink. My head was feeling a little spinny. My mouth was a little tingly.

"It's probably better you don't. I can just imagine how you would drive."

Dizzy now, I plopped my ass down on the bed. Respiratory alkalosis. I was hyperventilating. I concentrated on breathing more slowly. "Katie and I have been best friends for years."

"She was doing okay when they took her. Sloan, don't worry."

Ha. Easy for you to say.

"I'm heading to my car right now. I'll be there as soon as I can."

"Okay. Thanks." I'd been saying that word, "thanks," a lot lately. It seemed what independence I'd gained when I'd accepted the internship, I'd lost to some degree. I hoped I'd be back, standing on my own two feet soon.

It felt like Wagner took hours to get to the motel. But finally, just when I'd thought he'd been in a fatal crash or something, he called, letting me know he was down in the parking lot, waiting. Having already gone to the lobby to cash out, I left the key in the room, scampered down, and jumped into his car.

"What's the latest on Katie?" I blurted out before I'd even closed the door.

"I haven't called the hospital, but I'm telling you, she's fine."

Of course, I had my phone out and ready to dial. "What hospital?"

"St. Elizabeth's."

I looked up the phone number and rang the general line, asking for the emergency room. We were halfway back to my folks' place before I got any information whatsoever. All the nurse could do, since I was not a relation, was confirm that they did have a patient with that name under their care. That was not good enough.

"Can you take me to the hospital first?" I asked.

"Sure, but I can't stay. I need to get back to the scene."

"I'd be more comfortable going home if I could just talk to her, make sure she's really okay—"

"Let me see what I can do." Gabe called; and when he was eventually transferred to the emergency department, he informed whoever was on the other end of the line that he was one of the agents at the scene and needed to speak with the patient. He repeated his speech a few times and gave his name. By the fourth time that he'd recited his little I'm-an-important-FBI-agent speech, I had some serious doubts he'd get through. A few seconds later, he clicked off the speakerphone and handed me the phone.

I put it to my ear. "Katie?"

"Hello?" came a weak voice.

My heart jumped. A sob tore through my gut. "Katie! It's me, Sloan. Are you okay?"

"Sloan. Sergio saved my life. I'm tired and feeling a little strange, but the doctors said I'll be okay."

"I can't believe this. I can't believe it!" I repeated. "I didn't expect him to come after you. If I had, I would've warned you. To hell with FBI policy."

"Warned me about what?" she mumbled.

"It was the unsub we've been profiling. At least that's what we're guessing. Was there a lightning bolt right outside the house last night?"

"I don't know. . . . Wait, yes, now that I think of it, there was. I almost forgot. It was strange, because it wasn't even raining. But, Sloan, that's not what—"

"Oh, God, Katie." My hands were shaking. I was holding the phone with both of them, trying to keep it steady. If Sergio hadn't been there, Katie would be dead. *Dead!* I couldn't have dealt with that guilt, knowing it would have been my fault. "I'm sorry, Katie. So sorry." I wiped my face, realizing it was all wet. I was crying. "I'm so done with this job. It's not worth it, putting everyone I love in danger. I'm not even supposed to warn anyone if they might be in danger. Who the hell can live like that, just standing there—"

"Sloan, slow down. You're quitting? Why?"

"There are so many reasons. But I don't need to talk about that right now. I'm going to come up there, to the hospital. We can talk then."

"No, Sloan. You don't need to come up here. I'm fine. They're sending me home tomorrow. I'm going to eat, take a nap, do some reading. If you want to do something to help, then get that profile done and catch that guy . . . before you completely lose it." She clicked off before I had a chance to argue with her.

I dropped my phone into my purse.

"So?" Wagner asked.

"*Gah!*" I dropped my head into my hands. "My best

friend almost died. We need to profile this monster and figure out how to stop him. Today. Now. Right the fuck now."

"Yes, we do. So what are you going to do, Sloan? Are you going to quit? Or are you going to help us?"

"I guess I'll wait to hand in my resignation until after we're done with this profile."

Gabe didn't speak. He just nodded and smiled.

We met up with JT and Chief Peyton at the crime scene. The chief gave us a quick rundown of what had been found, and what hadn't. There was no mark outside a window, but the blow-dryer in Katie's bathroom had been shorted out. She was found lying on the bathroom floor.

"She's not a Fitzgerald High student. My cover must have been blown," I pointed out. This didn't surprise me. I'd waltzed into a crime scene with an FBI agent. Of course, the unsub made me.

"I don't think that's what happened here. But, just in case I'm wrong, I'd like to keep you under protective custody until the unsub is caught," Chief Peyton informed me.

I wasn't over-the-moon thrilled by that news, but it didn't come as a surprise. I knew what I was dealing with, and I had some notion of how to avoid being attacked. But Katie was still vulnerable. And so were over twelve hundred Fitzgerald students. We needed to quit poking around and get to work. "What about Katie?"

The chief and JT exchanged looks.

The chief said, "We'll take care of her too."

I watched the team of crime scene techs bustle through the living room, carrying their gear. One of them stopped, informed the chief, "We're finished up here."

"Thank you."

I watched them head outside. "I think we need to present what we have to the BPD. We can't wait for more details. They not only need to know we're dealing with two unsubs, but they need to understand that one of them can

change forms and identities. He's not just any predator. He's
virtually unstoppable."

"You'll present," the chief stated. "I insist."

"If you insist." I motioned toward the door.

And we all headed out together.

Walking into the BPD within twenty-four hours of being
interrogated for breaking and entering and assault was insanely uncomfortable, to put it mildly. I felt physically ill,
and slightly paranoid. It felt as though everyone was watching me, waiting for me to say or do something suspicious.

Yes, I do realize how that sounds. But if you haven't been
interrogated, you have no appreciation for what I had been
through.

Entering today, I was flanked by JT on my right and the
chief on my left. Both were muttering little words of encour-
agement as we made our way back to the room where the
day shift of Baltimore's finest had all gathered.

As he had the last two times, Commissioner Allan, of the
Baltimore Police Department, gave me a friendly welcome and
shook my hand. After greeting Chief Peyton and JT, he motioned to the front of the room. "We're ready when you are."

I forced myself to take a few deep breaths before stepping
up to present our profile.

I cleared my throat, and the room went silent.

"I'm Sloan Skye, and I'll be presenting our profile of the
Fitzgerald High killer today," I stated. My stomach clenched.
Sweat beaded on my forehead. "We have generated a prelim-
inary profile for the unsubs—plural—who are responsible
for the murders of Stephanie Barnett, Emma Walker, and
Hailey Roberts, and the attempted murders of Jia Wu and
Katie Lewis. As I mentioned, we are looking for two individ-
uals. I'll profile each one separately.

"The first is a mythical creature called an *impundulu,*
lightning bird, or *thekwane.* A creature of South African
folklore, the lightning bird is able to take the form of

human-sized black-and-white bird. Depending upon which myth you read, he is able not only to produce lightning at will, but is able to take the form of lightning, traveling at the speed of light. He is also able to take the form of an attractive man. In this form, he is able to seduce young women. What makes the *impundulu* virtually unstoppable is his ability to shape-shift. He is able to change his identity at will, and hasn't appeared as the same male twice. Additionally, he is capable of traveling at impossibly high speeds. In his lightning form, he cannot be caught and contained. It is a commonly known fact that energy cannot be destroyed. He is capable of using any form of electrical conduction to move in, out, and through buildings."

I paused to give everyone a chance to take notes.

"Our best chance of stopping the *impundulu* is to identify and apprehend his owner." I made air quotes with my fingers when I said the word "owner."

"This individual has complete control over him, and is using him as his or her weapon, enacting revenge against enemies. We do not know the gender yet. He or she is highly intelligent, and most likely psychopathic. We would classify him or her as an organized killer, and would expect he or she is taking measures to evade capture and hide his connection to the murders and the *impundulu*. I believe this individual's motivation will be instrumental in identifying him or her. Looking for some history of conflict with all the victims, both deceased and those who are alive, should present a pattern over time. And that pattern should point to this unsub."

"Can you give us more details on the second unsub?" one of the officers asked.

"Sure. We have profiled him or her as aged fifteen to eighteen, a student attending Fitzgerald High School, popular and well liked among his peers and teachers."

"So we're looking for a good kid?" another officer asked.

I nodded. "We are. He or she is smart. Charming. But with a dark side, which he may not always be able to hide. Based upon the level of severity of the crimes, we have concluded we are looking for an individual with a very high IQ. Highly intelligent psychopaths are notoriously difficult to catch. They masquerade as well-adjusted, successful people. But they are manipulative, cunning, impulsive, demanding, narcissistic, and egocentric. Someone out there has seen the real face of our unsub. The trick is finding that someone." I glanced around the room, catching more than one squinty eye. For the first time, I sensed the officers weren't 100 percent on board. If we were going to have any hope of stopping him, I needed them to believe in our profile. Ironic, it was the profile of the Homo sapiens that they seemed to have the hardest time swallowing.

"I realize some of you may have some doubts on this case," I continued, "but our profile is based upon the study of dozens of similar cases, known profiles of convicted offenders, and a knowledge of human behavior. We are convinced it is entirely accurate." I glanced at the chief, who was nodding in agreement. "That concludes our profile. Thank you for your time. If you have any questions, please feel free to contact anyone on our team. We want these two stopped as much as you, and are here to help you."

I hurried toward JT, passing Chief Peyton, who was heading toward Commissioner Allan for a little tête-à-tête.

He gave me a little smile. "You did great."

"Thanks. But I think they're having a hard time with this one."

"I've done plenty of studies on antisocial personality disorder and have profiled my share of psychopaths. I can say, with a great deal of certainty, your profile is spot-on."

"Well, thank you. At least I have that. I can profile a murderer, human or not."

Commissioner Allan took my place at the front, clearing his throat. "I'd like to thank the FBI's PBAU for its assistance in this case. At this time, we've ruled out several persons of interest. Mike Barnett is clear. He was under surveillance when Walker was killed. And we also checked out Ben Gardener's story. Several students were able to confirm his whereabouts when Roberts was killed. We've run a background on Hollerbach. It's clear. But we're still investigating him. His whereabouts were unknown when Wu was attacked. He's still a person of interest—our only person of interest at this time. And, unfortunately, it seems he doesn't fit the profile." His gaze swept the room. "Which means we have a lot of work to do. I don't need to tell any of you how vital it is we wrap up this case now. These individuals are dangerous. They need to be stopped. And I don't give a damn how many hours it takes—we're going to stop them."

The officers applauded.

JT gave me a bump with his elbow. He whispered, "Come on, let's head out."

"Sure, I'm so excited about getting back to my cubicle."

He waited until we were in the hallway to say, "We're not going to Quantico. So sorry to disappoint you."

"Where are we headed, then?" I asked as we walked toward the exit.

"Fitzgerald. Something you said struck me. I want to check it out."

"Okay, lead on. I'm just a lowly intern. Your wish is my command."

"Your wish is my command?" Two steps ahead of me, he sent a smirk over his shoulder. "Now those are words to live by, Sloan Skye."

In everyone's life, at some time, our inner fire goes out. It is then burst into flame by an encounter with another human being. We should all be thankful for those people who rekindle the inner spirit.

—Albert Schweitzer

22

"JT, before we go to the school, do you think we could make a little detour?"

JT was driving. He laughed. He laughed some more. "What happened to 'your wish is my command'?"

"I meant that. But I want to check on Jia and see how she's doing. She called me yesterday and said she was being released."

"She was released a little bit ago. BPD has a man on her, watching for any signs of lightning strikes."

"Can we go see her?"

"I guess. I haven't had a chance to interview her."

"Excellent."

We pulled up in front of the Wu house and parked. JT put in a call to the chief, letting her know where we were. I headed up to the front door while he hung back, still talking on his phone. A woman answered on the second knock. She was petite. Roughly late thirties. Asian. I was guessing she was Jia's mother. I offered my hand. "I'm Sloan Skye, a friend of Jia's."

"You're the one." The woman's eyes narrowed. "You broke

into our house." She had an accent. I guessed Mandarin was her first language, and English her second.

"I did. And I'm sorry for entering your home without permission. But your daughter called me, and I believed she was in extreme danger."

"I think you're lying. You were the one who attacked her." She pushed the door, narrowing the opening. "What do you want?"

"I'm here with an FBI agent. I'd like to talk to Jia, ask her about the attack."

"What agent?"

I thumbed over my shoulder. "He's on the phone. He'll be here any second." I glanced back, wishing I'd waited for him. He was loping up the front walk. "Here he is."

JT stepped up. He glanced at me; then he glanced at the suspicious woman hiding behind the front door. "I'm Agent Thomas." He passed a card through the opening, and the woman snapped it away, squinting at it.

"What do you want, Agent?" she asked.

"I'd like to interview your daughter."

"What for? The police are investigating." Her gaze jumped to me and stayed there. Her meaning was clear.

JT said, "Miss Skye is part of a team of professionals who are working with the police department, attempting to capture the individual who attacked your daughter."

Mrs. Wu glowered at me. *"Her?"*

"Yes, her."

"Jia said she was a student. Failing student."

"She was working undercover."

"She is not a student?"

JT shook his head. "No, *Ms.* Skye has just completed her Masters degree and holds two bachelor's degrees. She graduated from high school a long time ago."

The woman studied me for a moment. "Still, I heard policeman say she is dangerous."

"No officer would say that. Nobody has reason to believe Dr. Skye is the person who attacked your daughter. And if she had been, why would she call for medical? Now, if you wouldn't mind, we'd like to interview your daughter so we can continue with our investigation."

The woman didn't move for several long, painful seconds. Finally she opened the door and stepped aside. "This way." She ushered us into the living room. "Wait here. I will get Jia."

JT and I exchanged relieved looks as we waited. I scanned the room. All the furnishings looked like antiques. Asian. And the wall to ceiling bookshelves running the full span of one wall were loaded with old books, top to bottom. I recognized the writing on the spines, though I couldn't read it. Upstairs, we heard chattering. Jia's mother was speaking Mandarin—I was right—warning Jia not to trust us, or get too close. I translated for JT, and he sighed.

"I know why you did it, Sloan, but if you'd called for backup before coming here in the first place . . ."

"I know. I thought I was good with Wagner."

"He isn't an agent," JT pointed out.

"I was worried. She's a nice girl. A smart girl. I didn't want to see her hurt."

"I know. I get it."

Jia walked slowly around the corner; her mother followed closely. She looked like she'd been sleeping. Her long hair was tied into a sloppy knot on the top of her head. She was wearing a huge T-shirt that could probably fit two JTs. And a pair of shorts.

"Sloan?" She glanced at JT.

"You look tired." I motioned to the closest seat. "Please." She sat and stared up at me. "What's going on?"

"This is Agent Thomas with the FBI. I . . . work with him. In an effort to aid in the identification of Stephanie Barnett's, Emma Walker's, and Hailey Roberts's killer, I went undercover, pretending to be a student, hoping I'd gain some information leading to his arrest."

"And . . . did you?"

"No. If I had, you wouldn't have been attacked."

"You're a cop?"

"Not exactly."

Now, she was looking at me with the same squinty eyes her mother had been. "You pretended to be my friend, just so you could get information from me?"

I could hear the hurt in her voice.

"No, I didn't pretend."

"How old are you?" she snapped.

"Not much older than you. Maybe . . . three years? I graduated from high school early."

Her lips thinned. "You used me."

I wanted to say I hadn't, but the truth was, I had. "We're doing everything in our power to capture the person responsible for your attack. We don't want another girl to die. Isn't that worth lying for?"

"I don't know." Her gaze hopped back and forth between me and JT. "What do you want now?"

JT stepped in. I moved back to let him take over. "We'd like to ask you some questions about your attack."

"Okay." She flopped one knee over the other, and crossed her arms over her chest. "Go ahead." Her mouth said yes, but her body, no. Her gaze flicked to me, then to her mom.

"Did you see your attacker?" JT asked.

"Yes. I told the police detective I saw him, and I provided a detailed description."

"Could you describe him for me?"

"Yeah. I guess so. He was"—she glanced up, and to the left—"tall and really good-looking. With blond hair."

I wondered what she was lying about. When I'd first found her, she'd said she'd been attacked by a male. And he'd kissed her.

Her mother broke in, speaking in Mandarin, "It was a man? You didn't tell me!"

"I'm sorry, Mama," she answered in English. "I was ashamed."

JT asked, "Did this man have any unique characteristics? Tattoos? Birthmarks?"

"None that I saw. He was just really good-looking."

She'd said that twice. Clearly, our unsub preferred to take the form of extremely good-looking young men. I'd always been a little leery of men that attractive. Now, after this case, I'd never look at a man that gorgeous the same way again.

"Was he old? Young? Your age? Did he seem familiar? Had you seen him anywhere before?" JT asked.

"Maybe a little older than me, and no. I didn't know him."

"Did you see how he entered your home?"

"No. He just . . . appeared. As strange as it sounds, it's the truth."

"We believe you." JT nodded. "Did you wonder why a strange man was standing in your . . . ?"

"Bedroom," she finished for him.

"Bedroom," JT echoed. "Were you shocked to find a stranger in your room?"

"Yes."

"Did he say anything to you? Did he touch you anywhere?"

"Jia," I broke in, "You didn't tell me about the rumor that Derik killed someone. Why? Was it him? Are you afraid to tell us?"

"No. It wasn't him. Derik's creepy, but that rumor's a lie." She leaned forward, her shirt slumping slightly. I noticed a scattering of small red marks sprinkled across her chest. Was it a rash of some kind? Her arms tightened, and she began visibly trembling. "Why did he attack me? Why? What did I do?" Her eyes reddened. She lifted her shaking hands to her mouth. I knew he'd kissed her, at least. Possibly more. "I'm so scared. Is he going to come back?" She started crying, quaking harder. "I'm so sorry, Mama. I know I've brought disgrace to our family. So sorry."

"That's enough, Agents." Her mother wrapped her arms around Jia. "My daughter cannot answer any more questions today." She started ushering her from the room.

JT slid his notebook into his pocket. "Thank you for your time." He jerked his head toward the door.

We left.

I didn't say a word until we were in the car.

As I was buckling myself in, I said, "I think she lied when she was giving the unsub's description. Why would she do that? I already knew it was a male. Attractive."

JT cranked the key. "I have no idea. Maybe . . . she was just looking to the left for no reason? Now that you've seen she's okay, let's get to the school. Like you said in your profile, we need to focus on the other unsub. And someone has seen his or her dark side. We need to find that someone."

The car zoomed away from the curb. We were zipping toward the high-school parking lot and conversing along the way.

"Before we get to the school, Skye, I just need to ask—"

"What? That I don't do anything stupid? Like assault another student?" I smiled, letting him know I wasn't taking this personally, though I kind of was. I had never kneed a man in the crotch before. Of course, that was because I'd never been in a situation where I'd felt so threatened—not even when I was being bullied back in high school.

JT merely sighed. "I'm not trying to insult your intelligence, I swear."

"Let me guess, it's procedure, right?"

"Exactly."

That slightly awkward conversation over, we were both prepared, hopefully, to find that someone who had indeed glimpsed our unsub's ugly side.

"I want to share some of our profiles with the principal," JT explained ten minutes later as we were parking in the school's lot. "But we can't share the information about the paranormal nature of unsub one."

"Of course not."

He steered the car into a spot. "We haven't talked about this directly, but I thought I should explain how we can discuss the fact that our unsubs are mythical beings with the BPD, but we can't mention it to anyone else."

"I'm assuming the BPD has seen so much evil, both the human and nonhuman, that it was easy for them to accept the fact that mythical beings really do exist. In contrast, the average Joe hasn't?" I asked as I unbuckled.

"You're right. Kind of. Have you noticed we haven't done a lot of profiling in other districts?"

"I have. And I also realize most FBI agents think we're a joke. So . . . ?"

JT unbuckled, but he didn't open the door. "The BPD's connection to the paranormal dates back to the mid–nineteenth century. At that time, a certain well-known and respected poet and author lived in Baltimore, and it was he who brought to the Baltimore PD's chief the truth about mythical beings. That chief was quietly asked to retire shortly after he started telling his officers about the vampires and other unmentionables walking among them. But there was no stopping the spreading of the truth. The officers began to see and accept what they had witnessed, and they soon came to believe there were such beings walking among the humans. Both law-abiding and criminal entities."

"And let me guess. . . . That poet was . . . Edgar Allan Poe."

JT nodded. "None other."

"Interesting. But why hasn't the truth spread beyond BPD?"

"The officers, fearing they'd be laughed at, or worse, started taking a vow of silence upon joining the force. To this day, I believe they still take that vow."

"And so they keep their secret. But somehow, we have to spread the word."

"That's not our job, to spread the word about Mythics. That's for the risk takers, the poets, the authors, the movie-makers, the press. Our job is to profile the unsub and provide support where it's wanted and needed. Nothing more. It took a long time for the FBI to form our unit, though there was a similar unit back in the '60s. That one's focus was more on researching reports of alien visits and abductions. But it was disbanded after word was leaked to the public. The backlash was ugly, reports that taxpayers were footing the bill for frivolous projects. We have to protect the FBI's reputation, or it'll happen again."

"Okay, I get it."

JT pushed open his door. "Now let's go in and see if we can get this profile wrapped up."

"I'd love that. With a roommate in danger, I'm not going to sleep until both of them are caught."

We headed inside the school—our footsteps echoing on the tile floor. Our first stop was the administration offices to talk to the principal. After about a ten-minute wait, we were greeted and escorted back to Principal Glover's office. He sat. We sat across from him.

"How can I help you, Agents?" Principal Glover's gaze slid to me. "Miss Skye?"

I cleared my throat. "As you know, we've been working with the Baltimore Police Department, profiling the individuals who are responsible for the deaths of your students."

Principal Glover's bushy white eyebrows jumped up a little. "Did you say 'individuals'? Plural?"

"Yes, the killing is being carried out by one person, a male, who is being controlled by a second."

"And you need my help with what?" To JT, he said, "You're not bringing Miss Skye back in, are you?"

"No."

"Good. I've had two parents approach me about it, one threatening to take her complaint to the board. I want to stop this person—these persons—as much as you do, but I can't have your agents assaulting the students."

"I'm sorry," I said. "I never meant to cause trouble. I only took action when I was physically threatened." I hated having to address that issue, because it would only distract from what was really important. But I felt I needed to clear the air. "Derik Sutton trapped me, more than once, and sexually harassed me. I have no interest in pursuing any action against him. I merely wanted to explain why I had to do what I did."

"I see."

It didn't sound like he saw anything, but I was more concerned with steering the conversation back to the topic at hand. I said, "At any rate, we're here to interview some of your staff members. We'd like to present the preliminary profile of the second unsub—unidentified subject—and see if anyone recognizes him or her."

"Did you want to present your profile to them all at once?" Principal Glover asked.

"If possible," JT said.

Principal Glover crossed his arms. "That's easier said than done. I can probably arrange for them all to be here next week sometime."

Next week? We couldn't wait that long. I slanted a help-me look at JT.

JT leaned forward. "I realize what we're asking is difficult. But next week may be too late. The way this unsub is going, there could be another victim by tomorrow."

Looking regretful, the principal lifted his hands. "It's summer. Half my staff isn't here. I'd need to call them in and there's no guarantee I'd get them here."

"I see. Okay." JT looked at me. "We'll take whoever we can get. Today."

"Today?" the principal echoed.

Really? Did that surprise him? Children were dying. We were trying to stop it.

"Yes," I said. "We're prepared to present our profile now." I glanced at the clock. The second bell of the day was about to ring. Roughly half the students—the ones only attending morning classes during the summer session—would be leaving. And the others would be heading either home or to a fast-food restaurant for lunch.

"Let me see what I can do." He picked up his phone, dialed, and pointed at the door. "If you wouldn't mind waiting outside."

JT and I headed out to the waiting area and watched as a flood of students filled the hallways. A few minutes later, everything was quiet. Then my economics teacher arrived, looking slightly annoyed. He glanced at me. His brows rose.

"Sloan? Have you returned to school?"

"Not exactly."

A second teacher arrived. Then a third. Within five minutes, there were twelve teachers gathered in a small room. They sat and—looking annoyed, but slightly curious—waited for JT to speak.

"My name is Agent Jordan Thomas. I'm with the FBI. Sloan and I have been working with the Baltimore Police Department, helping to track down the killers responsible for the deaths of your students, Stephanie Barnett, Emma Walker, and Hailey Roberts. We believe at least one of the killers is a student at this school, and we'd like to share some profile information with you, to see if you can think of anyone who might fit the profile." He motioned to me.

I cleared my throat. "We are looking for a student who is outwardly friendly, charismatic, intelligent, well spoken. He or she is the last person you would think would be capable of murder."

"That description fits a large number of our students," Principal Glover said. "As a matter of fact, I can't imagine any of them would be capable of killing another human being. Not even our most troubled students. Your profile is too broad."

"There is one trait we haven't mentioned yet," JT added. "It should help you identify students who might fit the profile. This person is hiding a dark side—an impulsive, cruel side, which someone here might have seen, but may not have told anyone else about. Have you seen any students act out of character? Do something that seems so off, you almost didn't believe they'd done it?"

JT's question was answered by twelve silent head shakes and bewildered stares.

"Nothing?" I asked.

More head shakes.

"Can you give us anything else?" Principal Glover asked.

JT continued his address. "This person is using someone else to do his or her dirty work. He merely tells the killer which students to go after. The killer does the rest. The killer, the second unsub, will not be as bright or as socially accepted as the first."

"Unsub," Principal Glover inserted, "means unknown subject."

"Thank you," JT nodded. "The second unsub has a hard time relating to his peers. Maybe you've seen a pair of students fitting these descriptions?"

More head shakes.

This was getting us nowhere.

JT pulled some cards out of his pocket and doled them out. "We won't take up any more of your time. Thank you. If you do come up with a name or any information, please call me. We'd like to get this pair off the streets before another student is hurt."

The teachers filed out.

JT stuffed his hands in his pants pocket. "So much for my idea."

"It was a good one. We haven't talked to all the teachers yet. Could be we haven't found the right one yet."

"I just hope we find him or her before it's too late."

Principal Glover motioned to us. "I can give you some names, if it'll help. But these students don't exactly fit your profile. They've all had some trouble with the law. Are you sure you're looking for the right person?"

"I'm sure," I said.

JT nodded. "But we'll take that list of names, anyway. Who knows, maybe it'll lead us somewhere useful."

A half hour later, we were back out in the parking lot. JT had filled at least twenty pages of his pocket-sized notebook, but I knew in my gut we still didn't have our killer. Every student mentioned by the principal failed to fit our profile for one reason or another—either they weren't getting decent grades or were struggling socially or had rap sheets.

"Damn it," I grumbled as I slumped into JT's car. "This kid is good. Everyone is fooled."

"We'll figure it out."

"But how much longer is this going to take?"

"I have news for you, Skye," JT said as he started his car. "These cases aren't usually wrapped up in less than a week, like our first two."

"Yeah, I've always known that. But it still doesn't make this any less frustrating. My best friend was nearly killed. So was Jia. He's hitting too close to home for my comfort."

"Interesting, though, that the last two survived."

"Katie wouldn't have, if Sergio hadn't been there."

"And Jia probably wouldn't have, if you hadn't been there either."

"I like to tell myself that, so I don't feel so damn guilty for barging into her house." I glanced at JT's profile. He was looking straight ahead as he drove us toward the street. "What would you have done?"

"The same thing you did." He yawned and turned onto North Adams Avenue.

"Tired?"

"Yeah. A friend of mine called in the middle of the night. She had a little misunderstanding with the police."

"Did she?" I chuckled. "That must've been irritating, having to go pick up her sorry ass at some ungodly hour."

"Nah, I didn't mind. Not a bit." He yawned again. "But I think I'm going to head home. I can do what I need to from here."

"And what about your friend?"

"She's in protective custody. She'll be staying at my house until we stop this goddamn *impundulu*."

I felt myself grimacing. "That's gotta put a crimp in your personal life."

"This has nothing to do with duty. She's my friend. I wouldn't have her stay anywhere else."

I set my hand on his, which was resting on the gearshift. "Thank you."

"You're welcome." He yawned yet again. "Besides, if she's at my house, and doesn't have access to a car, she can't sneak out and get herself arrested again. I need some sleep."

I laughed. "Fair enough."

My phone rang before I had a chance to say something witty and humorous. Katie. I answered, heard the great news, and then clicked off. "JT, if you do one teeny-weeny favor for me, I promise I won't break any laws until at least nine o'clock tomorrow morning."

He gave me a very exaggerated, exasperated look.

"Katie's being released. How about we pick her up and stay the night at Mom and Dad's place? It's plenty big. We can each have our own room and our own bed. You won't have to inconvenience Brittany, or potentially put her in harm's way by leading the unsub to your doorstep. And I think you'll agree, with our unsub being able to travel at the speed of light, your place isn't going to be any safer than anywhere else."

"No broken laws until at least nine A.M.?"

I raised my right hand. "I promise."

"Okay, Sloan." Smiling, he shook his head. "You drive a hard bargain."

It seems to me that any full grown, mature adult would have a desire to be responsible, to help where he can in a world that needs so very much, that threatens us so very much.

—Norman Lear

23

It is in the room with her. The air is cold and dead, and that soul-stealing emptiness seems to be seeping through her pores, invading her body like a disease. She squeezes her closed eyes harder and silently prays for it to leave.

A frigid gust drifts over her, and the hairs at her nape stand on end. Goose bumps prickle the skin of her arms, back, and shoulders. It is coming closer. Oh, God, it is coming for her. The scent of rotting flesh fills her nostrils and her eyes tear.

Please leave me alone. Please.

Something hard, sharp, scrapes down her arm, and she shivers.

Please go away. Not again. Oh, God, not again.

Someone screamed.

"Sloan? Sloan. Wake up!"

I jerked upright, gasped. I was covered with a cold sweat, trembling. I blinked in the darkness, finding those creepy, glowing eyes staring at me.

"Elmer!"

"Yeah, it's me. Who did you think it was?"

"You scared me."

"Thank you. Glad to hear I still have the mojo."

A light flipped on, blinding me. I blinked a lot, squinted. Was I seeing things? Or was someone standing next to Elmer?

"What's wrong now?"

"Nothing's wrong. I wanted to come over and share the good news in person."

"What good news?" I squinted harder. Yes, that was someone standing next to Elmer. And that someone looked like a female.

Elmer stepped forward, pulling his guest with him. "I'd like you to meet the future Mrs. Elmer Schmickle, Olivia. Olivia, this is Sloan."

My jaw went slack. "What?"

The woman—the beautiful woman, who could pass for a model—extended a hand to me.

"Hello, it's nice to meet you at last," she said.

Mute, I shook her hand.

"Elmer has told me a lot about you," she added.

This woman had agreed to marry Elmer? Why? She was absolutely gorgeous. I had no doubt she had men lined up outside her door, waiting for her just to give them a glance.

Was she blind? Insane? Desperate?

"Whatever he's told you, I'm sure it's all lies," I answered. *What the heck are you thinking?* I silently chastised myself. *Elmer found a wife! I am off the hook.*

I pasted on a grin the size and brilliance of a supernova. "I'm sorry. I was still half asleep. Nice to meet you, Olivia."

The future Mrs. Elmer Schmickle scrunched her perfectly plucked eyebrows together. "Elmer lied? You aren't working for a top secret unit in the FBI?"

"Well, I guess you could say I am. Technically, I'm—"

"Then he hasn't lied. You're embarrassed? Don't care to boast? I get that. But don't worry, I find it refreshing that a woman should go into a field of work that is primarily inhabited by men. I'm an electrical engineer myself. You don't see a lot of women in my line of work either."

An electrical engineer? Intelligent? Beautiful? Where did Elmer find this woman?

"I would imagine." I motioned toward the hallway. "Um, can I get you something to drink?"

"Sure. Thank you." Holding Elmer's hand, Olivia tailed behind me. "I owe you thanks for another reason as well."

"Really?" I whispered, keeping my voice low so I wouldn't wake up JT as we stepped out into the hallway. He was sawing logs in the next room. Even with the door closed, I could hear him. Downstairs in the kitchen, I flipped on a light and I opened the refrigerator, taking inventory. "What would you owe me thanks for?"

She slid her arm through Elmer's, giving his shoulder a pat with her left hand. A huge, sparkly rock glittered on her ring finger. It was no wonder she was looking so happy. "For setting my sweet Elmer free, so he and I could be together."

She certainly didn't need to thank me for that. I pulled out a couple of vitamin waters; then I went to the cupboard for some glasses. "I'm very glad to see him happy. And you too."

She batted her eyelashes at her fiancé. "I'll be even happier once we're married."

"When's the wedding?" I asked, cracking one of the waters open. I was about to pour it into a glass, when she suddenly snatched it out of my hand and chugged half of it.

She swiped at her mouth with the back of her hand. "We'll be married on the next full moon. My ring. Isn't it absolutely gorgeous?" Olivia's eyes were all twinkly as she showed off her ring. She sighed, misty-eyed. "This is the first time I've been able to wear this outside of my house. The engagement is very secret. You're the first person we've told. You can't tell anyone. Elmer said you're trustworthy. We've signed an agreement with the production company to keep it quiet until after the show's full season has aired. That's not for another two months. It's going to be so hard to hide for so long the fact that we're married."

"I can imagine." I watched as she polished off her bottle of water.

"But a contract is a contract," Elmer said.

Evidently, Elmer only respected contracts when they worked in his favor.

"What would you like to drink?" I asked him, giving him some mean eyes.

"Do you have any champagne? I'm in the mood to celebrate."

"I don't know. In case you hadn't noticed, we're not at my place. But the folks have a wine cellar in the—"

"Who needs champagne? I know how we can celebrate." Olivia turned to Elmer and flung herself into his arms—and that was something to see, since he was a good twelve inches shorter than her. She planted a huge kiss on his mouth.

"I'll just go down and take a look." I tried to hide my grimace as I headed for the basement.

As I hit the bottom step, I realized someone was down in the media room, watching a movie. *Titanic.*

I heard heavy breathing.

What the heck?

I hurried up to the row of reclining chairs.

Katie.

And Sergio.

They were draped across a couple of chairs, making out hands everywhere, clothes askew, hair mussed. And totally oblivious to the fact that I was standing there, gawking. Evidently, both of them liked that whole mouth-to-mouth thing and had decided to do more of it—particularly now that a life wasn't hanging in the balance.

I just hoped this man wouldn't dump Katie like the last few had. Lately she'd been changing male companions more often than I changed my computer log-in password.

Trying to ignore the moans and sighs, I headed back to the wine cellar, found a whole section of champagne, grabbed the first bottle I touched, and headed back upstairs . . . to discover Elmer and his soon-to-be bride doing the exact same thing as Katie and Sergio.

Feeling a little left out, I took the bottle to the kitchen, popped the cork, and poured myself a nice, big glass. I tasted. I gulped. *Wow, is that champagne smooth!* It went down easier than water. I guzzled half the glass before I'd realized it. Then I downed the rest.

Now, pour some more? Or put it away, and go do something else, something productive?

Fuck that.

I poured myself another glass. These last few days had been pure hell. I deserved an indulgence. The second glass went down easier than the first. And the third, even easier.

Do I feel good! Warm and a little tingly all over.

Smiling, but a little wobbly, I went upstairs to my room and shut the door. I sat on the bed, used the remote on the flat-screen TV hanging on the wall, and clicked through the whole channel lineup. Somehow I ended up stopping on a porn channel, where a girl was lounging on her couch in a negligee, batting her eyelashes at the refrigerator repairman, who'd come to take a look at her compressor.

Really, the writers could do better.

For some reason, I watched her carry on with the man for a while. The whole time, I was wondering why she'd do that, since he was kinda creepy-looking and she was so beautiful. It was a complete mismatch, not unlike Olivia and Elmer. Evidently, Miss Porn Star was simply too horny to care.

I wasn't sure yet what Olivia's motivation was.

When the plumber showed up, to join in the fun, I clicked to the next channel, an infomercial for some overpriced skin care regimen. Then I tossed the remote on the bed and went in search of my phone.

I was lonely. Everyone had someone to swap DNA with—except for me. And I wished there were something I could do to change that.

Where is my . . . whatever he's called? Boyfriend? If we're officially courting, is that what I should call him?

I decided I needed to ask him that. So I dialed his number, and he answered.

"Hello, Sloan. I've missed you."

Wowzers, does he have a nice voice! Sexy, sultry.

"Where have you been?" I blurted out. Evidently, the champagne was making me be a little more direct than I normally would've been.

"Handling something for my mother. But I'm on my way home. I can't wait to see you."

"I can't wait to see you too. Katie and Elmer both have friends over to play, so I'm all alone."

"That's completely unacceptable." I heard the laughter in his voice.

"I concur." I hiccupped. "'Scuse me." I giggled.

"Have you been . . . drinking?"

"Yes. I had some champagne. It's been a rough week."

"I'm sorry to hear that."

"But the champagne was good." I licked my lips, tasting it. I briefly considered having another glass, but I vetoed that notion. I needed to function tomorrow, to think clearly. Another glass of champagne would no doubt make my head more than a little foggy.

"Um-hm."

"Really good."

He chuckled. Even though he was God-only-knows-how-many miles away, the sound seemed to vibrate through my whole body.

"I think you should probably put it away for now, if you haven't already."

I fanned my face. "Are you trying to tell me what to do?"

"No, of course not."

"Darn, I might be in the mood for that right now."

"What are you in the mood for?"

"You, me, playing a sexy game of Simon Says," I said in my best sex-kitten voice.

"Then it's a good thing I'm sitting here, in the airport in Dallas."

"Good thing for you. Not for me." I heaved a sigh he could probably hear all the way in Dallas, without the phone.

His chuckle told me he had heard it. "How about dinner tomorrow night? With my mother?"

"Already?" I squeaked. *Poof,* all those warm tingles were gone. Now I was covered with goose bumps as a cold chill swept up my spine. We were at the dinner-with-parents stage already? Really?

"There's no need to panic." He must've heard the anxiety in my voice. I did. "My mother may be a queen, but behind closed doors, she's just a woman. And she has a great sense of humor. I expect the two of you will get along just fine."

So glad he thought so. Me, I wasn't sure. I'd met "Mom, the queen" only once, at my parents' wedding. Because there were so many other royal subjects waiting in line to pay their respects, I didn't have much of a chance to talk to her. My first impression hadn't been all that great. She'd acted pretty stiff, like I would expect a queen to act. Reserved.

"Sloan?"

"I'm still here." My phone clicked. "I think I have another call."

"I'll say good night, then."

"Okay."

"Sweet dreams. I'll see you tomorrow, at six."

"Yes, sweet dreams to you too." I clicked over to the other line.

The caller said, "I need to talk to you. Now."

Never underestimate people. They do desire the cut of truth.

—Natalie Goldberg

24

Jia had called me, and she didn't sound very happy to talk to me. In my slightly (more like, very) intoxicated state, I wasn't prepared to handle an angry teenager.

"Hello, Jia," I slurred.

"I need to talk to you," she repeated.

"So you said."

"Now."

I flopped onto my back, resting my head on my free arm. "I'm listening."

"No, not on the phone."

"What? You want me to drive over to your house?" I could literally hear her eyes roll. I hadn't realized that was possible until now.

"Yes, I want you to drive over to my house. My parents will beat my ass if I leave the house this late. And I'm scared to go anywhere after . . . the attack. I watched the weather report. There's a chance of thunderstorms tonight."

I shook my head. *Whew, the world gets a little tipsy-topsy when I do that.* "Sorry, I can't drive right now."

"Why not? Are your parents going to beat your ass too? Oh, that's right, you're too old to be living at home with your mommy and daddy."

I glanced around. Yes, it was ironic. "Actually, I'm under

the influence of alcohol," I told her, thinking honesty was the best policy here. "I can't drive."

"Well . . . damn it."

"Can't you tell me whatever it is you need to say over the phone?"

"No."

"Then I'm sorry, it'll have to wait until tomorrow."

Silence.

"Fine. Bye."

I stared down at the screen. *Wow, that was interesting.* If nothing else, she'd sparked my curiosity. "Good talking to you too. Oh, and you're welcome for saving your life," I said to the glowing screen. Shoving my not-so-kind thoughts about the testy teen out of my head, I plugged my phone into the charger and went back to bed.

Tomorrow is another day. A better day.

Because I am going to have dinner with my boyfriend's mother!

That was bound to inspire some scary nightmares tonight. That, and the shocking sight of Elmer and his fiancée making out on my parents' couch.

I don't know how Olivia got past the stench of death. It hit me in the back of the throat the instant he came near me.

It must be true love.

She was screaming. Or was it . . . singing?

I blinked open my eyes, and realized nobody was screaming. And, technically, nobody was singing either. Some really awful song was playing on my clock radio. I hit the button, shutting off the alarm and logrolled out of bed. After my shower, I dressed in something adequately FBI-esque and clomped down the steps in search of caffeine. I sniffed. Was that . . . ? Had someone beat me to the coffee?

I rounded the corner, and there was Katie, standing next to the machine, a cup held under the spout, catching those precious first drips.

"You're up early for a Saturday," I said to her.

"I never went to sleep." She blinked in slow motion.

"No offense, but you look like you pulled an all-nighter. Why didn't you go to bed? Homework?"

"Not exactly. I went to bed, but I didn't sleep." Her face turned the shade of a pomegranate as she swapped her full cup for the empty cup I handed her.

"Sergio?" I asked, sipping.

"You know, he's more than just a pretty face."

"Of course, he is. But what about Viktor?"

"Screw him. He's not interested. His loss, Sergio's gain."

"But you said it was love at first sight with Viktor."

"Maybe it was for me, but clearly it wasn't for him." Her cup full, she pulled it away, replacing it with the empty carafe. Then the two of us went to the breakfast bar and sat.

"Maybe he's busy with prince stuff," I suggested. "Like Damen. He's been gone too."

"Really, too busy to call? Sorry, but I'm not buying that." I wasn't buying it either. Maybe that was why Damen's invitation had shocked me. Outside of the gift, he'd pretty much disappeared too. Sipping, Katie hit the remote, powering up the small TV hanging in the kitchen. An image of an already traffic-jammed I-95 displayed, and the traffic reporter jabbered about an accident over the *chop-chop-chop* of helicopter rotors. "Doesn't matter. Sergio is a great guy. He's intelligent. Did you know he has a master's degree?"

The pool guy? "In what?"

"Er, art."

"Art?" I echoed. I couldn't see Katie having anything in common with an artist.

"Actually, it wasn't exactly art. I can't remember exactly what he said it was. But you should see his room. It's full of paintings he did in school, and they are unbelievable. He has real talent."

Which was why he was working for my parents, answering the phone and skimming the pool, shirtless. "I bet he does." I was more willing to believe he had real talent in bed, based on the sparkles I saw in my best friend's eyes. *"Real talent."* I gave her a nudge, and that color in her face deepened a few shades. She hopped off her stool. "Bagel?"

"No thanks. I'd better get JT going. There's an accident on I-95. It's going to take us forever to get to work. We have to go pick up Mom's car in Baltimore first." I took a few more swigs of coffee before transferring what was left into a travel cup. "See you later."

"M'kay."

I dashed upstairs, where I discovered JT was already dressed and ready to head out. He made a pit stop in the kitchen for a vitamin water and breakfast to go. Meanwhile, I ran outside, threw my bag and my laptop onto the passenger seat of his car, then strapped myself in. And off we went, facing at least an hour and a half of congested freeway traffic. Almost two hours later, I was carting my laptop and an empty travel mug into the PBAU. JT had dropped me off next to Mom's parked car, after making me promise I'd go straight to the unit. I'd done exactly as he'd asked.

Here I was. In our office. The cubicles were all empty. I glanced up at the conference room door. It was open, and light was spilling out into the main open area.

Damn, I'm missing a case meeting!

I dashed into the room, expecting to see the whole gang. But there were only three people sitting around the far end of the long table—the chief, JT, and Fischer.

I jerked back, thinking this was one meeting I might not be expected to attend.

"Skye." The chief motioned me in. "Have a seat. We were just talking about you."

"Were you?" I had a feeling I knew what they were saying. They were discussing how to get rid of me. My insides twisted, and I reminded myself that it was for the best, if they did let me go. Granted, my bank account would suffer, which would leave me with two choices—find another job or ask my father for help. Neither made me feel particularly joyful, but at least I wouldn't have to worry about my mom being stalked by a vampiric predator or my roommate being electrocuted by an overgrown *Turdus merula*—common blackbird. Mentally bracing myself, I slid into the closest chair.

Chief Peyton waited until I was seated. "Thomas tells me you'd like to resign."

"I have been thinking about it."

"I wish you would reconsider." This surprised me. I would have thought she'd be glad to get rid of me after all the trouble I'd caused her.

"My best friend nearly died—"

"About that," the chief interrupted. "Sloan, she wasn't attacked by the unsub. Her hair dryer shorted, and she got a zap."

I looked at JT. Then at Fischer. They both nodded.

"I've known since that day," JT confessed. "I convinced Katie to keep the truth from you, so you would feel compelled to keep working the case."

"What?"

"It's true," the chief said. She looked guilty as hell. But JT looked guiltier.

"Wow. You lied to me. You all lied. Katie too?"

"Hers is more a lie of omission," JT said. "And the chief didn't realize what I'd told you."

"Unbelievable. What about our last case? Was that thing with the *aswang* and my mother a lie too?" I glared at JT. How could he trick me? I'd worked my ass off these past few weeks, trying to profile these unsubs. And this was the thanks I got? "Are you trying to manipulate me into working here? Now that I think about it, that makes sense. It seems my family and close friends have become targets for our unsubs only since I've started working with the unit."

The chief's expression soured. "I didn't know about your mother." She slid a dark look at JT.

"That was real," he said. "I swear."

The chief sighed. "We're sorry. Considering the circumstances, I can understand why you would want to resign. Someone should have told you the truth immediately, as soon as he realized there'd been a misunderstanding." She slanted her eyes at JT.

"Agreed."

I was so mad, I didn't know what to say. Finally, through gritted teeth, I said, "Will you accept my resignation?"

She shook her head. "No."

So much for that. "I see."

"What I will do is promise we will keep you informed at all times. And I will continue to do as I have more recently done, keeping you off the streets, where you're less likely to draw the attention of the unsubs." Her eyes narrowed slightly. "We've discussed this before. I made a mistake by putting you in the field undercover when you are only an intern. I'm regretting that decision, despite the fact that we were able to profile two unsubs and aid in their capture. You'll be working primarily in the office, but I won't keep you locked up in here for the rest of the summer. You will be able to accompany me or Agent Thomas on occasion."

That sounded like so much fun. *Not.* Especially the part about working with JT. He was at the top of my shit list at the moment.

But then again, it meant I'd get to keep my job and, hopefully, avoid any direct contact with another unsub. "I guess that'll work."

"As far as your friend goes, I am sorry she was injured. I hope she's recovering okay."

"She seems to be doing better."

"No long-term injuries?"

"None that I'm aware of. Not even a burn. . . ."

The image of Jia's chest, and those little red marks, flashed in my head. "I need to make a phone call."

The chief flicked her eyes to the door. "Carry on, Skye."

I hurried back to my desk and called Katie. She didn't answer. I left her a message, then powered up my laptop.

Red marks. Those hadn't looked like bite marks, now that I thought about it. They looked more like burns.

"Skye?" JT strolled up and leaned against my cubby wall. "Are you okay?"

"Fine," I said, skimming a Web page on electrocution and lightning strikes.

What the hell were those red marks?

Metal, belts, jewelry, those kinds of things, heated up when someone was struck by lightning. Had Jia been wearing a necklace? If she had, why were there so many marks, scattered all over her chest?

"Do you have a photo of Jia Wu after her attack?" I asked JT. I was proud of myself for not unloading on him, the lying rat. Now was not the time. I'd deal with him later.

"Sure. We should have one in the file. Why?"

"I noticed something odd when we were interviewing her." I motioned to my chest. "Some marks. Here. I don't remember seeing anything like that on the other victims."

"What are you thinking?"

"Nothing yet. I'm just wondering if the marks are significant."

"Let me grab the file. We can look through all the photos."

"Great. I'll be right here." I scanned the results of a Google search for the terms "electrocution burn marks."

Seconds later, JT was rolling his chair into my cubby and making himself at home. He smacked the file down on my desktop and flipped it open. "I guess we can start from the beginning and work our way to the most recent victim." We both scrutinized the photos of Stephanie Barnett. She had some marks. One on her hand, where she had clearly been wearing a ring. And another on her wrist. Nothing on her chest. On her back was a large red mark with bent spokes branching off. The mark looked a lot like the mark outside her window.

"Nothing but the large mark," I said.

"Okay," JT replied. "Next up, Emma Walker."

We both stared at the photos of Emma Walker, noting a burn on her stomach and on her neck, where she must have been wearing a necklace. Like Jia, she did have a mark on her chest. One mark, however, not dozens. "Where's the picture of Jia?" I asked.

JT flipped through the file and pulled out a photo. He pointed at the small red marks on her chest. "I don't know how I missed those."

"They weren't as red as this. I initially thought she had a rash or acne." I took a closer look. "Don't they look like they're actually sets of two marks, scattered randomly over her chest?"

JT took the picture from me and studied it. His mouth twisted into a snarl. "They do."

We flipped through the photos of the other victims. None of them had marks like Jia had.

"Those look like burns," JT said.

"I agree."

"Maybe she was wearing some kind of jewelry when she was electrocuted and it moved?"

"Why didn't it happen to the others? Why only her?"

"I don't know."

I studied Jia's picture some more. "No fang marks. And where's the main point of contact? Where's the telltale lightning-strike mark? Something about her story isn't adding up."

"Do you think she lied?"

"About what? Everything?"

He shrugged.

"Why would she make the whole thing up?"

"Hmm." JT spread all the photos on the desk. Jia was in the center. There was no doubt that her picture stood out from the others. "Good question. I think we should have another chat with her. Coming with me?"

I fiddled with my mouse. "I should stay here and—"

"Skye . . . Sloan, come with me." His head was tipped. His eyes were pleading. "I'm sorry for lying to you. I have no excuse. It was wrong."

Yes, it was wrong. Very wrong. But my refusing to work

the case with him—just because I was angry—wouldn't change anything. "Okay, fine. I'll go."

"I don't know why you're making me go through all of this again. I told the police everything."

JT was standing in the Wu family's foyer—his little notebook in one hand, a pen in the other. Jia was standing across from him. I was waiting for the right time to ask her why she'd called me.

JT said, "Humor us, please. We're just doing our job."

Jia scowled at both of us. Evidently, she didn't care for our jobs. Or maybe she was still irritated with me for lying about being a student. Now that I'd been the victim of a lie, I could relate, somewhat. Or maybe she was getting scared, realizing we were this close to unraveling her lies.

"Okay. So I had just taken a shower and was getting ready for bed, when this man showed up in my room. Out of nowhere, it seemed. He grabbed my arm with one hand and kissed me. Then he placed his other over my chest, and I felt this horrible sensation, so painful. I couldn't breathe and hurt everywhere. One second, I was standing, and the next I was lying on the floor."

"Okay, go on." JT was taking notes. Me, I was watching her every movement: each flick of her eye, each twitch of her fingers. She hadn't shown any outright signs of deception yet. But I still had the feeling she was hiding something.

What?

"Then he let me go, and all of a sudden, he ran to the window and leapt. I thought I heard someone downstairs and I tried to call out for help, but I couldn't talk. I lay there until I could eventually move, crawled to the door, pushed it open, and shouted for help. It wasn't long after that, when Sloan burst in."

"How long were you lying there?" JT asked.

"I don't know. I might have drifted in and out of consciousness for a while."

Which meant I hadn't scared off the unsub. Something or someone else had. Who? Or what?

JT glanced at me. "Anything else?"

I shrugged. "I guess we're finished. Thanks, Jia."

"Sure." Moving slowly, she ushered us to the door.

JT headed out onto the porch, but I hesitated, turning. "If there's anything you're not telling the police for some reason, say . . . about Mr. Hollerbach . . . I want you to reconsider."

"What makes you think I'm not telling everything?"

I kept my expression blank. "Nothing in particular . . . except maybe a phone call . . . ?"

"I've told you everything I know." She leaned closer and whispered, "It wasn't Carl. I'm not trying to cover for him, if that's what you think."

"Okay," I whispered back. "If you say it wasn't *Carl,* then I guess I have to believe you. Why did you call me?"

"To let you know you got what you wanted. He's a jerk," she snapped. "An asshole." She wasn't whispering anymore.

"What happened?"

Her lips sealed up, as if she was trying to hold back. But a second later, she blurted out, "He told me he can't see me anymore."

"I'm sorry." I wasn't sorry he'd dumped her. That was for the better, in the long run. But I was sorry for the pain I saw in her eyes.

"No, you're not sorry. You're happy we broke up." She stabbed a finger at my chest. "It's your fault. You told. You bitch. How could you? He's being investigated. He might be fired."

"Wait a minute. I didn't report him to anyone. But I'm not sorry he's in trouble. What he did was wrong. You're a student."

"I'm legal," she hissed.

"He's a teacher."

"So what?"

"He's married."

"Again, so what? It isn't illegal to have an affair." Affair? She'd told me they hadn't done anything.

Yet.

Jia glanced over her shoulder—probably looking for her mother. I doubted Mrs. Wu had any idea her daughter was having a sexual relationship with the teacher. "Besides, he was leaving her. He just had some things to take care of first."

I shook my head and stepped through the doorway. "I'm sorry you're hurt. That's what I'm sorry for. I can see this has torn you up inside. I'm telling you the truth when I say he wasn't ever going to leave his wife. He was telling you that so you'd keep seeing him."

"That's a lie! He loved me." Tears spilled from the girl's eyes. "He told me he loved me, that we'd get married. I'd have his children."

"Jia, did you know Hailey Roberts—"

She slammed the door.

Standing next to the car, JT watched me walk up. "Wow, what was that about?"

"That girl needs help. I hope her parents realize that. I'm not the enemy, here. I genuinely want to help her."

"I know." He tipped his head, indicating I should get into the car. I did. I sighed as I snapped myself in. And after he buckled himself up, he spoke. "Skye, you have to keep your emotions out of this. That's your problem. When you get involved, you start to make bad decisions. You take risks, and that's dangerous."

"That's my problem. And I don't know how to follow procedure, right? And what else? It's not so easy, shutting off my feelings."

"No one will ever tell you it's easy." He stuffed the key into the ignition and cranked it. "Why do you think I fucked up with you?"

"Sorry this was such a waste of time."

"It wasn't a waste of time."

"Where to now?"

"We're done for the day. I need to run home, check on Brittany, and grab some fresh clothes." He pointed at his gas gauge. "I need to fuel up. We're on fumes."

We sputtered up to the BP station. While he was pumping gas, JT's phone rang. I powered down the window to let him know.

"Who is it?" he asked.

"Carl Hollerbach."

"Go ahead, answer it."

I hit the button. "Hello?"

"Hello, I'm calling for Agent Jordan Thomas," Hollerbach said.

"I'm sorry, he's not available right this minute. Can he call you back in five to ten?"

"Sure. I guess. There's something he should know. I'd like to meet with him as soon as possible."

"He can come to your—"

"No, if what I've heard is true, it won't be safe for me to be seen with him. I need to meet him somewhere private, discreet."

"Very well. It's late, but he can meet you tomorrow morning. Seven A.M. How does Einsteins' bagel store in Ellicott sound? Safe enough?"

"That'll work."

"We'll see you then." I handed the phone back to JT. "That was Hollerbach. He's under investigation for sleeping with at least one of his students. I'm not sure he's credible. But if he can tell us something, I'm willing to listen."

"Good."

"I told him we'd meet him at Einsteins' in Ellicott. Seven o'clock, tomorrow morning."

He scowled. "My favorite place."

I chuckled. "Sorry. It was the first place that came to mind."

Fantasy, abandoned by reason, produces impossible monsters; united with it, she is the mother of the arts and the origin of marvels.

——Francisco de Goya

25

Damen picked me up at six P.M. on the dot. Maybe he wasn't the best at calling, and this whole courting thing was a little antiquated. But I'd give him credit where credit was due: he was punctual, a trait I admired greatly.

His eyes sparkled as he watched me descend the stairs. I swear, I've never felt so admired. When I hit the bottom step, he said, "You look absolutely stunning."

I felt my face heating. What girl wouldn't? I had to admit, I looked good. But "absolutely stunning"?

"Thank you," I answered.

He handed me a box.

"What's this?" I asked.

"A gift."

"Another one?"

"It's sort of an apology."

"Well, thank you." I hadn't anticipated him bringing another gift. That was two for me and none for him. Not exactly even. I felt more than a little guilty. Then again, I hadn't disappeared for days.

"Please don't feel you need to return the favor," he told me.

Is he reading my mind?

I opened the box, finding an e-book reader.

Evidently, he had been reading my mind.

He grinned. He had one heck of a killer smile. "I get the impression you do a lot of reading. I thought you might like one of these."

"It's . . . perfect. Thank you."

"You're welcome. This way, if you ever have another fire, you won't have to worry about losing all your books."

"Let's hope that never happens. I lost a lot more than my books. Just in case, I'll keep this safe. I definitely won't leave it in my car. Or in my apartment." I set the e-book reader on the table; then I checked my purse to make sure I had house keys.

"Give me time, and I'll have all of your other things replaced too."

I gave him a pretend glare. "You'd better not."

"Ready?" he asked, smirking.

"You bet."

JT was standing in the hallway, arms crossed over his chest. He said nothing. He didn't have to. The stink eyes said everything.

I felt a little bad, leaving when JT was camping out at Mom and Dad's house, playing bodyguard, per the chief's orders. But I was leaving with a man who was fully capable of providing for my safety. That fact, he couldn't argue with. And I would only be gone for a couple of hours.

Damen held the door for me—so gentlemanly. I thanked him as I stepped outside.

We strolled down the front walkway toward the waiting limousine. "I hope you don't mind. My mother prefers to dine outside." He stepped aside, motioning for me to take a seat first.

I climbed aboard and sat down. There was a man sitting near the front, staring out the window. Our chaperone, I presumed. He said nothing. "It's a gorgeous evening. I don't mind at all."

"Good." Damen made himself comfy next to me and slid

his hand under mine. Our fingers wove together, and a wave of heat seemed to ripple through my body. I couldn't remember ever feeling so excited and anxious on a date. Not ever. Then again, I hadn't gone on many dates, and never with a prince.

His hand squeezed mine. The door slammed shut; and within seconds, we were zooming down Mom and Dad's winding street. "You're nervous."

"I am," I admitted.

"Don't be."

"Ha! Easy for you to say." I gave him a little playful smirk. "You're not about to have dinner with a queen you've barely met."

"That's true." He set his other hand on top of mine, so that one was under mine and the other on top. "But I assure you, my mother is not what you're expecting." That hand started slowly smoothing its way up my arm.

"Not formal and stiff and regal?" I asked, checking to see if Mr. Chaperone was watching us.

He was.

I glanced back at Damen. His eyes were twinkling. "Stiff? Formal? Not at all. You'll see." A mischievous slant curled his mouth. He was so sexy when he was looking at me like that.

"What do you mean, I'll see?" I fanned my face. Did the driver have the heat on or what?

"You won't believe me."

"Try me." I powered down the window a little, letting a light gust of fresh air blow into the vehicle.

"It's better if you see with your own eyes."

The car stopped, and I glanced outside. "We're here? Already? What street is this?" I powered the window down all the way and took a look around. We were parked in front of what could only be described as a castle. The stone building was situated in a clearing, surrounded by a thick forest. It was so gorgeous—it almost seemed surreal. "We're less than five minutes from my parents' place, and yet this doesn't look familiar at all."

"It's farther than you think."

A tall wood-and-metal gate swung open and the car rolled inside, through thick stone walls. The driveway curled around the front garden in a wide U shape. We finally stopped in front of a set of double doors, manned by a uniformed guard, who reminded me a little of the English guards at Buckingham Palace.

"This place is unbelievable." I sounded as breathless as I felt. "Is this where you live?"

"No, it's where my mother lives." Damen leaned in and brushed a kiss on my cheek; then he pulled back. "You're in for a treat." With that, he took my hand in his, preceding me out of the car. As I stepped out onto the brick walk, I stared in awe at the carved woodworking around the windows and the glorious doors. The guard, dressed in a crisp black-and-white uniform, acknowledged Damen with a slight tip of the head, and the doors next to him swung open.

We stepped inside.

My gaze swept the wide-open space: ornate trim everywhere, artwork, beautiful furnishings. My shoes *tap, tap, tapped* on the stone floor as I followed Damen's lead.

"This place is unreal," I remarked in awe.

"Have you looked up yet?" He pointed at the ceiling.

"No . . . *ohhh.*" There was an amazing mural painted over the entire surface: a sky scene with clouds and creatures and beautiful winged men and women and children. *"Wow."*

"It's a Michelangelo original," he informed me.

"*The* Michelangelo?"

"*The* Michelangelo. It's called *The Choir of Mythics.*"

"I've never heard of it. His works were primarily religious, Catholic."

"Not many people have heard of it."

Looking at the figures, I could believe it had been painted by Michelangelo. But there was one problem with Damen's claim: Michelangelo lived in Italy, in the fifteenth and six-teenth centuries. There was no way he could have painted this ceiling. "It's beyond words."

"Come, this way." He gave my hand a little tug as he con-tinued through the huge room. "Mom will give you the grand tour later, after we've eaten. It's one of her guilty plea-sures. She's so proud of this crusty, old place."

I could think of at least a dozen adjectives to describe this place. "Crusty" wasn't one of them. "And you're not proud of it?"

"It's a little antiquated for my taste. I prefer something more modern. Sleek. Contemporary."

"I understand. Living in a place like this would feel like living in a museum." I hesitated next to a chair that had to be at least two hundred years old. I hesitantly traced the curved wood-carved top with the tip of my index finger. "I'd be afraid to touch anything."

"I can't tell you how many priceless antiques my broth-ers and I broke. We used to skateboard through the hall. Right through here." His arm swept across the front of his body. "We drove our nurse crazy. Poor woman had to retire last year."

"I bet. I've met a few of them. They were . . . all very dif-ferent. Do you have any sisters?"

"Only one."

"Poor girl. I can imagine what kind of hell you all gave her."

"Actually, we treated her pretty well." Reaching a set of tall French doors, he pushed one open, revealing a lush courtyard beyond.

Out we stepped, onto a covered stone patio. "Mum will be out back, in the gazebo. That's where she spends most of her time these days."

"With property this gorgeous, I could see why." I fol-lowed him down a stone path, cutting across the world's most pristine lawn, toward the white building set in front of a thick wall of trees. We found the queen standing at the rear of the building, facing the woods.

"Mother."

The queen turned around, and I sucked in a breath. She looked different—younger than she had at the wedding. She was extremely beautiful, with long, shimmering blond hair, which tumbled down her back in heavy waves; her skin was as smooth as an infant's and ivory white; her eyes so blue, their color was almost too brilliant to look at. She smiled. "I'm glad you're joining me tonight. I've grown weary of dining alone."

"You look beautiful, Mum." Damen kissed each of his mother's cheeks.

"Thank you." She reached for me. "And so does our guest. Sloan, it's good to see you again."

"Thank you for having me." I started to do that bow-curtsey maneuver I'd done at the wedding, but she gently pulled on my hand, stopping me.

"No, no. Please, no formalities. We're here, in my home. And I insist you call me Hildur."

"Okay, Hildur."

"Come, let's walk." Leaving me no option but to follow, the queen pulled me toward the exit at the back of the gazebo. We stepped onto a narrow path, which curled through the woods. The air smelled sweet and earthy; and the only sounds I heard were the scuffle of unseen animals skittering around us and the crunching of our feet on the wood chips. The queen inhaled deeply and smiled. "This is where I feel most at peace."

I was feeling a lot calmer too. "It's lovely."

"I don't know how much you have learned about our people, but we have thick ties to the natural world."

I surmised that by "our people," she meant elves. "I don't know much at all."

"Interesting. You'll visit me often, then. I'll teach you. Have you discovered your power yet?"

My power? No one had ever told me I would have a

power. If Mom had anticipated that, she would have told me. "Um, no."

"Even those who are half-elf would have a great power. It's in our blood. It's in your blood. Skuld, half-sister of Hrolf Kraki, who was half-elf, could raise her slain soldiers from the dead."

Raise people from the dead? I'd love to have that power, considering my current job. "I don't believe I'm capable of that."

"Have you tried?"

"I admit, I haven't."

"Then perhaps you should."

"Perhaps." Was this conversation for real? I flicked a glance at Damen. He was looking quite amused, which made me wonder if it was a joke.

The path took a sharp turn to the left, then curled around to a clearing, which led out to a sparkling lake.

The queen smiled.

"Wow," I said on an exhalation. The lake was gorgeous, just like everything else on this property. It wasn't the largest lake—thus from my vantage point, I could see the opposite shore. What I didn't see was one single house. No boats. No people. It looked untouched and private, completely undisturbed. The glorious sky was reflected upon its smooth surface. A few swans swooped down in front of us, splashed some water on their feathers, and waddled up onto the beach, where two white towels were laid out. In the next blink, their bodies changed. Their wings shortened; their legs lengthened. They grew taller. Their feathers morphed into ivory skin. And within two heartbeats, I was staring at two men, with striking blue eyes and platinum hair. They each wrapped a towel around their hips, hiding everything between their belly buttons and their knees—a good thing.

"My youngest sons," the queen said proudly. "They weren't in attendance at your parents' wedding. Fridrik and Dagur."

They acknowledged me with a nod, then ran off, down the path. "You'll excuse them. They're young and foolish."

"It's all right." Once again, I flicked a glance at Damen, wondering if he did that shape-shifting thing too. And if so, what bird or animal might he turn into? He was darker than his brothers. I could imagine him shifting into something strong and dangerous and sexy, like a panther.

Something tinkled, like a little chime. The queen said, "Ah, dinner is ready." Back down the path we went, winding among old oaks and maples and pines. When we arrived back at the gazebo, a table had been set up; it was loaded with covered metal dishes. The queen motioned for me to sit next to her, leaving Damen to take the chair opposite us. She uncovered the plate in front of her, a salad. I did the same, but I didn't lift a fork until she had.

"Wine?" Damen asked, taking a bottle out of the ice tub.

"Absolutely. Thank you." Hildur held her glass for him and he filled it with the amber-colored liquid. While he filled my glass, the queen dug in like she hadn't eaten in eons. After downing half her salad, and two glasses of wine, she looked at my plate and chuckled. "Humans and their table manners." Her salad was polished off before I'd consumed a quarter of mine.

Dinner was rather uneventful. No one shape-shifted, though watching a woman scarf down enough food to make a linebacker sick was somewhat amusing. Damen ate slightly less. Me, I consumed more than a mouse, but not much.

When the servants arrived to clear the table, Hildur announced it was time for the grand tour of the house. Off I was swept, into a castle that was fit for any queen, filled with priceless antiques and rare artworks. I "oohed" and "aahed" as I was led from one room to the next. When we reached our starting point, the room with *the* Michelangelo on the ceiling, the queen gave me a twinkly-eyed smile. "Thank you for your delightful company. It was a pleasure."

"Thank you for having me."

"We'll see each other soon." She waved her arm; and in the next blink, she was a golden eagle, soaring out the open French doors.

I turned to Damen. "That was some exit."

"Mom has a flair for the dramatic. She once told me she'd dreamed of being an actress, when she was a girl. I could see her doing films."

"She's certainly beautiful enough to be in movies. She looked . . . different today."

"Yes, today you saw her as she's always appeared to me. To fit in with humans, she ages herself, to avoid drawing attention to the fact that she doesn't change."

"I see."

"She likes you." Planting his hands on my hips, he turned me to face him.

"How can you tell?" I stepped closer; my gaze was locked on his handsome face. My heart was doing flip-flops. Or maybe it was doing loop-the-loops. At either rate, I was feeling a little giddy and dizzy. I needed to hold on to him. I ran my hands up his chest to his neck, and curled them around so I could play with the waves skimming the back of his collar.

"She didn't turn you into a toad."

"Glad she didn't do that."

"I know. I would have to change into a toad too, if she had."

"Would you do that for me? Turn into a toad?"

"I'd turn into anything you want." His gaze flicked to my mouth, and the air seemed to crackle between us.

"Where's our chaperone now?"

"Hmmm. Probably in the car." That was an excellent place for an unwanted chaperone to be. Better than here. His head started dipping down, toward mine. He licked his lips. I licked mine. And just as my eyelids fluttered shut, his mouth brushed softly over mine.

It was both the gentlest and the most thrilling kiss of my life. Lips smooth, not hard; damp, but not wet. He tasted; he tempted; he kissed me into a near coma. When the kiss ended, I almost fell over. Luckily, I was still holding him, and he was still holding me.

"Wow," I said.

"Marry me, Sloan."

"Wow," I said again.

Light thinks it travels faster than anything but it is wrong. No matter how fast light travels, it finds the darkness has always got there first, and is waiting for it.

—Terry Pratchett

26

Unlike a lot of girls, I never tried to imagine what that one special moment would be like—when the love of my life would ask me to marry him. But still, evidently, I had some sort of scene planned out in my head. Because this proposal took me completely by surprise. I was speechless. Completely shocked. Unable to utter more than a syllable.

"Wow," I said a third time. Then, "Um. I. Oh."

He chuckled. The low rumbles vibrated through me. "I take it you didn't see this coming."

"Yes. And no." My gaze swept around that insanely huge room again, drifted up to the ceiling before slowly falling back down to Damen's hope-filled eyes. He was serious. He genuinely wanted me to marry him. My knees started to soften. "I . . ."

"Do you need to sit down?"

"Yes."

Sliding an arm around my waist, he led me to the chair I'd touched earlier. I sat, and he lowered to one knee. That position made me feel even dizzier.

He took my hand and cradled it between his. "Are you all right?"

"I'm . . ."

"In shock?" he finished for me.

"Yes."

When I didn't say anything else, he asked, "Is it a bad shock?"

"I don't know." That was three syllables. An improvement.

"Are you happy at all?"

"I'm not sad."

"I suppose that's a good thing."

"It is." I took a few deep breaths. "I'm sorry. It's just a lot to process. My circuits are overloaded."

One side of his mouth curled up. A lopsided grin looked so good on him. "Take your time. I'd hate for you to have a complete meltdown." He winked, and my heart did a happy, little pitter-patter.

Was I looking into the face of my future husband? Was he really *the one*? How could I possibly know after only going on a couple of dates? When I'd agreed to the courtship, I had expected—despite what my father had said—for it to be a long courtship. At least twelve months. I wasn't mentally prepared for this yet.

"We don't know each other," I pointed out.

"Why should that stop us? My parents met on the morning of their wedding."

"Was it an arranged marriage?"

"No, my father was just an extremely impulsive man. He knew the minute he saw my mother for the first time that he was the one." He gazed down at my hand before lifting his eyes back up again. "I feel the same way. I've never met anyone like you. And I can't imagine a future without you."

Oh, my God! "It's so soon." My heart started thumping hard against my breastbone and a wave of heat crept up my chest. My palm was starting to sweat. And my mouth was dry. I tried to swallow but I couldn't. "I mean, I knew what our courtship meant, but still . . . I thought we'd have time to get better acquainted. We've only been seeing each other for just over two weeks. There's so much I don't know about you yet. And you don't know anything about me."

"We can have a long engagement, if that makes you feel better."

It did, to a certain extent.

It wasn't that I sensed there was anything wrong with Damen. The exact opposite, actually. He was amazing. He was mysterious. He was interesting. He was insanely handsome.

The problem was, he was too perfect.

I cannot marry him until I knew what his flaws are.

Oh, my God, did I actually say to myself that I'd marry him?

I stared into his eyes and tried to imagine what our future would be like. I saw the two of us standing in front of a large Colonial—two little boys, who looked just like their father, ran around us while we laughed. It was a happy picture.

"Sloan." He stuffed his hand into his pocket and pulled out a ring-sized box. "I took this out of the safe, just in case."

He flipped the lid, revealing a ring—and it took my breath away. A square-shaped center stone, the color of the queen's blue eyes, was ringed in sparkling white diamonds. More diamonds flashed on the band, the top, and both back and front. It was so sparkly; I had to blink a few times.

"It's a family heirloom, a blue diamond they call 'the Eye of the Goddess.' It was a gift from the king of the dwarves."

"I've never seen anything like it."

He plucked it out of the velvet box. "I've been waiting to give this to the right woman. I know I've found her." He slipped his free hand under my left hand and slowly slid the ring onto my finger.

It fit perfectly.

I stared down at it, mesmerized by the facets cut into the stone. It was so pretty. And huge. And I'd never imagined that I'd wear a ring like that, so . . . extravagant. But, oddly, it felt like it belonged on my finger. And when I gazed into Damen's eyes, I felt like I belonged to him.

"A *long* engagement," I said, emphasizing the word "long."

"Absolutely."

"Okay." I laughed. This was crazy, and scary, and exciting, and I was completely overwhelmed with emotions. That only got worse, when Damen jumped to his feet, giving a big whoop of glee as he did it. He hauled me into his arms and swung me around in circles until I was so dizzy that I couldn't stand. Then, holding me tenderly, so I wouldn't fall over, he kissed me until I couldn't breathe.

"Thank you," he said. "You've made me the happiest man on earth." His twinkling eyes said as much, if not more. "Tell me you're happy—that you can't wait to shout out your news to the whole world."

"I'm too overwhelmed to say what I feel."

He cupped my cheek. "It's okay. In time, you'll feel as I do. Are you okay, at least? Able to walk?"

"I believe so."

"Good." He placed his hand on the small of my back, which, as it turned out, was a sexy touch. It was an intimacy I hadn't anticipated. He led me to the door in this fashion.

I reached.

He said, "Sloan, before you—"

I pulled.

Flashes blinded me for roughly thirty seconds. I blinked, then lifted my hand to shade my eyes.

"What?" I said, jerking back. I bumped into Damen. He steadied me, hands on my hips.

"Prince Damen! Is it true? Have you proposed?" someone shouted.

"Prince Damen!" someone else yelled.

Dozens of people were crowded around the front door. They shouted questions. Flashes blinked. Cameras caught the image of me, frozen like a deer in headlights.

"Miss Skye!" someone yelled. "Is that an engagement ring on your finger?"

My gaze jerked to Damen.

Damen, my fiancé, was smiling. At least one of us knew how to handle this kind of thing. Me, I was still frozen, confused, completely taken by surprise.

"Miss Skye has accepted my proposal of marriage," he said, looking absolutely thrilled.

I decided I'd better don a happy face, rather than looking like a girl who'd just stepped into a bear trap.

"May we see the ring?" one reporter asked.

Damen stepped up to stand at my left. He slid his elbow under my hand, allowing me to hold his arm while providing the mass of paparazzi a glimpse of the ring. "It's a family heirloom," he said proudly.

"Miss Skye, do you have any comments?"

I swallowed, hard. "Today was one of the most amazing, surprising days of my life. I'm looking forward to many more."

"Have you set a date yet for the wedding?" another asked.

I let the pro handle this one.

"Not at this time," Damen said. "We'll be updating the press as arrangements are made."

I wore my fake-happy face for another lifetime while a zillion photos were snapped; finally the crowd broke up. Damen walked me down to the limo and we climbed aboard.

I slumped back in the seat, nestled against Damen's side. His arm was slung over the back, making me feel protected and cozy.

"Whew. That was quite a fiasco."

"I was about to warn you when you opened the door."

"I guess I forgot you're a prince. To me, you're just a regular guy."

"'A regular guy'?" he echoed, grimacing.

"I mean that in the very best way. Please don't take it as an insult."

"I don't. That's actually one of the reasons why I decided to propose to you in the first place. You see me as a man first, then a prince. Most of the women I've courted saw me as a prince first, man second."

For some reason, a little chill swept up my spine at those

words. He'd courted other women. I blurted out, "Did you court many?" I didn't want to know the answer to that question. I *really* didn't.

"Two others."

Ugh.

But looking at it from a different angle, at least I now knew he hadn't proposed to the first girl he'd courted. That made me feel a little better about my impulsive decision to accept his proposal.

The facets of my ring caught the light and I glanced down at it. It still looked huge and extremely flashy. I wondered how long it would take for me to get used to wearing it. And, even more important, I wondered how long it would take for me to get used to what it meant.

We chatted about this and that during the short drive home, completely avoiding the topics of marriage and weddings. Damen walked me to the door, where he gave me a toe-curling kiss, which actually made my heart rate shoot into the danger zone. Then he opened the door for me so I could stumble inside.

I headed for my parents' kitchen first. I needed a drink. Or something.

Katie and Sergio were lounging on the couch in the family room, watching TV. JT was nowhere to be seen.

"Hey, Sloan, how was your date?" Katie asked.

"Um. Full of surprises." I felt my face warming. And my hands clasped together. My right index finger traced the perimeter of the blue stone.

"What kind of surprises?" Katie scooted upright. "Good surprises or bad?"

"Um . . ."

Katie tipped her head to the side. "What?"

I lifted my left hand.

"Sloan? Is that a . . ." She vaulted over the back of the couch and sprinted across the room. Fighting the momentum, she practically smashed into me. "Sloan?" She grabbed my hand and stared at the ring. "Is that an *engagement* ring?"

"Yes."

"Damen asked you to marry him?" she practically squealed.

"He did." I braced myself for a bouncy hug.

It didn't come.

"So fast?" Katie asked, her excitement fading slightly.

"I know it's extremely fast. I told him I needed a long engagement."

"You're going to be married." Katie was staring at my ring, her brows scrunched. Her gaze lifted, and she must've seen something on my face, confusion perhaps. Her lips curled up. I guessed it was supposed to be a smile, but it wasn't. "I'm happy for you, Sloan."

"I don't want things to change between us," I told her, hoping it might ease her conflicted emotions. I knew Katie well. I had no doubt she wanted me to be happy. But at the same time, she and I had been living together all this time, acting as if we'd be roommates for the rest of our lives. Maybe that had seemed possible a few months ago, but not any longer. I understood her reaction. To be honest, I probably would have reacted exactly as she had if the situation had been reversed and she was the one telling me she'd just accepted a marriage proposal.

Katie gave me a hug, but it wasn't an exuberant one. It was, however, a warm one. "If you're happy, then I am too."

"I'm not going to push things. We're taking time to get to know each other, to make sure. This," I said, waving my left hand, "is a formality."

"That's one hell of a formality." Katie grabbed my hand and really studied the rock. "Yes, it is. I've never seen a rock so huge."

"I agree, it's a little flashy. I almost feel strange wearing it."

"It's very pretty. Is it a sapphire?"

"No, blue diamond."

Katie's eyes bugged. "That's a diamond? It's huge. Like . . . British crown jewels huge."

"I guess it's a family heirloom."

My phone rang. Honestly, I was glad for the distraction. I wasn't a materialistic girl. This talk of priceless crown jewels was making me uncomfortable.

It was my mom. "Oh, my God!" she screamed.

My heart jerked. "Mom, what's wrong?"

"Nothing! Your father and I were watching the news on the Mythic cable network. We saw you! You're getting married? My daughter's marrying Prince Damen?"

"Mom. Stop. Yes, I am."

"I need to get on a plane and get home right away. We have plans to make, dresses to fit, cakes and flowers and—"

Yikes! "Mom, wait. There's no reason for you to cut your honeymoon short. We have plenty of time for planning. Damen and I agreed we should have a long engagement."

"I figured as much, but still, Sloan, you need to get on this immediately."

"But, again, it's going to be a *long* engagement. I'm thinking we have at least a year."

Mom laughed.

"What's so funny?"

"A year?"

"Yes, a year. At least."

"Sloan, there's no such thing as a yearlong engagement to an elf."

"Well . . . there is now."

"Honey, the average elf engagement is two weeks. Look at your father and me."

"I thought he pushed for a quickie wedding because you were married before."

"Our first engagement lasted for three days. We eloped."

Something big and thick coagulated in my throat. I tried to swallow it down, but it was stuck. "Three days?" I squeaked as I sat at the breakfast bar.

"Three *long* days. It almost killed us to wait."

"I can't be married in three days. Or even three weeks. I need some time to make sure we're right for each other."

"You know, you could pay a visit to Allegra Love. You remember how she reads couples' auras to determine whether they're compatible?"

How could I forget? That was the woman who'd performed my parents' ceremony. She was most definitely unforgettable. "I remember."

"She said your father and I were soul mates."

"She said the same thing about me and JT. And at the wedding—"

"Go see her, Sloan. In the meantime, I'm going to call in a few favors and get the ball rolling. What do you think about an outdoor wedding?"

The lump in my throat doubled in size. And I was hyperventilating again. "I'm not ready to talk about the wedding yet."

"The golf course where your father and I married the second time was lovely, but there are other options. Oh! I have an idea! I can check Maryvale Castle and see if there's been a last-minute cancellation. I couldn't be married there, but maybe my daughter can."

My lips were tingling. "Mom—"

"This is so exciting! What are your favorite flowers?"

My head was spinning. "Mom—"

"Lilies are always lovely. I think you should have all white. No, maybe some other colors. Orange?"

I was starting to see stars. "Mom—"

"Ah, I remember, you don't care much for orange. What about yellow? Yellow's very cheery. It's a nice color for summer. A July wedding would be lovely."

I stuck my head between my knees. "Mom, stop! It's much too soon to be talking about wedding plans. And . . . July? Are you suggesting we get married . . . tomorrow? July's three-quarter's over. I did accept Damen's proposal, but I have every intention of putting off the nuptials until I'm good and ready."

"Of course you are, dear. Honey! Our daughter is getting married! Your father wants to speak with you."

"Mom—"

"Here he is!"

"Hello, Sloan?" my father said.

The stars were gone. I slowly lifted my head. "Yes, it's me."

"Congratulations. Damen is a good man. I've known him a long time. Good choice. Very good, though not as good as Elmer."

"Dad—"

"The queen will insist you have the wedding at Willow Hill."

"Where's that?"

"Her home. The grounds are nice, if you'd like to have an outdoor ceremony."

"Dad—"

"And her favorite color is blue."

My gaze dropped to my ring. Blue. "Dad, I think I've made a mistake."

"No, you haven't. You've made an excellent choice in a husband. First rate. I'm sure you'll both be extremely happy. Gotta go now. Your mother is clawing the phone out of my hand. I love you."

"Sloan, I heard what your father said," Mom practically shouted. "I think we should try to get Maryvale Castle, anyway. But blue and white sounds lovely. Blue is a good color for me. I'm assuming I'll be the matron of honor . . . right?"

The twinkling stars were back. "I haven't thought about it yet."

"Of course, you haven't. This is all very sudden. I remember what it was like when your father proposed to me the first time. I was overwhelmed, but my mother wasn't happy about my engagement. She didn't help me with a single thing. That's why I will make sure I don't let you down. I'll be there every step of the way . . . once I get back in town. Your father's checking on flights as we speak."

"Don't hurry back on my account. Like I said, I don't plan on marrying anyone before the end of summer. No, I'm thinking next spring sounds good. Late spring. Like . . . May."

"We'll see how far you get with that." My mother giggled. "Honey, stop that. I'm still talking to our daughter. Oh! You naughty, little urchin. Must go. Bye."

Click.

I stuck my head between my knees again.

Katie stooped down, peering at me. "I take it your parents are happy about your engagement?"

"Happier than I am."

Katie's brows furrowed. "What's up with that?"

"It's just that . . . they said Damen is going to expect a speedy wedding. I can't do a speedy wedding. I'm not ready. We barely know each other."

Katie laughed. "This is insane! Thank you for making me feel better about Viktor dumping me."

"That wasn't my intention, but you're welcome, anyway."

Celebrate endings—for they precede new beginnings.

—Jonathan Lockwood Huie

27

I rolled into the parking lot of the Einsteins' bagel store at exactly thirty-two minutes after seven for our meeting with Carl Hollerbach the next morning—accident on the Baltimore-Washington Parkway. JT had left an hour and a half earlier, saying he wanted to take care of some personal things before the meeting. He made me promise I wouldn't stop anywhere along the way, not even for gas. He called me several times to make sure I was okay. As I pulled in, I'd expected to find a slightly annoyed JT waiting for me—not a fire truck, two police cars, and the ME's truck.

I had a sick feeling, but that didn't stop me from hoping that the sick feeling was wrong. Looking down at the giant rock on my finger, I slid off the ring and put it in my purse. I wasn't ready to explain my engagement to JT yet.

As I approached the yellow tape and an armed police officer I didn't recognize, I looked for JT.

"I'm Sloan Skye, FBI," I told him.

"ID?" he demanded.

"Um, I don't have ID. I'm an intern."

The officer gave a little grunt.

With no other choice, I dug my cell phone out of my purse and called JT.

"Finally," he said. No hello.

"I was thirty-two minutes late. Thirty-two minutes isn't

so bad—all things considered. The backup was miles long. Tell me Carl Hollerbach isn't dead."

"Okay, Carl Hollerbach isn't dead."

I let out a long sigh. "What a relief. Who is it?"

"Carl Hollerbach."

"Ugh."

"Why aren't you in here yet?" He sounded annoyed and crabby.

"The friendly officer standing guard out front won't let me by."

JT's sigh was audible. "I'll be out there in a minute."

"Thanks."

I stood at the tape and stared at the policeman.

He stared back.

JT finally ambled over. "Officer, Miss Skye is a respected member of our team. I'd like to ask you to let her by."

The officer's eyes slitted. He jerked his head. "Go ahead."

"Thank you." I bounced past him. "So what's the story?" I asked JT.

"Electrocution and exsanguination. Same marks as our other victims. Similar MO. And a witness said they saw an attractive man talking to the victim shortly before he died. But the victimology is off. This is the first one that isn't a student and is an adult male."

"Even so, I know it's our unsub. Damn it. Now I wish I hadn't put off the meeting until today. It gave the unsub time to find out what he was up to."

JT shook his head. "I'm done here. There's nothing more to look at. I'd like to head over to his house and see if we can dig up something useful there. These unsubs are on a rampage. We need to stop them."

"I agree. Do you have an address?"

"Yes, come on. We'll take your car. Mine is pinned in."

* * *

By the time we arrived at Carl Hollerbach's house, several of BPD's finest were huddled outside. They hadn't gone in yet.

"I'm guessing Mrs. Hollerbach insisted on a search warrant. They're waiting for the judge to sign off," JT said as I angled the car up to the curb. "It's going to take a while to get the warrant, but Forrester's probably already inside, questioning the wife."

As we strolled up the front walk, my gaze snapped to the tricycle parked in the driveway.

This guy had children. Now, most likely thanks to his extracurricular activities, they would grow up fatherless. I knew what that was like. My heart ached for them. "I wonder why he did it, why he slept with those students?"

"Some guys don't think. They just . . . let their penis do the thinking for them."

"A penis can't think. That's a physical impossibility."

"It may be, but it's more common than you know." JT slid me a look I didn't like very much. I wasn't sure what he was trying to get at. Right now wasn't the time, anyway.

"I'd rather not talk about this now."

"Fair enough." JT knocked. And knocked. After about thirty raps, the door opened. Forrester motioned us inside. "Good, maybe you can get somewhere with this woman. I've been questioning her for over a half hour. So far, all I've gotten is her date of birth. She's refusing to talk."

"Sloan?" JT gave me a little nudge. "You're a female. I think in this case, you're the only one who stands a chance at getting her to talk."

"Okay. I'll do my best." I approached her with the same caution I might give a cornered wild animal. "Mrs. Hollerbach, I'm Sloan Skye. I work for the FBI."

She didn't even look at me. She was standing in front of the fireplace, arms crossed over her chest, hands cupped over her mouth. She was staring at a family portrait and crying. My heart twisted.

Under her breath, I could hear her saying something, but I couldn't make out the words.

"Mrs. Hollerbach? We'd like to find out who did this to your husband."

Still, nothing.

"Is there anything you can tell us that might lead us to his killer?"

Finally she turned to look at me. Her eyes were the color of a stop sign. They were watery. Her face was splotchy. Her hands were shaking. She sniffled.

After noticing a box of tissues next to the couch, I handed it to her.

"Thanks." She pulled a few tissues out, blew her nose, and dabbed her eyes. "I don't know what to tell you, Agent I'm shocked. I want to believe it's all a bad dream and I'll wake up, and then everything will be back to normal."

I set the box on the fireplace mantel, within reach. "I'm sorry. I can only imagine how confused you are."

"'Confused' doesn't even begin to describe how I feel. I'm hurt and furious and sad and torn. Last night, my husband told me he's been having an affair with a young woman, a student. And today, he's dead. I don't understand what happened."

Damn it, this was awful. "What a terrible shock."

"*Terrible* is right. What am I supposed to do now? Our boys. They don't have their father anymore. They need their father. All children do."

"Yes, they do. We've been working with the Baltimore Police Department, helping them profile the people who killed your husband. There's nothing I want more than to catch them. What did your husband tell you last night?"

"He told me he was sleeping with a student, that things had gotten out of control, and he'd tried to stop it, but she was threatening him."

"Did he mention a name?"

"No."

"Did he say anything about his plans today?"

"What plans?"

I motioned to JT. "He called Agent Thomas last night, telling us he had information relating to our case. Did he say anything about that to you?"

"Nothing." She picked up the framed photograph and traced the image of his face with her index finger. "I feel like I didn't even know him—that the man I'd married, the man I loved, wasn't real. I wonder if he even loved me. Or the boys."

"I'm sure he did."

"Then why'd he sleep with her? Why'd he do it?"

"I wish I could tell you. Did he ever mention the name 'Jia Wu'?"

"Yes. She's one of his star students. . . ." Mrs. Hollerbach's eyes widened. "Is she . . . Is she the little tramp who was threatening my husband?"

"I can't say."

"Why? Was there more than one?"

I didn't know how to respond to that question.

Mrs. Hollerbach took my silence as a response. "There was?" She clapped her hands over her face and sobbed. The sound seemed to knife into my gut. I felt useless as I stood next to her, wishing I could say something that might give her some comfort. "How many?"

"I don't know if there were more or not. And even if I did, I don't think telling you would be helpful right now."

"Yes, yes, it would." She put the picture back where it was, then knocked it facedown. "If I can hate him, maybe it won't hurt so much." She turned those watery, tear-filled eyes to me and wrapped her arms around herself. "Help me hate him. Will you, please? Tell me my husband was a cheating pedophile. Maybe then I'll be able to live with this hell." She clapped her hands over her mouth, smothering the sobs. Shoulders shaking, she cried. She swore. She cried some more.

I had no words; I merely shook my head. When she stopped crying, I asked, "Will you please allow us to search your home for clues? Sooner or later, you're going to want answers. Maybe not now, but later. I would like to give you those answers when you're ready."

She stared at me.

"Please."

"Fine. Go ahead. Dig through all our secrets." Her hands curled, cupping her upper arms. "What the hell? Everyone knows my husband was a psycho, anyway. Right?" She stomped away, shutting herself in a bathroom.

I returned to JT, who'd been watching from a safe distance. "She didn't give me any names, but she did give us the go-ahead to search the house."

"Good. Excellent work, Skye." JT waved at Forrester; and when he had his attention, he gave him a thumbs-up sign. A few minutes later, a team flooded the house.

"Now what?" I asked.

"I say we step aside and let the BPD do their job here. I'd like to head over to the school and see if there's anything interesting in his classroom."

"You really think he was careless enough to leave something in his desk drawer?"

"I've heard of weirder things happening."

JT gave Forrester a departing wave, saying, "Call us when you have something."

Walking together, we headed out to my car. We were at the school within minutes, checking in with the principal. We were told Hollerbach's classroom was empty—they hadn't had enough advance notice to call in a substitute, so the students in his class had been combined with another. We were free to search his things, and we were the first to have the chance.

JT led the way back to the classroom. Once we were shut in, he rubbed his hands together. "If you were a teacher, having illicit affairs with your students, where would you hide the evidence?"

"Nowhere. I wouldn't have an affair with my students," I said, squelching a shiver of disgust.

"Yes, of course, you wouldn't. But our job is to think like a criminal. So that's what we need to do."

"Fine." I glanced around the room. "It wouldn't be somewhere any students might stumble upon it. Or administrators. Or the janitor. Which leaves . . . nowhere. We're wasting our time here."

"Hmm." JT was standing next to the door, visually searching the room. His gaze snapped to the storage cabinet standing against the wall, behind Hollerbach's desk. He tried it. "Locked."

"Someone must have a key." At Hollerbach's desk, I tried a drawer. The top two opened. Not the third, the largest at the bottom. "This drawer's also locked."

JT headed for the exit. "I'll check with the office, see if they have copies."

"I'll keep looking." Pulling Hollerbach's chair back, I sat in his seat and stared out across the expanse of empty desks. There was a time when I'd considered teaching. I'd decided it wasn't for me years ago, after tutoring a nice but not very bright student named Patty Eccles. But, with the rising doubt in my suitability for the FBI, I might reconsider. Teaching might have its moments. Then again, recalling that situation with Derik Sutton, I thought maybe not.

Using care not to disturb Hollerbach's belongings too much, I rummaged through the top drawer. Not much there: some pens, pencils, whiteboard dry-erase markers, chalk, scientific calculator, lots of pads of unused sticky notes.

Again, feeling as though we were wasting time, I searched the second drawer too. All I found were teacher things . . . and a stash of protein bars and Doritos.

JT returned just as I was wrapping up my search. "It seems Hollerbach's keys have gone missing. The janitor's on his way down to see if he can break into the cabinet."

"Interesting."

JT and I kept ourselves busy until the custodian came in; he was armed with a screwdriver. He pried. He cussed a little. And then he shook his head. "I can't damage it."

I checked the hinges. They were hidden. No way to pop them off and get in that way. "I guess we're out of luck."

JT called Forrester and told him we were on the hunt for a set of keys. He "uh-huhed" a few times, then clicked off. "Forrester has some keys for us to try. Let's run over and grab them."

"I could stay here and keep working."

"No."

"It'll only take a few minutes. I can lock the classroom door."

He stared at me and sighed.

"I can get a lot finished while you're gone. Look, I can search through those papers." I pointed at the mountain on the shelf under the window.

He sighed again. "But what if—"

"I'll be fine. I can lock the door. Nobody but Principal Glover knows I'm here."

"Okay. But don't leave this room. Not for anything."

I raised my hand, as if swearing in. "You have my word."

After locking the door behind JT, I pulled a chair up to the shelf under the window, and started flipping through the stack of graded student papers. A few minutes passed, and a doorknob rattled. Assuming it was JT, I glanced up.

Derik Sutton.

How did he get in here?

"I thought I saw you," he said, a slow smile spreading over his face. "Couldn't stay away from me, could you?"

"I'm here on official business, and you need to leave."

His eyes sharpened. "What official business?"

"You need to go now." I slid my hand into my purse, fishing for my phone. That was it, I needed to buy a clip-on phone holder, something to keep it closer at hand. Today.

He took a few steps closer. "You look scared."

"I'm not scared."

"Are you sure?" He stepped closer still.

"How did you get in here? The door's locked."

He thumbed over his shoulder, at the door I hadn't noticed before now. "This one wasn't locked."

I didn't move away. I didn't want to appear weak or afraid. Derik Sutton was a bully. I knew from personal experience that any show of fear would only spur him on more. Instead, I jerked up my chin and glared at him. "Back off, or I'll humiliate you again."

He snorted, then placed a flattened hand on the window behind my head and angled in real close. "That was a lucky shot. I underestimated you. Won't happen again."

The unlocked door swung open.

I breathed a sigh of relief.

Derik backed up slightly, allowing me to see it was JT, who had opened the door.

"What's going on here?" JT asked.

"Nothing." Derik turned, but not before sending me a warning glare. "I'm a friend of Sloan's. Just getting reacquainted."

"Reacquainted" was a slight misrepresentation.

JT grunted, then jerked his head toward the door. "You need to leave."

The kid left.

JT locked the door; then he turned to me. "Why were you just sitting there, letting that punk intimidate you? And how the hell did he get in here?"

"First, I wasn't just letting him do anything. I was waiting for the right moment to make my move. And second, as you may recall, I was disciplined for doing something about it the last time he did that."

"That's the kid?"

"Yes, that's the kid. And third, I locked that door. I didn't notice the other one."

JT's eyes narrowed. "I'll talk to the chief." He stuffed his hand into his pants and pulled out a ring with four keys. He shook them. "Now let's see what secrets Carl Hollerbach kept in his drawers." Standing in front of the storage cabinet, he tried a key, a second, a third. "Damn it, I thought we had the right ring. Turns out Hollerbach had one hell of a collection of keys." He pushed the last one into the lock and turned it. "Yes." He pulled the door open, revealing shelves loaded with paper, books, stacks of ungraded student papers, and tests.

JT and I both sighed. In unison.

"If you were expecting the smoking gun here, like kiddie porn or letters to young, impressionable women, it's not jumping out at me," I said as I started pulling stacks of papers off one of the shelves.

"If there is a smoking gun in here, it probably isn't going to be front and center. It'll be hidden way in the back. How about you step aside and let me clear that top shelf first?"

"Sure, be my guest." I moved out of the way, keeping busy by flipping through a set of tests. "Ah, stoichiometry, one of my favorite topics."

"Definitely not one of mine." JT placed his loot on Hollerbach's desk in a teetering pile. "This will keep me busy for a while, if you'd like to search the lower shelves."

"Sure."

I pulled out boxes of classroom supplies, lots of papers, but found nothing interesting. After an hour, I was convinced the smoking gun was not in that cabinet. I put everything back where I'd found it. As I was loading up a stack of graded tests, JT stood up suddenly. His shoulder slammed into my elbow. The papers sailed through the air.

"Oh. Sorry." JT stooped down to help me gather them back into a tidy pile.

"Not a problem." One test caught my eye. The name on it—Derik Sutton. His handwriting looked eerily familiar. "Look, here's my good friend Derik's test. Would it be petty of me to see how he did?"

"It would."

The glaring, red-colored A surprised me. "I guess he's a better student than I thought. Look at that." I waved the test at JT. "Almost a perfect score. Huh." I slapped it on the top of the pile and shoved the whole thing back into the cabinet. "Okay, so we found absolutely nothing in there. I'm guessing the desk will be clean too."

"I can't leave without checking." JT tried one of the keys. "Bingo." He gave it a sharp turn and pulled. The drawer slid open.

It was empty.

"No smoking gun?" I asked.

"Nope."

The irrationality of a thing is not an argument of its existence, rather a condition of it.

—Friedrich Nietzsche

28

"I didn't expect this. It's empty?" JT fingered the steel drawer bottom. "Damn it."

I bit back an I-told-you-so and asked, "Have you heard anything from Forrester?"

"They hadn't found anything yet when I went over there to get the keys. I'll call him when we're through here." JT pulled the drawer back farther. He was looking for something hidden in the back, I suppose.

"It's empty." I stated the obvious. "Let's go."

"Why would he lock an empty drawer?"

"Maybe out of habit? I don't know."

JT fiddled with the drawer's back and bottom a few seconds more before grunting, sliding it closed, and fisting the keys. "I guess we can give these back to Forrester. Hungry?"

My stomach rumbled. I hadn't grabbed anything before leaving the house this morning. I'd assumed I'd be getting something at the bagel shop. "Yes."

"Let's get an early lunch. Then we can check in with Forrester, see how they're doing at the Hollerbach house." On his way out of the classroom, he glanced over his shoulder. "Damn it, I thought we'd find something here."

"He was cautious. What he was doing would cost him his job, probably his marriage."

"Yes, but . . . I had a feeling we'd find something here."

"Sorry."

We headed to the office to let the school staff know we were leaving. As we were strolling toward the door, a low rumble of thunder echoed overhead.

"A thunderstorm."

We exchanged looks.

A tiny shudder swept up my spine. "This job is getting to me. I'm visualizing giant man-birds every time I hear thunder."

We stepped outside and stood under the overhang protecting the front doors.

JT said, "I can run out and get the car. Bring it up for you, if you want."

"No, that's okay. I'm not made of sugar. I won't melt."

A huge bolt of lightning sliced through the sky. An eardrum-shattering bang followed in less than a blink. I jerked backward at least five seconds too late.

That was definitely too close for comfort.

I stepped back another six inches or so. "On second thought, maybe we should wait for a few minutes. There's no sense risking a lightning strike."

JT's face paled. "Agreed."

We went back inside to wait out the storm. I sat on the bench just inside the doors. JT walked a few feet away, murmuring into his phone. A half hour later, a wicked storm had blown past. Knowing a stray bolt could come out of nowhere after a storm, I didn't walk to the car—I jogged. JT did too. I drove him back to the bagel shop. His car was right where he'd left it, no longer blocked in by fire and police vehicles. My phone rang as I was heading inside to grab a quick something to eat. JT was outside, talking to the chief.

My phone call was from Elmer—or rather, his phone.

"Hello, Sloan. This is Olivia. Elmer suggested I call you."

Isn't that something? The little rat fink was hiding behind his fiancée. "Thank you for calling, but I need to speak to him directly."

"Oh. He told me you'd be glad to hear from me. Something about if you returned the favor he paid you, maybe he might be compelled to return what you have so generously offered him. Those were his exact words."

I didn't offer him anything. He tricked me. "Humpf. Maybe?" I echoed. "What do you want?"

"I was hoping you could help me with the wedding plans. You know—go with me to try on dresses, pick china, plan the bachelorette party. That kind of thing."

"That's it? That's all you want?" Wedding planning was not my favorite thing in the world to do, especially not now. If anything, I wanted to avoid all thoughts about weddings. But if it got me back the memory he'd stolen, I had no problem volunteering. "Fine. I'll do it."

"Good. I would like to go shopping for dresses this afternoon."

"This afternoon?"

"How about . . . one o'clock? I'll meet you at your house." She hung up before I'd responded.

I glanced at the clock on my phone. It was noon. She didn't expect much. Evidently, the world revolved around Olivia.

Elmer deserved her.

I headed outside, carrying my lunch in a bag. JT waved me over.

"The chief called me in for a meeting. She wants you to stick with me."

Of course she did. "I have some personal business I need to take care of. Can I meet you later? In an hour or two? Or more?"

His jaw tightened. "Are you telling the truth? It's personal? You aren't going to kick anyone in the nuts or break into anyone's house?"

I lifted my hand. "I promise. I'm heading back to Alexandria. I won't be anywhere near Baltimore."

"Fine. I'll meet you at your folks' place later."

"Thanks."

He went west. I went north.

"Thank you so much for agreeing to help me. A little bird told me you're engaged too!" Olivia bounced like a preteen who'd just been told Taylor Lautner was on his way over to watch a private screening of *Twilight* with her. "Oh, my God! I'm so happy for you! When are you getting married?" Her gaze flicked to my left hand. Her brows scrunched. "Where is your ring?"

"It's . . . erm, getting sized."

"Ah. Say, here's an idea, why don't we get married together? Wouldn't that be a riot?"

Not.

It was a little after one o'clock and we were on our way to Annie's Bridal Boutique, located in Alexandria. I hated to burst Olivia's sparkly bubble, but there was no way I was going to agree to a double wedding. Not on the next full moon. Not on the one after that. Not in a year. "Since we haven't set a date yet, that probably won't work. But thanks for the offer. That was very sweet of you."

"But if you haven't set the date, what's stopping you from getting married with us? Don't feel you have to decline to be polite. It's really okay. I don't mind sharing the spotlight with another bride."

So much for me trying to let her down easy. "I'm not being polite. *Honest.* We're not ready to start making plans yet. We have other issues to tackle first."

"Issues?"

Really, how could I expect a woman who had met her undead husband-to-be on a reality dating show to understand where I was coming from? Not to be rude, but she couldn't possibly relate. Clearly, she was far more adventurous than I was.

"Yes, family stuff."

Her eyes widened with comprehension. "Ah. Yes. It can be tough if the families don't get along."

"That it can." Desperate to steer the conversation away from my upcoming nuptials and toward a safer topic, I asked, "How does your family feel about your appearance on the reality show?"

"They were one hundred percent behind me. They just love Elmer." She gave me a happy, sparkly-eyed look and sighed. I had to say, her bubbly, happy act made me feel better about dumping Elmer. I'd known from the get-go that he wasn't for me, and I had worried he wouldn't find a woman who would be over-the-moon crazy for him. How wrong I'd been. This girl practically had a spasm every time she spoke his name.

"That's wonderful." We parked in the lot outside the boutique. "You know, isn't this whole trying-on-dresses thing usually reserved for the bride and her mother?"

"I suppose so, but Mom couldn't make it. You don't mind doing this with me, do you?"

"No, of course not."

"Maybe you'd like to try on a dress or two also?" she threw over her shoulder as she galloped into the store.

"No, I think I'll hold off until we have a date set."

We stepped inside, and I nearly went blind: bridal-gown blindness. Too much white. I went mute.

Olivia had quite another reaction. "Oh, my God, just look at all these dresses! How could you resist?"

I mumbled, "It'll be tough, but I think I'll manage."

"I can't." She heaved a happy sigh. "I'm going to have to try on every dress in this store."

"Every one?" I almost whimpered. "Don't you think you should narrow it down a little?"

"Absolutely not! You never know. A dress that looks like crap on a hanger could end up looking absolutely delish on. I can't risk missing the perfect dress."

A woman who looked very familiar glided up to us, saleslady game face on. She beamed at Olivia, who was "oohing" and "aahing" at the selection, before she flicked a glance at me. Her brows sank and that game face dimmed. "How may I help you ladies?"

She recognized me.

A little over two weeks ago, my mother had come here to shop for gowns when she was remarrying my father. As it turned out, Mom had a reaction to something, swelled up like a puffer fish, and ruined a designer wedding gown. As a result, our friendly saleslady passed out, and I had to drive both her and Mom to the emergency room for treatment. "Miss Saleslady" ended up with a concussion from slamming her head on the ground when she collapsed. But she was released within a few hours. After getting an injection of Benadryl, Mom deflated and was as good as new.

But the dress, the poor dress—a lovely hand-beaded Mizelle worth a small fortune—didn't make it.

I pointed at Olivia, who was already pulling gowns off the racks. "My friend is getting married."

"It seems you know a lot of people getting married," Miss Saleslady said.

"It does."

The woman gave me a look, which I interpreted as a warning. "Very well." She stepped up to Olivia and started the drill she'd gone through with Mom, asking her questions about her "dream" wedding gown.

Meanwhile, I found a comfy place to sit, pulled out my phone, and started poking around on the Internet, looking for more information on the *impundulu*. My overall opinion of cell phone Web service has always been low. It became even lower after I'd been enduring the torturously slow loading of Web pages and a parade of one perfectly nice wedding gown after another for over three hours. Finally I heard the words I'd been longing to hear since we stepped foot in the store.

"That's it. I'm done."

The angels were singing.

Olivia was back in her street clothes. Her hair was mussed. And she looked as beat as I felt.

"Which one did you pick?" I asked.

"The one you told me to."

I didn't recall choosing one. "Ah. Excellent." I dropped my phone into my purse. "Ready?"

"I'm beat and hungry. Want to get something to eat?"

I hadn't eaten since lunch. "Sure."

We both climbed into the "Mom-mobile." I buckled up and shoved the key into the ignition. Twisted. "Where to?"

Click. Clickclickclick.

I knew that sound. It was the unmistakable sound of a dead battery. "Well, damn." Knowing it wouldn't work, but figuring I'd lose nothing by trying, I turned the key again.

Clickclickclick.

"What's wrong?" Olivia asked. Everyone knew what that sound meant. Obviously, Olivia knew nothing about cars. And she'd said she was an electrical engineer?

Red flag. There was no way she was an electrical engineer.

"We need a jump start. The battery's dead."

"Oh. How do we do that?" she asked.

Elmer, my friend, you have no idea what you're getting yourself into.

"We call the auto club and they send a truck. And then we get food in the drive-through, so we don't have to get it jump-started a second time, and then drive to the closest mechanic."

Olivia wrinkled her nose. "That sounds very complicated. Can't we just call someone to come pick us up and have the car towed?"

"No."

That wrinkle across the bridge of her nose got deeper.

"I mean, you can do that. Me, I can't." I tried not to focus on the fact that she had expected me to sit for hours in a stupid bridal shop and wait for her to try on every dress they had in stock, and all without complaining. Yet, she couldn't be bothered to sit for a half hour and wait for the auto club to send out a truck to start my car? Really?

I was beginning to have some serious doubts about the future Mrs. Schmickle. She wasn't only a diva, but a lying diva to boot.

"I think I'll call for a cab. I'm much too hungry to wait, and I do not eat anything that is served through a window. Period."

"Ah, is that a new diet plan?"

"You could say that." She dug in her purse, which I just noticed had a Gucci logo on the buckle, pulled out a cell phone—which was more bling than phone—and poked at the buttons with her manicured fingernail. I, on the other hand, extricated my well-used phone from my clearance-sale faux leather handbag with the paperclip-repaired strap and called the auto club to request a jump start. Her call ended before mine did. When I clicked off, she shoved open the door.

"My ride will be here any minute."

The distant rumble of thunder echoed off the brick store.

I shoved open my door—couldn't open the power windows with no power. After taking an assessment of my lightning-strike risk, I poked my head out (as little as possible). "We're about to get a storm. You may want to wait inside."

"I'll be fine. How often do people get struck by lightning?" She tossed a dismissive hand.

Another jagged bolt lit up the sky. I flinched. "About six hundred times a year."

"What?"

"People get injured by lightning approximately six hundred times a year. That's in the U.S. Worldwide, the figure is much higher, over two hundred thousand people are injured every year. About ten percent die. The odds of your being struck by lightning in your lifetime are roughly one in ten thousand." *And significantly higher, with an* impundulu *running amok in the area.*

Her jaw dropped. "What are you? A walking encyclopedia?" I'd heard that question once or twice in my lifetime.

Another flash zigged down from a nearby cloud. The heated air produced a loud *craaack,* which made me wince and my ears ring. "Please get back inside the car."

Olivia glared at me.

"Please."

"Fine." She *click-clacked* back to the car and opened the door.

And I was blinded as a brilliant light suddenly exploded next to us. When I realized what had happened, I unclicked my seat belt and crawled over the car seat to look down.

Olivia was lying on the ground. Still. Too still.

"Damn it!" Hanging half out of the car, I dragged the upper part of her body inside and checked her pulse. Nothing. "*No, no, no, no!* You can't die." On my knees, bent over the center console and her head, I tried to perform chest compressions. I had no idea if it was working, thanks to my position, but I couldn't risk going outside. It seemed we were being showered with lightning strikes, brilliant blue bolts zinging down around Mom's car. I'd never seen anything like it. I knew it wasn't natural.

My hands shaking from the adrenaline charging through my body, I checked again for a pulse. I felt something, a weak beat beneath my fingertip. I grabbed my phone and dialed 911; then I concentrated on getting Olivia's legs into the car and her door closed to protect her. The bolts increased, becoming thicker, brighter. Blinding. Faster. More and more of them, until it was like the car was being walled in by electricity.

Squinting, I tried to start the car. No luck. I was sweating and the inside of the car was heating. Would we bake to death?

"Where are you?" I screamed above the nearly constant booming thunder. "What do you want?"

A dark shadow appeared in the blue-white wall. It grew larger, larger. A bird. The man-bird. At least six feet tall with feathers that were inky black and a wingspan of no less than fourteen feet. Its beak was hooked, like a raptor's. And its eyes were small and sharp. It opened its beak and a shrill shriek—so loud that it hurt—cut through the car. I clapped my hands over my ears.

"You're being made to do this!" I yelled. "But you don't have to. You have a choice!"

It turned its head, one eye staring at me.

"I can help you."

Its feathers rippled, as if a wind gust was blowing up from the ground. Within seconds, they were gone, and I was staring at Damen. My fiancé.

I couldn't speak for at least a minute. It might've been longer. An hour. "It's you? You're the *impundulu*?"

He said nothing. He lifted his hand and the wall of blue-white light instantly vanished. The air went still. Everything went silent, except the ringing in my ears.

My eyes were watering, and my nose burning. I thumbed away a tear. "Why? Why did you kill those innocent girls?" Suddenly cold, I wrapped my arms around myself. I couldn't believe this. Damen? It was Damen?

"I had no choice," he said, looking regretful.

"Why?"

"She's forcing me to."

She? "Who?"

"I can't say her name. Can't speak it. Just as I can't refuse her."

"Then I have to stop her."

"Stop her, Sloan. For me. Please." He rounded the front of the car, stopping next to Olivia's feet. He stooped down and put his eyes level with mine. "I think you might be her next target. Once she gives the command, I won't be able to refuse her."

He extended a hand. "I'm sorry about your friend. Once I release the current, I can't control it. And this one was too close to the car. Forgive me."

Another flash.

He was gone.

"Ooohhh," Olivia moaned. "What happened?"

I opened my mouth. Nothing came out. Two police cars bounced to a stop in front of the car. A fire truck and an EMS vehicle were right behind them. Within minutes, Olivia was being checked out by medical, and I was relating to the police officers a highly edited version of what had happened.

Inside, my heart was shattered. The man I'd just promised to marry was our unsub. Make that *one* of our unsubs. Could I believe what he'd said? Was he really under the unsub's complete control? And if he couldn't tell me her name, how would I find out who she was before she gave the command?

Whoever undertakes to set himself up as judge in the field of Truth and Knowledge is shipwrecked by the laughter of the gods.

—Albert Einstein

29

I now knew the identity of one of our unsubs. And I was under obligation to report it to the chief. But I wasn't sure I could do it. Damen—my Damen—had killed innocent teen girls. Not because it was his choice, but because he had been commanded to do it. What did that make him?

Guilty?

Not guilty?

A cold-blooded murderer?

Or a victim?

I needed to talk to someone who wasn't directly involved. Someone objective who could see this situation from my point of view . . . or at least a more neutral point of view. Someone who wasn't in the FBI or BPD.

Of course, that was prohibited. We weren't permitted to discuss a case with anyone outside of the bureau. But I needed some help sorting this whole thing out. I needed to understand the legal ramifications of Damen's actions. I needed to have some idea of what would happen, once his identity was known to the authorities—which was inevitable.

Sitting in the waiting area at a mechanic's shop, the buzz of hydraulic wrenches humming from the garage, I stared at my phone, browsing through my contacts. Who could I talk to? Katie? Mom? Dad? Someone else?

No one. Damn it. I couldn't call anyone.

But I did need to call my father. I needed to meet with the queen. It was time for a heart-to-heart with the woman who was supposed to be my future mother-in-law. But I wasn't going to tell my dad about Damen. I couldn't.

He answered on the third ring. "Sloan?"

"Dad, I need your help." I swallowed a sob.

Damn it, I am not *going to cry. Not now. Not here in this ugly, old mechanic's shop.*

"What's wrong?"

"A lot." I swiveled in my chair, facing the dingy corner as much as I could. "But I can't go into it."

Or could I?

Before marrying Mom for the second time, Dad had been the queen's head of security. He knew the queen's family. He knew Damen well.

Could I trust him?

"Dad, you know Damen. But did you know *what* he is?"

"What?" my father echoed. "As in, an elf?"

"No, *what* as in *impundulu*." Feeling the shivers coming on, I wrapped my free arm around myself. This case was hell. And I wasn't sure I could deal with it.

"Oh. That." He knew.

"You knew? Damn it."

"Yes, but I'd taken a vow of silence. I couldn't tell you."

"Well, his secret is a secret no more. I know. And soon the FBI and the entire Baltimore Police Department are going to know too. Dad, how many people has he killed?"

"None that I'm aware of. That was why I had no qualms about keeping it secret."

"That's changed recently." The doorbell chimed, signaling the arrival of someone. I glanced over my shoulder, saw it was a woman, and turned back around. I lowered my voice. "He's killed three teenage girls, and I believe he nearly killed at least one more."

"Oh, damn. Someone found out. They've performed a linking spell."

"They have. Is it true that he can't refuse a command once it's given?"

"That's true. One of my primary responsibilities was to protect him so that no one found out. Their power is absolute."

"I need to find out who is controlling him. Is there any way to do that?"

"I don't know. He can't tell you who he or she is."

"That I know. Can he write his or her name? Sign it? Give it to me in Morse code?"

"No. He isn't able to use any form of communication to reveal her identity."

"Damn it. Dad, do you know what this means for him? If he's powerless to resist a command from someone else, is he legally culpable?"

My father didn't answer right away. "His attorney will no doubt enter a defense of automatism, alleging that he had lack of control over his actions. Therefore, he cannot be held responsible."

"Will it work?"

"It *might.*"

Or it might not.

My gut twisted, and I realized suddenly that I genuinely cared for Damen. I didn't want to see him spending the rest of his life incarcerated for a crime he was unable to stop himself from committing. But I was also concerned for his future. If he fell under the control of someone else, what other heinous crimes might he be compelled to carry out? How horrible, to live under the constant worry of someone discovering your vulnerability and using it against your will.

"Sloan, if you're thinking you can save him somehow—"

"I need to help him." My eyes were burning again, damn it. I dragged the back of my hand across them. "How? What do I do?" There was no thinking. I had to save him.

"There's only one way, but it's dangerous. He's dangerous. And with every kill, he becomes more deadly. You have to take control over him."

"Okay."

"To do that, you'll need to kill the person who's controlling him now."

"Kill?" My voice cracked. I hadn't killed anyone before. I haven't even killed an animal. How could I drum up the courage to end someone's life? My insides did a flip-flop. "Isn't there another way?"

"No. Once a linking spell has been completed between the *impundulu* and its master, it can only be broken by the master, or by death . . . of either of them. Though, if the *impundulu* dies, its master dies too."

I imagined myself face-to-face with a young teenage girl; I held a gun in my hand, pointed at her. "I can't do it. I can't kill anyone."

"Then I'm afraid there will be no stopping him or her. Or Damen. There's something else, Sloan."

I was sure I didn't want to know. "What?"

"Like I said, with each kill, Damen becomes more dangerous. He loses more of himself, his soul. If you don't stop him, he'll eventually become a killer with no remorse, no regret. He'll have no capacity to love, to care about another person."

"The good news just keeps coming." A sob-sigh slipped from my mouth. "In other words, it's either his master's life or his?"

"His life or all the victims his master has set his or her sights upon."

"I understand. Thanks." My finger hovered over the red button. I wanted to end the call, but I blurted out, "Dad?"

"Yes?"

"One more favor. Can you arrange for me to meet with the queen? I'm hoping she might have an idea of who's done this."

"Let me see what I can do."

"Thanks."

After I clicked off, I dropped my phone into my purse, bent over, folded my arms on my knees, and cried.

By the time my car was done—which didn't take long—my tears had dried up and I was somewhat ready to face the next step. Once I was in my car, I dialed my father first, to see if he'd had any luck with the elf queen. Somehow I needed to figure out who Damen's puppet master was. And after that? Well, I was hoping I'd find a way to get around the whole must-kill-one-of-them thing.

Dad answered on the fourth ring. I admit, I was getting nervous by the second ring. "Hi, Sloan. I have good news. The queen has agreed to meet with you tonight."

"Good. Where do I go?"

"She'll be sending a car for you. Go back to the house and wait for it there."

"Okay. Thanks, Dad. I owe you." I paid for my new battery.

"Don't worry about it, Sloan. That's what fathers are for." After a beat, he added, "I wasn't there for you for all those years. I figure I have a lot of making up to do."

I entered Mom's car, shoved the key into the ignition, and turned. The engine started. My next call was to JT. Of all the members of the PBAU, he was the one I trusted most.

"Sloan, I heard about the attack." He sounded worried. "Are you okay?"

"I'm sort of okay," I said as I turned out of the parking lot, heading toward Mom and Dad's place. "I learned who the first unsub is—the one who's been doing all the killing."

"Good! Who is it? One of the students at the high school?"

"No, it's Damen Sylver."

"I recognize that name. Wait, isn't he the one who—"

"Yes. He's the one. It's worse." I dug my ring out of my purse and slid it onto my finger. "He . . . asked me to marry him. I accepted." My insides knotted. "We're engaged."

"Shit. Sloan, we need to take this to the chief right away. You should be pulled from the case. There's no way you can be objective, and you need to be protected. What if he finds out—"

"He already knows that I know. He told me. I don't believe he wants to hurt me. Please, JT, don't tell her to pull me. I agree, I can't be completely objective, but I want to work this case. Damen is under the control of someone else. He can't stop what he's doing."

"If that's the case, he'll have his day in court to explain it."

"If we're going to stop him, we have to find out who is pulling his strings. I have connections nobody else at the PBAU has. You need me to get to the unsub." I glanced over my shoulder, easing onto the freeway.

"Sloan."

"JT."

"I'm calling the chief. I'll explain everything and see what she says. Where are you now?"

"On my way home."

"Good. Once you get there, stay away from all electrical appliances. And don't go anywhere until you hear back from me. We have to handle this situation with care. We can't risk losing the case in court."

"You see, that's the thing. I'm waiting for someone to pick me up. I've set up a meeting with someone who is key in the case."

"Damn it, Sloan."

I jerked the wheel, and the car lurched off onto the shoulder. My hands were shaking so badly, I could hardly shift the vehicle into park. I hit the hazard lights. "If I have to quit the PBAU right now, I will. JT, we're not talking about some stranger who's running around slaughtering people unmercifully, we're talking about a man who is being forced to kill against his will. He's suffering. He's in danger. He needs my help."

"Let me get in touch with the chief. I'll call you back in a few."

"Fine. Bye." I clicked off, shifted back into drive, and hit the gas. My car was pointed toward Mom and Dad's place. I didn't care if the chief sent over a SWAT team; I was going to help Damen—no matter what.

I noticed the first car tailing me when I was a couple of miles from my parents' house. A second one joined the parade, a half mile down. And then a third shortly after that. By the time I pulled up in Mom and Dad's driveway, I was leading a fairly sizeable caravan. All the miscellaneous cars parked up and down the street—their drivers were all watching and waiting for me to make my move.

Or waiting to shoot down Damen, if he risked showing up at my house.

I thought about calling him, then second-guessed myself. Was my cell phone being monitored? Might I lead the BPD right to his front door? I couldn't risk it. Instead, I texted him three words: Danger. Stay away.

When I scurried inside, Katie caught me practically the moment I shut the door behind me.

"What's going on, Sloan? We've had two police officers watching the house for the last twenty minutes." She parted the curtains, peering outside.

"There's more than two out there now."

"Why?"

"Damen is the one who killed those girls."

"Your Damen?"

"Yes."

She smacked her hands over her mouth. "Oh, my God! Sloan!"

"He isn't doing it because he wants to. He's being controlled by someone else. It's very complicated."

Katie's eyes widened to at least twice their normal size. "Oh, my God. What are you going to do?"

"I don't know. Somehow I need to find out who is doing the controlling, so I can stop her."

"Can I help?"

"I don't know." I sank into a nearby chair and concentrated. It wasn't easy. I was slipping into panic mode. My synapses didn't fire when I was in panic mode. "I need to think. How am I going to find out who she is?"

Katie peered outside again. She flopped her hands. "Sloan, there's a mobile police station parked outside."

"Are you kidding me?" I peeked out. "Shit! The queen is sending a car over to pick me up so I can talk to her. That isn't going to happen if the crew out there throws us all to the ground, slaps cuffs on us, and drags us in for questioning."

"Maybe you should sneak out now."

"And go where?"

"I don't know."

"Can you call her? Arrange for her car to pick you up somewhere else?"

"I don't have her number. My father arranged the meeting." I was already pulling out my phone.

"Call him."

"On it." I dialed. The phone rang once, twice, three times, four, five, six, seven times, eight. "He's not answering."

"Call Damen."

"I'm afraid to. What if they can trace the call somehow?"

At the window, Katie pulled the curtains aside to peek out again. "Sloan, some guys in black are surrounding the house. They have guns."

"This is crazy! I'm unarmed. So are you."

My phone rang. It was JT.

I glared at it, then poked the button. "The chief called in a SWAT team. I'm surrounded by armed officers!" I yelled.

"I'm sorry, Sloan. She had no choice. It's protocol."

"He's not here, JT. It's just me and Katie."

"They're not going to shoot you," JT said. I supposed that was meant to be reassuring. It wasn't. "They're there to protect you."

"Right. I feel so protected, with the serious end of all those guns pointed *at* me."

"Chief Peyton's on the way. She'll take care of it when she gets there."

"I hope so. I'm wishing I had a bomb shelter right about now."

"Hang in there, Skye."

"Okay, bye." I clicked off, then dragged Katie away from the window. No sense taking any unnecessary risks. In fact, we opted to pay a visit to Mom's media room downstairs, where we'd be less likely to be struck by stray bullets. Of course, we stayed away from the electronics too.

After a moment's hesitation, I dialed Damen's number. He answered right away.

"Hi, Sloan. I received your message," Damen said. "What's happening? Are you okay?"

"I'm fine. It's not me who's in trouble. It's you." A tear dribbled down my cheek. I wiped it with the back of my hand. "They know, Damen. I had to tell them." I sniffled.

"It's okay, Sloan. When I warned you, I expected this. What's going on?"

"There's a SWAT team outside, the entire FBI, as well as the Baltimore and Alexandria Police Departments. They've set up a mobile police station in front of my parents' house."

"Sloan, I'm so sorry I dumped all of this on you." His sigh was audible. "I need to see you."

"You can't come over."

"I'll be there in a second. Don't worry. They won't see me."

Simultaneously an electric *crackle* sounded in my phone and a house-rattling *boom* of thunder followed in my backyard. I heard the humming of electricity buzzing all around me.

Katie practically crawled on top of me. "What the hell?"

"Sloan, where are you?" It was Damen. He was in the house. Already.

"Down in the basement!" I yelled.

The steady *thump, thump, thump* of his footfalls signaled his descent.

Katie's hold on me tightened. "I don't like this. What if his owner has ordered him to kill us?"

"I'm guessing he would have warned me if she had."

He stopped at the foot of the stairs. It was the same Damen I'd known since my parents' wedding. Same hair. Same mesmerizing eyes. Same model-perfect body.

"I'm sorry, baby. I told you because I wanted to warn you. I didn't want this." He waved an arm toward the staircase.

"Neither did I. But I had to tell someone. Unfortunately that started a cascade of dominos." Dragging Katie along— she was wrapped around me like an overly affectionate python—I stepped closer. As I came nearer, I noticed the little blue arcs of electricity sizzling from him. I'd never seen those before. As much as I wanted to touch him, to be held in his arms, I wasn't about to risk it.

"It's safe," he said, seeming, once again, to be reading my mind. "She hasn't ordered your execution. But I have a feeling that's just because I've been avoiding her. If she learns how to issue the command without speaking directly to me, I'm in trouble."

"Can she do that?"

"She can. And she is aware of it. She just doesn't know how to. Yet."

"I'm scared."

"I'm scared for you. If she forces me to . . ." His jaw clenched. His eyes darkened. "I think it may destroy me. Already, what she's done has poisoned me. I've been fighting against the darkness. If she uses me again, especially against someone I care about, I don't think I'll be able to hold off anymore."

Damn it, I felt so helpless, and yet so desperate to do something, even if it was almost guaranteed to fail. "Tell me what to do."

"You must stop her."

"But you can't tell me who she is."

"No."

"Can you lead me to her?"

He considered my suggestion. "Perhaps, if I didn't know you were following."

"Understood." I was already formulating a plan. "Wait, you didn't drive over here. How would this work?"

"That's the least of your problems," Katie said. "There's an army out there. You're not going anywhere if they have anything to say about it."

"Hmm," I said.

"Hmm," Damen said. "It's not going to work. I'll know you're following. Your best bet is getting to my mother. She'll know what to do."

"Fine. That's what I'll do then."

"There's just one problem. You can't be followed. The car won't be able to pull onto the property if it's being tailed."

"Okay, so I not only need to get out of the house without being detained, but I also need to make sure we're not being tailed. Hmmm. We need someone to stand in for me," I said. "She needs to be quick. Smart. Lead the police on a wild-goose chase. Someone who is young and female. . . ."

We both looked at Katie.

Katie's eyes nearly bugged out of her head. "Are you

kidding me? You want me to lead around a pack of armed policemen?"

Hearing it said aloud, I couldn't help scowling. "Truthfully, I don't like this plan either. You're right. It's too dangerous. Plan B. What is Plan B? Maybe I can lead the pack and you—"

"No, I'll do it. I think I can handle it." Katie visibly gulped.

"I can help her," Damen offered. "Protect her. And I can tweak her appearance a bit, too. To make her look more like you."

When this case was over, I was going to owe Katie bigtime. "Thank you. You have no idea how much I appreciate this." I hugged her. She hugged me back. "But no, I'm not going to let you risk your life for me." To Damen I said, "Can you get her out of here?"

"Sloan!" Katie yelled. "I said I'd do it."

"No, you won't. But . . . you aren't safe here, either. Once they realize I'm gone . . . and if Damen . . . no, I want you to go somewhere safe and I don't want you to leave until I call you. Now, I have a question for Damen." I turned to him. "You say you can protect Katie from the police, but is she safe from you?"

"Sure. I wouldn't hurt anyone, if it were up to me. My mistress must give the command, and she must name the target, by their full name. She won't know Katie's name."

"Okay. So now all we have to do is figure out how you two will leave the house without attracting the attention of all of those armed guys out there."

"Not a problem," Damen said, looking completely confident. Of course he was confident. The man could turn into a bolt of electricity. Katie couldn't.

"That's fine and dandy, you can leave. But what about Katie?"

"That won't be a problem," Damen said. "I'll help her get out of the house. Then I can call for one of Mum's cars. We

an arrange to meet the car close by. I'll make sure she's
safe, Sloan." He placed a call, then told Katie where the car
would be parked. "Katie, you may not see me, but I'll be
with you every step of the way."

"O-okay." Katie was petrified. And I was petrified for
her. And for Damen, too. I hoped this was worth it, and his
mother would know what to do.

It seemed we'd thought our way over most of the hurdles.
"Okay, if that's settled, we just need a second limo for me."

Damen stuffed his hand into his pocket, pulled out his
phone again, made a very brief call, hung up, and announced,
"You ask and you shall receive."

"Keep that up, and I will marry you before next summer,"
said jokingly as I headed toward the stairs. My progress
was suddenly impeded by one scrumptious *impundulu*. He
caught me around the waist and hauled me up against him.
With his cupped hand, he tilted my head back.

"I'm looking forward to making you keep that promise."
And then he smashed his lips on mine. I swear, currents of
electricity were zinging all through my body, as if I'd grabbed
hold of a live wire. I couldn't let go of him, couldn't back
away, couldn't break the kiss that was making my heartbeat
so irregular and my gray matter turn to mucilaginous mush.

His tongue shoved in my mouth, and I savored the taste
of man and need and sensual hunger. Our tongues did a little
naughty dance together, twining and stroking. By the time
he finally released me, I could barely stand and my brain had
completely shut down.

"Wow," I said, staggering backward.

He looked mighty pleased with himself as he helped steady
me. "That's just a hint of what's to come—after we're married,
of course."

If that was true, I wondered what reason I might have
for leaving our bedroom. I tried to shove aside the myriad
images that flashed through my head. It was time to focus.
My best friend was about to walk into an ambush of epic

proportions. And I was on my way to visit the queen again in the name of saving a man I'd come to care about. Surely fate would be on my side, and I'd succeed. After all, I was on the side of the just.

Right?

"Sloan, Mum's car will pick you up at the intersection. My powers are limited now, because of my mistress. I can cast a temporary spell on both of you, making you more difficult to see, but not completely transparent."

I half-walked/half-staggered upstairs, Damen behind me and Katie taking the rear.

"Whatever you can do to help, Damen. Thanks." I checked my phone. It was fully charged. I waved it at Katie. "Make sure you call me the minute you get somewhere safe. Don't do anything dangerous."

Katie scowled. "You know how I feel about dangerous." I did. Katie blew things up on a regular basis. She wasn't as fearful of danger as she liked to let on. "I'll be extremely careful."

"Please do. I hate that I've put you in harm's way. If only I could be in two places at once, I'd lead the police on a chase through town, giving you time to get away."

Katie shrugged as she checked her phone. "Sorry, Sloan, but evidently people can turn into electricity and zap from cloud to cloud, but they can't instantaneously clone themselves."

"Hmm," I said again. I recalled what the queen had said about me having some kind of magic power. I closed my eyes and concentrated, imagining a perfect duplicate of me standing next to me. I opened my eyes.

No deal.

Either I didn't have any special magic power, or it wasn't magical cloning. Either way, I was out of luck.

I grabbed Katie and gave her a big hug. "I'm sorry."

"Don't be. I'm not."

"I'm heading out," Damen announced, nuzzling my neck. "You remember where the car is?" he asked Katie.

"I remember." Katie rolled her eyes. "Just because I don't have a Ph.D. yet doesn't mean I can't remember where a car is parked. I'm this close to finishing my thesis." She pinched her thumb and index finger together. "Rather, I was that close before my research burned up."

"Don't worry, we'll be calling you 'Dr. Katie' in no time." I hugged her again. "By the way, I forget where I park all the time." We laughed. Hard. To near tears. I think it was the stress. We were both freaked out. We needed the outlet. After ten minutes of *haw-haw-hawing,* I felt better. I think Katie did too.

I tipped my head. I could hear movement outside.

"The first car is pulling into position," Damen said.

"All right. This is it. Here we go." I gave Katie's hand a squeeze, then hugged Damen.

"We're going to fix this," I told him.

He smoothed his hand down my hair. "Thank you, baby. And don't worry, Sloan. When the time comes, Gelf can shake any tail."

"Gelf?"

"Mum's driver. He'll be driving Katie's car."

"I'm not worried," I said, smashing my cheek against his broad chest. "I mean, I am scared. But—" He kissed me again. This time, the kiss was more gentle and sweet, a promise, a whisper. Still, when it ended, I was dizzy. "What was I saying?"

"You're leaving now." He cupped my cheek. "I'll see you soon, Sloan Skye." He snapped his fingers at me, and a buzzing charge hummed all around me, soaking into my skin. Again, he snapped his fingers, this time over my shoulder. "Hurry. The spell won't last long." And then he changed into a ball of blue-white, crackling energy that hovered in front of me before drifting toward an open window.

Behind me, I heard Katie say, "Whew, he sure does know how to make an exit."

I swiveled around. My breath caught. She looked like she was made of translucent mist. "He gets it from his mother. Let's hope that's the last dramatic exit he has to make for a long, long time."

There has to be evil so that good can prove its purity above it.

—Buddha

30

Katie and I exchanged final hugs and good-luck wishes. Then Katie gulped in one long, deep breath before opening the back door, leading out into the backyard. She looked in my direction, but seemed to be looking through me. "This is weird. I can barely see you. I hope this works out okay, Sloan. I'm scared for you."

"I'm scared too. For you. And for Damen."

We faced the French doors, peered through the glass. There was an army out there, guns pointed at the house. She inched open the door, wider, wider, until she could squeeze through. She put one foot out, the other. Then she broke into a sprint.

I watched her zigzag around potted plants and clusters of police officers. She circled the pool and ducked between the trees lining the back of the property. Finally, once she was completely out of sight, I stepped outside.

Instinctively, I lifted my hands, held my breath. Could they see me?

No one moved. No one spoke to me. I took a few hesitant steps, then a few more. Then, feeling fairly confident I was okay, I dashed across the backyard, toward the back fence. Over the fence I went. Down the street. I stopped.

The queen's car—my target—was surrounded. Its doors

were open, and the driver was standing with his hands on the trunk, in your typical subject-being-searched position.

One officer waved toward him, motioning him back into the vehicle. Good. All I had to do was get to him now. Almost there. Just a few dozen yards. I picked up the pace, adopting a race-walk. Then a jog.

Nobody told me to stop, lie down, or do anything, so I kept going, making as little noise as possible. As I made my way down the sidewalk, my gaze swept the area. There were police cars everywhere. Officers dotting the sidewalk, small groups huddled together. Clearly, they'd surrounded my parents' house on all sides. I was glad Katie had gotten out. I hoped she'd made it to the queen's car by now. I listened, trying to eavesdrop into the officers' conversations as I inched forward. As I approached the waiting limo, I had to pass a large group of officers. One of them glanced my way. My heart jerked. My skin burned.

He squinted.

I froze.

His gaze narrowed even more.

I felt panic setting in. *He can't see you*, I told myself.

The tingling got worse. Hotter. More intense.

Was the spell wearing off already?

"Stop right there!" the officer pulled his gun and pointed it at my chest.

I stopped.

Roughly ten years later, or so it felt, I was standing next to a police car, surrounded by policemen, answering the same questions over and over. The queen's limo was idling in front of Mom and Dad's next door neighbor's house, the driver also speaking to a small horde of police officers.

I was about to explain for the zillionth time that I didn't know where Damen was when an SUV pulled up, tires skidding on gravel. The chief practically bounded from the vehicle. I'd never been more relieved to see her.

"Sloan!" She wound through the wall of men circling me.

I motioned to the limo. "I'm trying to get some information on the unsub. It seems they don't want me doing that."

She waved me over. "Come here. We'll get this all worked out."

Trusting her, I scurried over. She grabbed my hand, tugging me toward the mobile police station. "I wish you'd called me first, Sloan. Getting Thomas involved has put me in a predicament."

"I'm sorry." Boy, was I ever.

Inside, we sat at a small table. The seats were swivel-style chairs, bolted to the floor.

She rested her elbows on the table between us; her fingers were steepled beneath her chin. "Now tell me what's going on?"

"I was out running errands with a friend, when I was surrounded by a wall of lightning, for lack of a better descriptive. The person responsible for the lightning revealed his identity to me out of concern for my safety. As it turned out, he's a close friend of mine."

"Thomas said he's your fiancé." She gave a pointed look at the rock on my finger.

"Um, yes. Technically, he is. We are engaged. But it's going to be a *lengthy* engagement."

"Okay. So until today, you had no idea your fiancé was our unsub?"

"No clue. Why would I even consider it? He has nothing to do with those girls. I don't know how he got tangled up in this, but he is. And the killings are not being committed willfully. He's being forced to commit them."

The chief looked skeptical. "Are you certain?"

Of course I was certain. I was willing to risk my own life, as well as my friend's, because I was so sure. "I have no reason to believe otherwise. He's one of us, an agent. Somehow the second unsub discovered his vulnerability and learned how to use it to her benefit. He can't tell me who she is, but he's trying a different strategy, leading my roommate,

Katie, to her. I have no idea if it'll work. In the meantime, I was going to pay his mother a visit and see if I can figure out how he is connected to unsub two."

"Okay." The chief pursed her lips. "That's everything you know, correct?"

"Yes. Chief, am I in trouble?"

The chief's gaze flicked to the window. "Let's just say you need to proceed with extreme caution, Sloan. Not only are your actions under a lot of scrutiny, but so are mine. We can't screw this up."

"I understand."

"Let me talk to some people. Don't move. Not a fingertip. I'll be back shortly."

"I'll wait right here."

And wait I did. I waited for eons. At least, that's how it felt. I watched black-clothed SWAT officers come in. I watched them go out.

Finally Chief Peyton returned. "All right. We have a plan."

I hoped it didn't involve shooting Damen upon sight. "I'm ready to go when you are."

"Protocol calls for you to be removed from the case immediately. But there's a bit of a problem with that. The car's driver has been in contact with the owner, and she has agreed to meet with me, *only* if you are present. So you're coming along. But you will not take any action whatsoever without my clearing it. You won't even breathe without permission. Got it?"

"Message received."

"Sloan, I warn you, this is serious. You're straddling a very fine line here. I don't want to see you ruin your life over one small misstep. Trust me. Do what I say."

"Okay."

We left the SWAT mobile together and boarded the limo. I watched the congregation around my house disperse as we rolled down the street, past landmarks that had become familiar to me. Behind us, a small caravan of unmarked police cars followed.

The chief, sitting across from me, looked a little uncomfortable in the limo. "I understand your father set up this meeting. But when we arrive, I need you to let me do the talking. You're a fly on the wall. Got it?"

"Sure." I thumbed over my shoulder. "You might want to call off the troops. We won't be able to enter Her—erm, Mrs. Sylver's property with them following."

"I'll see what I can do."

While the chief placed a call to Forrester, I checked my phone. No call from Katie yet. My insides twisted. Maybe it hadn't been such a good idea, sneaking her out of the house? Maybe she was safer there? She'd already been hurt once. Speaking of that, I needed to find out how that had happened. If Damen hadn't been responsible, then who or what had been?

"I appreciate your help with this situation," I said after the chief ended her call, my voice cutting through the heavy silence. "Thank you."

"You've done a lot of good work for the bureau since you started. I don't want to see someone with so much promise fall into an ugly mess."

She said absolutely nothing the rest of the ride.

I stared out the window. At one point, just as we passed a Walmart, a deep shadow engulfed the car. It didn't last long, no more than a split second, and then we were driving along a winding country road, flanked on both sides by heavy forest. And the caravan behind us—gone. I had a feeling this road wasn't on any map or GPS. The chief, busy poking buttons on her cell phone, hadn't noticed a thing. Just like I hadn't the first time I'd paid a visit to Willow Hill with Damen.

When the car pulled up the long, U-shaped drive, I unfastened my seat belt. My heart was thudding so hard—I could count the beats.

"Hildur Sylver is an eccentric woman," I warned. "No
like anyone I've met before."

"Eccentric or not, her son is wanted for questioning. We
need her to talk."

I was pretty sure the chief wasn't going to get what she
was after. Not if she approached the queen like that. We
debarked and the car rolled away. At the front entry, the
uniformed guard opened the door for us.

We stepped inside.

My gaze went up.

The mural was gone.

I checked out the walls.

The paintings were gone too.

The queen, looking arthritic and bent, shuffled into the
foyer, pushing a walker. This was the queen I'd seen at my
parents' wedding. "Welcome," she said, motioning to a smal
sitting area off to the side. "Agent Peyton, won't you have a
seat. Miss Skye." Her eyes twinkled as she greeted me.

I nodded, keeping my expression sober.

"Thank you for meeting with me," the chief said. She sat
and I took the chair next to her. "We need to ask you some
questions about your son."

Her Majesty lifted a bent finger. "Before I answer a
single question, I must speak with Miss Skye. In private."

Chief Peyton stood. "I'm sorry, but I can't allow you to
do that."

The queen studied the chief for a handful of beats. "Then
I'm sorry, our business here is done." The queen stood as
well.

I was torn. I didn't want to see this whole thing fall apart.
I had a feeling Her Majesty had information we needed. "It's
okay," I said. "Whatever you have to say to me, you can say
in front of my superior."

The queen's eyes narrowed. Her lips pursed. Clearly, she
didn't want to say anything in front of the chief. A lengthy
very painful silence followed. The chief stared at the queen
the queen stared right back. They reminded me of two cats

that had just discovered each other and weren't sure if they should fight or not.

"Very well." The queen took her seat again. "I have a message for you. Your friend lost track of Damen."

"Damn it," I mumbled, hoping she wouldn't hear me. That made this interview that much more important. "Thank you for relaying the information."

"You're welcome."

"Do you know whether she's safe?" I asked.

"I assume she is. I haven't heard otherwise." To the chief, she said, "As you will soon discover, tracking my son's movements is impossible. Unless you're able to shift into some form of energy?"

The chief cleared her throat. "We're more interested in finding out the identity of the person who has taken control of him."

Something flickered in Her Majesty's eyes—distrust, perhaps. "We all are."

"You don't know who she is?" I asked.

The chief gave me a warning glare.

Her Majesty shook her head. "Nobody but the two of them do. I did everything in my power to protect him."

"He mentioned no names?" the chief asked, taking control of the interview.

"None. He wouldn't be able to. At least, not once the link was formed."

The chief leaned back, one leg crossed over the other. "Do you know when this link occurred? The killings are recent, within the last week."

The queen mirrored the chief's position. "I assume it's very new. Probably within twenty-four hours of the first killing."

"Do you remember anything unusual happening in that time? Did he go anywhere? Talk to anyone?" the chief asked.

"No, other than Sloan's parents' wedding the first week of July."

The chief dug a file out of her briefcase. "We have a reason to believe the unsub could be one of these young women. Do any of them look familiar?" She opened the file, revealing a stack of photographs.

I studied each one as the queen leafed through them.

Her Majesty said, "I trust Sloan. She can help him. I know it." She hesitated as she came across one photo I recognized. "Hmm . . ."

A huge swan swooped into the room, entering through the window. The queen lifted a finger, set down the photos, and walked to the bird. "Excuse me, please." She picked it up and carried it outside, closing the door behind her.

The chief's brows flew to the top of her forehead.

"Like I said, she's eccentric." I lifted the last picture that the queen had been looking at. "She stopped when she got to this one."

"That may mean nothing."

My soon-to-be mother-in-law shuffled back in. Before I could ask her about the picture, she said, "I have more news. Sloan, he's received his next command."

My gaze locked to hers, and a shiver swept up my spine. "It's me, isn't it?"

"It's you. And of course he knows you're here."

The rumble of thunder echoed in the distance.

It is weakness rather than wickedness which renders men unfit to be trusted with unlimited power.

—John Adams

31

The queen was at my side within seconds, arms waving. had no idea what she was doing. A blink later, a jagged lue bolt struck the ground right outside the French doors. was blinded for an instant. Afterward, my vision was locked by the shadowy afterburn. I blinked frantically, earing scuffling and voices. The chief yelling. Her Majesty elling back.

"Mum." It was Damen's voice.

He was here.

To kill me.

My fiancé.

"I haven't done anything to anyone," I said, still blinking ny eyes to try to clear them. Someone was tugging on my rm—the chief?—but I fought her. "Why would she want ne dead?"

"It's her command. I must obey." Damen's voice was low nd full of regret.

Still blinking, I looked him in the eye. "Can't you fight it omehow, Damen? Please, can't you try?"

"Sloan, we're leaving. Now." Once again, the chief tried o drag me away.

"Please, Damen. Fight it. For me. If you love me, you'll ight it."

His hands curled into fists. His jaw tensed. "I've tried Sloan. Believe me, I've tried. That's why it took me this long to get here."

The chief yanked harder, and I nearly fell. "Sloan, if I must, I'll handcuff you and drag you out of here." She meant every word. I knew it, but I wasn't going to leave. No, I needed to stay, to help Damen. Maybe it would come to a point where it would be his life or mine. But it wasn't there yet.

"Can't you change her mind?" I threw out, inching toward the door to appease the chief.

"I tried that too, warned her that you're not the only one who's on her trail. She thinks if I kill you, then stop killing for a while, the investigation will be called off."

"Not a chance," the chief said.

"I tried to tell her that. She doesn't trust me. She knows I was lying earlier."

"Call her, we'll tell her ourselves," the chief suggested.

"I can't do that. It might reveal her identity. As it turns out, I'm unable to do anything that could threaten her safety. That's why your friend failed to follow me."

I felt myself scowling. "It was worth a try, I guess."

"It was." Damen's expression was so dark—his eyes so clouded—my heart was breaking. "I didn't want it to come to this."

"I know, Damen."

"Come with me, Sloan. Right now." The chief was pretty much shoving me through the door, and I wasn't doing much to stop her.

However, while I was walking toward the waiting limo, my mind was racing. Jumbled thoughts bounced around in my head like atoms in an overheated nuclear reactor core. *If only I can figure out who she is. If only.* I thought about our case up to this point, the girls we'd interviewed. The girls who'd died. I was missing something. That *something* was the key. *If only I had more time . . .*

Standing framed in the doorway, Damen lifted his hands

I couldn't miss the anguish I saw in his eyes. "Sloan, I don't want to do this."

His mother mirrored his position. She scurried in front of me, hands flat, chest high. "Son, you know what I'm about to do."

Damen nodded. "I do."

"I love you, son."

"I love you too."

"What? What are you going to do? What's happening?" I asked as the chief shoved me aside. "Chief, there's nothing you can do. If he releases a bolt, it's going to strike you, or it's going to strike me."

"Better if it's me," she said.

"No." Now I was the one doing the pushing. But the chief was strong and she was determined. She wouldn't move out of the way.

"You're safe," the queen said. "He's going to discharge a stream of electricity. I've opened a connection between us. Like a circuit. It'll circle the charge back to him."

"Will that stop him?" I asked.

"Eventually—though it'll likely kill him."

No!

My knees softened and I nearly went down. The chief caught me before I hit the ground. "Oh, God, isn't there another way?" I asked as I forced myself back to my feet. Damn it, I wasn't going to fall to the ground and wail like a little baby. I was going to think this through. I was going to solve this problem, just like I had every other problem I'd ever faced. "Tell me what to do!"

"Figure out who she is. That's the only way," Damen said. His hands started glowing, little visible arcs of white static jumping off his fingertips. "Sloan, this wasn't what I wanted for us."

A sob tore up my throat. I clapped my hand over my mouth. Frozen. I couldn't move, couldn't speak. I wanted to do something, to save him somehow. But what could I do? I couldn't stop electricity. And I couldn't change the fact that he was under the control of someone else. Right?

Right?

All you can do is what you do best. Think, Sloan, think!

My brain started piecing together all the clues: the marks on the girls, the names of the girls, the conversations I had with Megan and with Derik and with Jia.

The marks. Little marks. Pairs of burns.

The note *Your dead.* That handwriting. It was Derik's.

The profile: intelligent, respected, well liked.

She'd faked the attack.

To throw us off.

Figuring it was "do or die," I said, "She's Jia."

His fingers curled into fists. His lips clamped together.

This was it. Either he'd die or I would. I couldn't hold back. "That's who it is, isn't it?"

The chief had her phone out, dialing before I'd taken my next breath. "Thomas, head to Jia Wu's house. She's the unsub."

"I'm right, aren't I?" I yelled, hoping he could hear me.

He was glowing all over now; a blue-white aura surrounded his whole body. He lifted his hands higher and a shower of sparks jumped from his fingertips. "It doesn't matter if you know. It's too late. I have to carry out her command."

"Can't you wait? If JT brings her here—"

"Waiting puts her at risk. I can't do that." He was shaking now, trembling from head to toe. He was fighting it. I could see it in his face. I had to keep him talking—that seemed to be helping.

"What if . . . What if your mother brings her here? She's powerful. Surely, she can snap her fingers or something, and get her here."

His mother flicked her gaze to me. "I could do that. She'd be standing right there in a blink. But if I did, I'd have to break the circuit between myself and Damen. You'd be vulnerable. And my son knows that. The instant the circuit is broken, he can—will—strike."

My gaze snapped to his. Would he really do that? Or could he resist? "Well?"

His eyes were full of anguish. "She's right."

"Can you fight it? It's not going to take long. Seconds."

"I don't know. Maybe." His head fell back. "Sloan!" he cried out.

I glanced at the queen, then turned back to Damen. "If you can resist for only a moment, we might be able to save your life."

"Help me," he growled.

"I want to try."

I locked gazes with Damen. Took a few deep breaths. "Ready?"

"Yes."

I took one last breath. And before I had the chance to second-guess myself, I yelled, "Do it!" I did not break eye contact with him.

Time seemed to slow down; I concentrated so hard. Damen's eyes glowed silver. He raised his flattened hands, slowly moving them in place in front of his body. Little bolts of electricity arced from his fingertips. The sizzling white sparks floated there, in front of his hands, as more leapt from his fingertips. They moved closer to each other until they joined, forming a small ball in the air. More sparks joined the ball, and more; the shimmering ball grew oh-so-slowly in front of him.

How much time had passed? Ten seconds? Twenty? A hundred?

The ball was growing larger. Baseball-sized. Softball. Bigger. Soccer. Its hum was louder. The crackle of static over an AM radio station.

"Do it!" someone screamed.

I knew that voice.

"What are you waiting for? You must do as I say," Jia commanded.

Damen's bizarre silver gaze didn't leave mine. I concentrated hard on keeping the connection between us. "What do I do?" I yelled. "How do I stop her?"

"You must break their bond," the queen said.

"How?"

"I'm losing control," Damen said, his voice weak. The glow in his eyes amped up. Hundreds of mini lightning bolts jumped from his fingers.

"Sloan, I can complete the circuit," the queen said.

"No."

"Do it, Mother. Do it now," Damen muttered. He was losing the battle. Losing, but *hadn't lost*.

"No! Call him off, Jia!" I yelled.

"Fuck you."

"Mum. Sloan!"

Without taking my gaze from Damen's, I said, "Call him off, Jia, or I'll make sure you spend your every remaining moment in a living hell."

"You'll be dead. You won't be doing anything."

"You've lost. Too many people know," the chief told her. "You can't kill us all. Haven't you done enough? Haven't you hurt enough people?"

"Where's your humanity? Your heart? Your conscience, Jia?" I demanded. "Are you going to let hatred and vengeance consume you?"

"Mother!" Damen screamed. The ball was the diameter of a beach ball now. "Can't hold it."

The queen put up her hands. "I love you, my son."

"What's she doing?" Jia shrieked.

"Killing him," I said, sobbing. "Damen!"

"No!" Jia shouted. "You can't!"

Her reaction shocked me. "What's wrong?"

"If he dies, so does she," the queen told us.

"Then you've got nothing to lose, Jia. Call him off," the chief said.

"Stop! I command you." Jia turned to the chief and started crying. She covered her face with her hands. The chief wasted no time, grabbing her hands, shoving them behind her back so she could handcuff her.

"Don't say a word. Nothing. Got it?" the chief told her.

Still crying, Jia nodded.

The ball in front of Damen fizzled, but it didn't vanish.

"What's happening?" I asked. I wanted to run to him, to throw myself into his arms, but not with that ball of energy there.

"Mother, do it." Damen's shoulders slumped. His gaze left mine, jerking to the queen.

"Damen, my son, no. Why?"

I started trembling. What was he doing? What the hell was he doing?

"Just . . . do it." His head dropped.

"No!" I ran to him, stopping directly in front of the buzzing, zapping ball of lightning. "I won't let you."

"It's better this way." His gaze met mine, and I knew his mind had been made up. "Nobody can use me to hurt anyone else again."

"What about Jia? If you let your mother do this, she'll die too."

"She doesn't have to. That's her choice. If she releases me, she won't die."

I swung around. "Release him. Save yourself."

Jia's gaze jerked to Damen, to his mother, to me, then back to Damen again.

"Kill them all!"

Damen swung his arms in an arc and the ball shot at me so fast that it looked like a white blur. Then it zoomed around me, slammed into him, and exploded.

He collapsed to the ground.

It was done.

The *impundulu* was free.

Jia was next. She slowly sank, like an inflated doll losing its air.

It was done.
We had stopped the killer.
It was my turn to collapse.
It was done.
My heart was broken, my soul shattered.

Time passed in a blur after that. Somehow I ended up back at Mom and Dad's house; somehow JT ended up there with me, holding my hands, a silent, strong presence. A friend. Katie was there too, sitting next to him, a box of tissues on her knees.

"How did Damen become tied up with Jia?" I asked, pulling a tissue from the box. I dabbed my burning eyes. "I don't see where the connection came from or understand how she was able to find out about his . . . vulnerability. Or how to use it to her advantage."

"The BPD searched his home," JT told me. "They found some schoolbooks, some notes with the name 'Fridrik Sylver' on them. Damen lived close to Fitzgerald. We think one of his brothers was living with him, attending Fitzgerald. That brother met Jia Wu through the tutoring program. The BPD also found some letters at Wu's house. From Hollerbach. And from Fridrik Sylver. They both were in love with her. I'm guessing Fridrik told her about his brother for some reason."

"But how did she know what he was?" I asked, struggling to make sense of what had happened. "How did she know how to take control of him? Did Fridrik tell her?"

"He didn't have to. You can find just about anything on the internet," Katie said.

"Jia Wu didn't need the internet," JT corrected. "Her mother has an extensive collection of old books. You remember seeing them? In their living room?"

"Yes, I do."

"She'd been reading books on witchcraft, searching for a love spell."

Ironic that a teen's search for love had led to the death of o many people. That fact only made this case that much nore tragic.

"And the note? From Derik?" I asked. "Was it a threat?"

JT shook his head. "It was a warning. Derik didn't know exactly what Jia was doing, but after Stephanie Barnett's death, he had a suspicion Hailey Roberts was next."

"Poor Damen." Feeling a sudden chill, I wrapped my arms around myself. "God. I can't imagine living in fear all he time. And then, when his worst fears came true, having o . . . hurt those girls. . . ." I cupped my hands over my mouth to stifle the sob which was surging up my throat. "I can't imagine how terrible it must have been for him, being forced to do something so wicked. It ripped pieces of his soul right out of him."

"You know what your problem is?" JT said a bit later; his voice was soft and gentle.

"Yeah"—I blinked through my tears at him—"I let my feelings get in my way too much."

"No," he said, pulling me into his arms. "You think too much, Sloan Skye. Don't ever stop feeling, following your heart. You're perfect, just the way you are."

Friedrich Nietzsche once said, "Whoever fights monsters should see to it that in the process he does not become a monster. And if you gaze long enough into an abyss, the abyss will gaze back into you."

I was an anomaly, the offspring of imperfect genes, imperfect parents. In some ways, I felt like I had more in common with the monsters than I did with the average Jane.

Was it the job? Was it the FBI? The PBAU?

Or was it . . . me?

If you enjoyed BLOOD OF DAWN,
find out how Sloan Skye got her start in

BLOOD OF EDEN.

Turn the page for a special excerpt.

A Kensington mass-market paperback
and e-book on sale now!

Man can believe the impossible, but can never believe the improbable.

—Oscar Wilde

Rotten eggs and sulphur. Oh, the sweet stench of home.

The gray cloud of *parfum de sewer* rolled out of my apartment door as I juggled my keys, two mocha lattes—heavy on the whipped cream—and bagels. Standing in the hallway, I shouted, "Is it safe to come in, or do I need my gas mask?"

That was not a rhetorical question. My roommate, Katie Lewis, was playing with chemicals again. And I was guessing this morning's experiment was an epic failure.

She'd converted our kitchen into a chem lab last year. Made sense, since neither of us cooked food. Since then, I've learned to live with safety gear at the ready, at all times. Splash goggles. Gas mask. Fire extinguisher. Fabric deodorizer. It goes without saying, *Casa* Skye/Lewis isn't the average home of a couple of grad students. But every now and then, having a chemist at my beck and call, 24-7, came in handy. Especially now that Mrs. Heckel in 2B has stopped reporting us to the DEA. We've been raided twice.

"Sloan?" Katie was sporting her everyday wear—apron, goggles, heavy rubber gloves . . . and slippers with stuffed Albert Einstein heads on the tops. It wasn't a look every girl could pull off, but she did—and still managed to look cute.

If she wasn't such a sweetheart, I might have hated her for it. "Did you happen to get cream cheese? We're out."

"Sure did." Taking my cue from Katie, who wasn't wearing her gas mask, I hurried inside and shut the door. "Whew, whatever you just blew up reeks. Do you have the exhaust fan going?"

Grimacing, Katie waved a hand in front of my face. "Yeah. The smoke should clear up in a few minutes. Sorry." She slid her goggles to the top of her head and swiped one of the coffees from the cardboard tray.

"Did you figure out what went wrong this time?"

"Not a thing. It was supposed to do that." Katie took a slurp and smacked her lips. "Mmm, good coffee. They used just the right amount of chocolate this time. Not too little, not too much."

"Good." After I set my coffee and the bag of bagels on the coffee table, which served double duty as our dining table, I headed straight back to my room. I checked the clock on my nightstand. It was a twenty-eight-minute drive to the FBI Academy. That left me exactly four minutes to finish getting ready.

"Are you geeked about your big day?" Katie hung back, standing just outside my bedroom as I rushed around, digging out my laptop case and tossing the essentials into it. Pens, notebook, spare change, cell phone, Netbook.

"I can't tell you how nervous I am." I sighed. "I gotta pee again. This is the third time in an hour. I swear, I have the bladder of a sixty-year-old mother of twelve."

"I'm so excited for you!" As I shuffled past her, toward the bathroom, Katie caught my shoulders and gave them a quick shake. "My best friend's working for the freaking FBI. You'll tell me absolutely everything, right?"

"Sure, I'll tell you everything that isn't classified." I dashed into the bathroom and took care of my personal issue, hoping I wouldn't get the urge to go again in the next three minutes.

"Call me later," Katie yelled through the door.

"Will do." I dropped a throwaway toothbrush into my purse, zipped it shut, and, heading out into the hall, scooped up the laptop bag I'd left next to the door. Racewalking across the living room, I slung my bag over my shoulder and grabbed my lukewarm mocha latte and a dry bagel while on the way to the exit. "Don't burn the place down while I'm gone." Before heading out, I doused myself in Febreze.

Katie pushed her goggles in place and headed toward the kitchen. "You have nothing to worry about."

I'd heard that before, exactly one minute before the last explosion. And the one before that. What can I say? We both like to live a little dangerously.

With not even a second to spare, I yanked open the door and almost crashed into my mother, her hand raised to knock. She was wearing her threadbare hot pink bathrobe—and God only knew what underneath. Two different shoes poked out from beneath the ratty hem, and her hair—today it was the shade of a new penny—looked like it had been styled with an eggbeater. A huge suitcase sat next to her feet, and an unlit joint as thick as my thumb was protruding from the corner of her mouth.

Nothing new there.

I grinned, plucked the joint out of her mouth, and dropped it into my purse. "Hi, Mom. What a pleasant surprise."

"Honey, I need your help. The power's out in my building again and the landlord says it's my fault. He's exaggerating, of course."

"Of course," I echoed.

"It's not my fault the building's wiring is outdated. I was just trying—"

"It's okay, Mom. You can stay with us until it comes back on." I gave her a peck on the cheek and handed her my coffee as I hurried past. "I'm sorry, I've gotta go. It's my first day with the FBI. There's bagels inside. Your favorite. I'll call you later." After ditching the contraband in the scraggly shrubs next to the building's main entry, I sprinted out to my car, my laptop case bruising my hip and my empty stomach rumbling. I hit my mom's landlord's phone number on my cell, programmed on speed dial, prepared to give the usual "it'll never happen again" speech.

I'd already handled my mother's little problem and was in the middle of an emergency handbag repair—making creative use of a couple of paper clips and a broken pencil—when my new boss, Special Agent Murphy, finally emerged from his office. "There's been a mistake," he informed me. "We won't be able to use you this summer. . . ."

Of course, there's a problem. There always is. The question is, what can I do—

"We've selected another intern. . . ."

Another intern?

"I'm sorry." Murphy scowled and glanced down at his cell phone. "Excuse me for just a moment."

I should have known it was too good to be true. But after two decades of dreaming and studying and hoping, I—Sloan Skye, the only offspring of a schizophrenic philosopher-self-proclaimed inventor and delusional biology professor—wanted to believe I'd landed the internship of my dreams. I didn't expect it to blow up in my face my first day on the job.

As I struggled to recover from the bomb that Agent Murphy had just lobbed my way, Gabe Wagner—who should have been doing grunt work for some senator in DC, not anywhere near the FBI Academy in Quantico, Virginia—came strolling by.

That was it; I knew exactly what had happened. His internship had fallen through, so somebody had pulled a fast one on me.

Again.

As a few choice expressions played through my mind—all of them involving specific anatomical parts and physically impossible actions—I gave Gabe, my frenemy since freshman year, a blindingly bright smile. "Hey, Gabe, does this mean the dream job with the Waste Management Department is still open?"

"No, I'm pretty sure that one's been filled. Sorry." Looking as evil as ever, Gabe sauntered within reach, but I resisted the urge to snap his neck like a toothpick. "Why? Were you interested in applying?" Lucky for him, I possessed an iron will, an allergy to prison air, and—I'd never admit this to Gabe—I secretly enjoyed our little verbal tussles. They made life interesting. "If you're really hard up, I could ask my dad to pull a few strings, get you an interview at the meatpacking plant in Baltimore."

Argh! Animal guts give me hives.

"Gee, thanks. I'd love to spend my summer elbow deep in big intestines, but I'd hate to impose. I'm sure Senator Wagner has more important things to do, like slip his pet pork barrel projects into the latest bill the Senate's debating. You never know, that nineteen-million-dollar study on cow flatulence might solve the energy crisis someday."

Murphy returned, giving each of us a bland look. "Good morning, Mr. Wagner. I'll be with you in just a moment, if you'll wait over there." He motioned toward a grouping of chairs a few feet away, next to a table with a coffeepot, cups, and a mug full of primary-colored swizzle sticks. Once Gabe was out of my reach, Murphy turned to me. "Miss Skye, I tried to call you this morning, after I discovered the administrative error, but it was too late. We're looking into something else for you. I'll give you a call as soon as I know something."

Translation: Don't call us. We'll call you.

"Thanks, Agent Murphy." I fought to look cheery, but I knew I wouldn't fool anyone, especially Gabe. I was, without a doubt, the world's worst actress. In my defense, I don't think even Reese Witherspoon could have pulled this one off.

Feeling a little defeated, I slumped into a nearby chair. It rocked back, almost dumping me on the floor. Not to sound like a pathetic whiner or anything, but this was unbelievably unfair. It's not that I expect life to be one big wonderful world full of happiness and justice for all, but I'd been preparing for this job my entire life. And when I say "entire life," I'm not exaggerating. As I lay in my crib, my mom fed my brain a steady diet of everything from analytic philosophy to quantum physics, a thick joint tucked between her lips and a cloud of pot smoke circling her head like a halo. As a result, not only had I memorized the work of just about every major player in the world of psychology by the time I'd graduated from elementary school—Freud, Jung, Adler, just to name a few—but I could square eighteen digit numbers faster than most people could add two. And I could recite the *Divine Comedy* . . . in Italian. "I'll just mosey on home and wait for your call. Thanks again."

"Good luck with the job hunt." Gabe waved from the coffee stand. "Call me if you want me to hook you up." He had the nerve to actually waggle his eyebrows.

I threw up a little in my mouth.

What a day. Thanks to Gabe, I was not only out of a dream internship but out of a steady paycheck as well. I received an annuity payment every fall, which kept us afloat for the year and helped pay my tuition. I had my dad to thank for that. But I'd promised to pay my mom's landlord a thousand dollars to cover the damage she'd caused. My bank account was on the brink of imploding. How would I pay next month's rent? Electric bill? And, more important, how would I take care of Mom? SSI barely kept a roof over her head, even when she wasn't causing minor catastrophic damage. If I didn't subsidize her pathetic income, she'd end up living under a bridge, smoking marijuana and talking to invisible zombies . . . again.

Damn it!

All of my dreams for the summer—kicking ass and taking down bad guys, anyone?—were slipping from my grasp. But I have never been the kind to stand in stunned silence and let everything fall apart. I had to do *something*.

But what?

I looked down at my hands and, just like that, I had an idea.

Lucky for me, Gabe was called away to handle some super-important, top-secret intern stuff before I had to throw myself at Murphy's feet and beg for a job. Quickly, before I lost my nerve, I muttered, "In case the other thing doesn't work out, I'm pretty handy with a broom." Sweeping the Behavioral Analysis Unit's offices was better than the alternative.

"Oh?" Murphy glanced at the paper clips in my hands, then at my cheap Prada knockoff purse, its broken strap dangling off a nearby desk like a dead eel.

"And a vacuum," I added, hoping I was making my point clear. For a guy who puzzled together clues on a daily basis, Murphy seemed to be having a hard time getting my drift.

"Yeah." He nodded, glanced at his phone again, and lifted a finger. "Just a minute."

"Sure." I beamed a silent thank-you, hoping I'd soon be the recipient of some good news. Anything, and I mean *a-n-y-t-h-i-n-g,* would be better than last year's summer job, cleaning behind a pack of greasy, belching, middle-aged mechanics who thought the word "wash" had a letter *r* in it and a high-school diploma constituted an advanced degree. I have never been an intellectual snob—it's a lot more fun laughing at people who think they know everything—but come on. There was only so much a girl could take.

I'd been lucky to get that job last year, even with two bachelor's degrees and a master's in the works. And this year, things were even worse. The guy who was sweeping my uncle's garage this summer had a master's degree in mechanical engineering.

I finished up my handbag repair, and was about to tackle the broken chair, which posed a genuine threat to national security, when Murphy returned with a woman who looked like an older version of myself. The agent's dull brown hair, the same shade as mine, had been scraped back from her face and tied into a tight knot at her nape. Her nondescript polyester suit had fashion disaster written all over it, just like mine. And little-to-no makeup enhanced her unextraordi-nary features—also, sadly, just like mine.

"I think we've found a solution to our problem." Murphy motioned to the woman. "This is Special Agent Alice Peyton. She's chief of a new unit in the FBI, and she could use your help."

Yes, yes, yes, the angels were singing! And I was ready to join them in a lively round of Handel's "Hallelujah Chorus."

I had no idea what kind of work Chief Peyton's unit was involved in; I didn't care. All that mattered was I had a job, and it was within the hallowed halls of the FBI Academy. Gabe hadn't ruined my summer, after all. And dear old mom wouldn't be sharing the overpass with Crazy Connie, the bag lady—who wasn't crazy at all, if you ask me.

Sane has always been a relative term in my world.

I cranked up the wattage of my smile and offered a hand to my soon-to-be boss for the summer. "Sloan Skye."

"Alice Peyton. It's good to have you with us."

"Glad to be here." That was no lie.

Murphy turned my way. "Special Agent Peyton will take care of transferring your paperwork. I hope you have a good summer, Miss Skye."

"I will now. Thank you." I shook his hand.

Chief Peyton motioned toward the elevators. "Let me show you where you'll be working. We're one floor up."

"That would be great. I'll get my things." As I snatched up my purse and laptop case, I caught Gabe's openmouthed gawk. I couldn't help noticing he held a coffee cup in both hands.

Within Gabe's earshot, Chief Peyton said, "I'm hoping you can do more than fetch coffee. Do you have a valid pass-port?"

Karma was my new best friend.

I tossed Gabe a little smirk. "You mean I'll be traveling with the unit?"

"Of course, Skye. Wherever we go, you go too." Chief

Peyton stopped in front of a bank of elevators. "Speaking of which, Skye is an unusual name."

"Yes, I suppose it is, statistically speaking. According to GenealogyToday-dot-com, it was the sixty thousand one hundred eighty-fifth most popular surname in the . . ." *I'm doing it again.* ". . . Sorry, I get a little carried away with statistics sometimes. . . . Um, I was told my father was Scottish."

"I thought he might be. What does he do?" Chief Peyton pushed the elevator's up button.

"Well, my father's dead. He was a professor at the University of Richmond."

"I'm very sorry." When the elevator door opened, Chief Peyton motioned me in first, then followed.

I stepped toward the back of the car. "It's okay. He died when I was young."

She hit the button for the third floor. "I see. He was a professor of . . . ?"

I wondered for a second or two why Chief Peyton seemed to be taking such an interest in a man who'd been dead for more than twenty years. But I quickly shrugged it off as small talk, her way of making me feel more comfortable. "Natural science—specifically, biology." I left out the part about how he'd been shamed into giving up his position at the university after publishing an article arguing for the existence of fictional creatures—vampires, werewolves, ghosts, and goblins, that sort of thing. I was fairly certain that would be low on Chief Peyton's need-to-know list.

"That's very interesting." As the elevator slowly rumbled up to the third floor, Chief Peyton began explaining, "The PBAU is a brand-new unit within the FBI. We'll be handling our first case this week, and we're very fortunate to have you on our team." When the car bounced to a stop, she motioned for me to exit first, then followed me out.

Wondering what the acronym PBAU stood for, I headed straight for the open area where the unit members' desks sat in tidy rows. It was exactly as I'd imagined the Behavioral

Analysis Unit, aka BAU, would look. Semitransparent half walls separated a half-dozen identical cubicles from each other. And around the back ran a raised walk, which led to a couple of rooms closed off from the main space. But this wasn't the home of the BAU; it was the *PBAU*. And instead of a bustling room full of busy agents, it was eerily silent.

"I'm very happy to be a part of the team. I'm eager to get started," I said.

"We'll be meeting for our first case review in a few minutes. I want you to join us."

Join them? I almost giggled like a little girl, I got so excited. I never giggled, not even when I was five and I'd built my first robot, using LEGOs and a few electronic bits I'd "borrowed" from various sources around the house. Mom didn't need that old drill, anyway. Or the toaster. We never ate toast. And the computer . . . it had been useless, outdated and begging to become spare parts for Heathcliff, my new best friend. "Sure."

My new boss tapped the back of a chair, tucked under a nearby cubicle desk. "This'll be your work space. We'll get you a computer, supplies, and phone by the end of the week."

"I get a desk of my own?" I peered at the inhabitants of the adjoining cubicles, thinking I'd introduce myself, but both had their backs to me.

"Sure. Of course you get a desk," Chief Peyton answered.

"Well, thanks. Don't worry about the computer. I brought my own." I lifted my computer case.

"We'll need to have it checked for security before you can log into our system."

"No problem." I set my case on my desk and unzipped it. "This is great. It's like I'm a permanent part of the team." Trying not to think about the fact that this whole thing sounded too good to be true, I tried the chair out for size. It was a perfect fit.

"Perhaps you will be someday." Chief Peyton patted my shoulder, then announced, loud enough for everyone to hear,

"Case review in five minutes. Let's take it up in the conference room."

Scuffling and chatter followed; in less than five, I was introduced to the three other members of the PBAU.

Of course, there was Chief Peyton. Also on the team were Special Agent Jordan Thomas, Special Agent Chad Fischer, the media liaison, and Special Agent Brittany Hough, the computer specialist/techie geek. They had all transferred to the PBAU from other units. That meant I was the only clueless newbie. Each greeted me with a friendly smile and a handshake.

Finally, with the introductions over, we all took our seats. Standing in front of a whiteboard, Fischer taped up a color photograph of a dead body. Fischer launched into his presentation. "The Baltimore PD is asking for our help solving a suspected murder case. At this point, all indicators are pointing to a nonmortal suspect. . . ."

Did he just say "nonmortal"? No way.

". . . Bite wounds on the victim's neck suggest we may be looking for a vampiric predator. . . ."

Vampiric?

". . . It's too early to say what the cause of death is, but local law enforcement doesn't want to wait. The media's hot to cover the story, and they can't be held off for long."

Had Chief Peyton known all along who my father was and what he'd researched?

No. Okay, maybe. Crazier things have happened.

". . . It appears to be a single vampire killing, blitz attack. We don't know much, but one thing is certain. This unknown subject—unsub—won't stop until we catch him."

They all looked at me.

What were they expecting? Should I have whipped out a wooden stake and led the charge, yelling, "Die, you bloodsucking bastard"?

My phone, set on vibrate, started buzzing.

"Skye, what are your thoughts?" Chief Peyton asked.

"Well . . ." Lucky me, not only was my mother calling, asking me to solve another crisis, no doubt, but it also seemed I'd just been dubbed the FBI's Buffy the Vampire Slayer. There was only one problem. My mother had taught me plenty—Latin, vector integral calculus, quantum physics. For some silly reason, though, she'd eschewed vampire psychology and comparative biology of shape-shifters.

I didn't know a Sasquatch from a yeti.

When no coherent response came from my direction, Chief Peyton turned back to Fischer. "I agree. If the unsub is a young vampire on a feeding frenzy, there will be more. And soon."

Vampire. They were actually thinking this crime was the act of a vampire?

Again, I should've known it was too good to be true. This had to be some kind of joke. A freaking brilliant, absolutely hilarious one. Gabe Wagner was behind this. It had his name written all over it.

"Not only must we profile our killer's personality, but also his species," Chief Peyton said.

Species? God, this was good. Anytime now, one of Gabe's friends was going to pop out of a corner and shout, "You've been punked!" Then everyone was going to laugh, including me. And then I'd be escorted to my real boss, and I'd find out I don't get a nice desk and my own computer and phone, but rather a rusty old file cabinet, a yellow legal pad, and that crappy broken chair, shoved into a supply closet.

"Excellent point," Fischer said. "The being's physical characteristics will influence his behavior as much as psychological factors."

Yep, any minute now . . .

My phone, sitting in my lap, started vibrating against my leg.

Gabe?

No. Mom again.

I ignored the call and played along with Peyton's game,

nodding at the appropriate moments, raising eyebrows, and scribbling notes on the pad of paper that I'd dug out of my laptop case.

Very interesting. The body had bite marks on the neck.

Oh, yes. Fang marks were most definitely a sign of a vampire attack.

It appeared blood was missing from the victim's body, but if so, the body hadn't been completely drained.

Hmm. "Perhaps the unsub had been interrupted midfeeding. *Cena interruptus,*" I offered.

Everyone concurred with a nod.

Okay, this practical joke was stretching on too long. I leaned back and tried to peer around the corner. I didn't see any sign of Gabe or his posse. Where was he? This had to be a joke. It couldn't be real.

I checked my phone, thinking maybe I'd missed his call. Nope. Nobody had called but my mother.

At the end of Fischer's presentation, the team members stood, each one giving me a look as they filed out of the room. Finally Chief Peyton walked to my side of the table, pulled the chair out next to me, and sat down. "We'd like you to come with us."

"You would."

"To Baltimore. We'll be leaving in just over an hour."

"Oh. Um, I don't know." I am so rarely struck completely mute, but this situation had done just that. There were so many questions clogging my brain, I couldn't think.

"This case is local, but I should mention every member of my team has to keep a 'go bag' with them at all times, stocked with the basics—a couple changes of clothes, toothbrush, makeup, hairbrush—"

"Excuse me, but what exactly does PBAU stand for?" I asked.

"Paranormal Behavioral Analysis Unit. Like the BAU, the mission of the PBAU is to provide behavioral-based investigative support to local FBI field offices. Unlike the BAU, the cases we are called to assist with all involve acts of violence that have some tie to the unknown, the paranormal, or the occult."

Seriously?

I couldn't help asking, "You don't really believe there are Edward Cullens running around, chomping people in the neck. Do you?"

"Not the kind of vampires you see in movies, no. Of course not." Finally this very sensible-looking woman was saying something reasonable. I pulled in a lungful of air and let it out slowly. "I have yet to see a vampire that sparkles," she added, looking dead serious. "Now, come on, I'll tell you more in the car. I thought we'd all drive together. It'll give us a chance to discuss the case." She checked her wristwatch. "Time's tight. We need to get going. Sunset's a few minutes after nine tonight." Not waiting for me, she headed for the conference room door.

I followed her. "Is it too dangerous to be outside after dark?"

"We'd like to get as much time as possible at the crime scene during daylight hours. It's hard to see after sunset."

Why did I feel like I'd just said something totally stupid? "Gotcha."

She waved Jordan Thomas over. As I'd noticed earlier, he was the closest to my age. Fischer and Chief Peyton were older, thirties, maybe early forties. I'd noticed another thing about him too—he wasn't hard on the eyes. He had nice . . . glasses. "JT, I need you to give Skye a rundown of our policies and procedures before we leave."

"Sure, Chief."

Chief Peyton tapped my arm and looked me straight in the eyes. "Are you with us, Skye?"

That was the fifty-thousand-dollar question, wasn't it?

The way I saw it, I had two options: either forget about an

internship with the FBI, and let my mom down; or chase imaginary monsters.

When I looked at it that way, spending three months profiling vampires and werewolves couldn't be any worse than emptying Porta-Potties in the county parks. And that I'd done, for more summers than I cared to remember.

I shrugged. "Sure. I'm in."